DJUNA

∎ ∎ ∎

Also by Phillip Herring

Joyce's Uncertainty Principle

■ ■ ■

DJUNA

The Life and Work of Djuna Barnes

PHILLIP HERRING

VIKING

VIKING
Published by the Penguin Group
Penguin Books USA Inc., 375 Hudson Street,
New York, New York 10014, U.S.A.
Penguin Books Ltd, 27 Wrights Lane, London W8 5TZ, England
Penguin Books Australia Ltd, Ringwood, Victoria, Australia
Penguin Books Canada Ltd, 10 Alcorn Avenue,
Toronto, Ontario, Canada M4V 3B2
Penguin Books (N.Z.) Ltd, 182–190 Wairau Road,
Auckland 10, New Zealand

Penguin Books Ltd, Registered Offices:
Harmondsworth, Middlesex, England

First published in 1995 by Viking Penguin,
a division of Penguin Books USA Inc.

1   3   5   7   9   10   8   6   4   2

Page 386 constitutes an extension of this copyright page.

Portions of this book first appeared in different form in *De Gids* (Amsterdam), *Eire-Ireland, James Joyce Quarterly, Journal of Modern Literature, Library Chronicle, Modes of Narrative: Approaches to British, American, and Canadian Fiction* edited by Reingard Nischik and Barbara Korte (Konigshausen & Neumann, Wurzburg), and *Review of Contemporary Fiction.*

ILLUSTRATION CREDITS
Photographs 1, 4, and 5: Peter Barnes; 2 and 3: Nicholas C. Barnes; 6, 7, 8, 9, 11, 13, 14, 15, 17, 20, 22, 24, and drawing opposite "Lullaby": Papers of Djuna Barnes, Special Collections, University of Maryland at College Park Libraries; 10: National Archives (photo appearing in *1933* by Philip Metcalfe, Permanent Press); 12: Irwin Cohen; 16: Fabienne Benedict; 18: the Estate of Carl Van Vechten, Joseph Solomon, Executor, and the Harry Ransom Humanities Research Center, The University of Texas at Austin; 19: Harry Ransom Humanities Research Center, The University of Texas at Austin; 21: Emily Coleman Papers, University of Delaware.

LIBRARY OF CONGRESS CATALOGING IN PUBLICATION DATA
Herring, Phillip F.
Djuna : the life and work of Djuna Barnes / Phillip Herring.
p.   cm.
Includes bibliographical references and index.
ISBN 0–670–84969–3
1. Barnes, Djuna.   2. Women novelists, American—20th century—
Biography.   3. Lesbians—United States—Biography.   I. Title.
PS3503.A614Z68   1995
818'.5209—dc20   95–7630

This book is printed on acid-free paper.
∞

Printed in the United States of America
Set in Bodoni Book
Designed by Francesca Belanger

Para Lydia de los ojos bonitos

Drawing by Djuna Barnes, date unknown.

Lullaby

■ ■ ■

When I was a young child I slept with a dog,
I lived without trouble and I thought no harm;
I ran with the boys and I played leap-frog;
Now it is a girl's head that lies on my arm.

Then I grew a little, picked plantain in the yard;
Now I dwell in Greenwich, and the people do not call;
Then I planted pepper-seed and stamped on them hard.
Now I am very quiet and I hardly plan at all.

Then I pricked my finger on a thorn, or a thistle,
Put the finger in my mouth, and ran to my mother.
Now I lie here, with my eyes on a pistol.
And there will be a morrow, and another, and another.

DJUNA BARNES

Acknowledgments

■ ■ ■

A fellowship from the University of Wisconsin–Madison enabled me to spend six months in the enormous Djuna Barnes collection at the University of Maryland; I am also grateful for two summer fellowships from Wisconsin's Graduate School Research Committee. Research prompted me to visit many libraries and courthouses, and to interview many who knew Djuna Barnes. Her surviving relatives were mostly cooperative but cautious: I am especially indebted to Kerron Barnes, N. C. Barnes, Peter C. Barnes, and the late Saxon Barnes.

For permission to quote unpublished material I am indebted to Herbert Mitgang of the Authors League Fund, 234 West 44th Street, New York, N.Y. 10036, for the Djuna Barnes Estate. I give thanks to Joseph Geraci, Executor of the Estate of Emily Holmes Coleman, for quotations from letters and diaries of Emily Holmes Coleman, and to Karole and Julia Vail for permission to quote from the letters of Peggy Guggenheim. I am obliged to François Chapon of Fonds Littéraire Jacques Doucet for permission to quote from the letters of Natalie Clifford Barney. For permission to quote a passage from John Glassco's *Memoirs of Montparnasse*, I thank Oxford University Press Canada. Quotation from Susan Chitty's *Now to My Mother: A Very Personal Memoir of Antonia White* is by permission of Curtis Brown, London, Ltd. Chester Page and Charles Henri Ford have with great generosity allowed me to quote from unpublished memoirs of Barnes and themselves. Mrs. T. S. Eliot has kindly allowed me to quote from her review of *I Could Never Be Lonely Without a Husband,* a few letters from T. S. Eliot to Barnes, and an editor's blurb by Eliot for Barnes's *The Antiphon.* I have relied heavily on the published work of James B. Scott, Ph.D., and Hank O'Neal and have benefited from interviews with them.

Due to space limitations, the rest of my gratitude is spread through what unfortunately looks like a telephone directory: I am indebted to Berenice Abbott, Ruth M. Alvarez, Jay Arnoldus, Eleanor Barnes, George Barker, Joella Bayer, Fabienne Benedict, Shari Benstock, Francesca Belanger, Danielle Bergey, Anette Hannemüller Bretschneider, Jackson Bryer, Kenneth Burke, Lawrence Campbell, Agneta Carlson, Andrew Chappell, Susan Chappell, Cara Chell, Susan Clark, Irwin Cohen, Roger Conover, Daniel Conaway, Kathryn Court, Janet Dempsey, Elizabeth de Veer, Betsy Draine, Blanche Ebeling-Koning, Donald Farren, Noël Riley Fitch, Susan Stanford Friedman, Egon Hanfstaengl, Rosalind M. Harris, Phillip Harth, Loni Hayman, Cathy Henderson, Standish Henning, Wolfgang Hildesheimer, Carly Jablonski, Agnes Kobin, Renée Lang, James Laughlin, Irwin Leiser, Jane Marcus, Douglas Messerli, David Oliphant, Hank O'Neal, Darryl Pinckney, Grady Pearson, Leigh Ponvert, Sherry Reames, Klaus Reichert, Peter du Sautoy, Bonnie K. Scott, Thomas F. Staley, Caroline Stokes, Jane Strong, Howard Weinbrot, Larry Wallrich, Caroline J. White, and Joseph Wiesenfarth.

Contents

■ ■ ■

A section of photographs follows p. 162

Introduction

■ ■ ■

In 1968, a Philadelphia librarian, planning an exhibit centered upon Djuna Barnes's novel *Nightwood*, one of the great novels of the 1930s, wrote to the author herself, wanting to know something of the circumstances of the novel's creation and her life. Barnes's indignant answer was that writers do not reveal these circumstances, and if she had already done so, the librarian would have read about it. A door slammed in the face of the curious was the typical Barnesean response to inquiry.

Since she died in 1982, Djuna Barnes's door may now be opened a good deal wider than it has ever been. She was in fact torn between two conflicting impulses—the desire to scream to the world of the outrages that had been committed against her, and the more ladylike wish to endure her bitterness in silence. This ladylike second impulse, however, would manifest itself as anger at attempts to pry into her personal affairs, and during her lifetime she would have opposed by every possible legal means the writing of this biography. The first impulse she satisfied in her best writing, which at its gentlest is satirical and at its angriest involves acts of vengeance against family, friends, and lovers. Djuna Barnes dazzles readers with her wit and brilliance, but in the absence of a good biography has left them puzzled as to her motives.

She valued her privacy with a fanaticism seen in only the most reclusive of writers, but then revealed all the secrets worth telling in a fictional form that is often inscrutable, even indecipherable, without some knowledge of her life. This is the major reason why Barnes is too little appreciated today as the writer of genius who was befriended by James Joyce, sponsored by T. S. Eliot, lectured on by Dylan Thomas, only to fall into forty years of obscurity, confined by poverty and pride to a hermit's life in Greenwich Village. Yet the bushel never completely obscured her light, for in the 1950s she became a close friend of Dag Hammarskjöld, secretary-general of the United Nations, who so admired her play *The Antiphon* that he helped translate it into Swedish.

James Joyce advised Barnes to write about the ordinary and to leave the extraordinary to journalism. But like most writers, she wrote about what she knew best, her own life, which was indeed extraordinary. Then, too, giving to "airy nothing a local habitation and a name" was not her way. As she told a friend, "I can't imagine spending years writing fiction, things made up entirely out of thin air, and without a foundation in some emotion."[1] Invention was not a priority because in remembering her past she found no end of emotional subjects. She simply couldn't have invented fiction more compelling or bizarre than her life had been.

Born in a log cabin on a mountain overlooking the Hudson River, Djuna was the second child in her family. Living with her was her grandmother, Zadel Barnes, whose philosophy of free love led to a sequence of disasters that divide her family to this day: letters point to a possible sexual affair with her grandmother and to Djuna's claim that her virginity was taken in a violent rape at sixteen when her father brought in a middle-aged neighbor to introduce her formally to the pleasures of the boudoir. Or was the neighbor perhaps really the father? Or was it the brother of the father's mistress? Something terrible enough to cause bitterness for a lifetime happened to Djuna Barnes at an early age, but precisely what it was may never be known.

One can see her need for reticence: "I like my human experience served up with a little silence and restraint. Silence makes experience go further and, when it does die, gives it that dignity common to a thing one had touched and not ravished."[2] Yet in her best work Barnes herself ravished in ways that would make the crassest biographer blanch; powerless in life, in her art she paid back ravishment in kind, in a series of creative acts the execution of which she said were all that kept her from suicide.[3] The first major instance was *Ryder*, an autobiographical novel of her early life, a witty family history cloaked in experimental style but clearly based on fact. The book ends with the image of her polygamous father stumbling about at night in the company of beasts, on whose sexual behavior he had based his disastrous natural philosophy. *Ryder*'s last line and ultimate refrain is: "And whom should he disappoint?"

Djuna Barnes called her famous novel, *Nightwood*, the soliloquy of a "soul talking to itself in the heart of the night,"[4] but it, too, is a kind of ravishing, which takes as its subject Djuna Barnes's eight-year lesbian relationship with a Saint Louis artist named Thelma Wood. Writing this novel allowed Barnes to purge herself of the overpowering anger and bitterness she felt when Thelma left her for another woman. In *Nightwood*, the abandoned lover is inconsolable, at one point telling her departing mistress: "In the resurrection, when we come up looking backward at each other, I shall know you only of all that company." Her ex-lover responds: "Don't wait for me" (*N* 58–59). To Emily Coleman, a dear friend, Barnes wrote that Thelma "was that terrible past reality, over which any new life can only come, as a person marching up and over the high mound of a grave. . . . I have *had* my great love, there will never be another."[5]

Though tragic, *Nightwood* is wickedly satirical, as is Barnes's *Ladies Almanack*, a takeoff on Natalie Barney and her lesbian circle, written to pay Thelma's hospital bill; but through *Nightwood*'s play of styles one hears anguished voices protesting that life seems a vicious joke. Djuna's mother understood her daughter's pain when she said: "You have condensed your agony until its pure platinum."[6] Coleman saw Barnes's grim talent rather differently: "You make horror beautiful—it is your greatest gift."[7]

Once called, rather unimaginatively, "the Garbo of letters," Barnes was a mysterious figure during her lifetime; her beauty and apparent genius, her sense of style and veneer of sophistication, camouflaged a bohemian background and an erratic education that was strongly centered in the arts but weak in every other category. She was born in 1892, just north of West Point, on the Hudson River, to an English mother, who wished to be a celebrated poet, and an American father, an itinerant musician, painter, and writer, who was content to be supported by his own mother's journalism while he fiddled and sowed his seed wherever a field was in want of a plowshare. When Djuna was a child of five, her father, Wald, took a mistress named Fanny (his mother's friend) into their log cabin and had children with her as well as with his wife, so many that Djuna Barnes spent much of her childhood caring for siblings and half siblings, which scotched any desire to emulate the fertility of the two mothers in a house where children were welcomed into the world with diapers of burlap.

After a series of moves, the family settled on a farm in Huntington, Long Island. Her beloved grandmother, Zadel, taught her to write, and her father gave her lessons in drawing, painting, and music. Young Djuna read many novels and grew to know great poetry and painting, but such unpleasant subjects as math and spelling were brushed aside. She resented her mother, feeling that her four brothers were more loved than she. In *The Antiphon*, the bitter Barnes has her surrogate say: "Of that sprawl, three sons she leaned to fairly: / On me she cast the privy look of dogs / Who turn to quiz their droppings."[8]

Zadel Barnes was a spiritualist and an early feminist; a friend of Elizabeth Cady Stanton, she was an activist in the suffragist movement. She wrote a novel, a biography, and a volume of poetry that was praised by Whittier and Longfellow. During the 1880s, she had a literary salon in London, where her friends included Lady Wilde and Karl Marx's daughter Eleanor. Later she lived with her son's expanding family and helped Djuna launch her career as a journalist.

Though the names are changed for fictional purposes, *Ryder* tells us of the day on their Huntington farm when Djuna's father was told by his increasingly exasperated mother that he had to choose between his wife, Elizabeth, and Fanny. By this time Wald's dual ménage had grown to nearly a dozen in number, far too many for their meager resources. When the agonizing decision was made, Elizabeth and her children were exiled to the slums of New York, where Djuna labored to support them. The day after a divorce was granted, Wald married Fanny. Now Djuna had several grievances, any one of which would have been sufficient for a lifetime of bitterness: she felt betrayed by her own grandmother, with whom she had slept for many years; she claimed that her father arranged to have her raped at sixteen; she was sent off to provide comfort for a soap salesman three times her age; and finally she was forced into exile to earn wages for the family her father had deserted. Compounded, these grievances left Djuna Barnes in a state of nearly permanent rage.

At times her mother and siblings seemed destined for starvation, but spurred on by need, Barnes became a successful journalist in New York, where her articles and interviews (accompanied by drawings, often in the decadent style of Beardsley) gained her wide attention. Eventually she wrote stories, a few poems, and three plays. One of the great beauties of Greenwich Village, she was attached to the Provincetown Players when Eugene O'Neill was there, and had lovers of both sexes. Sexual freedom had been imbibed in girlhood, and despite her sense of violation, she was never to feel guilt about sexual experience, whether with men or with women. Once, when a friend asked her if she was a lesbian, she replied: "I might be anything, if a horse loved me, I might be that."[9] This typically witty deflection of inquiry also acknowledged her bisexuality; one fell in love with the person, not the gender, as Barnes's friend Charles Henri Ford once said.

But there was more grief to come, for Djuna Barnes was unlucky in love. Barnes probably never loved any man with greater intensity than she did Ernst "Putzi" Hanfstaengl, a Harvard graduate who was to become Hitler's secretary for the foreign press until forced to flee Nazi Germany for his opposition to the Führer's policies. But that was later. When declared an enemy alien during World War I, he broke off his engagement to Barnes to find a fellow German suitable for carrying on his aristocratic lineage.

Early in the 1920s, Barnes went to Paris as part of the great writerly migration and came to know the expatriate writers and artists

in residence, including Gertrude Stein, James Joyce, Robert Mc-
Almon, and Ezra Pound. She was especially close to Mina Loy and
Natalie Barney, subjects of *Ladies Almanack*. Much of *Nightwood* was
written or revised in the company of Peggy Guggenheim (and circle),
who gave Barnes a stipend for much of her life, a sort of permanent
if meager Guggenheim fellowship, designed to be supplemented. In
the early 1930s, Barnes became a close friend of Emily Coleman, a
novelist and poet who championed Barnes and *Nightwood* and was
primarily responsible for attracting the attention of T. S. Eliot to Djuna
Barnes's work.

From 1940 until her death, Djuna Barnes lived a very private life
in a tiny flat in Greenwich Village, where she wrote poetry but published only a few poems and a bestiary called *Creatures in an Alphabet*. In those years she also wrote her greatest work after *Nightwood*,
The Antiphon, composed in a style reminiscent of the Jacobean dramatists and set in her mother's English town of Oakham. Severely alcoholic for many years, Barnes was able to conquer her debility only
by immersing herself in a full frontal attack on her family, to explore
and explain her sense of victimization and injustice. The play's Djuna
figure, who has sacrificed all for art, finds that her mother has always
preferred her sons, crass businessmen who plot against the two women
as financial burdens. When she finds that her daughter has been right
after all and her sons have abandoned her in the ancestral mansion,
the mother in desperation crushes her daughter's skull with a curfew
bell. A letter from one of Barnes's brothers claimed that *The Antiphon*
was written as revenge against her family; Djuna claimed her motive
was "justice," not revenge, but the distinction seemed obliterated by
the fury of her judgment. Djuna Barnes died embittered, though surrounded by a few friends who cared deeply for her.

This biography derives from a particular moment in time, when, in
1988, I was looking for more novels by women for my Modernism
course. I wanted to teach *Nightwood* but felt frustrated by my futile
attempts to understand it; before I could understand the novel, I believed, I had to understand Djuna Barnes. The only Barnes biography

in existence was disorganized, incomplete, and conceptually flawed, so that it is impossible to assess any well-reasoned discourse on Barnes or *Nightwood* on the basis of what was known about this most elusive of modern writers. In view of the Barnesean politics being generally offered, I was unable to account for her brilliantly satirical description, which seemed to have as its objective its own brilliance rather than the subversive strategies for which Barnes was becoming famous. The writing of this biography thus springs from my own ignorance and confusion, and from my certain knowledge that this important writer had eluded us modernists so completely that her textual strategies continued to perform tricks while she hid behind a curtain of obscurity, smiling at our gropings.

Djuna Barnes Chronology

■ ■ ■

1826 Birth of Henry Chappell, DB's maternal grandfather, in England.

1828 Birth of Ann Chamberlain, DB's maternal grandmother, in England.

1831 *13 January:* Birth of DB's paternal grandfather, Henry Aaron Budington, in Massachusetts.

1841 *9 March:* Birth of DB's paternal grandmother, Zadel Barnes, in Connecticut.

1857 *26 October:* Henry Aaron Budington marries Zadel Barnes in Leyden, Mass.

1862 *3 November:* Birth of DB's mother, Elizabeth Chappell, in Oakham, County Rutland, England.

1865 *14 January:* DB's father, Wald Barnes, originally named Henry Budington, born in Greenfield, Mass., to Henry A. Budington and Zadel Barnes.

1877 *February:* Zadel divorces Henry in Middletown, Conn. *3 May:* Zadel marries Axel Gustafson in Middletown.

1880–89 Zadel, Axel, and DB's father (Wald) live in London.

1889 *3 July:* Wald Barnes marries Elizabeth Chappell in New York City.

1892 *12 June:* Djuna Chappell Barnes is born to Wald and Elizabeth in Cornwall-on-Hudson, N.Y.; no birth record.

1897 Fanny Faulkner (Mrs. Elizabeth F. Clark) moves in with DB's family.

1902 *1 July:* Zadel buys two parcels of property in Half Hollow area of Huntington, Long Island.

1910 *Summer:* Common-law marriage between DB and Percy Faulkner. They live in Bridgeport, Conn. Probably later in summer, DB leaves Faulkner and returns to family farm in Huntington.

1912 *17 July:* Elizabeth separates from husband and takes Djuna and her brothers to New York City. *30 September:* DB enters Pratt Institute in Brooklyn. *6 November:* Divorce of DB's parents granted. *November:* DB and family living at 1320 Ward Avenue, Morris Park, Bronx. *13 November:* DB's father (calling himself Harold B. Barnes) marries Fanny Faulkner.

1913 *19 March:* DB leaves Pratt Institute. *29 June:* DB's articles begin appearing in the *Brooklyn Eagle.* *27 August:* Zadel writes Jack London a pauper's letter.

1914–16 DB love affair with Ernst Hanfstaengl.

1915 DB moves from mother's dwelling to Greenwich Village: 42 Washington Square South, then 220 West 14th Street. *November:* DB publishes *A Book of Repulsive Women.*

1915–16 DB attends Art Students League of New York.

1916 DB meets Baroness Elsa von Freytag Loringhoven.

1917 *16 May:* Zadel dies of uterine cancer in Huntington; burial is in Middletown, Conn.

1917–19 DB lives with Courtenay Lemon in Greenwich Village.

1921 DB is sent as correspondent to Paris by *McCall's. September:* DB in Berlin. Meets Thelma Wood in Paris.

1923 DB's story collection *A Book* is published by Boni and Liveright. *September:* DB now lives at 173, boulevard Saint-Germain, Paris, with Thelma Wood.

1924 *14 October–16 February 1925:* DB in Cagnes-sur-Mer with Thelma Wood.

1927 *30 August:* DB and Wood move into recently purchased flat at 9, rue Saint-Romain, Paris.

1928 *Ryder* and *Ladies Almanack* are published.

1929 DB and Wood separate. Boni & Liveright publish *A Night Among the Horses*, revised version of *A Book*.

1930 DB lives in New York.

1931 *May:* DB begins friendship with Charles Henri Ford. *13 August:* DB operated on for appendicitis in Paris. *September–October:* DB and Ford travel to Munich, Vienna, and Budapest.

1932 *August:* DB spends month with Peggy Guggenheim and entourage at Hayford Hall, England.

1933 *April:* DB arrives to stay with Ford in Tangier. *13 June:* Returns to Paris for abortion. *12 July:* Arrives in Southampton en route to Hayford Hall. *Fall:* Returns to live in New York until 1936. Works on *Nightwood*.

1934 Wald and Fanny Barnes die in Philadelphia. *Spring:* DB begins affair with Peter Neagoe.

1935 DB works on *Nightwood*.

1936 *February:* DB works for the WPA, compiling a guide to New York City. *May 1:* Sails to Paris; to London May 16. Much of year is spent in London and Paris. Faber & Faber publish *Nightwood* in London.

1937 DB in London and Paris. *Summer:* DB begins affair with Silas Glossop. *27 July:* DB's Paris apartment is sold. *6 August:* DB moves to London. Harcourt, Brace publish the American edition of *Nightwood*.

1938 DB's alcoholism now very serious. *November:* DB travels to Megève, Haute-Savoie; stays there with Laurence Vail and Kay Boyle until end of January. Ends affair with Glossop.

1939 DB returns to London. *February:* Peggy Guggenheim takes DB to a nursing home for treatment of alcoholism. *1 July:* DB moves to Paris, lives at Hôtel Récamier. *12 October:* Sails to New York on *Washington*.

1940 *March:* DB sent by family to sanatorium on Lake George, New York. *May:* Travels to Arizona ranch to live with Emily Coleman; returns to New York in June. *September:* Moves into 5 Patchin Place, Greenwich Village.

1943 *18 January: Time* magazine interview with DB.

1945 *15 March:* DB's mother, Elizabeth Chappell Barnes, dies.

1950 *22 July:* DB's last voyage to Europe, on *Queen Mary.* DB stops drinking.

1958 *The Antiphon* is published.

1959 *28 January:* DB elected to National Institute of Arts and Letters.

1961 *17 February: The Antiphon* premieres in Stockholm's Royal Dramatic Theatre.

1968 *April and June:* DB undergoes double hernia operation. *6 June:* Estate of Albert Lewin leaves DB $5,000.

1970 *February:* DB has part of large intestine and gallbladder removed. Peggy Guggenheim grants Barnes $300 a month. *December:* Thelma Wood dies of spinal cancer in Connecticut.

1971 *21 December:* DB closes sale of her papers and manuscripts to University of Maryland.

1972 *February:* Natalie Barney dies, leaving DB small annual stipend.

1974 *13 June:* Emily Coleman dies at Catholic Workers' Farm, Tivoli, N.Y.

1982 *April:* DB taken to nursing home in Doylestown, Pennsylvania. *19 June:* Dies in Patchin Place. *Creatures in an Alphabet* published.

Abbreviations and Archival Information

■ ■ ■

N: Nightwood, by Djuna Barnes. New York: New Directions, 1946.
R: Ryder, by Djuna Barnes. Elmwood Park, Ill.: Dalkey Archive, 1990.
SW: Selected Works of Djuna Barnes. New York: Farrar, Straus & Cudahy, 1962.
A Night Among the Horses, by Djuna Barnes. New York: Boni & Liveright, 1929.
NY: New York, by Djuna Barnes. Los Angeles: Sun & Moon Press, 1989.
I: Interviews, by Djuna Barnes.
Smoke: Smoke and Other Early Stories, by Djuna Barnes. College Park, Md.: Sun & Moon Press, 1982; 2d ed., 1987.
Diaries: Diaries of Emily Holmes Coleman. Unpublished manuscript, University of Delaware Library.
OC: Out of This Century, by Peggy Guggenheim. New York: Dial, 1946.
C. Page: Chester Page, "Memories of Djuna Barnes." Unpublished manuscript.
Ford: Charles Henri Ford, "I Will Be What I Am." Unpublished manuscript.
O'Neal: Hank O'Neal: *Life is painful, nasty and short* . . . New York: Paragon House, 1990.
Time Morgue: James Stern's notes from *Time* interview with Djuna Barnes, 18 January 1943.

Unless otherwise noted, the letters to Djuna Barnes are located in the Djuna Barnes Collection, McKeldin Library, University of Maryland at College Park. Copies of many letters from Barnes to other people are also in this collection. Some letters from Barnes to Emily Holmes Coleman are at Maryland, but most are in the Special Collections Department, University of Delaware Library, Newark, Delaware, as are Coleman's diaries. Letters from Barnes to Natalie Clifford Barney are in Fonds Littéraire Jacques Doucet, Bibliothèque Sainte-Geneviève, Paris. Letters from Barnes to Robert McAlmon are in the Yale

Collection of American Literature, Beinecke Rare Book and Manuscript Library, Yale University. Letters to E. E. Cummings, Marion Morehouse, and Bradley S. Phillips are at the Houghton Library, Harvard University. Relevant manuscripts and letters of Charles Henri Ford are at the Harry Ransom Humanities Research Center, University of Texas at Austin. Permission to quote from letters to and from Djuna Barnes has been granted by these libraries, and this is acknowledged with gratitude.

DJUNA

Zadel

"There is no timber that has not strong roots among the clay and worms."[1]

Djuna Barnes sometimes wondered if she had not become her grandmother, so indelible was the imprint of the woman's influence and her fascinating life. To understand, one must begin with a detailed knowledge of her grandmother, Zadel, in whose footsteps Djuna Barnes followed during a considerable portion of her life, and whose remarkable career she wrote of again and again in her best fiction.

On 26 October 1857, Zadel Turner Barnes (born 9 March 1841) married Henry Aaron Budington (1831–1921), a few months after he graduated from Wesleyan University. One would have expected them to marry in Middletown, Connecticut, where Zadel was born and raised and where Henry had studied. That they did not is the first indication of the sort of untraditional behavior described in Djuna Barnes's *Ryder*, a novel whose facts and characters are almost without exception autobiographical.[2] There Zadel's counterpart, Sophia, confesses to her seduction of her Latin tutor, who marries her when her pregnancy is discovered. Sophia tells her daughter-in-law Amelia that she went for a lesson in Latin and came back a mother, having conjugated the Latin verb "to lie" and demonstrated literally her understanding of its usage. A page of Djuna's notes speaks of "her running away and of her consequent disgrace and forced marriage with the tutor Henry Budington."[3] Another fragment of Djuna's memoirs confirms that

Henry was indeed a tutor in Zadel's house. In any event, Zadel was only sixteen, and they married in his hometown, Leyden, Massachusetts. She was the first of her sisters to marry.

Zadel's wealthy father, Duane Barnes (1814–1900), whose parents were Elisha Barnes (1773–1841) and Lucy Jones Barnes (1774–1854), was, like Zadel, born in Middletown, in the Long Hill district, where his family had settled.[4] Duane's first wife, Cynthia Sexton Turner Barnes (1815–1867), one of seven beautiful daughters, as Djuna Barnes was fond of saying, was also born in Middletown; they married on 20 April 1834. Duane took great pride in his town and gave liberally of his time and money for civic improvement: his pet projects were building the railroad, planting shade trees, widening the river, and looking after the quarry, from which he took stone to build an interesting Gothic cottage on High Street, Clovernook, now the infirmary of Wesleyan University. Duane was first a teacher, later a builder, book dealer, and a "friend to just principles and right ideas," as his obituary said. He was happy to lend his beloved books to others or to sell books, provided they were not immoral. Students and faculty at Wesleyan often dropped by his store simply to read. Duane also wrote verse and was probably the first to teach Zadel the art, for she took poetry seriously from an early age.

The naming of Zadel and her siblings at the least showed imagination, though more probably it reflected a commitment to spiritualism. In order of age they were Marilla, Llewellyn, Hinda, Zadel, Lillian, Reon, Gaybert, Culmer, Kilmeny, Justa (she and Lillian lived but a year), and Everett.[5] Djuna thought Kilmeny the most strikingly beautiful, remembering a photo of her "in a tight thirty-button bodice with leg of mutton sleeves and a dash of mid victorian lace."[6] Zadel seems to have been especially devoted to her brother Llewellyn, who had pink cheeks and a fine beard, and who never returned from the Civil War.[7]

Zadel's article on Sir Walter Scott for *Harper's* (September 1871), called "The Bard of Abbotsford," begins with a glimpse of her father's library, where she indulged her girlhood reading tastes. Books were shelved from floor to ceiling in the large room, from which one could view the Connecticut River.

In a page of notes, Djuna recorded some details of Zadel's girlhood.[8] She was evidently a temperamental girl, for during a quarrel she threw a knife at a brother, which "stood quivering above his head in the moulding." Once, she ran away from home.

Zadel was taught at home and by tutors, but in 1856 she attended Wesleyan Academy in Wilbraham, Massachusetts (now the Wilbraham-Monson Academy), a coeducational Methodist school founded by the governing board of Wesleyan University.[9] Since Zadel lingered only briefly at these schools, she was probably looking beyond them to a writing career, for at thirteen she was publishing in local papers, and two years later her poems appeared in *The Home Journal*. When she married Henry the next year, few teenagers (then or now) could have matched her achievements.

After his marriage to Zadel, Henry taught in various schools. He was Assistant Assessor of Internal Revenue at Greenfield, Massachusetts (1862–69), and also an insurance agent, with an office on the courthouse square and a house on Davis Street (1865–69). During the Horace Greeley campaign of 1872, Henry (a supporter) founded and published the *Franklin County Times* in Greenfield. In 1873, the family moved to Springfield, Massachusetts, forty miles south along the Connecticut River. There Henry ran an advertising agency on Main Street and published spiritualist tracts.[10]

In moving to Springfield, Zadel left behind a small town, as well as her in-laws. Her new home, she found, was a small city, located a few miles from her old school in Wilbraham, with arguably one of America's best newspapers, the *Springfield Republican*. She would have been welcomed by editors and journalists impressed by her credentials. For the *Republican* she wrote poetry, stories, and literary reviews.[11]

The firstborn of Sophia Zadel in *Ryder* died in his sixth month (*R* 34); if this is based on truth, Zadel and Henry had three sons, two of whom survived childhood: Justin Llewellyn Budington, born 22

August 1859 in Middletown, and Henry Aaron Budington (Djuna's father), born 14 January 1865 in Greenfield.[12] Except for musical training, young Henry had little formal education beyond Boston Highlands High School (and would seldom be formally employed). Since Zadel later allowed him to choose his name, he changed it often during his lifetime. To spite his father, for whom he was named, Henry used the names Harry, Harold, Wald, and, in later years, Brian Eglinton Barnes (we will call him Wald).

Djuna's uncle Justin graduated from Cornell University in 1881 and attended medical school in New York, where he later practiced medicine of the eye and ear and specialized in removing cataracts.[13] His office was located at The Sydenham, Madison Avenue at Fifty-eighth Street, in New York. Family lore has it that Justin built the house in which Djuna was born, called The Chalet, on Storm King Mountain, above Cornwall-on-Hudson, New York, but land records do not support this, and he may have simply leased the property. It was on the east side of Mountain Road, diagonally opposite the entrance of the Mountain House Hotel, several hundred feet up the road.[14] Justin died in New York on 13 April 1907, cared for by his mother, who by this time had plenty of experience with the dying. He was buried in New Windsor, New York.

If Zadel caused a scandal in marrying Henry Budington, she caused a greater one when she divorced him—this time back in her hometown. She left Springfield and Henry in July of 1876 and took the boys to live, first, with her father in Middletown, then to Boston Highlands (now Roxbury), Massachusetts. She divorced Henry in February 1877; since divorces were rare, the court proceedings must have caused a sensation, though perhaps not for the Barnes family: Zadel's sister Marilla had divorced her first husband in about 1865.[15]

Zadel charged "intolerable cruelty and such conduct on the part of the defendant . . . as [to] permanently destroy the happiness of the petitioner and defeat the purposes of the marriage relation." Although this charge is found in Henry's petition to remarry, filed in Springfield in 1879, the judge found that since he had been of good character during the preceding six years, he might marry again. It seems to be a very odd judgment.[16]

Zadel's notes in preparation for her divorce trial paint a frightening portrait of Henry as an abusive man easily provoked to fury. According to her, Henry once threw her down a hall so forcefully that she fell against a door. When Justin was but a day old, Henry scuffled with one of Zadel's brothers next to her bed. He regularly knocked their two boys about, even though Justin had an enlarged heart and needed to avoid excitement, while Djuna's father, Wald, was supposedly prone to attacks of brain fever. Once, Henry struck Justin across the cheek with a carving knife; another time, he dragged Wald by his ankle down the hallway, knocking his head against a doorframe. Zadel also says that Henry carried a pistol, with which he intimidated her and demanded her signature to a life insurance policy to escape charges of embezzlement.

According to her notes, Zadel herself suffered from a heart malady and required solicitous treatment, but Henry refused to follow the physician's prescriptions. They had verminous flour and rancid butter. Henry was a brute in sexual matters, having no regard for the pain he caused her; he demanded intercourse during menstruation. So repugnant did Henry make himself that when he came in for meals, Zadel lost her appetite and "felt chill and faint."

Henry seems to have been a fanatical spiritualist. In her divorce testimony, Zadel says that he forced her and the boys to spend three weeks annually at a spiritualist camp meeting, saying that provisions would be available to them only there; if they wished to eat, they would attend.[17] Zadel herself seems to have been responsible for converting both her husbands to spiritualism, so adept a spirit medium was she. Apparently it took hold only too well, but if it seems odd that she would detest such meetings, it seems normal that she would detest the husband she describes.

Zadel's written conclusion to her plea for divorce from Henry Aaron Budington in Superior Court, Middlesex County, Connecticut, in February 1877, was as follows: "These things and others of a nature agreeing with them, have made my life with him intolerable to me, and by robbing me of sleep, appetite, peace, and health have more than once brought me close to the grave, and have made death seem of all things most to be desired, but for the condition in which my darling boys would be left." She was thirty-six at the time. Certainly her sons took her part, for they chose to take the surname Barnes, though Justin later reverted to Budington.

There is no record of Henry Budington's rebuttal, nor is it clear whether or not he contested the divorce, but one can speculate that he was glad to be rid of Zadel, being irritated by her success as a writer and by her outside activities, which may have included infidelity. She certainly outdid Budington, despite his Wesleyan education, and she had the drive to succeed as a writer, which he probably resented. At a time when her husband was gearing up to publish esoteric spiritualist tracts, Zadel had already published widely and well: for seven years she had contributed articles and poetry to *Harper's* (she would continue to do so until 1889).

Throughout her career as a journalist and creative writer, Zadel displayed a passion for social justice, a love for humankind, and a desire to call attention to the talents of notable American women, such as the actress Genevieve Ward (1837–1922) and the writer Maria Gowen Brooks (1794?–1845). Much of her writing would today be called sentimental, but it suited the taste of the time and the literary marketplace. For instance, the dedication to her novel *Can the Old Love?* (1871) begins:

> For those who know themselves to be travelling down the hill of Life, it may be a consolation to remember that old hearts need not be cold ones; To remember, that beyond the faltering step, and fading eye, and trembling hand, and gray hair fluttering in the evening wind, and the abrupt yawning of the inevitable grave,—lies the fair, free Hereafter of Eternal Youth, wherein all souls shall find what life and light and love do fully mean.

In a similar vein, her sentimental story "Where Is the Child?" begins: "The ends of the yule-log are in shadow, but its heart is a heart of fire," and goes on to explore the injustice and human waste of modern society. When Zadel wrote to touch the heart, she also expressed political concerns, as in her poem "The Prisoner." The first stanza reads:

> For years upon his dungeon floor
> He sat and counted o'er and o'er
> The hopeless links that, grim and fast,
> Chained out the Future and the Past;
> Trailing in rugged ruthless twist
> Down to the ankle from the wrist,
> Thence gliding, like a living thing,
> To grapple with an iron ring.
> He sat and counted, vaguely smiling,
> Himself with gibberish beguiling.
> For years like this; and then one night,
> Awaked as by a piercing call,
> Aroused as by a blinding light,
> With groping hands upon the wall,
> He caught his breath, remembering all!

The galloping cadence recalls Poe. One poem by Zadel that received national attention was "Little Martin Craghan," at once a memorial to a boy who died in a mine fire, trying to save older miners, and a protest against the exploitation of children.[18] Among Zadel's other pieces of political journalism was an important newspaper article on capital punishment (it has yet to turn up), which Appleton's *Cyclopaedia* says attracted "general attention." "Is It All There Still?" tells of a poor girl of the slums who dies dreaming of a beautiful week spent on a farm, a visit made possible by a charitable organization.[19]

Zadel did a considerable amount of unsigned writing, but her *Harper's* stories and verse earned her a national audience. Her long poem "The Voice of Christmas Past," with eighteen illustrations (*Harper's*, January 1871), is about Charles Dickens's *A Christmas Carol* but also manages to bring in for cameo appearances most of the interesting characters in Dickens. It was so successful that Zadel wrote another long poem, called "The Children's Night" (*Harper's*, January

1875), which featured familiar characters from bedtime stories. Zadel was an eclectic journalist; the variety of subjects she covered for *Harper's* is remarkable, from the Flemish artist Nicaise de Keyser to Moses Montefiore to Saint Cecilia. Once she wrote an article on Afghanistan, which contained purported truisms of Afghan character that today would be considered embarrassing ("As the Afghans are a nation of thieves, and live upon the fruits of this vice, they are lenient toward it").[20]

It is unclear whether Zadel pursued famous people, or they her, but she certainly developed connections. In 1877, Henry Wadsworth Longfellow sent her a picture of himself taken in London that year.[21] There was also a letter from John D. Rockefeller. Djuna used to say that Zadel knew Abraham Lincoln and "helped in the Underground Railway."[22] Her sister in Washington makes a meeting with Lincoln plausible, and her strongly abolitionist sentiments would have fostered such a meeting.

In Zadel's library were two volumes of John Greenleaf Whittier's poetry inscribed to her in friendship by the Quaker poet: *The Vision of Echard* (inscribed in 1879) and *St. Gregory's Guest and Recent Poems* (inscribed in 1886). His friendship with Zadel had been something of an embarrassment to him. When her collection of verse called *Meg, A Pastoral* came out in 1878, Whittier wrote her on Christmas Eve to say: "I have read *Meg* with delight. It is a charming New England Pastoral, very sweet and tender, and musical as the songs of our thrushes and song sparrows." About her tribute to William Cullen Bryant, the second poem, he said: "But the elegy on Bryant! I can only compare it with Milton's 'Lycidas'; it is worthy of any living poet at least." The poem begins:

> Thus sang a glorious voice, that, full and free,
> Filled all the atmosphere from star to sea:—
> Speed hither, winds, and blend in noble mirth
> The many-chorded harmonies of earth;
> Bend, cloudless heavens, thy quickening golden eye
> Beyond the mountain snows that crest on high . . .

Since it does not get much better, Whittier's praise was a real stretcher, as Huck Finn would have said, an exaggeration that returned to haunt him, because Zadel promptly showed the quotation around to promote her book. A literary editor of *The Critic* (New York) who expressed his doubts about the veracity of Whittier's praise in "The Lounger" column for 11 October 1884 was forced by Zadel to retract, for she cited Whittier chapter and verse in a letter to "The Lounger" sent from London on November 13. Whittier had perhaps forgotten his lavish praise and then denied it, saying, "no one could dream of comparing the 'simple, unpretentious poem' with anything of Milton's," but Zadel set them straight on the facts of the matter.

In any event, Zadel's *Meg* was praised by important connoisseurs of poetry. Edwin P. Whittle said that "On the Sands" and "The Prisoner" ranked "with the best English verse"; Bryant, whom Zadel eulogized in *Meg*, said of her poem "Flower of May," which he saw before publication, that it was "the most exquisite dress that flower has ever worn in the English language." Longfellow said that *Meg* "placed her beyond doubt in the foremost ranks of the younger poets," and he suggested that she dramatize her story "Karin," about a Swedish commoner girl who married into royalty.[23] Like most writers, she enjoyed discussing the praise she earned.

When Zadel moved to Boston in 1876, she was entering the world of Henry James and his novel *The Bostonians* (1886), which he began writing in 1883 and which takes as its theme the suffragists and by implication the radical and reformist movements to which Zadel was attracted. As an experienced medium, she may also have moved in the spiritualist circles the novel describes. It is possible that she actually met James, since they shared the same Boston publisher, James R. Osgood.[24]

Zadel could hardly have moved in those circles for a day without hearing about, and wanting to meet, Elizabeth Peabody, the unworldly Miss Birdseye of James's novel, who was at the center of nearly every progressive movement in Boston. James's narrator says of Birdseye: "she was heroic, she was sublime, the whole moral history of Boston was reflected in her displaced spectacles."[25]

Soon after her divorce—on 3 May 1877, to be exact—Zadel was married to a Swedish immigrant named Axel Carl Johan Gustafson on his birthday in a Middletown church ceremony. Axel is listed on their marriage certificate as a clergyman residing in Cambridge, Massachusetts.[26] Born in Lund, Sweden, on 3 May 1849, Axel emigrated in 1871 to the United States, worked on farms in the West, taught school, and eventually became a citizen. Interested in the temperance movement, he wrote an article on the granting of licenses to serve alcohol in Göteborg. When he met Zadel in Boston, he must have been doing editorial work. According to Wald's son Duane, Axel and Zadel had a son, Emmanuel, who died shortly after birth, then appeared occasionally in Zadel's séances, as little more than a contented smile.[27] The year after they married, Zadel dedicated *Meg: A Pastoral* to Axel, "in token of his wife's love." They lived at 5 Linden Avenue, Boston Highlands.

Zadel continued to write. From childhood on, she had been interested in Maria Gowen Brooks, whose nom de plume was Maria del Occidente. A Massachusetts woman who had married and settled on a Cuban coffee plantation, Brooks was a poet and the author of *Zóphiël, or The Bride of Seven*, a romantic work that had been greatly admired by Robert Southey and Charles Lamb, and which so captivated Zadel that she edited a new edition for publication in 1879. In 1872, Zadel began corresponding with Brooks's relatives, as well as with descendants of the English Romantic poets who knew her, Southeys and Coleridges, and eventually she published an article on Maria del Occidente in *Harper's* (1879).

Zadel was sent to London in 1880 by *McCall's* magazine, and though she and Axel traveled extensively (they went to Sweden in 1880 or 1881), London remained their base until 1889. The preface to her biography of Genevieve Ward was dated London, 27 August 1881. It was probably in 1882 that the Gustafsons met Samuel Morley, (1809–86), a very wealthy wool manufacturer, philanthropist, reformer, and member of Parliament for Bristol, who persuaded Axel to write on the abuse of alcohol rather than tobacco, as he had planned.

Morley, who headed the City of London Total Abstainers' Union, had earlier favored persuasion on the question of alcohol abuse, but by 1878 he advocated legislation and was willing to spend money on the cause. One result was Axel Gustafson's *The Foundation of Death* (London, 1884), one of the most successful temperance books of the last century. It was written between March 1883 and May 1884 (and later revised twice), and its influence on the Women's Christian Temperance Union and similar organizations was apparently profound.[28]

Morley bought a hundred copies of Axel's temperance book to present to friends he wished to influence. Edwin Hodder quotes Morley's accompanying letter to William Gladstone, which calls for the Prime Minister to lead his Blue Ribbon supporters to "a final and victorious onslaught against the greatest of all modern social evils," alcohol.[29]

Axel's book rapidly went through three editions, and the final one lists Zadel as coauthor; it included an exhaustive bibliography on the evils of alcohol, a historical overview, and chapters on various aspects of alcohol abuse. The book was translated into seven languages and put Gustafson in demand on the lecture circuit. In 1884, with Morley's help, the Gustafsons founded and edited the *National Philanthropist*. Along with Zadel, Axel was instrumental in establishing the prohibition parties of England (1887), Sweden (1889), and the state of Victoria, Australia (1890). Axel also started and led the Anti-Compensation campaign in England in 1889.

The Gustafsons lived well in London. Not only did Morley subsidize publishing costs; he paid the Gustafsons well enough so that, together with the earnings from Zadel's articles for *Harper's*, the *Pall Mall Gazette*, and other journals, they could have a respectable address, where Zadel kept an influential literary salon.[30] (Her counterpart in Djuna Barnes's play *The Antiphon* is called the Middletown Récamier "free-soiler, free-thinker, nonconformist, mystic—Abolitionist, Hyde Park orator—)" (*SW* 148–49).

From a window overlooking Trafalgar Square on 13 November 1887, Zadel observed "Bloody Sunday," a police riot that attacked an illegal socialist demonstration led by the famous literati George Bernard Shaw and William Morris, then she drew a sketch of the events, showing where Cunningham Graham was bludgeoned.[31]

As in Boston, Zadel was drawn to radical, literary, and reformist circles in London: she knew Lady Wilde, some of the Pre-Raphaelites, Robert Browning (1812–89), the actress Mary Anderson (1859–1940), the actress-comedienne Lotta Crabtree (1847–1924), Karl Marx's daughter Eleanor (1855–98), the blind poet Philip Bourke Marston (1850–87), and his friend Herbert Edwin Clarke, whose *Poems and Sonnets* was published in 1895, and the eccentric Richard Hengist Horne (1803–84), mentioned in Zadel's introduction to *Zóphiël*. She was a friend of Charles Reade (1814–84), the author of *The Cloister and the Hearth*.[32]

Of especial importance in Zadel's London years was Lady Wilde (1826–96) (and to a lesser extent her son Oscar Wilde [1854–1900]), with whom Zadel had much in common beyond an interest in literature.[33] Lady Wilde was an Irish nationalist who had written her share of inflammatory articles for *The Nation*, and she was a feminist who wrote in "The Bondage of Women" that "We have now traced the history of women from Paradise to the nineteenth century, and have heard nothing through the long roll of the ages but the clank of their fetters."[34]

Lady Wilde's first salon had been at the elegant address of 1 Merrion Square in Dublin, where all were welcome, and many presumed upon her hospitality. In London, as in Dublin, "the rooms, lit by lamps and candles, were shuttered and closely curtained even in the afternoon when the sun was shining out of doors."[35] At Lady Wilde's one could have met American visitors such as Oliver Wendell Holmes, Henry Ward Beecher, and Bret Harte.[36]

Lady Wilde, known as Speranza, was well over six feet tall and of great girth, and she typically sported a costume such as "two crinolines under a silk gown that swept the floor, . . . an oriental scarf, flounces of lace, a number of rings and brooches" and a black wig crowned with "a gilded Laurel wreath."[37] Richard Ellmann, with memorable wit, describes how she "sailed among her guests with swelling canvas."[38] It was probably Zadel's impression of Lady Wilde's figure that Djuna recorded in "Julie von Bartmann": "[She] wondered, under the subdued lights, why Mme Wilde looked so monstrous in dotted swiss."[39] Tall Speranza and the petite Zadel would have made an odd pair at the famous salon, where Oscar passed the teacups and notable people packed into the small rooms with the curious (in two senses), but as a journalist and liberal thinker, Zadel likely found these gatherings of immense interest.

From 1883 through 1889, both Speranza and Zadel contributed articles to the *Pall Mall Gazette*, edited by William Thomas Stead (1849–1912). In its pages also appear articles by Matthew Arnold, Leslie Stephen, G. B. Shaw, and Oscar Wilde. This magazine, the most passionate voice for reform in Britain in the 1880s, was represented by Zadel while she was in the United States in 1886.[40] Stead's favorite topic was Ireland, and curiously enough, like Zadel's husbands, he became an ardent spiritualist.[41]

Three letters from Zadel to Lady Wilde are records of their friendship from 1882 to 1888. In one dated 23 June 1882, written from 14 Brunswick Square, Zadel thanked Lady Wilde for a pamphlet she wrote on the Irish question and a photograph of her son Oscar, who recently entertained them at the Falstaff Club. Zadel promised a photo of Axel in return. She endorsed Lady Wilde's views on the oppression of Ireland and expressed her wish to travel there: "I want to go among those poor evicted ones & return to sing their wrongs in burning verse to the guilty ears which heed them so little."

In June of 1882, Zadel wrote Lady Wilde to say that she would attend her party and wished to bring along not only Axel but Eleanor Marx, "a very accomplished & clever girl, & I believe as good as she is attractive." She and Axel admired Lady Wilde's political pamphlet, regretting that Speranza was not in Parliament or Downing Street, a view unlikely to have been shared by many in government.

From her London lodgings in 30 Cromwell Grove, off Shepherd's Bush Road (the semidetached house, with garden, still exists), Zadel inquired of Lady Wilde whether she might bring some American friends, "into the liberal sunshine of your presence" (she forgot mo-

mentarily the gloom in which Speranza's guests were received), signing it "Faithfully always, Yours & Ireland's" (1 August 1888). In a
postscript, Zadel invites her on the following day to a private discussion on the Irish question with Mr. Gill, M.P. "I am urged to bring
friends & you are my friend are you not—Speranza."

Late in life, Barnes told her young friend Chester Page, a frequent
companion in her last years, that her grandmother was a "great friend"
of Oscar's brother Willie and that Oscar admired Djuna's father's
curls.[42] Barnes used what Zadel probably told her in a scene in *Ryder*,
where Willie Wilde presses Sophia Zadel's little hand in hot pursuit,
while her husband, Alex (as Axel is called), can be heard in the other
room whispering sweet nothings in Mary Anderson's ear (*R* 19). Still
later in the book, Wendell/Wald describes Oscar Wilde as "a man of
beauty, who looked through a privy-ring at the stars" (*R* 166); seeing
him in a cab in troubled times, Wendell turns away to avoid being
recognized and feels himself damned for cowardice. As a young man,
Djuna's father may have felt guilty about his inability to show support
for Oscar Wilde, the son of his mother's friend, condemned to prison
for homosexuality.

Zadel shared Lady Wilde's political views: a fragment from *The
Antiphon* describes the Zadel figure, Victoria, as "abolitionist, free-
thinker, *raconteur*, abstainer, known for her turbans; seizures; wit."[43]
She is the model woman writer, who keeps a salon where advanced
thinkers from the arts and politics rub shoulders and communicate
ideas. But unsuspected by Zadel, the model would have a darker side:
the woman writer who is struck with adversity in old age, who falls
into poverty and neglect.

For Djuna's father there was perhaps also a legacy, for he must
have been impressed by Lady Wilde's conviction that everyone who
visited her salon, including himself, was destined for greatness. Re-
inforced by Zadel, his belief in his own artistic abilities and eventual
fame never left him. In his pursuit of greatness, Wald thought that it
helped to have a distinguished name and, perhaps, a noble lineage to
be a success, a belief Djuna parodied in *The Antiphon*, where it is
said that Titus/Wald, pretending to the "earldom of old Pendry" and

to be the "Baron of Castaigne . . . / Went scratching in the barnyard straw / Searching his escutcheon" (*SW* 160). In *Nightwood*, this becomes a trait of the Volkbeins.

Around 1 July 1882, Eleanor Marx, called Tussy by her friends, was introduced by Zadel to Lady Wilde, who subsequently invited her back. Eleanor wrote her sister Jenny later in July to say that she had been "asked . . . to a 'crush' at Lady Wilde's . . . the mother of that very limp and very nasty young man, Oscar Wilde, who has been making such a d——d ass of himself in America. As the son has not yet returned and the mother is nice I may go."[44] For many years, Tussy had supported the Irish cause and so would have been sympathetic company for Zadel and Speranza. She was the favorite daughter of Karl Marx, who had obstructed her desires in love and vocation, greatly affecting her health. Tussy was to scandalize many by setting up housekeeping with a prolific author on socialism and atheism, Edward Aveling (1849–98) at a time when such arrangements were a rarity. Zadel, however, would have approved of this "free love" arrangement.[45]

Eventually Zadel set up her own salon at 30 Cromwell Grove, an obscure address then and now. An autobiographical blurb Djuna wrote for Harper & Row places Zadel's salon at a far grander address, Grosvenor Square (the American embassy is there). It was said to have been attended by Oscar Wilde and Robert Browning. On other occasions Djuna added to the list the Pre-Raphaelites, and the actresses Mary Anderson and Lotta Crabtree. A glimpse of what the salon may have been like is visible in *Ryder*, in which Sophia collects young women friends and asks them to call her "Mother," a tactic she imagines they cannot resist. Eleanor Marx might have been tempted to do so, having grieved so over the loss of her own mother. Zadel's letters to Djuna Barnes's mother are typically signed "Mother."

Victoria Woodhull (1838–1927), the radical feminist, spiritualist, reformer, and advocate of sexual freedom, was already in London when Zadel arrived. Woodhull, who had moved there in 1877 after the death of her benefactor, Cornelius Vanderbilt, had pleaded for women's suffrage before the judiciary committee of the House of Representatives in 1871. She divorced her husband a year before Zadel divorced Henry Budington. The year after Zadel moved to London, Woodhull married a rich English banker, John B. Martin. In 1871, she had been the first woman to run for President of the United States; the next year, she published the first English translation of Marx and Engels's *Communist Manifesto*. Her views on free love would have been shared by Zadel; Djuna Barnes certainly saw the connection, because she named Zadel Victoria in her play *The Antiphon*.

On March 4, 1888, about a week after giving a reception for the great American suffragist Elizabeth Cady Stanton, Zadel sailed to New York with Stanton and a group of women who were delegates to the first International Council of Women Convention in Washington, D.C., which was assembled by the National Woman Suffrage Association and held from 25 March to 1 April.[46] Zadel, representing the National Prohibition Movement of Great Britain, gave an eloquent address on women's suffrage, alcohol abuse, and other social issues, which was published in *The Women's Tribune* for 5 April.

There was obviously an important link between the vote for women and prohibition, because many thought that women's suffrage would in effect mean prohibition.[47] And in fact in London, Zadel, Axel, and Wald began to be snubbed socially; Djuna recalled her mother's account:

> They went off to the salon that had once so much admired them, your father and his mother, to Lady Gray, and there they were snubbed and returned. Why, well goodness why not, did not your grandmother and her renegade husband stump on prohibition, and yet there always were decanters in her what-not, if I recall.[48]

Zadel returned to the United States in May 1889; on 3 July, she attended the wedding of Djuna's parents in New York City. Later that month, she traveled west, en route to Australia; her business card of the period lists the address Bella Vista, Parliament Place, East Melbourne, and says she represented *Frank Leslie's Weekly*, *Leslie's Monthly*, and *The Judge*. Perhaps the Gustafsons were there to help found the Prohibition Party in the state of Victoria. Zadel stayed in Australia from about August 1889 until March 1890, when she sailed on the S.S. *Mariposa* to Europe.

During the 1880s, Zadel and Axel had received much of their support from Samuel Morley, but he died in 1886, and the royalties on *The Foundation of Death* were likely at an end. Also nearing an end was her marriage to Axel. By August of 1890, the separation must have been final, since she cut the name Gustafson from a letter of 22 August, but they probably never divorced formally. He may have had an affair with a younger woman.[49] Zadel mourned the separation from Axel for a decade; in one letter, she said that she had tried to save a man who couldn't save himself. This may mean that the author of *The Foundation of Death* was himself an alcoholic.

Djuna's story "Oscar" describes Emma Gonsberg (Emma Goldman + Zadel) as a "little creature, lively, smiling. She had been married twice, divorced once, and now a widow in her early thirties. Of her two husbands she seldom said anything. When she did, it was always this: 'Only fancy, they never did catch on to me.' "[50]

What is implied is that Emma's husbands didn't "catch on" to her infidelities, though Zadel seems to have been hurt by Axel's. Djuna referred to her grandmother's many amours in conversations with Chester Page and gave the same description in *Ryder*, where among Sophia's prized possessions is a Swedish trunk with seven locks, which contains compromising letters from many married lovers. If Zadel's husbands did not actually catch her in bed with other men, they surely heard at length her philosophy of sexual freedom. In any event, after their breakup, neither Zadel (though she tried) nor Axel seems to have published or to have carried on with a public career. Axel returned to Middletown and is listed in the 1891 city directory as living with Zadel's father, Duane, at Clovernook. When Duane died, in 1900, Axel stayed on in Middletown and held down odd jobs; he worked for I. E. Palmer, which made Arawana Hammocks, and later was a hospital attendant and then a night watchman. Like Henry Budington, and certainly under Zadel's influence, Axel began to experiment with the occult in later years. In 1919, he faded without a trace from directories, but one source says that he died in 1914.[51] Zadel's certificate of death, in 1917, listed her as a widow.

In the 1890s, Zadel traveled a fair amount. In a 9 October 1895 letter to Djuna's mother, she mentions caring for her brother Gaybert, who was to die four days later, at the age of forty-eight, in his house at 670 Tenth Street in Brooklyn. Her description of his passing is memorable: he was formerly "beautiful with the beauty of strength, as now he is beautiful with the loveliness of patiently accepted weakness." Times of great stress seemed to bring out the best in Zadel.

Zadel's career as published author was pretty much at an end by 1898. On 31 January of that year, journalist, labor reformer, and champion of the oppressed John Swinton (1830–1901) wrote her that a manuscript of hers had been rejected by the publisher O'Loughlin, mainly because it dealt with the "sex question"; he suggested that she send it to *The Truth Seeker* in Brooklyn. It never appeared.

By 1900, when her father died, Zadel was a tired woman of fifty-nine, who richly deserved retirement and an easier life. Her well-to-do son, Justin, might have made her later years more comfortable, but she was on uneasy terms with his family. Instead, she had to support herself, her son Wald, plus his wife and mistress and their children, a commune at one time numbering thirteen. She worked for some time for what seems to have been a fund-raising organization called the Patriotic League of the Revolution, in Brooklyn, but it cannot have brought in enough money. Letters show that she worked there as early as February 1906 and as late as 1911.[52]

Djuna Barnes re-created the scenario for her grandmother Zadel in *Ryder*, when Sophia goes to each child in turn, pledging love and care (*R* 169). The entire burden of support of the Barnes family rested on the shoulders of an aging woman whose earning power was diminishing, but it would have been out of character for Zadel to be the disciplinarian, insisting that her son become gainfully employed, and Wald wouldn't have been Wald if he had been realistic about the future. The eternal optimist, he continually devised schemes for instant success as either a composer, a writer, or a painter. He even made an offering to Buffalo Bill, for on 6 April 1899, Colonel William F. Cody of Nebraska wrote to thank Wald for sending a painting that he particularly admired. He carefully avoided asking Wald to travel with the show.

The fictional counterpart of Wald Barnes's mistress in *Ryder* angrily insists on having as many children as she likes, regardless of Sophia/Zadel's age and burden, despising such mean economies as giving the children bread made from cow fodder—despising, too, the stupid absence of planning that had brought about such a crisis (*R* 170–71). Zadel, who came from a family of eleven children herself, initially must have thought it both a desirable situation and a challenge. However, when Wendell, the Wald of *Ryder*, asks his mother what one does with nature, she answers: "A humane man would occasionally give it respite" (*R* 172).

Yet for Zadel, Wald could do no wrong, and they ardently shared the free-love philosophy. Her letter of 13 March 1906 contains the line: "I simply shrieked when I read that Papa [Wald] had made a hole in Mrs. Jones." But Wald certainly lacked the approval of his father, who on 24 May 1913 sent Djuna his genealogy of the Budington family, which asserts that Zadel had led her son "to a course of life ill adapted to produce a successful and correct life." As late as 1912, Henry Budington was apparently offering financial aid if Wald would take his old surname back, an idea Wald rejected as "bribery."

In a letter to Djuna dated 11 March 1913, Zadel says: "You will remember my long established shabbiness of wardrobe & can guess what further lapse of time has done to it!" By the summer of that year, she was taking desperate steps to increase the family income, including writing to friends and acquaintances for money, and she kept her extended family from the poorhouse for some ten years with such letters (see *R* 14–15, 176ff.). On 27 August 1913, a supplication was sent by Zadel to Jack London (1876–1916), whom she had never met, ostensibly requesting free books. Zadel's draft survives (question marks preceding words indicate uncertain readings on my part):

It is now two years and six months since, trusting in the large nobleness of mind I find in your works, and under pressure of a great crisis in my life, I broke through strangerhood and distance and wrote you a letter, to which your reply is, I think, the most beautiful and royalhearted letter ever written from stranger to stranger and transforming strangerhood into vital friendship—for I have felt that that single exchange of letters made us friends, and I did not write again because the situation and ?conditions concerning which I wished for your counsel and help could only be dealt with adequately by consultation, face to face . . . in the hope that you might possibly be coming to New York so that I could talk with you. Perhaps after all this time you will not remember me at all—unless you remember my delight in the exquisite story of Elam and Dede and your Dede's pleasure in my delight. Your wish that we lived near each other, and your invitation to visit you on your ranch if I ever came to California—and your friendly charge to remember that your latchstring was out are a memorable and permanent ?sweetness in my life—and I ought to have told you so more promptly—but the very impasse under the stress of which I first wrote you—has continued . . . to exact all the time and strength I possess in the struggle with it. I can't buy anything beyond bare subsistence—and not even that only by observance of the most diabolical economy—ergo, I can't buy books . . . and therefore have only heard, not seen your books that have been published since "Burning Daylight"—so, if you have more copies of any of them than you need—or have not planned otherwise to dispose of—for dear ?love's sake send them to me—who read your big soul in, as well as between the lines of them—and write your name in them. . . . I sympathize with you and Charmian if the press reports of the burning of Glen Ellen be true. I wish I could hope they are not true—I think most regretfully of what Elam and Dede may have lost. . . . Fire is so kind a servant and so relentless a master. Fifty-three years ago my own home, a new two story ten room cottage on a pretty terraced plot in a New England town, was destroyed by fire.[53]

On a separate sheet, Zadel listed the real reasons she was writing, and these were doubtless inserted in the actual letter. They read

"Mortgage foreclosure impending. loss of home—consequent catastrophe to present & future—precious grandchildren—invalidism of an only son were involved but these hard problems were enclosed in the network of a harder problem than all put together which I could discuss with you—but could not write about."

It was said in *Ryder* that "Into those hundreds of begging letters went all of Sophia Grieve Ryder, her cunning, her humour, her deceit, her humbleness, and always, with unerring faithfulness to her original discovery of the way to the heart of man, they were signed 'Mother' " (*R* 15).

Jack London's wife, Charmian, answered Zadel's letter promptly on 12 September, ignoring the plea for help and the request for an interview. Under separate cover she sent autographed copies of *The Sea Wolf* and *Adventure*. Zadel wrote the Londons once more, in 1915, again receiving a response from Charmian, in Honolulu, dated 24 May 1915. While the Londons were preparing for a voyage to Molokai, Zadel was preparing for death. A letter of December 1916 indicates that she was receiving radium treatment for uterine cancer, for which Djuna, by now a successful journalist, lent her money.

So with love and infinite patience, Zadel sacrificed herself for her family, wearing a thirty-year-old pauper's cloak to knock on doors in New York City, forgiving her bigamist son, who was content to whittle, to putter about their farm, and to play the piano while his wives and children were supported by the frantic struggles of an aging woman who was suffering from cancer.

Zadel's death scene is evoked at the end of *Ryder* (237ff.), as Wendell sits weeping in terror. One smells the unpleasant odor of cancer, undisguised by the violet toilet water, and feels the warmth of the wood stove. His mother's small body occupies but half the bed, and on her left hand, the bloodstone ring given her by the king of Sweden encircles a finger that points to George Eliot's novel *Adam Bede*.[54]

In a shockingly callous unpublished narrative called "History of an American Family," of which only pages 1 and 2 survive, Djuna Barnes described the hours following the death of Zadel in the family's

Huntington, Long Island, farmhouse on 16 May 1917 as remembered by Fanny, Wald's mistress now his wife. Djuna had paid a last visit to Zadel some two hours before her death. Fanny said that Wald had wanted to clean his mother before the undertaker arrived; with Fanny's oldest son, Duane, helping (he was asleep on the floor when his grandmother died), Wald had taken one leg and she the other, but they were shocked when cancerous matter shot from Zadel's vagina onto Fanny. When some got into her mouth, she spit and took salt water to vomit.

Barnes evokes the image of Wald, in sheepskin coat, boiling medicinal rags in an outdoor laundry cooker. Not being present herself, Barnes has Fanny say that the undertaker took Zadel's body out in a wicker basket, to be sent to Middletown for burial. Wald is defensive about not accompanying the body. Asked what she felt about Zadel's death, Fanny answered that the dominant feeling was resentment at the odor and the horror of Zadel's last days, when her body was so little in control of its functions.

After Zadel's death, Djuna, crying, excused herself to work on a newspaper story, but she really had only one idea, to escape the smell of her grandmother, which she felt would linger in her nostrils throughout her life. She found her escape in sexual intercourse with her then lover, Courtenay Lemon, an especially passionate encounter with "extra strong climax to drown out the sound of those death splatterings of my beloved" grandmother, her "first love."

Amid many barbs, Djuna paid tribute to Zadel in her writings.

> That old lady knew how to be old.
> Bent double, as a sailor from the sea
> Low slung in gifts
> She came at you, blazing like a grot
> Hung in the offerings of her children's love.[55]

During the last months of her life, with undiminished wit, Zadel was in the care of Dr. H. H. Janeway, in appreciation of whom she wrote one of her last poems.

The ailing ones—along the Hospital laneway,
Watch daily for your coming—Dr. Janeway!
You—whose trained mind, and heart humane and pure,
Guide your skilled hands—to our relief and cure:
You who, however closely claimed and weary—
Give ever the kind smile—and verdict cheery,—
Give ever of your store of healing power,
From day to day,—through ever waking hour,
Inestimable, heroic service—thine!—
Only the grace of grateful blessing,—mine!

Zadel was buried to the left of her mother in the Barnes plot in
Pine Grove Cemetery, Middletown. There is no grave marker.

Storm King

"Man lives between the dreadful press of groin and grave."[1]

I n 1888, under the name Wald Gustafson, Djuna's father published a twelve-page pamphlet called "Practical Air-Navigation," which described a model airship that was to be bicycle-driven.[2] He was truly eclectic: his many talents included wood carving, whittling, painting, drawing; he wrote in prose or verse, could build a house, was able to fix things, plow, plant, and reap, and slaughter animals for food. He could write operas with full orchestra score, carve a flute, play the piano well, other musical instruments a little, and give music instruction to his children. Wald Gustafson, the name of the moment, was listed on an engraved certificate of recommendation signed by Gustav Ernest, Professor of Music, Crystal Palace School of Art, Science and Literature, in London, dated November 1888.[3] The recipient probably intended to use the certificate to attract music students.

Zadel was convinced that Wald was a misunderstood artistic genius who needed a long sabbatical in order to produce the one great musical or literary work that would capture the imagination of the art world, but except for the art of seduction, in which he excelled, he lacked the perseverance to be expert in anything. Being a dilettante was good enough for Wald, and his mother supported him for the first fifty years of his life.[4] Chapter 10 of *Ryder*, written in Chaucerian couplets, describes Wendell Ryder's many occupations, prefaced by these lines:

Now ye of all good virtue, bring your sewing,
For herein sleeps a dog beyond your knowing.
And all ye Burghers rowdy, drink and spit
For this be wholë cloth of Wendell's wit.

In her 1943 interview with *Time*, Djuna said that her father "was a cabinet maker, a painter, a novelist, a poet, a musician who played five instruments, a composer who wrote librettos for his own operas, a man who could never stay put. He was more nervous than I am. While I scream when someone comes near my door, he simply fainted away." Wald's relaxed attitude toward vocation derived from the certain knowledge that his once celebrated mother believed in his talent and indulged his polygamist views. Minor peccadilloes were forgiven with a jolly embrace. As James B. Scott noted after interviewing Barnes in 1971, "Wald was in many ways a gifted man, a man of vision." He "trusted nature, distrusted society," and had "a messianic impulse to reform . . . society, using nature as his prototype."[5] His beliefs were close to those of Henry Thoreau, but with an admixture of Brigham Young, plus Zadel's feminist social conscience and spiritualism. Preaching a philosophy that justified his promiscuity, he imagined a world of musicians and poets, free from societal constraints and religious oppression, hopping joyfully from bed to bed. He must have observed such a scene in the radical London circles in which his mother moved. These beliefs and practices caused his children to feel shame, to lack respect for him as teacher and provider, and to long for a conventional home life. Among themselves, however, Wald was also the source of much laughter.

As early as 1895, Wald was using as his pen name Brian Eglinton Barnes, and this was the name he kept longest. In *Ryder*, Wald is called Wendell, and in *The Antiphon* he is Titus: both characters share many characteristics with their counterpart, including his birth date. He has "a hawk nose, a long lip that upon the nipple seemed too purposeful, a body like a girl's," and red hair (*R* 17). In Barnes's notes, Titus is "a damned self-indulgent rustic," with big thumbs, good for puttying windows, nice teeth, "knee britches, and a flowing tie."

He plays "six instruments—badly."[6] *Ryder*'s Wendell recalls working as a drug clerk in London for three weeks before being fired for mixing up a pharmacy order; after a similar experience, Wald never worked at a steady job again until three years after his mother died, when he was fifty-five.

Indulged by Zadel from childhood, Wald had it in his nature to shirk responsibility and to look to his mother to solve his problems and provide for his needs and wants. His son Saxon said that Zadel spoiled everybody, especially Wald,[7] making him unfit for work. She controlled him so completely that he resented both his father, Henry, and his stepfather, Axel, with whom he had to share his mother's affection. It is little wonder that he was a poor provider.

Barnes has her fictional father confess to having been sexually initiated by a kitchen maid, which, if true of Wald, would have greatly amused Zadel (*R* 167). His mother seems to have acted as his procuress at times, binding young women to her with charm and promises, then standing aside to delight in her son's successful seductions. So it was with the wooing of Djuna's mother.

Elizabeth Chappell came with her sister, Susanna, to London to study violin at the Academy of Music in about 1886 and lived next door to the Gustafsons. In May of 1924, Elizabeth wrote to Djuna in London to have a look at Cromwell Grove in Shepherd's Bush, "where I met my fate." She was born on 3 November 1862 in Oakham, in the county of Rutland, to Henry Chappell (born 1826) and Ann Chamberlain (born 1828). In *Time* in 1943, Djuna called her mother a "beautiful, dour Englishwoman."[8] Wald teased her about being English and would say with scorn, "You British!" He claimed to be anything but English himself, chiefly Scotch and Irish, though in fact he was mostly of English stock.

Djuna never knew her maternal grandparents, for they were dead by the time her parents married. Her grandfather Chappell, partly of French Huguenot descent, with a touch of Irish blood, was a builder specializing in slating and plastering, but his first love was cabinetmaking. Elizabeth Barnes told Djuna her family history in great detail, noting that grandfather Henry was the silent type and "was as kind as necessary, as fecund as possible, a sturdy worker." Henry's family belonged to the Church of England; he rode to services on horseback, after which he hunted hares.[9]

Djuna's grandmother Ann Chamberlain had been a farm girl from Hambleton who had earlier fallen in love with a rake named Rayworth, but her family insisted that she marry a responsible fellow like Chappell.[10] Family legend has it that Ann's sister Elizabeth was mistress to the duke of Cambridge, Queen Victoria's uncle, until he married her off to a Captain Bailey.[11]

The Chappells lived in Flore House, which Barnes would later visit and remember vividly; it is the setting of her late play *The Antiphon*. Djuna's mother left Flore House and Oakham for London when her widowed mother died, and the parents' estate was divided up among the children. Elizabeth's small inheritance was later turned over to Zadel and Wald, an act she would never cease to regret; they eventually used it to buy the Long Island farm and then turned her and her children out.

Elizabeth was enticed into the Gustafson sphere by the idea of developing as a poet under Zadel's tutelage, and perhaps the prospect of playing duets with Wald. Zadel praised her poetry and told of many connections in the publishing world. To the end of her days, Elizabeth felt aggrieved that Zadel had filled their lives with so many empty promises, which had given them—especially Wald—an unrealistic view of future prospects. Two years before her death, Elizabeth wrote Djuna: "Even unto today I seem to feel & expect miracles."[12] Augusta, Elizabeth's counterpart in *The Antiphon*, says: "Was I, a country girl, to disbelieve her? May I be forgiven, I believed her utterly; she was so tender and perfidious . . . she had my purse, my person, and my trust in one scant hour . . . and I but rock-salt to her stallion son" (*SW* 153–54).

In *Ryder*, the fictional equivalent of Djuna's mother, Amelia, has accommodations in Shepherd's Bush, in a house with a garden wall and gooseberry bushes (*R* 32).[13] She studies the violin and gradually comes to know her next-door neighbors, and once she knocks Wendell off the wall (*R* 125–26); it seems he teased her while feeding his white mice. Soon thereafter, Amelia gives up the violin and signs over her inheritance.[14] All of this appears to be based on truth.

Elizabeth could hardly fail to be impressed by Zadel and Wald, for she had not yet found her direction in life. "Lizzie," recovering from a minor illness back home in Oakham before they all eloped for America, received from Zadel advice on matters of health: If she would but keep her word to take care of herself, then it would be

> possible for us to love you as you want to be loved—utterly. That is the way I want to love you & trust you & so have you for my true womanly companion and friend, a real daughter & confidante. Will you be that dear? I have never before asked any woman to be that. My life has been too tragical. . . .[15]

The letter is signed: "Love from Little Mother." An effective manipulator like Zadel had a way with motherless daughters like Tussy Marx and Lizzie Chappell, and Djuna's mother was not the first to be asked to play daughter. Whatever seductive strategies were used, they certainly worked. Without parents or prospects, Elizabeth was free to emigrate in the lively company of these seemingly well-connected Americans. Then, too, she probably loved Wald.

From evidence in Elizabeth's letters to her sister Sue, it seems that Zadel, Wald, Elizabeth, and perhaps Axel sailed to New York from Plymouth in November of 1888, moving, in the words of *The Antiphon*, "to a cabin, cocked in Pendry Cove . . . to Spuyten Duyvil [where the Harlem River meets the Hudson] . . . to a house he liked to call 'Hobbs Ark' " (*SW* 128). From there our new Noah set out to populate the world with Barneses.

Wald proposed to Elizabeth Chappell under the Arc de Triomphe in Paris in the previous year and, under the name Wald Harold Barnes, married her in New York on 3 July 1889, with the Reverend John E. Gorse officiating.[16] The ceremony was held among eye chart and optical instruments in brother Justin's office, which was located in a three-story row house in Manhattan. Not long after, Elizabeth was seeking to publish stories. A letter from her wedding guest and Zadel's sometime lover, Henry M. Alden, says that two of her stories were "too juvenile" for *Harper's Young People*.[17] Alden, who became managing editor of the magazine in 1869, had sent them on to *St. Nicholas* and listed other children's publications which might consider her submissions, but they probably never saw print. Alden sends his regards to Harry (the current Wald persona) and promises a visit soon.

The couple worked as caretakers of Justin's estate on Storm King Mountain, where Wald built a log cabin. The Chalet, where Justin lived, still stands, without the original porches, but the log cabin is gone.

The Barnes family moved there to Cornwall-on-Hudson in about 1890, perhaps because of Justin and Wald's love of nature, or possibly because Zadel knew Sarah Hussey, a relative of Zadel's favorite poet, John Greenleaf Whittier, and a woman with whom she would have had much in common. Hussey had been a nurse in the Civil War and had founded a newspaper in Cornwall before retiring to solitude on Round Top, part of Storm King Mountain. She was a temperance advocate and a supporter of progressive causes, and she would have welcomed a friendship with Zadel.

Elizabeth hated housework and resented being a maid in her brother-in-law's house, but she resented even more Zadel's inviting her friend Elizabeth Frances Faulkner Clark (1867–1934) to move into their small cabin. Two Elizabeths were one too many. Fanny, as she was called, was the daughter of Harriet Ussher, an opera singer, and John Faulkner (c.1830–c.1888), an Irish landscape and marine painter known for his watercolors. Both of Fanny's parents were from County Wicklow. According to the historian H. L. Mallalieu, Faulkner was elected to the Royal Hibernian Academy in 1861 but was expelled in 1870 and left for America; he later settled in London.[18]

Fanny was born in 1867 in Philadelphia and, like Elizabeth Chappell, was a neighbor in Shepherd's Bush in London who fell under Zadel's spell. Fanny married the painter George Merritt Clark and lived in Buffalo, New York, but they reportedly separated when his alcoholism became excessive. A shapely young woman who had something of a career on the stage—photos survive of her in stage costume—Fanny in later years became obese and rather indolent, though good-natured, fun-loving, and witty. Wald once wrote an uncomplimentary poem celebrating her rotundity, which nevertheless probably amused her:

> A thin little fellow had such a fat wife,
> Fat wife, fat wife, God bless her!
> She looked like a drum and he looked like a fife,
> And it took all his money to dress her.
> God bless her!
> To dress her!
> God bless her!
> To dress her![19]

Her counterpart in Barnes's notes for *The Antiphon* has "tow-colored hair" and "the broad butt of a librarian looking for a good book on a low shelf."[20] There is also a page of notes where Djuna revealed considerable animosity toward her mother's rival, whose name she wrote in the margin:

> Bridgette who scuffed through the cabage [sic] leaves of the Haymarket, was a solomn [sic] sluttish wench, who was always knitting . . . or sewing interminable roses into the linen centers of embroidery hoops . . . when she was not reading the papers, or drinking tea, her faintly bearded chin moving [shaking] to the words [deleted] as she read.[21]

Djuna Barnes certainly resented Fanny; in *Ryder*, she called her Kate Careless, her mother a street singer from Cork and her father a Pre-Raphaelite painter of seascapes. Kate has eloped with a painter, eventually settling on a houseboat on Lake Erie (*R* 101–2). Fanny herself lived for a time on the houseboat *Bohemian*, docked mostly at Niagara Falls or at Tomkins Cove on the Hudson River, just south of Cornwall. Zadel spent the early days of 1899 with Fanny in Tomkins Cove. It wasn't long before Wald, "wived in righteous plenty," as *The Antiphon* tells us (*SW* 208), and now preaching polygamy, began a sexual relationship with Fanny that was to bring more children into the household for Zadel to support.[22] Fanny moved in when Djuna was five, in 1897, which is also the date given for the fictional event in *Ryder* (84).

Wald's cabin was, in effect, the ark "Bohemian," a small two-story log structure with two rooms, one on top of the other, connected by a ladder through a trapdoor. Located among the pine trees just north of Justin's Chalet, the cabin was "fifteen feet high and twenty-nine feet wide," and the furnishings described in *Ryder* must have been similar to those in the Barnes cabin (see *R* 84, 86–87).

Sleeping arrangements were unusually flexible. In *Ryder*, the Justin figure has a German mistress. Djuna told her friends that Wald rode circuit in the neighborhood to have sexual encounters with women and kept a sponge tied to his horse's saddle to wipe his private parts. Opposite page 1 of *Ryder* is a drawing by Djuna depicting Wendell mounted on a horse, wearing the lamb's wool coat he wore in all seasons, his women in the background, and the sponge dangling.

Wald justified promiscuity on both natural and moral grounds. Humans were animals, and most animals are not sexually exclusive; one does well to imitate nature. "Be fruitful and multiply" was a command he found easy to obey, for children were pleasant in the getting and gave him pride in his potency. If people were easier about sex, Wald argued, there would be no prostitution. *The Antiphon* says: "He claimed himself a Saint of such day would sweep the world of whores . . . he said he was the stud to breed a kingdom" (*SW* 160–61). But the condition imposed on Elizabeth, Fanny, and Zadel would perhaps not bear defining.

Wald argued that polygamy would mean less poverty, fewer single mothers, and more social stability. In other words, it was moral to beget bastards; but after procreation, his moral responsibility seemed to end. In 1887, two years before their marriage, he wrote to Lizzie that he would take up his pen and state his views. Wald then composed a book-length "credo" about polygamy, entitled "Rescue of the Race," but destroyed it, fearing arrest. *The Antiphon* reveals: "When the law caught up with us, behind the wall—which he'd built up high for fear of tongues—he burned his credo, chucked up his account" (*SW* 159). Years after they left their Huntington farm, the neighbors remembered the Barneses as "the Mormons."

In *Ryder*, Hannel quotes his father as saying that "one should regard all the miracles of nature with an impartial eye. . . . See . . . the little girls stumbling to school; it's their future maternity that makes them stare into the hedges like that. Mark . . . the squirrels lifting their tails unabashed . . . that [is] pure reason and unobstructed inner vision" (*R* 162). This was the center of Wald's credo.

Djuna's siblings and half siblings arrived at short intervals. *Ryder* presents Amelia and Kate as simultaneously in labor; Wendell, not alarmed, refuses to send for a doctor (*R* 95–96). On 18 June 1890, Elizabeth had a son, named Thurn, and Djuna arrived on 12 June 1892; both were born in Cornwall-on-Hudson.[23] Then came Muriel, born to Fanny on 10 October 1899; next came Elizabeth's sons Zendon, on 8 January 1900, and Saxon, on 26 July 1902. Twelve days after Saxon, in Huntington on 7 August, Fanny gave birth to Duane, and on 25 March 1904 came Buan. On 24 May 1904, a son named Shangar (he later changed his name to Charles Chappell) was born to Elizabeth, her last baby. As is the Yankee custom, all the children had their mother's maiden name as a middle name, either Chappell or Faulkner.

Zadel's influence may be assumed in the matter of the children's unusual names, reflecting her siblings'. Djuna said that her own name came from Eugène Sue's *The Wandering Jew*, where there is an Indian prince called Djalma, which became spliced with Thurn's word for moon, "nuna."[24] Thurn's name recalls the Regensburg family of Thurn-und-Taxis, whose postal system, dominant in Europe for centuries, is familiar to readers of history and Thomas Pynchon's novel *The Crying of Lot 49*. Saxon seems clear; something might be made of Zendon from the Greek; Shangar was derived from their ancestor Shamger Barns [*sic*] (1670–1750), who was the first of the family to settle in Middletown. Odd names were very Barnesean, and Djuna continued this family tradition in her own stories.

On 14 October 1906, Fanny had her last baby, Sheila, but she died on 25 February of the next year and was probably buried in a small cemetery across the road from the Huntington farm. As Djuna later recalled, Zadel wrapped her "in her warmest fleece jacket, and the *last* of her Liberty silks, the fleece jacket because papa and I (mostly me I guess) thought she *would be cold,* it was winter and snow was on the trees and along the garden paths, and the undertakers were so damned jolly and breezy, it made one even colder, and more frightened."[25]

Much of the bitterness Djuna felt toward her mother in later years resulted from real or imagined grievances: she believed that Elizabeth had wanted only sons[26] and had seemed insufficiently demonstrative with her affection; and Djuna resented having to take care of her younger brothers, a hint of which can be seen in one of her articles: "Sin led to Hades, and love to a lot of male children doted upon by a mother who bore a sufficient number of girls to clean up after them."[27]

Nevertheless, Djuna was pleased at the birth of Zendon, for in "The Songs of Synge" she wrote: "Synge first touched the Irish in me as nineteen hundred touched the attaining of a long desire; mother that day had presented me with a brother. I remember the brother but hazily, the little pair of boots over the arm that held him, I remember plainly."

Things did not go smoothly in this strange household with two mothers. While Wald fiddled or whittled or gardened, the women burned with resentment or physical distress over the work occasioned by so many children. The hardship, plus assisting at Zendon's difficult birth in 1900, which was agony for her mother, killed in Djuna Barnes all desire to reproduce. She once wrote her friend Emily Coleman that "father and his bastard children and mistresses had thrown me off marriage and babies."[28] Neither Elizabeth nor Fanny had the benefit of anesthetic during childbirth; Djuna felt that childbirth was really awful and that no author had portrayed its true horror.[29]

Stories about Wald abound. One has to do with a bout of fever, which produced severe chills that made him shake so hard that "all the children would have to get on top of him to hold him in bed."[30]

Though small, about five feet seven, and of a nervous disposition, he could be brash. Saxon tells of his threatening to kill a Polish neighbor, a huge man, who had come to retrieve the team of horses he had lent Wald. The smaller man wasn't ready to return them and pretended that his honor had been impugned, surely knowing that his generous neighbor wouldn't punch him in front of the children.[31]

Wald had some strange ideas, a few of which seem to derive from one of his favorite books, Thoreau's *Walden*. Djuna often told the story of his insisting that his children eat a few pebbles occasionally: "since chickens ate pebbles to aid their digestion, a few pebbles in the diet of his children might be equally salubrious."[32] In one of her "Wanton Playgoer" articles, Barnes wrote of fashioning "a tricky pair of trousers from a ham sack to cover my brother, aged four. I think the ham was the better tailored."[33] This sounds like Wald's idea. Baby Saxon he circumcised on the kitchen table.

When the log cabin became too small, the family packed up and left. Wald signed a poem (never published), called "The Flying Dutchman," with his new nom de plume, Brian E. Barnes, in June of 1895, giving as his residence New Rochelle, New York. Correspondence reveals that they were at 27 William Street. In 1900–1, they lived on Valentine Avenue near 194th Street, Fordham, in the Bronx. Djuna told James Scott that it was in Fordham that she began playacting with her brother Thurn and writing poetry and plays. They were encouraged to write about daily events in their lives even before they could spell, and the results can be found in exercise books. Djuna helped plan a garden in May 1901 and took daily walks with her mother or father. At age nine she witnessed a quarrel—duly noted in an entry of 30 May 1901—when Wald asked Elizabeth for a pair of pincers.

Her mother answered "I would of told you bfore now if I new." and then my father sed that she was not nice to talk lik that it wasent ladilike to say that. And then my mother got mad and rased her voice a lettle louder and sed. 'it wasent nasty or bad.' and then papa called her a Darn fish wife (I think he was horrid to say that. Dont you.) after that she menning mother. she said that she was a lady and not a woman. and then papa said that you cold not make a lady out of a fish wife. and then mother said that if he only wold bring ladies into the house she might Be one her self, and then papa after a lettle talk about fish wives went out into the garden.

Djuna wrote about their walks near the Harlem or the Bronx River, along Pelham Avenue or the Boston Road. In an entry of 12 December 1900, Thurn wrote that Zadel wanted to play cards every night but Wald had little interest. On 5 February 1901, he wrote about a quarrel (spelled "corrill") with Djuna, when they crashed while sledding. Thurn describes her going to complain to their mother.

She went in and sed to mamma he hart me. That Boy is a fool. She is a grate name caller. . . . She cept saying dam you Thurn I hate you it is all a lye what you are saying when I was telling the troth. I thing she is natraly gifted to dserving or lying which ever you like. and her temper is like hot spies. She has in herited it from my father mand kind.

A travel notebook by Thurn records details of their voyage to Jamaica in December 1901.[34] The family packed forty pieces of luggage, and on a snowy evening, movers loaded the wagon and started uphill on Valentine Avenue, but the horses slipped and the wagon overturned. The four family dogs atop the load were unharmed. Eventually Djuna, her parents, Fanny, Thurn, Muriel, Zendon, and Zadel, plus the dogs and luggage, made it to dockside, where they boarded the *Altai* of the Hamburg America Line and sailed down the coast to Cape Hatteras and on to Kingston. Thurn complained about the small portions of food. In Kingston, the family rented a cottage for a few days and probably did not even unpack. Thurn was intrigued by the Jamaican accent and the swaying hips of the women, who so deftly carried loads on their heads, but Wald soon tired of Kingston and was ready to continue on to England. Zadel bought the tickets, and off they went again.

Wald and Elizabeth (with some of her inheritance) had bought land in Cornwall-on-Hudson, which they sold the last of in 1897.[35]

On 1 July 1902, Zadel, listing as her address Mamaroneck, New York, bought from Clarence and Caroline E. Carman two parcels of good orchard land in the township of Huntington, Long Island, for six thousand dollars. (In *Ryder*, Barnes called it "Bull's Ease.") The deed shows it to be 105 acres, encumbered as late as 1907 by a lien of ten thousand dollars. The parcels were divided by what was then Upper Half Hollow Road. Across the road was a small family cemetery. Until a developer illegally bulldozed it in 1992, the house where Djuna lived most of her years from the age of ten until about nineteen stood as one of the oldest farmhouses on Long Island, the first deed having been recorded in 1837.[36]

In her unpublished play "Biography of Julie von Bartmann," Barnes included a description that seemed to fit the farmhouse living room: "the drawing room [was] large, with three windows looking out into the road. Books, a sofa, a wall cabinet, rugs etc. Doors in the left wall and back centre right. Pegged beams, but pictureless walls. On a white marble pedistal [*sic*] stands a bust of Chopin."[37] Wald, an expert wood carver, made the rafter beams for the living room of the farmhouse. Using a penknife, he whittled candlesticks, totem poles, and even cedar spoons and forks.

On the farm there were cows, one of which "thought she was a bull. Thats the one I rode rashly and got my legs skinned for pay, she also had to have her horns cut as she tossed my fathers offspring about the hedges and used to milk *herself*, so had to wear a yoke." Wald taught Djuna to lasso and would practice with the children, catching them with his rope and dragging them around for fun.[38]

On a page of notes compiled for her poem "Rakehell," Barnes remembered the stationmaster's wagon, used in winter, which contained a stove and had "tenting over the top"; it must have brought Zadel on many occasions from New York City and the nearby Wyandanch train station.[39]

Duane, Djuna's half brother, named after Zadel's father, left to his son Kerron Barnes a narrative of some twelve pages, describing daily life in the Barnes family from about 1906 until 1908. He remembered "walks to the sunny hillside with tall grasses, on the way to Wyandanch, and a little brook in the springtime when the snow melted, big woods on the other hillside."

There was Biv, the Maltese cat, "with six toes on his front feet," and the garden where in the sandy soil there grew string beans, tomatoes, muskmelons, carrots, lettuce, some cabbage, turnips, onions, and radishes. Asparagus grew round about, and rhubarb. There was also an orchard; various kinds of apples were picked and then stored in the basement, along with pears, plums, peaches, and quince. Raspberries, strawberries, and blackberries grew wild.

Between the house and the barn there was a well one hundred feet deep, with "good spring water." When he was nine, Duane was persuaded to go down to the bottom to dredge out sand. In a painting owned by the local historical society one sees a windmill over the well, with "Stover" painted on the rudder (perhaps a brand name), which Wald, after catching his hand in the gears, took down and sold to a neighbor.

When the water refroze after a thaw in winter, there was sledding, or skating on leather shoes for lack of ice skates. Duane describes Dick the horse, who resisted being hitched until Wald bribed him with an apple. Dick had to be whipped en route to the store but reined in on the return, or he would race the automobiles on the parkway. Dick pulled a surrey, in which Wald kept a small stove for Zadel. An intelligent horse, he could count to six and would come to the kitchen door for precisely six apples in winter. After Dick died of tetanus, the children went shopping on their bicycles.

When Duane and Buan were older, they worked for Charles Titus, who lived to the east of the farm, mostly felling trees. (Djuna gave the Wald figure in *The Antiphon* the name Titus Hobbs.) The Barneses kept no pigs but did smoke ham and bacon, and they had chickens and cows. In their last year on the farm, Duane and Buan grew corn, cabbage, and potatoes, and earned a profit of a thousand dollars.

As a significant part of the Barnes family life on the farm in Huntington, Duane recalled the home concerts, the singing, the piano playing, Wald composing (in 1910, he composed an opera called "Allan Castle"), and Zadel's reading aloud works by Dumas or Dickens in the living room after dinner, by the coal-burning stove. Sometimes Zadel or Wald would tell stories of their own.

In later years, Djuna spoke to James Scott about her early education, then corrected his transcript of the interview, censoring the information she had given him and making additions where required. Barnes's education reflected family agreement that the instruction offered by the public schools was inadequate and in many ways even detrimental to a child's development. Learning was an intense and ongoing process for the whole family; it was a way of life. There were "lessons," of course, but probably of greater importance was the emphasis on the arts in their curriculum. (Barnes's additions to Scott's narrative are noted in brackets.)

> In the evenings Zadel read [aloud] from a wide spectrum of authors. Gathered about the fireplace, they heard Dickens, Dumas, Henty, George Eliot, George Sand, Lewis Carroll, Grace Aguilar, L. T. Mead, Swift, Grimm's fairy tales, Shakespeare, Kate Greenaway, Mother Goose, Turgenev, the poetry of Poe, Kipling, [Whitman,] Swinburne (Wald's favorite), Wordsworth, Longfellow, . . . Hans Christian Andersen, Louisa May Alcott, dime novels, the Bible, [*Pilgrim's Progress*] . . . Her recalled favorite authors included Dostoevsky, Dickens, Chaucer, Montaigne, Donne, Shakespeare, and [later Proust].[40]

> Some evenings were musical. Again, if lessons were important, even more were evenings devoted to playing in ensemble. Wald could play a number of instruments [wind & wood as well as the organ &], the piano. [Here Barnes deletes the words "quite well."] He composed [symphonys—songs] operas, he [painted—wrote novella & poems] wrote his own libretti. [His daughter] learned to read music [painted in water colour, wrote poetry, novella] and to play the banjo, [guitar], the violin, the french horn.

Elizabeth and Wald mostly shared the piano playing, but the instruments often rotated among family members. Nearby was a sandpit, where Thurn sometimes practiced trombone for the echo.

In *Ryder*, Sophia reads nightly to the children, but since Wendell would weep at death scenes in novels, they were usually skipped

(*R* 122). Although Djuna credits Zadel with most of her education, Elizabeth and Wald probably did their share of instructing, since Zadel was often away. Djuna could never spell properly or do much with numbers, but at an early age she wrote the one-act plays that she performed with Thurn. When the children were not reading, there were the games children play and, of course, the farm chores and activities, horseback riding, and animals to tend.

In "Julie von Bartmann," Djuna Barnes describes the arrival to the Huntington farmhouse of a famous European opera singer, supposedly modeled on Marguerite Amelia d'Alvarez, who may have been Wald's mistress for a time. Barnes harbored resentful feelings toward her, for she once wrote that the singer "has the most Gothic Roof in the singing architecture of the Mouth ever seen."[41]

Wald's lifestyle, sanctified by his views on the social benefits of sexual freedom, was most probably a source of gossip around Huntington, and Zadel and Wald naturally sniffed danger lurking in the local school board. After the divorce, Fanny's children began to attend more regularly, but earlier Wald insisted on bending the rules in favor of home instruction. A letter of 5 November 1903 from A. N. Brockway, M.D., to the attendance officer in Huntington, John N. Cromwell, provides a medical excuse for truancy:

> I certify, as their physician, that the children of Mr. Wald Barnes of Wyandanch are of such a constitution, mentally, nervously, and physically that their education, at home, is a matter of necessity to their health. They will be thoroughly educated, in every way, in their own household.

In *Ryder*, the local people aren't so easily satisfied on the issue of truancy, and in Chapter 30 they gather in the schoolhouse for a hearing.[42] With chutzpah, tricky rhetoric, and intimidation (the school's well has been contaminated with a dead cat), Wendell manages to convince the superintendent that his family is more trouble than it is worth and that he alone should be responsible for his children's education.

Although Djuna always said that she had no schooling, there is some evidence of her irregular attendance. Barnes's first biographer, Andrew Field, cites a letter he received from an elderly woman, who said that Barnes attended school "with her on Long Island, although it is true that she was frequently truant."[43] This was likely the case. Djuna arrived at the Half Hollow farmhouse when she was ten, and would have been required by law to attend school until she was fifteen.

In the summer of 1912, Djuna Barnes experienced a catastrophe from which she never completely recovered—the divorce of her parents and, at age twenty, the responsibility of a large part of the financial support of her mother and brothers. The reasons for the divorce were partly financial: Zadel could no longer support twelve people on her meager income, and Wald could not grow enough vegetables to make a difference. Barnes saw it differently, for in *The Antiphon*, she says of this event that her father "turned us out like bastards, being none . . . that he might make at least one hussy legal" (*SW* 159).

Seeing depressing reality, seemingly for the first time, Zadel devised a plan that gave them all excruciating pain: the families were to be separated, with the financial aid of her brother Reon, who could be trusted not to refuse in an emergency. Reon Barnes, four years younger than Zadel, was a widower who had been living on Staten Island.

In her 1917 address book, Djuna records the sad event: on 17 July 1912, Elizabeth separated from Wald and took Djuna and three of her brothers to New York City. In the deleted fragment from *Nightwood*'s "Go Down Matthew" chapter, Barnes focuses on this tragic event.

> And then I came to New York, when the family broke up, and father drove us all down in a pickle cart, and said good-bye forever, and he did not wave to us, nor turn his head, and my little brother had been lying on his face in the straw all the way and has grown up all different because of that. And so I had to earn a living for me and some for them. (*N* 256)

Saxon cried all the way to the train station. Four days later, Elizabeth and her children returned to the family farm for a visit, feeling quite depressed about the separation. For the foreseeable future, Elizabeth and the children would live at 1320 Ward Avenue, Morris Park, in the Bronx. Writing on Saxon's birthday, 26 July, Zadel said that the entire family would need to attend the divorce hearing. Wald, Zadel, Fanny, and the children "clasped hands in a circle and all said 'Many happy returns dear Saxon.' Did you hear it?"

On 31 July 1912, Elizabeth officially filed for a divorce on the grounds of adultery, a charge that Wald could hardly contest. Still, it gave Zadel and Wald considerable pain to know that Elizabeth and her children were wisely heeding their attorney's advice to avoid contact with the Huntington branch of the family. On 6 November, Elizabeth Chappell Barnes was divorced from Harold Barnes. Thurn, now twenty-two, was living on his own; Zendon was twelve, Saxon nearly ten, and Shangar eight. Djuna was living at home and preparing to go to work as a writer.

On 13 November, Wald (using the name Harold B. Barnes) married Fanny (Elizabeth F. Clark), but he continued to insist that they were all one family. "From a spiritual (or higher) point of view, nothing is changed."[44] Djuna continued to correspond with Zadel and Wald for many years after the divorce, mostly about the farm animals and dogs, but she carried a deep sense of grievance that her career as a writer had been launched under such emotional duress. Contact was infrequent because of Djuna's time constraints, for she had to earn money and worked very hard, but she sought to reassure Wald of her love. In a letter of 20 January 1915, he responds to Djuna's remark that she was sending him fifty kisses and fifty hugs ("could I bear them?—Well I *did*, in spirit").

In the months that followed, there wasn't much to eat on the Huntington farm besides vegetables, the local currency, which Wald earned as an occasional laborer on neighboring farms. Although Wald claimed that his father would provide support if he would take back the name Budington, he refused what he called this "bribery."

Fanny and her children were chosen over Elizabeth and hers for fairly obvious reasons: Fanny was cheerful and easygoing and had no other source of support; Elizabeth, suffering the intense humiliation of a rival in her house, was difficult, spiteful, and argumentative. If push came to shove, Zadel's brother Reon could be prevailed upon to contribute support to Wald's legitimate family, but not to the illegitimate one.

In 1920, three years after Zadel died, Wald, Fanny, and the children decided to sell the heavily mortgaged farm to Dr. Herman Benjamin Baruch, the brother of Bernard Baruch. They moved then to Shillington, Pennsylvania, which was apparently the home of Charles F. Molly, a friend who had once been involved in buying and selling the farm. Duane and Wald first went to the area to find a house, then returned to help with the packing. Duane drove the moving van procured from nearby Reading, a Packard truck that moved at the breakneck speed of twelve miles per hour, and the rest of the family traveled by train to Reading. Wald was to manage fox farms. A surviving brochure shows him working at the Berks Lehmont Fur Farms, Exeter Township. He was now fifty-five and, except for a short stint working for a London apothecary, had never been formally employed. During their four-year stay in the area, the family also lived in Stony Creek Mills and Chester Springs.

One of the first purchases made in Reading was a used Weber grand piano, which cost five hundred dollars of the boys' farm earnings, for Wald strongly supported Duane in his desire to become a fine pianist. Soon Duane was giving local concerts, and the Reading Music Club offered him a scholarship to attend the Juilliard School of Music in New York. Duane did not go because there was not enough money, but he continued to play until he had eighty pieces in his repertoire, his favorites being by Liszt, Rachmaninoff, and Chopin.

From Pennsylvania, Wald kept up a correspondence with Djuna, telling her that the Long Island farm had been a nightmare and that they had almost starved in the last years. He advised her to give up her pessimism and agnosticism. Despite Djuna's resentment of Wald, she urged him to write to her.[45] One of his letters to her reports that Duane and Muriel were practicing hard at the piano, Buan was driving a truck, and he, Wald, was writing mazurkas, which he hoped to sell. Unfortunately, the mazurka market was not vigorous that year.

Fanny, who shared Zadel's interest in spiritualism (this may have been one reason Fanny was chosen over Djuna's mother), consoled Wald by means of her mediumship. Spiritualism was all the rage in the 1850s, then faded; after the Civil War, many bereaved parents joined a massive return to the séance in hopes of making contact with their dead sons. Zadel's own interest in spiritualism may have had its origin in the death of her favorite brother, Llewellyn, in a Confederate prison camp late in 1864. In *Nightwood*, Nora remembers in a dream her grandmother's room, with his faded portrait on the wall.[46]

Zadel Barnes was a spiritualist in the tradition of the theosophists Madame Blavatsky (1831–91) and Annie Besant (1847–1933), whom she may well have known. Indeed, Djuna remembered her grandmother knitting a rag rug by a faded photo of Besant.[47] She once told Emily Coleman that Zadel "used to go into trances and speak in the voices of the dead. She used also to levitate objects."[48] A remarkable section of Duane's narrative confirms Zadel's and then Fanny's mediumship and the "occult happenings" in the Barnes family. Duane was unaware of Zadel's talent until he was playing a Liszt rhapsody one day and she said, "he can do it." Wald explained, "Liszt is here," and then Duane noticed that Zadel looked different. Later Wald told Duane about the spirits—"eaches" was his term for them—who were able to use Zadel's body to bring messages from the dead, an event he called "stepping aside."

Duane was completely convinced. During the séances, Zadel's face would change, becoming squarer when Franz Liszt was there, and her voice said things she would ordinarily never say. Curiously enough—and Duane never seemed to notice this—the messages for him always concerned his piano playing. Liszt repeatedly encouraged him to practice more and work harder, a view later corroborated by Chopin and Beethoven; all spoke English faultlessly. Photographs displayed on the farmhouse wall recorded Zadel's facial changes.

Zadel had two other spirit visitors. One was Jack London, who died in 1916, the year before Zadel. The medium's legs would uncharacteristically cross, her face would change, and London would discuss many things with the family. When her pain from cancer was excruciating, London would appear, to "take the pain" for Zadel. The other visitor was Lord Kitchener, who also died in 1916; he used her body to express his encouragement for the British in the Great War.

In his notebook, Duane recalled that Wald had told him of a son (Emmanuel) born to Zadel and Axel, who died shortly after birth and who used Zadel as a medium. Apparently speechless, he would just express a puff of air, smile, and disappear. Wald himself had seen his future before birth "and was hesitant to accept it. He was told 'it is yours to do,' after it is over it will seem as a few minutes, like a flash." These experiences convinced Duane that "the spirit life is without beginning and without end," and he only regretted that he himself did not have a medium's powers.

Duane ends his narrative with a series of imaginative speculations on unreality. One inexplicable aspect of his memories is that they exclude references to any of his half siblings or to his father's bigamy.

Wald remembered a time—apparently about 1897—when Zadel was gravely ill; the spirits told him that they wished her to see the future, that she would appear to be dead but would recover. Zadel remembered the beauty of that experience. After she died, Fanny apparently inherited mesmeric powers, for most of Zadel's spirits, as well as Zadel herself and the Irish patriot John Redmond, used her to communicate. Redmond had lived in the same house in which Fanny's Irish father was born, in Avoca, County Wicklow.

Djuna mocked Fanny's clairvoyance in a note, describing her as "pausing now and again to raise her head and to remark to anyone who chanced to be listening that she had a 'premenition' [sic]. She was given to sudden catastrophes of vision. Once she had seen Um Paul Kruger so closely knit before her, that she had fallen into a tub."[49] The note was destined for the The Antiphon, which refers to Fanny's counterpart, Kitty, as "A lost clairvoyant, that is all, poor creature. / Said she saw Lord Kitchener in a cloud / Chasing Oom Paul Krueger over Africa, / Waving the Doomsday Book before him as he ran" (SW 158).

In a notebook, Wald recorded in some detail Fanny's trances; the earliest are from March 1918, the latest from August 1920. If they were of a political nature, such as Lord Kitchener's pronouncements on Bolshevism, they were inevitably preceded by Fanny's reading of a relevant article in the newspaper. The obvious connection seemed to escape Wald. The messages were never gloomy or discouraging. One from Jack London said: "Cheer up—stiff upper lip! Wade thro! Fine weather coming!"

Lord Kitchener's messages of 1918 reveal that he was tormented by the Great War; one on 21 March says that the Allies could not fail. "Do you think all those beautiful souls have come over here in vain?" His ranting, chauvinistic messages are repetitive, with few specifics that could be interpreted as prophecy. For example, an entry for 21 June 1918 says: "F. came into the dining room with a military stride. K—— of course: He said—in a tremendous voice—'They will go forever, forever! The—Beasts! Oh! Oh! Oh! They are so rotten!' " He is disturbed by all the "beautiful souls" crossing over to the life beyond and, for all his ferocity, makes remarks such as "love is the greatest of all forces" (18 August 1918).

At times Jack London echoed Lord Kitchener's sentiments. On 24 June 1918, at precisely 2:00 P.M., he appeared with a rare prediction: "There is to be a big sea battle—the Germans coming out Kiel (of the Kiel Canal). Zeebrugge & Ostende bottled up more & more. They will be beaten. The rout is beginning. We have decided that the end must come." Lord Kitchener swiftly agrees: "They must be stopped as *I stopped* the Mahdi!"

In one of his many attempts to become famous, Wald communicated the results to newspapers such as the *Daily News* (London) and the *New York World*. At the head of a letter of 9 August 1920 (from the Huntington address, Route 4, Box 54), he noted "Spiritual Wireless No. 1." It concerned Lord Kitchener's dim view of the "Bolshevist Advance." The *World* published the letter on 12 August, and Wald responded that very day with thanks. He wrote a number of such letters, and all are basically the same: Using Fanny as a medium, Lord Kitchener, in simplistic, excited, patriotic language, condemns the Red menace. Here is an excerpt of Lord Kitchener's views in Wald's letter of 9 August:

My friend! It is to be a fight for your lives—for your living on the Earth! It must be a fight against the throwback of all the advancement made through the centuries of horrors! A fight against such awful horrors! It is worse because of the advancement already attained at such a terrible cost. It cannot be—it must not be—their success! The menace is too great! Oh! More boys to suffer—more lives to be lost! More useless waste! It can never last, this Bolshevism. But it causes such a delay (of the coming of the new era) such a delay. UP! FORWARD!! FOR THE GOOD!!!

Wald concludes with a remark of his own: "This message was delivered orally—and with it came an immense feeling of friendship for humanity."

On 23 August 1920, Wald sent the *World* a message from John Redmond, a supporter of Irish Home Rule who nevertheless backed the British in the Great War and opposed Sinn Féin and civil war. Rather out of character (but then who is to say that the dead can't change their minds?), and using Fanny as a medium, Redmond's spirit attributed Sinn Féin's agitation for independence to Bolshevism. What was wanted was more tolerance in Ireland. In conclusion, Wald's letter quotes the spirit of Redmond: "We here, in this life where I am, we are all striving to help you Earth people through this awful crisis now coming on you." As Captain Boyle, in Sean O'Casey's *Juno and the Paycock*, would have said, the world was in "a state o' chassis."

When the *New York World* stopped printing Wald's letters, he turned to the *Progressive Thinker* of Chicago, which published him on 25 September 1920. Wald sent more letters from his spiritual wireless, with Lord Kitchener's dire warnings about Bolshevism's threat to the world. His long letter of 1 September to the *Progressive Thinker* explains the basis of his belief in the authenticity of such messages; he gives to the journal exclusive right to print them but reserves the right to publish them in book form.

After Jack London transmitted her love in a message of 4 March 1918, nearly a year after her death, Zadel visited regularly, full of encouragement for the family. Fanny had watched Zadel often enough to know how to communicate on the spiritual wireless, and it must have given her great pleasure to see how delighted Wald was to believe that his mother had not abandoned him. On 14 April 1918, Wald went into the kitchen to kiss Fanny, "but found myself embracing my mother instead, she saying—'Brian, dear Brian!' & began to snuggle & kiss me—in her old way. 'My son—courage—a good fight! Dear son. Waldy!' (a pet name for me). Then more face snuggling & kissing. Very plainly mother—for no one else has *her* way of doing it. 'Lovin's!' said she, suiting action to word. Then a gradual withdrawal." Then minutes later, Zadel is greeting and kissing Buan and Duane in her characteristic way. Duane says, " 'Nice Gaga' (our pet name for Mother) . . ." Turning to Muriel, Zadel begins to hug and kiss her, saying, "I fink you is a weel coot person!"

The family's visitors (or eaches) were well acquainted with each other (Lord Kitchener once said that Jack London would soon pay a visit) and were quite solicitous about the Barnes family's welfare. In an entry of 8 April 1918, Jack London advises Wald to tell Djuna "that you are pleased to have her help you." He concludes his visit with: "Tell Djuna she will have good reason to be proud of her Pa." When London visited, Fanny was always tender and loving, as presumably suited London's character.

John Redmond, in his visits, seemed particularly anxious to have conscription enforced in Ireland, "to fight for world freedom." When Franz Liszt came to Fanny, as he had come to Zadel, he usually advised Duane and Muriel (whom he once calls "Girlie") to work harder at their music and success would not be far off. (Perhaps the eaches had given up on Wald.) He believed that they both had a great gift for music that might be wasted through lack of effort. One other visitor was Fanny's father, John Faulkner, who spoke with a pronounced Irish brogue, but his message was the same as that of Liszt: "*Patience* me boy," he says to Buan, and "Try the wather colors! Its in you to do it."

While in a trance, Fanny's face changed to resemble the controlling personality, but the experience placed such stress on her and left her so tired that she gave up being a medium. Then, too, her impact on foreign policy wasn't as dramatic as had been expected.

In 1924, the imported Canadian foxes became ill, and dame fashion turned her head away from fox fur. Wald Barnes decided that the family should move from Pennsylvania to California, a trip he had wanted to make for many years. On 1 July 1916, he had written Djuna's and Courtenay Lemon's friend Konrad Bercovici a fleshed-out revision of an earlier letter in which he proposed that the family pool their resources with the Bercovicis (Konrad was married and had several children), buy an automobile, and head west, sleeping in the car or in a nearby tent.[50] A two-wheeled trailer would be pulled behind for those who couldn't fit into the car, and the men would get out to walk up the hills:

> On reaching California . . . we could start in teaching Music IN A TENT—with a board floor for the piano to stand on—several such tents could be added just as fast as they would be needed. The climate of Los Angeles permits out-door living the entire year around. . . . Whether the idea of teaching in a tent would draw pupils, is of course, problematical, but handled in the right manner, I should think the novelty of it would decidedly make a possibility of it.

Djuna would be welcome to come along, and she or Zadel (who, already fatally ill, was expected to travel with them) could write it up' for publication. They could even pull a piano and give concerts en route, with Fanny singing solos. His naïveté knowing no bounds but his imagination, Wald was intoxicated with the possibilities of teaching music in California. In the margin of his copy of the letter, in a saner moment, he entitled it "The Gypsy Conservatory."

It turned out rather differently, and the trip would take eight years to happen. On 14 September 1924, Wald wrote Elizabeth that he would make the trip in October. After a strenuous journey, working their way across the continent, they arrived in Los Angeles, only to find no work, so they moved on to Oakland, where they lived in an auto camp. Muriel (now twenty-five) worked as a waitress in San Francisco, and Buan toiled as a roofer, but money was still scant. Easterners, they were told, were not welcome. Wald could get no work, and so on 8 December he wrote to his son Zendon, asking for help. As security, he was willing to put up the two Great Danes and the grand piano they had left behind. When Wald had managed to borrow fifty dollars for the trip back to Pennsylvania, the family began the return by way of Phoenix. They lived on bread and prunes, slept in the car, worked when they could, and were able to pay for enough eight-cent-per-gallon gasoline to reach Pennsylvania again.

Wald's family had an auto accident near West Alexandria, Pennsylvania, on 7 January 1925. Replacement auto parts took almost two weeks to arrive; Fanny and Muriel found a room, while the men slept in the damaged car. Eventually Wald returned to work on the fox farm, Muriel got a job at Sears, and Duane and Buan became truck-drivers. Duane, who would come to own a trucking firm in Philadelphia,[51] retained a lifelong passion for music and, in his spare time, composed and played the piano. Of the California trip, Elizabeth said, "their supreme optimism keeps them from too much suffering."[52]

The last address of "Brian Eglinton Barnes" and Fanny was 1820 West Albanus Street, Philadelphia. On 21 May 1934, Wald died laughing, apparently of a heart attack, as he rose in his seat while listening to *Amos 'n' Andy* on the radio; three weeks later, Fanny died of a stroke, having become disoriented in a grocery store. They were buried without headstone—like many others during the Depression —in Laurel Cemetery, Bala Cynwyd, just outside Philadelphia, the enormous Fanny on top of Wald, whose grave was opened to accommodate her in a special coffin that might have held their grand piano. The old lecher would have appreciated the humor of their position, and so would Fanny.[53]

After Elizabeth Barnes divorced Wald in 1912, her life became a predictable one of drudgery, loneliness, despair, and dependence on her children for love and support. Wald's father, Henry Budington, remembered her in his will when he died, aged ninety, in 1921, but she still depended on her sons.

Elizabeth was quick to censure Djuna and slow to recognize her talent and accomplishments. Still, she commended her daughter's sense of family loyalty—which extended even to Wald. On 19 December 1921 she wrote her sister that Djuna "is very sorry for her father and understands him better than some of the boys." Djuna, who also sent her impoverished aunt Susanna money whenever she could, was in later years furious that she herself was not the recipient of unquestioning generosity from her family.

If Wald had been an incurable optimist, Elizabeth and Djuna became equally incorrigible pessimists, though with much reason. In a letter of 1 July 1924, Elizabeth told Djuna: "I brought you a lot of misery that I shall never cease to suffer for." Sharing her husband and her house with another woman, who also bore his children, must have been a source of unending grief, yet in a letter of 17 June 1925 to Djuna, she recognized that art may have its origin in absurdity: "Thats the tragedy—your father is not natural dear, if he had been his life would not have been worth writing about."

In the years from 1912 to 1920, Djuna's brothers gradually became successful businessmen, at times distracted by the artistic urge that was characteristic of the Barnes psyche: Thurn wrote poetry, Zendon preferred woodwork, Saxon sculpted, and Shangar/Charlie painted and sculpted. Although they were educated to the joys of artistic creation, hunger had convinced them that a full stomach was the sweeter pleasure, and so they chose practical vocations.

Elizabeth Barnes, in her early years an unusually attractive woman, gifted with intelligence, some talent, and the creative urge, in middle age expressed, in carefully written poems that went unpublished, the bitterness of a life filled with tedium.[54] Largely correct in her belief that her chance for happiness had ended with her marriage to Wald, dependent upon her children for support during the last thirty years of her life, she came more and more to live vicariously through them, which they resented. In a letter of 8 February 1928, she tells Djuna: "I now no longer believe in marriage & if I ever live over my life again you'll find me a free entity shocking all the blue stockings." Family gatherings became distinctly unpleasant.

Elizabeth was a trial to her sons because of her possessiveness; she disapproved of the women they found interesting. Except for Charlie's first wife, Francesca, none were good enough for her boys: "I wonder if all girls are like the women my sons have chosen? If so! they are a lot of selfish egotistical empty heads. All they want of a man is his devotion & his pocket book."[55] The children also found difficult her conversion late in life to Christian Science and her wish to read to them from the writings of Mary Baker Eddy. The burden of Elizabeth fell especially heavily on Saxon, who suffered emotionally from her incessant demands. When he married Eleanor Kastner, he insisted that his mother live by herself.

Elizabeth Chappell Barnes died on 15 March 1945, and her ashes were deposited in the Saint Andrews section of Ferncliff Cemetery, Ardsley-on-Hudson, New York. Her voice lives on in *The Antiphon*.

CHAPTER 3

Dear Snickerbits:
Early Loves and Art School

"Melancholia, melancholia, it rides me like a bucking mare."[1]

n a fragment from 1932 called "Show Break," Djuna wrote about her feelings for Zadel and Wald:

> There were moments that were to stamp for me the early dawn as forever tragic—for I loved [Zadel] as a child usually loves its mother—I cared little or nothing for the rest of the family, and my father, who was to drive her down the three miles to the Wyandanch station, standing clapping his hands against the leather of his lambs wool coat, has been for me from birth a resentment that I myself did not understand. Their relationship was so close, their love for each other so evident, and yet though my grandmother was for me [up to a certain age] the greater of the two, my father always stood "outside."

Djuna was obviously exasperating to Wald and brought out his cruelty. She told Chester Page that as a child, "she remembered her father in a rage, trying to whip her with a horse whip. Her grandmother had intervened. 'Stop it,' she cried, 'she's just like you. She can't tell an untruth.' "[2] In a note, which reveals this cruel side of her father, Djuna wrote: "I remember when my father put me in a skip, and lowered me into a well hed dug in Cornwall . . . he cried how does it feel to be away from home and in this quaking fen he dipped my cage [me down] . . ."[3]

Rage may have led to violation, for Djuna told the poet George Barker that "she believed her Lesbianism to have been the consequence of her father raping her when she was a very young girl."[4] Yet she told James Scott a rather different story, which he recapitulated in a letter to Barnes dated Good Friday, 1971. The subject is Barnes's play *The Antiphon*, but the impetus is close to autobiography:

> I now "reconstruct" more by looking at "The Antiphon." I see a little girl named Miranda who had entered into a complex relationship with her mother. She felt neglected, for she sensed that her mother loved her sons more than her daughter. The little girl became strongly self-willed. She did things for which she earned endless punishment. Yet her punishment became "love," for at least it was some form of recognition. At age 16, she was raped by an Englishman three times her age with her father's knowledge and consent, while her mother did nothing to stop it. This, too, she endured as a "punishment" for an ill-defined sin: the sin of being, or at least feeling, unwanted. Still later, this girl, now a young woman, left her home to make her own way in the world; but her leaving was not an emotionally neutral thing. Although she went at her own desire, she still felt "expelled" from her home.

We shall return to this subject in Chapter Thirteen, for Barnes's rage at her early violation informs *The Antiphon*.

Fearing Wald in childhood, she turned for emotional support to her grandmother, Zadel, who became the single most important influence on Djuna, the family member Djuna always said she loved the most. One reason was her sensitivity and concern during troubled times.

When Djuna was five or six, her first pet died, a small canary, one of several pets that would cause Djuna much weeping. On this sad occasion, Zadel buried it in her best Liberty silk pink scarf, as later she would Fanny's baby Sheila.[5] Zadel had an instinctive understanding of the importance of such rituals, which endeared her greatly to the children.

Without Zadel's tutoring, Djuna Barnes would probably not have become a writer, have developed the necessary skills and sense of dedication to her craft. She followed in her grandmother's footsteps, entering the world of journalism and illustration as a way station to poetry, drama, and the novel. In later years, she wrote Emily Coleman: "I always thought I was my grandmother, and *now* I am almost right" (14 December 1935).

Djuna was in turn Zadel's favorite, the one in whom she put her faith for the future. Though she read to all the children nightly when she was not away, Zadel took special pains to teach Djuna all she could about journalism, literature, and art. Zadel often reminisced about the famous people she had known in her career, talking of what writers did, how they acted, and how pleasant it was to be an artist, living outside the world of moral conventions. Consequently Barnes knew at an early age that she would become a writer and an illustrator. Zadel remained an important presence in Djuna's life—as late as 1974, at the age of eighty-two, Djuna noted in her diary that 9 March was Zadel's birthday, a day to be remembered.

Zadel traveled frequently, or worked in New York, so that there is correspondence which provides in reflection a portrait of Djuna at thirteen. In a letter, she told her granddaughter to practice her writing and to do a lesson in geography. "Be *patient* with yourself & in *earnest* & *take pains*." Djuna was to spend twenty minutes daily reading music and was to learn the multiplication table, which gave her trouble. Of course, with eight or nine children about the house, Djuna was also expected to help her mother with the chores. Apparently she was not very nice to her half sister, Muriel; and so Zadel warned her against a character flaw, meddling in business that was not her own. "If you overcome this bad habit," Zadel says, "you will *escape* a lot of trouble,—*prevent* a lot of trouble,—you will be *happier* & be really a much nicer girl."[6] In her letters, Zadel expressed her love to all the children, but Djuna was her passion.

Zadel's passion for Djuna, however, has a peculiar twist: most of her surviving letters to her adolescent granddaughter carry sexually explicit messages. From Djuna's side, the only reference to this aspect of the relationship is at the bottom of the second page of a fragment about the death of Zadel. The page is torn, but at the bottom, one can make out Djuna's thoughts on sleeping for fifteen years beside Zadel and playing with her breasts, here called "Redlero" and "Kedler." Djuna's letters to Zadel from this period, few in number, are occasionally bawdy but provide little evidence of sexual involvement.

The family members had affectionate nicknames for one another. Zadel was "Gaga" to all, although in letters to Djuna she signed herself variously as Corkerditterdillercork or Waedler or Flitch. Djuna was Snickerbits or Starbits, and her breasts were "Cuddlers." Zadel's breasts, also called "Pink Tops" and "wedlers," are the subject of cartoons at the conclusion of most of her letters to Djuna. A letter dated 9 July 1905 (Djuna was thirteen) shows a sketch of Zadel with her breasts stretched out of shape to look like penises. One is labeled "Ronk-onk-oma!" (a town on Long Island), the other, "New York City"; on the side: "Dey's *stwetched* orful! (Pull gullet!)" A letter of 25 February 1909 shows Zadel's nipples as eyes, reading one of Djuna's letters. On 11 June 1908, Zadel wrote: "Pink Tops are simply gasping with love!" and on 4 March 1909: "Oh, Misriss! When I sees your sweet hands ahuggin you own P.T.'s—I is just crazy & I jumps on *oo!* Like dis. Wiv dis wesult." Next to this is Zadel's drawing of one nude woman atop another, breast to breast. The letter is signed: "ownest lishous grandmother." On 14 November 1909, Zadel wrote: "I'm huggin' you close to the Pinknesses, and they is cortlin' tremendous."

In a letter from this time but dated only "Thursday," Zadel tells Djuna; "I'm so *sorry* 'oo isn't feeling happy & are tired of effthing X *Don't* feel that way any more, my little sweetheart X. Sweetest Missrus X we is fayde our pinkyness will go pale if misriss isn't happy X." Each X was a kiss.

Indeed, in thinking of Zadel Barnes today, it's impossible not to reflect on the mystery surrounding those erotic letters she wrote around 1909 to her granddaughter Djuna, which suggest that they may have been involved in one of the rarest forms of incest. But precaution needs to be taken before one accepts the letters as an open-and-shut case for incest, because there are counterarguments. Barnes did write that she loved Zadel "as a child usually loves its mother." Regardless of whether or not incest occurred—and given Zadel's exuberance and freedom from convention, some variety of sex play may well have happened—these letters were written primarily as bawdy entertainment by two females who happened to share a bed, as everybody in this large, unconventional family seemed to do in their small farmhouse in Huntington. Since there are no living witnesses, the letters should perhaps be examined more as literary texts than as conclusive proof of incest.

A counterargument might proceed as follows: Humor played an important role in family correspondence. Zadel complimented Djuna on her humor in letters, which suggests that Djuna also read Zadel's letters as bawdy humor: "*Your* letter made me laugh till I was lame; you certainly are delightfully humorous."[7] Djuna responded in kind, for one of her letters to Zadel of this period shows a drawing of a sticklike woman laid out with a writing pen inserted between her legs as an illustration of how Djuna looked when no letter from Zadel came that day (26 February 1909). Letters from Wald Barnes, Djuna's father, invariably include attempts to amuse, for bawdy letters were family fun.

Djuna probably carried the letters around for everybody in the family to read. There would have been no need for secrecy about them, for certainly the family was not prudish about sex. Would not Djuna's mother have intervened if the letters had pointed to an unhealthy relationship between grandmother and granddaughter? Since Djuna did become prudish in her later years, surely she would have destroyed Zadel's letters if she had worried about their contents. Loving Zadel "as a child usually loves its mother," would she have sold them to a university library? Jealous of her privacy, why did she save the letters if they revealed incest? This seems to be the crux of the mystery.

Barnes easily became outraged at what she considered to be misinterpretation; for example, she was anxious to communicate the "truth" about the ending of *Nightwood* (that there were no sexual implications) to those in whom she had confidence. Then, too, if Zadel had a sexual interest in Djuna, it was certainly not accompanied by possessiveness, as is normally the case, for as we shall see, by the end of 1909 she was actively promoting Djuna's love affair with Fanny's brother Percy Faulkner.

Since in 1909 Zadel was sixty-eight and Djuna seventeen, the idea of incest is more than a little bizarre. But perhaps the word "incest" is too strong a word for what passed between them, which may have been nothing more than good-natured fondling. Barnes seems not to have complained about Zadel's sexual exploitation, as she did about her father's, though she blamed her grandmother for occasionally being untruthful. But what is one to make of the image of Zadel in *Nightwood*, "dressed as a man, wearing billycock and a corked moustache, ridiculous and plump in tight trousers and a red waistcoat, her arms spread saying with a leer of love, 'My little sweetheart!' "? Even as it evokes sinister implications, this image of cross-dressing seems distinctly parodic (*N* 63).

Even if the bawdy letters of 1909 point more surely to sexual involvement, or to a rather droll, untraumatic, innocent variety of entertainment than incest, that still leaves the question as to why a grandmother should write to a granddaughter in this way, drawing pictures of her breasts and fantasizing about the joys of the bed they shared. We may locate the answer in Zadel's philosophy of free love, which she had encouraged her son Wald to believe and which resulted in the peculiar arrangement of his two wives and two sets of children living in the same house, with Zadel as matriarchal head and sole means of support. Zadel wanted Djuna to be comfortable with her body and with her sexuality, just as she wished Wald to be comfortable with his bigamy. One way to do this was to treat the normal anxiety of girlhood with generous portions of humor, so as to make the idea of free love more palatable.

As we have seen, Zadel's liberal attitude toward sex began as early as adolescence; it was reconfirmed in the radical circles to which she gravitated as a journalist. In London, she would have found the company of thinkers who theorized that women would be better off without the bonds of matrimony, that love was sufficient grounds for sexual involvement, and (this is one of Wald Barnes's favorite lines) that both prostitution and the oppression of women would end if polygamy became widespread. Djuna Barnes told Chester Page that Zadel "believed in free love—everybody screwing each other."[8]

Zadel was a very physical, loving person in the family circle, so that the exuberance of her letters might have its parallel in her gushy hugging and kissing of the other family members, as is noted by Duane in his séance notebook. Still, when all is considered, Zadel believed that sex was fun, natural, liberating, and educational, and as Djuna's teacher and confidante, she would not have thought it immoral or irresponsible to instruct Djuna in the delights of the boudoir. Sex was not to be experienced just in marriage, and homoeroticism was obviously condoned.

The Djuna-Zadel relationship implies three distinct possibilities, none of them mutually exclusive: grandmother-granddaughter sex; evidence of bawdy wit, the letters being written in large part to amuse; and, last, evidence of Zadel's and Wald's philosophy of sexual freedom, the point of the obscene drawings thus being to liberate Djuna from sexual inhibitions by humorously playing down any negative consequences.

It is not necessary to go so far as to argue, as Mary Lynn Broe does, that the Zadel-Djuna relationship was incestuous and therefore beneficial as a refuge against patriarchal violence. Broe confuses a number of issues. She says: "Temporarily safe from the violations of the patriarchal household, Zadel and Djuna played in their symbolic, marginalized world, a queendom of 'nanophilia.' "[9] Broe argues: "Read as a text of patriarchal authority, the daughter's violation and Zadel's efforts to restore her were bounded on one side by the story of the father's attempted rape, his 'virginal sacrifice' of the daughter, then his brutal barter of his daughter-bride."[10] In effect, this is a reading of *The Antiphon* as straight autobiography, as if all were there and nothing traumatic suppressed.[11]

Whatever the truth may be, the effects of Zadel's love were seen in later years as Barnes's bisexuality flowered. Emily Coleman once reminded Barnes of what she had said on this subject: "when I asked you if you considered yourself really Lesbian: 'I might be anything. If a horse loved me, I might be that.' "[12] Though her sexual attraction was not restricted by gender, inquiries as to her sexual orientation were regarded as an invasion of privacy; here the probing is deflected with characteristic wit. One reason for Barnes's privacy may have been that she was undeniably fascinated by the notion of incest as an element in sexual attraction. In *Nightwood*, Nora describes her intense love for Robin: "For Robin is incest too; that is one of her powers" (*N* 156). Djuna told Chester Page that she had fallen in love with Thelma Wood (the novel's Robin) because she resembled her grandmother.[13]

A letter of 22 February 1909 from Djuna to a friend named "Dougga" gives us a glimpse of Djuna at sixteen. It mentions Thurn making a trapeze in the barn, on which the children loved to swing. At Christmas, Djuna had received a box of candy and Thackeray's *Vanity Fair* from a "gentleman friend" named Roy: no Prince Charming, but he is definitely interested in her, she says. Apparently Roy was *quite* interested in Djuna, for just four days previously, Zadel wrote Djuna advising her what to do if a certain young man should propose. She was to tell him that they were too young and unprepared for marriage, and "he *must not know* your views on marriage & sex questions—they would certainly become common gossip!" (18 February 1909).

By April of that year, it was no longer Roy but an older man, Fanny's brother Percy Faulkner, who occupied Djuna's thoughts, for on the twelfth, Zadel comments on a love letter from Percy forwarded to her by Djuna. She affirms that it is indeed a love letter and jokes about Percy's being in the soap business. Even here there is the drawing of breasts at the end and a puzzling code reference to "swinging the Chinaman."

Throughout 1909, Zadel encouraged Djuna in her relationship with Percy, even while Djuna's mother strongly disapproved. It is unclear whether this was simply another example of Zadel's bad judgment in domestic affairs, or whether she perhaps thought that Percy's financial support and a change of scenery might provide Djuna with the independence to develop her art. As for Djuna, she clearly seems to have loved Percy at first, or at least to have been flattered by his attentions. In May, she went to Brooklyn to stay with Zadel for a while, perhaps to get away from the family. The courtship continued through the fall, though not without misunderstandings, for on 21 December 1909, Zadel wrote Percy a long letter that patiently explained how to make Djuna happy.

> Djuna loves you truly & deeply, as would be her nature to do, if she loved at all. Of her love you may feel as sure as of your own. But she is one who needs the outward sign as well as the inward assurance. She is sensitive . . . the more so because of the adverse conditions in which she is placed. Her mother's disapproval & opposition; the relationship with Fanny which she cannot help disliking . . . these are depressing elements in her daily life, but fortunately, they need not mar her life in its final individual union with yours.

Zadel went on to warn Percy of a bad habit: "your way of not appearing to notice or reciprocate some of the sweetest tendernesses she bestows on you." He was at times "quite indifferent to her presence," so that "on the last day of your last visit, she loved you so much & so hated to have to part with you, that she frequently drew near you; leaned against you & wanted to put your arms around her & show her that you understood." But Percy seemed indifferent. Zadel quotes Djuna's response: "I know I shall need to be loved, to have love *shown* to me all my life, & if he finds it tedious to do so now, in this early time— how will it be later on?" Djuna approved the letter and her amanuensis.

In late May or early June of 1910, before her eighteenth birthday, Djuna reluctantly "married" Percy, for a letter from Zadel of 11 June indicates that the couple had arrived in Bridgeport, Connecticut. Saxon Barnes affirms that he remembered a kind of marriage ceremony without benefit of clergy in Zadel's room, which probably consisted of an exchange of vows with musical accompaniment.[14] Then the eighteen-year-old Djuna and the fifty-two-year-old Percy went off to

Bridgeport, to live at 941 Kossuth Street, near Ogden, in a very large white frame rooming house. In their single room, Djuna tried her hand at cooking stew, while Percy peddled soap. With an abundance of time on her hands, she managed to write some poetry and complete a painting of Bridgeport's Beardsley Park, complete with woodlands, ice-skating rink, and zoo.

Djuna was terribly lonely, and her family felt desolate without her, but Zadel thought it was for the best, for she was unwavering in her support for this (mis)match. In a letter of 13 June, Zadel addressed Djuna as Mrs. Percy Arthur Edward Walsh McCormick James Faulkner. On 11 June, Zadel had written to encourage Djuna[15]: she was sure that Percy would take Djuna to the best libraries; "And *now* dear, before you become the mother of a brood of darlings!!! you will have leisure & quiet for the development of your poetic gift." In an undated letter of this time, Djuna's mother advised her to read the classics, recommending *Paradise Lost*, *Faust*, and the *Iliad*. She said that Wald had read all the great writers except Dante, for when he came to the *Inferno*, "it was so infernally long, he couldn't stand it, so gave it up!"

Djuna probably soon grew restless living with Faulkner, for she was accustomed to her large family circle and their nightly readings, music, and other artistic pursuits, but Zadel must have felt that she needed to push Djuna out into the world. One can speculate that conditions on the farm were growing rather desperate and there was some relief in having one less mouth to feed, even if the family missed Djuna.

In an unpublished fragment intended for the "Go Down Matthew" chapter of *Nightwood*, we find an account of a character's love life, which must have been based on real events in the early months of 1909. Hess, now called Cathrine [*sic*], later Nora, explains to the doctor about her childhood:

"Then at sixteen, standing at the break of day in the dust of crossroads, a boy asked me to kiss him, and I kissed him, and he said, 'Thank you,' and I laughed because I knew that was not the answer, though what he should have said I hadn't the faintest idea. Then he went away because he was dying of something incurable and hot in him, though he was only a boy of eighteen. And then I had a lover and a doll,[16] and because he was a man who had held me on his knee when I was a child, and because I had a doll and ate caramels, and looked up at him and said 'yes,' he couldn't bear it. He thought, perhaps, that he was bored, but it was something else; he was an old man then and he wanted something simpler and older, so he took me away to a transients' hotel in Bridgeport, if you know what kind of an hotel that is—."

[Dr. O'Connor responds] "I should hope to say I do! Men going upstairs panting, and women going up slowly, saying, 'For the love of God, can't you wait.' "

"Like that, and it frightened him still further, beyond endurance, because I wouldn't cry, and he said, 'Go back home and don't tell anyone, because after all I never did intend to marry you!' And I picked up the carving knife then, seeing that night back on the hill, my brother playing the trombone somewhere so that it came softly up to the trees and I had said, 'No, I will marry you in my heart but I will not marry you in church.' Because there was a big new deal my father had in his head. Then I remembered the ceremony beside the Christmas tree, when my father and my grandmother stood by, and my mother by the door in her apron, crying and thinking God knows what; and he put a ring on my finger and I kissed him. Before that, it must have been two hours, I had gone down on the floor and hugged my grandmother by her knees, dropping my head down, saying, 'Don't let it happen!' and she said, 'It had to happen.'

"And I was in bed that first night, and he said, 'Christ! You don't bleed much.' And I said, 'It is all the blood it has.' And all before the door my mother had strewn flour—to give herself hope, hoping there would be no foot-mark in it going my way."

"So I took the carving knife and leaned across the table, strong and blind with something coming up in me out of what my father had in his head for women and love, and for the Christmas tree and the flour on the floor, and he jumped out of the window backward into the garden. And then I came back home and I wasn't crying. And I got thin, and fell when I walked, and my grandmother came to me and said: 'What is it that he has done that you are sent back home?' And I told her. And that too was my childhood."[17]

Some of the details of the relationship with Percy and the brief encounter with the eighteen-year-old boy with an incurable disease appear in Barnes's one-act play "She Tells Her Daughter," published in *The Smart Set* in 1923, wherein Madame Deerfont sets the record of her youth straight for her daughter, Ellen Louise Theresa. Madame has pretended to be more of a lady than she was. Her father was a chemist (Wald's only formal job had been in a chemist's shop in England). At fourteen, Madame met the consumptive Ramey and felt sorry for him because she thought he was dying. She took him into the garret, where they "read *Hamlet* together, and he recited bits of the 'Lily Maid.' "[18] It is implied that a sexual encounter followed. If the account is autobiographical, "Ramey" could have been an early lover of Djuna's, possibly Roy.

Madame has previously told Ellen that she was once "in love with a fellow named Percy,"[19] but her next lover is not named. They would meet at night and crawl into the hay of the livery stable his father kept, but after a few months he left. Madame continued to visit the barn, and when he returned she was there, holding in her hand a knife that she found in the hay. She implies that she stabbed him to death, perhaps as revenge for abandonment. Her father, who had recently "married again, a great lazy brute of a creature called Daisy," married her off to Ellen's father, to remove her from harm's way.[20]

It is doubtful that Djuna stayed longer then two months with Faulkner. She returned to the Long Island farm, feeling that she had failed in an important human relationship strongly promoted by Zadel and Wald, and she blamed them for having encouraged her elopement with a man nearly three times her age. (Later she would accuse Wald of conspiring to take her virginity by bringing in a neighbor—also three times her age.) Feeling betrayed by family and life in general, Djuna Barnes would in the years to come profess love, but finally little sympathy, for her first great passion, her grandmother. "Sophia offered her heart for food, Julie spewed it out on a time, and said, 'I taste a lie!' And Sophia hearing, cried in agony, but Julie went apart" (*R* 16).

After the fiasco in Bridgeport, Djuna stayed at the Huntington farm through the rest of 1910 and much of 1911, practicing writing under the tutelage of Zadel. Few letters of this period apparently survive—probably few were written—but on 30 June 1911, Djuna received a letter from Zadel's publisher friend Robert H. Davis, of the Frank A. Munsey Co., remarking on Djuna's "The Dreamer," a twelve-line poem in two verses. Davis said he admired one line: "Shivering across the pane, drooping tear-wise." By the summer of 1912, Djuna had several stories circulating, but "The Dreamer" would be her first publication.[21]

The years immediately following her parents' divorce were among the most difficult of Djuna Barnes's early life, for she felt an insufficiency of everything necessary for happiness and prosperity; and the entire burden of mother and brothers seemed to be on her own shoulders. She must have enrolled in art school as one means to get away from her family.

Zadel's brother Reon Barnes paid Djuna's tuition at Pratt Institute in Brooklyn and also helped support Djuna's mother and brothers, though with considerable ill will. His correspondence with Elizabeth and Djuna is heavy with irony and condescension, for he adopted the tone of a schoolmaster correcting unusually dim-witted children.[22] Even on these terms, his support was welcome. To eke out a bit more income, Djuna also posed (fully clothed, she said) for the painting class, and she practiced figure drawing so that she could illustrate her articles. (Her favorite teacher was Mr. Skidmore, but her most famous teacher may have been Elizabeth Ely Lord.)

Djuna entered Pratt on 30 September 1912 and left on 19 March 1913,[23] those scant six months and a few more at the Art Students League of New York being about the extent of her formal education. All considered, she did well at Pratt, making B's in most courses. Her best subject was pictorial composition, in which she improved from a B to an A in her second term. Despite her success, Djuna recalled that she was headstrong and resisted doing anything she was told. This is borne out in part by teachers' comments on her grade card, which also indicate that though she was educated at home, she did well on tests. Among the various notes penned are these: she was "bright," an "excellent student," and kept "evenly at B level work." At the end of her stay, on 19 March, one teacher said: "I have just seen some outside work of hers and I am greatly impressed. Individual, strong, full of promise. Hard to convince." Another said that she was a "genius" but "hard to teach."

A classmate at Pratt, Mary Ludlum Davis, wrote in later years to inquire whether Djuna remembered her, "a dark, stringy maiden with acne whose locker was next to yours." They had exchanged verses, some of which were about a teacher whom they both found attractive—Ernest Watson, who taught design and lettering. Davis inquired about a missing word in one of Djuna's poems about him: "You would know he is male by his ———." The word is forever lost, though perhaps not much needed. Djuna got a C in lettering in her first term, and Mr. Watson said of her that though she had "individuality," she could not "work out a stated problem," and indeed, problem solving was never to be one of her strong points.

After Pratt Institute, there was still considerable pressure on Djuna to support her mother, her brothers, and herself. Even on her meager salary as a journalist, Djuna did manage in 1915–16 to enroll in courses at the Art Students League of New York, where she studied drawing and illustration with George B. Bridgman (1864–1943) and Frank Vincent DuMond (1865–1951). Tuition was six dollars a month.

According to Lawrence Campbell, currently of the League, when Barnes was a student, males and females went into separate classes when there was a nude model; otherwise they were treated as mature professionals. Djuna seemed quite fortunate in her teachers, especially in George Bridgman, who Campbell says was "the best-known teacher of Life Drawing and Anatomy in the U.S. His methods were often considered somewhat radical even though he himself was part of the Beaux-Arts tradition and had studied with Gérôme at the École des Beaux-Arts in Paris."[24] Bridgman would not have admitted Barnes without an entrance examination. The skills she learned in art school served her well in illustrations for her journalism, *Ryder*, and *Ladies*

Almanack, and in later life, when poetry, drawing, and painting were her chief hobby and her principal escape from despair.

It was around this time that she moved out of the flat shared with her family in the Bronx, feeling that she had done what she could for them. She urgently needed more freedom and space. She also resented her mother's expectation that she sacrifice herself for her brothers. She would tell Emily Coleman: "My mother at that time was a bloody nuisance, weeping, lamenting, self pitying weak creature who would have sold *me* for dogs meat for the boys."[25] Being jobless, Djuna had even considered turning prostitute for them, but she packed her things and found a flat in Greenwich Village. In 1915, close to starvation at times, she managed to keep lodgings at 42 Washington Square South, then at 220 West 14th Street.

Barnes left Pratt in March 1913 and pursued a career in freelance journalism, but her articles didn't begin appearing in the *Brooklyn Daily Eagle* until 29 June; the hiatus has not been explained, but there may have been a training period to get her started. As a free-lancer, Barnes sometimes wrote for more than one newspaper simultaneously. She stayed at the *Eagle* until about Christmas, when Carl Van Vechten (1880–1964) hired her to write for the *New York Press*.

Barnes may have had brief affairs with both the English writer Richard LeGallienne's daughter Gwen and Carl Van Vechten during these years. Van Vechten, a native of Iowa, was a novelist, translator, and critic of music and dance, but he may be best remembered as a portrait photographer; he did a particularly fine photograph of Barnes. He also produced seven novels and five books of music criticism.

Much of Djuna's story is about impossible love affairs, and as the narrator of Ford Madox Ford's *The Good Soldier* says, this is the saddest story. If we forget the Percy Faulkner fiasco, we can say that after Zadel, the great love of Djuna Barnes's early life was Ernst Hanfstaengl (1887–1975), known to his friends as "Putzi."[26] The beginning of their affair coincided with her moving to Greenwich Village. The romance blossomed during 1914–16.[27]

Hanfstaengl came from Munich, where his father owned an art gallery. According to the author Philip Metcalfe:

The Hanfstaengls were prominent folk in Germany. They supplied three generations of privy counselors to the dukes of Sax-Coburg-Gotha while distinguishing themselves as patrons and connoisseurs of the arts. The invention of the photographic camera in the 19th century and a new process that put more colored dots to a square centimeter made Putzi's paternal grandfather a wealthy man and the Hanfstaengl name preeminent in the field of art reproduction.[28]

Putzi's mother was the daughter of a Civil War general from Connecticut. At Harvard (he graduated in 1909), he knew T. S. Eliot, Walter Lippmann, and other notables, and he performed at the Hasty Pudding Club.

In his introduction to *Unheard Witness*, the English translation of Hanfstaengl's autobiography, Brian Connell described Putzi as a magnetic character, famous for his enormous vitality, his love of mimicry, his piano playing, and his wit, qualities he retained even in later life:

> Putzi Hanfstaengl is a representative of that dwindling human species—a character. His appearance alone would single him out in any crowd. A towering six-foot-four, the thick hair on his enormous head is barely speckled with gray even in his seventieth year. The twinkling eyes above the bold nose and prognathous jaw reflect the endless stream of humorous comment and brazen *boutades* which provide his conversational fireworks.[29]

Once, while rowing for the Harvard crew team, he rescued a canoeist on the Charles River; Boston newspapers declared him a hero. In 1908, he visited Theodore Roosevelt at the White House (the President's son was Putzi's Harvard classmate), where he gave a concert and in his enthusiasm broke "seven strings on the presidential piano."[30] Teddy Roosevelt extended invitations to Putzi even after his retirement from office.

Putzi was a connoisseur of nineteenth-century German art and German wines, an incessant raconteur, a jovial tease, and a boisterous entertainer, apt at any moment to leap to the piano and play Chopin, Liszt, Beethoven, Wagner, or Harvard marching tunes.[31] In 1911, the year after his father died, Hanfstaengl took over the New York branch of the family firm, on the corner of Fifth Avenue and Forty-fifth Street, which specialized in prints, especially Holbeins. During this period he socialized at the New York Harvard Club with Pierpont Morgan, Arturo Toscanini, Henry Ford, Charlie Chaplin, and Senator Franklin D. Roosevelt.[32]

Djuna Barnes remembered that in 1916 she had "tinted Holbeins for the print store."[33] In later years, she related to Chester Page how she had walked into his Fifth Avenue gallery with a portfolio of drawings under her arm. By this time Djuna was a stunningly attractive woman—handsome rather than beautiful, as she always said, with auburn hair and a curvaceous body. Her passports describe her as five feet eight, gray-eyed, with a mole near her left eye. She and Putzi "sort of looked at each other and fell in love," she said.

They were engaged during the inauspicious years 1914–16, when anti-German feeling in America was at its height. Saxon Barnes was convinced that but for the war, they would have married; he remembered well Putzi's visits to the Barnes home in Morris Park.[34] Putzi was fond of Saxon, to whom he gave a stamp album. He was friendly and likable, but at the same time there was a soldierly quality about him. Saxon remembered how Hanfstaengl could go through a military drill with rifle in a convincing manner.

During her time with Putzi, Djuna was already an enterprising and adventurous young journalist, but one seemingly foolhardy scheme particularly frightened him: her editor's plan to send her up in a homemade airplane. Putzi offered her the twenty-five dollars she would have earned, and she did not go up. The plane crashed, killing all aboard.[35] Late in her life, Djuna told her friend Hank O'Neal: "[Putzi] saved my life twice, first in the airplane and then when he didn't marry me."[36]

Hanfstaengl was incensed about what he called anti-German hysteria in the United States during World War I, "in a population which came to regard dachshunds as fifth columnists."[37] He was spared confinement as an enemy alien, but his art gallery, which he said was worth half a million dollars, was confiscated and sold to rivals for $8,200. It may have been during this time that he taught painting and drawing on Christopher Street in Greenwich Village. Konrad Bercovici tells a different story, about how Hanfstaengl was behind the peace movements in New York City that were subsidized by the German embassy; and how, according to the Irish labor leader James Larkin, Hanfstaengl asked him for help in blowing up American ammunition factories.[38]

Instead of marrying Djuna, Hanfstaengl wed a German-American woman named Helene in 1920, and the next year, using a Swiss passport, he returned to Germany, where he pursued a doctorate in history at the University of Munich. Soon thereafter he heard one of Hitler's speeches at the Kindl Keller and was convinced that he had found a great political orator and potential leader, if only one could make him socially respectable. On hearing Hitler speak, Putzi's sympathies shifted from monarchism to fascism; on hearing Putzi play the piano, Hitler became a devoted fan.

In 1930, in Paris, Rudolf Hess approached Putzi Hanfstaengl about becoming chief minister of the foreign press, citing his extensive international connections; he accepted the position and held it from 1932 until 1937, claiming that he supported Hitler in hopes of influencing him on important issues. In essence, he said he was a patriot rather than a Nazi, but he was forced to stand by helplessly while Hitler turned to the most radical fringe of the party—to Joseph Goebbels and Hermann Göring.

Having lived in America, Hanfstaengl tried to convince Hitler that Germany could not win a European war if the United States entered it as an enemy. Hitler, ignorant of America's strength and resolve, took no heed, and it became increasingly clear that a major part of Putzi's job was to promote propaganda for the National Socialists, although ostensibly it was to receive foreign visitors and reporters who wished to know more about the new order in Germany. In his loyalty to Hitler, Putzi went a considerable distance down the road of fascism. He wrote marches for the Hitler Youth, and supervised and financed the filming of the life of Horst Wessel, a Nazi killed by communists in the 1930s and now a national hero. The film was banned by Goebbels as politically incorrect and had to be completely revised to reflect the life of a completely different subject, Hans Westmar; Putzi lost his shirt because of quixotic censorship.

Hanfstaengl was increasingly distressed by Nazi thuggery. Foreigners were regularly slapped or slugged when they failed to raise their arm in salute of Nazi banners and parades. This happened to H. V. Kaltenborn, the radio broadcaster, a Harvard friend of Putzi's. Increasingly Putzi was excluded from Hitler's inner circle, and the Führer even made contemptuous remarks to his face. As early as 1932, Bercovici witnessed enmity between Hanfstaengl and Goebbels in a Berlin nightclub,[39] and trouble between Putzi and Hitler may have begun in 1934.

Having seen how his moderate, democratic-minded colleagues were executed without trial, and surely suspecting that he might be next, Hanfstaengl fled to Switzerland in February 1937, just before his fiftieth birthday. He had been called to Berlin to fly a secret mission to Spain, where he was to land by parachute and deliver a message from Hitler to Franco. His pilot, who knew him, advised him that his parachute would not open. Allowed to escape, he hastened to Zurich, then went to England.

Djuna Barnes had lunch with Putzi in May 1938, while he was in London, but he upset her, apparently with a proposition she refused. She realized that "its always painful to have loved someone years back and find out what they grew up into, he was so much sweeter when I was twenty three."[40] Beyond seduction, what was on his mind was getting her to check the English in his autobiography, which she thought was odd for a Harvard graduate.

Interned in England, Canada, and the United States during World War II, roughly from 1942 to 1945, Putzi provided what information he could to the American government and was in frequent contact with the Roosevelt administration regarding the nature of Hitler and his inner circle. His loyalty to Harvard and the Class of 1909 had served him well. After the war, Putzi returned to Germany, where a denazification court cleared him of charges that he had helped Hitler gain power. He died in 1975.

Djuna sometimes wondered what might have happened had they

married, imagining opportunities she might have had to assassinate Hitler had she become part of his inner circle. She told Hank O'Neal that

> Putzi was one of the people who helped hide Hitler after the Munich affair, and he [Putzi] told her she could interview him [Hitler] for two dollars a word, but no one wanted to pay the bill in those days. She says this is too bad; she could have met Hitler and then turned him in and where might that have led?[41]

Djuna visited Putzi in Munich with her lover Charles Henri Ford in October 1931. There are photographs of the three of them standing in Odeonplatz, where Barnes is feeding the pigeons. Putzi's son, Egon, remembers Djuna coming to tea at Villa Tiefland, the Hanfstaengl house in Munich, on a number of occasions in the 1930s. Once, it was to interview Oswald Spengler. He remembers her metallic voice and incisive way of speaking (he knew no English). When Egon was old enough, his father would speak to him about his affair with Djuna, recalling such pleasures as scrubbing her back in the bathtub. Egon believes that his father may have always intended to marry a German to continue the family line, but according to Putzi, the specific cause of the breakup was Djuna's continuing sexual interest in women. This should have been apparent to Putzi early in their relationship: a letter from Wald Barnes to Djuna of 5 December 1913, when she was twenty-one, indicates his cheerful awareness of both her bisexuality and her new love, which was probably Putzi: "You say that you are *in love*—but that was always more or less kronik with youse wasn't it? Male or female this time? And who's th' lucky dorg (or dorgess)?" The letter is signed "Your Operapa." Putzi left Djuna for Mimsey Benson, a stunning blonde, before eventually meeting Helene, whom he married.

Djuna and Putzi remained in contact throughout their lives, though the friendship was mostly on his side. He sent her pastries and chocolates on holidays, and at various times offered money, which she rejected. On 19 January 1952, he wrote her: " 'Old love does not rest'—it seems—and our early afflictions remain loyal to us throughout life." He signed the letter with "and a big hug from your old seducer Putzi." O'Neal observes: "the only picture with any color in her apartment was a postcard, 'Violets' by Dürer," a memento of Putzi.[42]

Djuna Barnes probably never fully recovered from the very deep hurt she felt when Putzi Hanfstaengl told her that he must have a German wife for his children and broke off their relationship.[43] The devastating effect on Djuna was recorded in the deleted section of *Nightwood* where her persona narrates the events to Dr. O'Connor.

And I wouldn't take my hair down when a boy asked me to; and I wore ear-rings and played the fiddle. And another boy asked me to kiss him and I struck him, and then I was older, and another man—he seemed so tall and melancholy and humorous, with a head with the curve of madness in it—said, "Sit beside me." And I sat beside him. And he said, "I love you." And I said, "I love you." And we walked across Brooklyn Bridge, and he kissed me then and it was the first time I had been kissed or cared [for] in six years, and I loved him with all my heart, and I screamed and flew at him and I said, "I'd throw you down there into the water if I were strong enough!" And I struck at him, and he laughed, and I began running, and he walked quietly after me in soft long strides. And it went on three years and I said, "I will be married." And then the war came, and he was a German all the time in his heart, and in his mind he saw German families going down to death, and he thought German children must be born to take their place. And he came to me in a top-hat one morning with a can of cocoa under his arm and two rolls, because it was Sunday (we used to take the ferry) and he said, "I can't marry you, because you must be German for that now." And we cried until it was night; and he took me up to my garret room on Washington Square, and he stood under the trees and cried up at me, and I leaned weeping down at him from the window, and it was good-bye forever. And that Bulgarian, one floor down, a strange man, fat and devoured by a passion for cake, came up and stood in the doorway and said, "You mustn't do that," and how did he know that I had thought of killing myself—would I have? I think not. Two days later I couldn't stand it any more, so I rushed into the German's house and flung my arms about his neck and I said, "I love you anyway, and you can do as you like!" And he said, "The court would say the child resembles me." And my blood went away then, and he was quoting Shakespeare (he used to teach me Hamlet in German) and I was leaning by the table, my hands on it, gone terribly still, and I said, "That is a lie, a terrible lie—that I would get you into court, and it is against me and what I am!" And he said, "What is this that you are that I do not understand!" And he took me by the wrist and began turning my wrist. He was livid and turning and turning and I wouldn't scream though I began to go down with the pain in my arm. And he said, "Down, and say that there is nothing that I do not understand about you!" And I said, "You understand nothing, now I know you understand nothing!" And I kept saying, "Nothing!" and he had me down and back with my legs under me, still turning my arm; and then he was lying on me and trembling and crying and kissing me, and so heavy that I shook with his shaking. And I said, "Nothing! Nothing! Nothing!" Then it was over and he got up and I got up and he went to the window and I said, "She will *have* to be a German—now." And he said, "She will be German."

The "Go Down Matthew" fragment continues:

"And then there were others?"

"And then there were others. One was a Cuban, very gentle and pretty and sick. . . . And there was also a Cuban woman. "And I said then, 'How can this be, that I could love a woman?' And that was the first thought about it and the last because after that there was no difference at all, only just love."

It was at the *New York Press* that Djuna worked with Mary Pyne, and quite possibly she moved to the *Press* because of Pyne, whom Barnes came to love passionately.[44] Apparently little information on the Djuna Barnes–Mary Pyne relationship survives, and their passion is very difficult to date precisely. Barnes probably met her before Putzi, and they may have just been friends then. After her affair with Putzi, Djuna's feelings toward Pyne were definitely passionate.

Barnes told Chester Page that she used to leave presents of fruit at Mary's door, and Mary's father, who did not like Djuna, would kick them onto the sidewalk. Like Barnes, Pyne was a beautiful redhead who became associated with the Provincetown Players soon after they opened, in the summer of 1915. She also wrote poetry and was at this time attached to tramp poet Harry Kemp. In December, she appeared opposite Eugene O'Neill in his play *Before Breakfast*; in February 1917, she played Elena in Michael Gold's *Ivan's Homecoming*; in March, she was in Kemp's *The Prodigal Son*; and in January 1918, she was in Alice L. Rostetter's *The Widow's Veil*, all at the Provincetown. The next year, Pyne died of tuberculosis at Saranac Lake, New York, attended to the last by Barnes, who supplied oxygen and what comfort she could. Djuna sought to claim the body but was at first refused, since she had no money. Mary Pyne was the subject of a drawing in Barnes's story collection *A Book* and of her poem "Six Songs of Khalidine," which begins:

> The flame of your red hair does crawl and creep
> Upon your body that denies the gloom
> And feeds upon your flesh as 't would consume
> The cold precision of your austere sleep—
> And all night long I beat it back, and weep.

The painter Maurice Sterne remembers Barnes grieving over the death of the "Titian-haired beauty" Mary Pyne, "sobbing painfully, her head buried in her arms, saying over and over that she would never get over the loss. These were the only times I had even a glimpse of the true intensity her controlled facade covered."[45]

When she arrived in Paris in the early twenties, she told her friend the poet Mina Loy that she had had nineteen lovers, and that women were better in bed than men.[46] She might have been partial, being a woman herself; still, men had given her the most grief.

"I Could Never Be Lonely Without a Husband":
Barnes in the World of Journalism

"Ampee lived among his fellow beings as though he were the only pardonable mistake among a million errors."[1]

One day, probably in the spring of 1913, clad in a calico dress and carrying a basket, and looking rather like a milkmaid gone astray, Djuna appeared at the *Brooklyn Daily Eagle*. She applied for a job, concluding with the simple statement: "You need me." Late in life, Djuna described this scene a bit differently to Chester Page, claiming that she said "she could draw and write and they would be foolish not to hire her."[2] And so they did.

By this time she had published her first literary work, a twelve-line poem called "The Dreamer," in *Harper's Weekly*, where her grandmother, Zadel, was published frequently. During the summer of 1912, before she went to Pratt, Djuna was sending stories to the magazines Zadel had written for and recommended, stories with titles such as "Tomorrow Is Coming," "My Solitude," "A Cancelled Misdemeanor," and "A Painter of Pictures." They were rejected by *Smart Set*, *Harper's*, and *Life*. It wasn't until 1914 that she finally had a story accepted, by the *All-Story Cavalier Weekly*: "The Terrible Peacock." In dire poverty, bearing the burden of supporting her mother and brothers, in nearly constant depression, and frantic about the future, it is a wonder that Djuna was able to write at all; but in fact, adversity drove her furiously onward toward fame, achievement, and a measure of financial security.

At the *Eagle*, she was an illustrator and a reporter and drew a daily cartoon, for the handsome wage of fifteen dollars a week. Around Christmas of 1913, she went to the *New York Press*, where she wrote and illustrated theatrical interviews under the direction of Carl Van Vechten, who called her his "favorite genius." She stayed at the *Press* until August 1914, when she began to work for the *New York World Magazine*. Returning to the *Press* the following February, she went on to the *New York Morning Telegraph*, which paid Djuna to write illustrated short stories and articles for its Sunday magazine. During this time she covered murder trials, among them the "Gyp the Blood" case, which resulted in the electrocution of a number of gangsters.[3]

Barnes wrote quite a lot of freelance journalism, much of which was published unsigned, and probably a good deal of her work for these various newspapers was short term and contractual. For the New York bureau of the *Chicago Tribune*, where her boss was the publisher Burton Rascoe, Djuna wrote book reviews and drew illustrations of authors from photographs. She was a general reporter for the Hearst newspapers but was fired when she refused to write a story about a young girl whom ten men had raped. She gained admission to the girl's hospital room by saying she was a friend from school, but this invasion of privacy deeply distressed her.

During her early career, Barnes said, she worked for every English-language newspaper in New York but the *Times*. On her unsuccessful application for a Guggenheim fellowship, dated 4 November 1930, Djuna listed her accomplishments as a journalist: she had been a feature writer and reporter for the *Brooklyn Daily Eagle*; had contributed theatrical reviews, interviews, and drawings to the *New York Press*, short stories and drawings to the *New York Morning Telegraph*; had done features and illustrations for the *New York Tribune*, worked as a reporter for the *New York American*; was syndicate and feature writer for the Newspaper Enterprise Association; contributed gossipy features and illustrations to the *Theatre Guild Magazine*; and had written for *The Little Review, Dial, Charm, The Smart Set, Vanity Fair, McCall's, Transatlantic Review, transition*, and other magazines.

The money did come in. As Nancy J. Levine reminds us: "By 1917 Djuna Barnes was earning five thousand dollars a year as a free-lance feature writer. Fifteen dollars for an article was considered good payment in the 1910s; Barnes could, and often did, write several a day. By the time she left for Europe in 1920, she had published more than a hundred articles and over twenty-five short plays and fictions."[4] In all, she published some forty-five short stories. Writing for news-papers was in some ways advantageous for Barnes: it paid well; it gave her plenty of practice, for there were daily and weekly columns to fill; and the constant pressure must have taken her mind off her troubles.

Though Barnes called her journalism "rubbish" and discouraged interest in it, her juvenilia eventually came into the public domain, and she could not stop Douglas Messerli from republishing it. This is fortunate, for her interviews and journal articles deserve to be read not only for their historical and biographical interest but also for in-sights the serious Barnes reader gains into the techniques of *Night-wood*, in which, one could argue, Nora interviews Dr. O'Connor on the meaning of bohemian life.

In the early 1920s, James Joyce gave Barnes advice that he gave to other aspiring writers: in writing, the extraordinary event was the subject of journalism, while the commonplace was for literature. Or: "Never write about an unusual subject, make the common unusual."[5] But from the first, Barnes was attracted to the extraordinary, regardless of genre. She ignored Joyce's advice, then, in her literary work, forged his technique to a different shape.

But even in the earliest poetry, fiction, and journalism, the bo-hemian touch was there. In *Fancy's Craft*, Cheryl Plumb correctly points out that Barnes's writing owed much to the symbolists and decadents, for it oozed with the spirit of the yellow nineties, satirizing conventional virtues, criticizing middle-class American vulgarity and provincialism, and raising the flag of art for art's sake. Barnes pre-ferred artifice to honest realism, the fascinating cad to the simple provincial, the grotesque to the sublime. For the most part, the style is world-weary and blasé, the thought superficial; in other words, she gave readers what they wanted. If her decadent views mocked the readers of her journalism, they informed her more serious fiction of the 1920s and 1930s as well.

Barnes's journalism, especially the interviews, must also have provided for her a fantasy world of wealth and power to which she, as a beautiful female journalist, was able to gain admittance. But she was not part of that world, pretend though she might, for the truth was that her love life was a mess and her eagerness to serve art was largely frustrated. Excluded in various ways, Barnes divided herself into two parts in 1922, signing some of her journalism (Lady) Lydia Steptoe, perhaps so that she could reserve her real name henceforth for art.[6]

Success in journalism brought complications for Barnes. That which she valued little sold well; that into which she poured her soul was often seen by editors to be a less valuable commodity. If editors were interested only in sales and were right about what their readers wanted, then, Barnes concluded, American readers must be vacuous, superficial, poorly educated yahoos. This inverted sense of values contributed considerably to Barnes's anti-American attitude, her anxiety about her career as a writer, and her general feeling of depression. It wasn't until 1931 that Barnes considered herself securely enough established to reverse her vocational priorities and consider herself an artist first and a journalist second, though this had always been her goal.

The precariousness of her career probably tempted Barnes to dip too often into her well of bitterness for the decadent or sensational perspective that would plant a leer on the face of a harassed editor. This may be precisely what one would expect from the newly employed art school student, but the perspective was empowered by her inner feeling, affirming her pessimism about human nature, even human existence. It must also be said that Djuna's preoccupation with the horror of modern life is precisely the bridge between the journalism and her best creative work. Emily Coleman once remarked that making horror beautiful was Barnes's greatest gift.[7]

There was, however, a brighter side. Wit was a trademark of her work, and no matter how depressed Djuna Barnes felt about her life or her prospects, she never lost her sense of humor. She saved one newspaper clipping (date and source unknown), entitled "Women in Collision; Finery Strews Street," which is typical of Djuna at her wittiest. It describes a fight between two women on a street corner as if it were a traffic accident:

> A southbound woman and another woman standing on the corner of Sixty-eighth street and Broadway met in violent collision at 8:45 last night. Among the casualties were:
> One large summer hat, torn from the head of the southbound woman and thrown violently to the ground. Removed by some one who left neither name nor address.
> One shirt waist badly torn and discolored: will dye.
> Several rats, puffs and clumps of bona fide hair; suffering from shock.
> Two complete sets of feminine feelings: badly ruffled.
> The southbound woman was northbound at first in one of those semi-open cars that run up Amsterdam avenue, when she spied a man said to be her husband standing on the corner with woman number two. Leaving the car, the first woman started south and lost no time in getting into contact with the woman on the corner of Sixty-eighth street. At the first shock the latter's corkscrew curls were telescoped and her shirt waist backed onto a siding. . . .

Barnes's typically more decadent side emerged in her advice to any damsels who might be planning for distress, and other readers of *Vanity Fair*, when she published "What Is Good Form in Dying? In Which a Dozen Dainty Deaths Are Suggested for Daring Damsels." Insisting on good taste in all things, lamenting, tongue in cheek, the total absence of socially correct prescriptions for young ladies in the fashion magazines that bore the moral responsibility for their guidance, she advises women to match lethal technique with hair color. The real topic of the article was, of course, suicide, and how to look smartly decorous when found dead. In a world where form outclasses both substance and feeling, one must plan for every eventuality.

And so a blond must "hang sweetly, debonairly, and perseveringly by the neck," preferably from a Venetian mirror, while "the cold, cruel, the heavy-lidded vampire of the brunette order" must choose poison, preferably a "slow green" one.[8] A white-haired woman should jump off a tall building to end her ennui, while for the redhead (Djuna had auburn hair) only drowning would do: "But, it's hard to make them do it!" For fat women, "the pistol is reserved," though "she may have to use it two or three times; the position of her heart has to be ferreted out." But alas, the truly superior, the only possible death is by boredom.[9]

Most of the best journalistic articles by Barnes are collected in the volumes *New York* and *Interviews*, edited by Alyce Barry and published by the Sun & Moon Press. There are too many to be considered here, and most would be of scant interest if Barnes had not been destined for greater things; unless, of course, one had a particular interest in New York of the second decade of the twentieth century.

The articles of the early period cover a great variety of subjects, some timely and some seasonal. Four articles are on Coney Island, where dancing was a hot subject, especially the tango. Then there was women's suffrage, about which Barnes's attitude seems more bemused than supportive. Ethnicity was of interest, for she takes us to Chinatown, and to Brooklyn to see the Europeans and the Irish squatters. The latter visit gave her an opportunity to write Irish brogue, which she did less beautifully than her favorite playwright of the period, John Millington Synge. Djuna Barnes takes readers to "The Hem of Manhattan"—Greenwich Village, the Bowery, and then to the Bronx, where she dwells on girlhood memories from her time in Fordham.

We meet a dentist called Twingeless Twinchell, who practices in the open air from a platform erected on a touring car; we spend a day in court, seeing how prisoners and their loved ones react to sentencing; we listen to the debaters around Ben Franklin's statue; we attend a suffrage aviation gathering and then watch seventy trained suffragists "turned loose on [the] city." There is a back-to-school article, and visits to a floating hotel, a club for servants, a fashion show, and the Brooklyn Navy Yard. In the atmosphere of World War I, Barnes describes the soldier's life in New York and accompanies several doughboys on a tour of the city. The actress Mimi Aguglia, whose in-depth interview appears in the *Interviews* volume, apparently became

Barnes's friend and invited her to see a performance at the Italian theater, which Barnes wrote up in "Found on the Bowery."

From early age an animal-lover (her last work was *Creatures in an Alphabet*), Barnes saw nothing oppressive about the animals' lives in the Hippodrome Circus:

> A circus, if of pleasant kind,
> Doth give the animals a chance
> To note the foolishness of pants,
> And so it brings content of mind. (*NY* 191)

Animals also occasion witty if vacuous journalism: "An elephant, like an uninhabited mansion, is majestic. . . . I'm glad my mother does not know as much about me as those elephants" (*NY* 93).

At end of the Hippodrome article is a scene that seems to foreshadow Nora's meeting with Robin at the circus in *Nightwood*, where a lioness salutes Robin. Standing alone in front of the animals' cages at the Hippodrome, Barnes shares an introspective moment: "with nothing but my iniquitous past, I slowly and softly raised my hand—in salute!" (*NY* 197). In each case, what is recognized is the animality in us and the humanity in them.

At times in her journalism, Barnes feels empathy and does indeed show sensitivity. In the fall of 1913, she did for the *Eagle* a series of nine interviews of men (mostly Irish) who, by virtue of their advanced age, had merited retirement but were still on the job. There is a postman, a trolley conductor, a waiter, a fireman, an elevator operator, an engine specialist, a newsdealer, a court clerk, and a physical culturalist. Barnes movingly depicts their hard work for low pay and reveals the despair just beneath the surface as they peer into an empty future.

Barnes keenly evokes the sense of loneliness that a boxer feels when he knows the fight is over and he is going down for the full count:

> Then, like a bird thrown helpless against the bars of a cage, one of
> them is hurled against the ropes. With wet, shaking limbs he strives

to regain his footing. He strikes out, but his fists feel no shock of contact. His antagonist becomes a blank; his arm muscles seem numbed. But he still fights on, and to the audience his arms, moving ceaselessly and ineffectually, seem like the branches of a tree caught in the fury of the blast. A low groan escapes him as he vainly endeavors to combat this overwhelming force. Then comes an abrupt stillness. He hears the taunts of the crowd, but they do not affect him. Only a great loneliness, a sense of complete isolation, fills him as he slowly sinks to the floor (NY 171).

A carnival freak show inspires Djuna Barnes with horror as "the demonstrator comes forward, cane in hand; he touches the nearest freak on the shoulder and begins turning him around as if this turning were all that the unfortunate had been born for. He begins to enumerate this man's misfortunes as though they were a row of precious beads" (NY 279). She also saw that the Industrial Workers of the World had come to their revolutionary convictions through starvation: "By way of the empty interior they came to the shut door" (NY 200).

There are uncollected articles and interviews, such as her essay on the New York tea shops, entitled "Crumpets and Tea," and the particularly well-written "When the Puppets Come to Town," which commemorated the opening of a puppet show at the Little Theatre and revealed Barnes's fascination with this difficult art. "Three Days Out" described the tedious life of actors on the road who longed to return to the big city. "The Artist's Place in War" is an interview with the author and theater enthusiast Marguerita Abbott, who argues that during wartime, artists should not be sent to the front lines but be given optional duty, since artistic temperament disqualifies one for combat. Barnes gave no sign that she found the argument naive.

"On Going Fishing" describes a sojourn in Provincetown, at the tip of Cape Cod, where Barnes sailed on a fishing boat. Rich in images, the article serves to prove wrong an impression Barnes initially expresses about fish: "There is nothing in the death of a fish to bring tears to the eyes or horror to the heart. It is only something that has moved about a little while unseen, and will move about no more." On coming ashore, though, she is rather deeply moved by the mass slaughter of fish, particularly noting the panic of one fish: "The goose-fish rose with wide swinging jaws and frightened eyes. Terror convulsed it from quivering fin to the pit of its stomach, a belch of water gushed from its jaws."

A companion article to "Going Fishing" is "Doing the Dunes," where Barnes quotes the Provincetown writer Mary Heaton Vorse on activities for tourists. She hikes to a lifeguard station, is attacked by mosquitoes, wades through a cranberry bog, then returns to the uncustomary dining hours of this small village of Portuguese fisher folk and artists.

Articles selected for the *New York* volume cover the years 1913–19. Barnes enjoyed her journalism but could not help suggesting that she was meant to write for a more distinguished audience. Her occasional allusions to high culture hint of a restlessness for a more challenging literary form: she refers, among others, to Rossetti (*NY* 155, 353); Zola (*NY* 270); Nietzsche (*NY* 234); and Kipling (*NY* 184).

In the 1920s, Barnes published her best stories, *Ryder*, and *Ladies Almanack*. Between 1929 and 1931, when she was writing the early drafts of *Nightwood*, Barnes wrote a regular column for the *Theatre Guild Magazine*, called the "Playgoer's Almanac" (July 1930–March 1931) and then "The Wanton Playgoer" (April–September 1931), as well as an assortment of articles on the current stage and interviews with such stage personalities as Jig Cook of the Provincetown Players. The almanac idea derives, of course, from her recent success with *Ladies Almanack* (see Chapter Six).

The editor of *Theatre Guild*, Hiram Motherwell, had confidence in Barnes's talent. He wrote her that he wanted her to cover the "hits," the movies, any awards, such as the Pulitzer Prize for *The Green Pastures*, and gossip about leading personalities of the theater. "Once we have agreed on the right subject matter for the almanac, spread your wings and write as you like. The more the almanac is DJUNA the better it will be."[10]

One may read Barnes's journalism simply for amusement or as preparation for *Nightwood* and the later fiction, for the common denominator here is, as Nancy Levine has said, the grotesque.[11] Like any good reporter writing feature stories, she sought out the extraordinary, but her fascination with misfits is reminiscent of Nathanael West (especially *Miss Lonelyhearts*) and Flannery O'Connor. Despite Barnes's haughty airs, she felt a kinship with the outcast and at times would have taken the world's wounded to her breast, but she could also be wickedly satirical.

The result in *Nightwood* are cameo appearances by the militaristic Hedvig Volkbein, who dances a "tactical manoeuvre" (*N* 4), the Duchess of Broadback (Frau Mann), "whose coquetries were muscular and localized" (*N* 12), Nikka the Nigger, whose skin is a mosaic of tattoos (*N* 16–17), and the legless Mademoiselle Basquette (*N* 26), who patrols the Pyrenees on a rolling platform—all of them in rather short order. Nor are the major characters of *Nightwood* much less grotesque, though Barnes makes some attempt with them to engage the reader's sympathies. One might extend the idea of grotesque to style as well, for in her journalism Barnes yokes together with considerable violence and for general amusement ideas never before associated.

In later years, Djuna wrote to her friend Willa Muir that from an early age she had feared the poorhouse.[12] Consequently Barnes persisted in her journalism until she could become established as a serious writer. If in her youth the feature stories and interviews kept bread and butter on the table, in the 1920s they helped her to live in style. Having good taste required money, and being able to dress fashionably so as to complement her beauty gave Djuna much-needed self-confidence. She was never in any doubt about her artistic integrity or her ultimate literary objectives, but she had a real talent for journalism and a keen eye for fashion, for detail, and for a celebrity's quintessence or formula for success. One sees her values reflected in the care with which in recording interviews she presented the ideas of those she most admired.[13]

Three of the stories that Barnes published in newspapers in the summer and fall of 1917, which were doubtless written hastily for an editor's deadline, provide a fair sample of her work during this period. They are of little artistic significance in themselves, but they look forward to the major work. For instance, the national and racial stereotypes of *Nightwood* have their origins in Djuna Barnes's stories and reflect the international character of her acquaintances on Long Island farms, in Manhattan, and in France. They also express the intense alienation from both family and nation that Barnes felt during her adult life, for one would be hard put to make the case that she saw herself as a truly American writer. Her values and loyalty were much more English, and what she knew of the United States was mostly New York. She became convinced that European culture was superior to American; other than love and friendship, art and culture were about all that she valued.

One of the strangest (and most intriguing) stories Djuna Barnes ever wrote was "The Head of Babylon" (1917), about a prosperous Polish-American farmer named Pontos ("sea" in Greek), who had eleven children, one of them a daughter, Theeg, whose limbs are paralyzed. Her designation as "Head" shows Djuna's perhaps unwitting insensitivity. Though the title hints at a Middle Eastern ambience, it actually refers to Babylon, Long Island, just south of the Barnes's Huntington farm, where there were Polish neighbors.

The story takes place on Theeg's wedding day, when she is borne in upon a litter and placed upon a dais like a sacrificial victim. Less a victim than it would first appear, she is much loved by her family but has decided to leave them for a new life. She speaks a poetical prose from the King James Bible:

> Yea, the land and the moving things thereon, and all the young year that has begun, are theirs. All the grass that has found renewal, all the flowers that bloom, all the old hopes and the old manner—but this, this is mine. This new man and this new day are mine, and mine this task to make this lonely head a wild, grand thing upon its helpless pedestal (*Smoke* 118).

One does not expect much subtlety in newspaper stories, but "The Head of Babylon" is a bit enigmatic. Theeg seems to echo the judgmental voice of a John the Baptist (Barnes was surely thinking of Oscar Wilde's play *Salomé*). Ultimately the main point of the story seems to be that the rewards of the imagination are to be preferred to the physical labor and conventional prosperity that farmers prize.

Theeg is an artistic type, and her story is one of unconventional strength and courage, but Barnes may be responding to the more grotesque implications of a young woman powerless in the physical sense, relying on a moral authority deriving from her disability, entrusting herself to a man who seems attracted to her merely because she is exotic.

One of the most haunting of the earlier stories is "Fate—the Pacemaker" (1917), later called "No-Man's-Mare," about the death of Pauvla Agrippa, whose name suggests that she is one of the progeny of Herod the Great. *Salomé* is again recalled. Pauvla had been content enough to die, leaving behind her baby and siblings in her remote fishing village, but left with the need to discover a way of transporting the corpse to a cemetery, her family conceives the extremely odd plan of fastening Pauvla with a fishing net to a wild old mare who grazes near the sea. No-Man's-Mare, presumably recognizing a kindred antipatriarchal spirit, for the first time allows her old bones to be burdened but fools them all when, led along the strand, she suddenly becomes energized enough to plunge into the sea and swim out of sight. A particularly dramatic, if tentative, solution to a pressing problem, No-Man's-Mare now becomes a polluted no-man's-*mare*, Latin for "sea." Barnes probably did not think beyond the ending to see the waves accomplishing a less than triumphant return of the burial problem, now much greater than before.

The tone of "Monsieur Ampee" (1917) is sardonic throughout; the story tells of a disreputable wine merchant, cold, indifferent, dishonest by nature. The epigram, later to become a Djuna Barnes trademark, is on target here: "Ampee lived among his fellow beings as though he were the only pardonable mistake among a million errors" (*Smoke* 150). The epigrammatic phrasing recalls Joyce's *Dubliners* story "A Painful Case," which is also about a cold, unfeeling mercantile type. Ampee swindles his investors through an explosion that kills his honest wife, and thereafter he keeps company in the evenings with nihilists who deride his bourgeois values. The point is rather obscure, but it probably revolves around the thought that it is better to be a poor revolutionary dedicated to making society better than a dishonest capitalist who wins a fortune only to lose his reputation. Still, Ampee is true to his wormlike nature, and the world depicted by Barnes may be beyond saving. The story oozes cynicism.

As for the effect of this mood on her fiction, the Baroness Elsa von Freytag Loringhoven once said: "I cannot read your stories, Djuna Barnes. . . . I don't know where your characters come from. You make them fly on magic carpets—what is worse, you try to make pigs fly."[14] The reaction is extreme but the sense not far afield, for despite Barnes's occasional triumphs in the genre, what is usually missing is psychological depth or believable motivation in characterization. Even when we are told where the "characters come from," their origin seldom explains how they got to be the way they are. The absence of clear motivation, a dependence on description, the emphasis on literary style—in this the stories look forward to *Nightwood*. Given her view that life is monstrous, the ghoulish drawings of Barnes's Beardsley period were appropriate accompaniments to the stories and plays. Furthermore, the stories resemble Barnes herself, whose sense of privacy cast a shadow over her past, impenetrable to all but a few of her closest friends, a privacy cloaked in stylishness—a black cape, expensive clothes, auburn hair hidden under a modish hat—a brilliant discursiveness cloaking a sense of vulnerability.

Two sets of articles by Barnes in the *New York* volume are especially noteworthy: a series of four pieces on Greenwich Village, and three stunt articles. In the Greenwich Village series, "The Last Petit Souper" takes us on a tour of bohemian cafés; "Greenwich Village as It Is" introduces us to the Brevoort, the Café Lafayette, the Liberal Club, and the Washington Square Players. Appropriate names are dropped, including Charles Edison, who Djuna said once proposed to her, and Guido Bruno, who had in the previous issue of *Pearson's Magazine* (September 1916) published an article entitled "Greenwich Village as It Was," complete with a drawing of Barnes.[15]

"Becoming Intimate with the Bohemians" capitalizes on the public's thirst for glimpses of the risqué behavior and atmosphere of the arty crowd, while Djuna tweaks the tourists' collective nose in the persona of Madam Bronx. The familiar haunts are visited, and more names are dropped, such as Harold Stearns, Floyd Dell, and Marsden Hartley (who rates a drawing), all of whom Barnes knew well. One arresting image of a female drunk stays with us: her eyes "are set in her face like a child's peering over a wall where all the refuse of life has been whirled and caught" (*NY* 237). "How the Villagers Amuse Themselves" continues the themes of its three predecessors: "So the Greenwich Villager sets out to amuse himself. It's sordid and hard, but it must be done" (*NY* 246).

Andrew Field has written at length about the apparently disreputable Guido Bruno (1884–1942), sycophant of Frank Harris and prominent publisher of the risqué and avant garde in *Bruno's Weekly*, which he published from his garret on Washington Square. Among the literary works appearing in the Bruno's Chapbooks series were pieces by Alfred Kreymborg, Oscar Wilde, Sadakichi Hartmann, and, in November 1915, Barnes's poetry chapbook, *The Book of Repulsive Women*.[16] He also exhibited her Beardsleyan drawings and the war drawings she did for *Trend* magazine.

If one truly cared for Djuna Barnes, one would say very little indeed about *The Book of Repulsive Women*, for she and others often wished that these eight disgusting "rhythms" accompanied by five drawings had never been published. For this we have Guido Bruno to thank. The poems portray lesbian life in the most horribly negative terms imaginable. "We'd strain to touch those lang'rous/Length of thighs;/And hear your short sharp modern/Babylonic cries" is one absurd image in "From Fifth Avenue Up." Another from that poem, the worst image of the lot, depicts one woman "sagging down with bulging/Hair to sip,/The dappled damp from some vague/Under lip. /Your soft saliva, loosed/With orgy, drip." Hideous images are a Barnes stock-in-trade even in the later poems, but they focus on life in general as a dirty, mean trick.

Barnes had many dealings with Bruno and with Albert and Charles Boni, proprietors of the Washington Square Bookshop, who exhibited Bruno's posters. Barnes didn't like Bruno much, and to her friends she complained about his bad breath.[17]

At twenty-two, Djuna wrote articles she called "stunt stories" for the *Sunday World*, which involved adventuresome and potentially dangerous acts—such as going up in an airplane as one of the first women to fly, which ill-fated stunt, as we have seen, Putzi dissuaded her from undertaking.

Given Barnes's high-strung nature, sensitivity to matters of privacy, and horror of medical examinations, it is scarcely imaginable that she could have submitted to force-feeding, but this she did in order to write "How It Feels to Be Forcibly Fed." Many suffragists died in British prisons from that mode of torture. Existing photographs show that this incident took place on 16 August 1914. Andrew Field describes the scene:

> Miss Barnes was placed on an operating table and attended by four men, one of them a doctor. Just before she mounted the table to begin the procedure, she caught sight of the yard of red rubber hose and also of her own face in a mirror, ghostly white. Three of the men pressed down on her ankles, hips and head, while the doctor painted her nostrils with a mixture of cocaine and disinfectant and then examined her nasal passages and throat with a bright light prior to introducing the tube into one of her nostrils.[18]

"There it is," she says, "the outraged will. If I, playacting, felt my being burning with revolt at this brutal usurpation of my own functions, how they who actually suffered the ordeal in its acutest horror must have flamed at the violation of the sanctuaries of their spirits" (*NY* 178).

"The Girl and the Gorilla," a tongue-in-cheek interview with Dinah the "bushgirl," a three-foot African specimen caged in the Bronx Zoo—who died soon after she met Barnes—could also be seen as a stunt story. Djuna puts words into Dinah's mouth to describe a taxi ride and her curiosity about chewing gum. Her embrace is like a garden hose, "at once impersonal and condescending, and yet rather agreeable" (*NY* 183).[19]

The final "stunt" piece, "My Adventures Being Rescued," was the result of her April 1914 visit to a basic training school for firemen on Sixty-seventh Street. Like the force-feeding, her stunt there took courage. On her first descent, she went out of a window and shinnied down a rope from about a hundred feet up. The second time, a fireman descended from the roof in a sling and took her to the net in an embrace. Then she made a solo descent down a slippery ladder. As on other occasions, she insists that any grisly fate that might await a lady must be endured in good form. To mark the occasion, Barnes was photographed landing in the net.[20]

A few of Barnes's dialogues with celebrities are included in the *New York* volume; most appear in *Interviews*; and some have not been reprinted.[21] *New York* contains such pieces as interviews with two Broadway song composers, Hal Atteridge and Harry Carroll, and a series of quick fixes on superstition from the viewpoints of various people, including Enrico Caruso and Frank Harris. In Barnes's interview with the actor David Warfield, which has not been reprinted, he advised her not to write sad plays, observing that farces were much more difficult and more profitable. It was advice Barnes did not heed.

In *New York*, the reader is introduced to Police Commissioner Enright, who turns out to have a passion for Voltaire, a surprising taste that Barnes attempts to make interesting. A female deputy police commissioner, Mrs. Ellen O'Grady, proves to have a social conscience, if a dated one, when she expresses her concern with the roles of women in society and how to keep them out of trouble. "There are plenty of places in public life where they can serve. They are excellent secretaries; they make good waitresses; they are librarians of the most careful type." But she thought that "housework is, after all, their master art" (*NY* 314). Curiously, she failed to mention police work. O'Grady's complicity with patriarchal oppression goes unnoticed by Barnes, who seems more interested in the fact of a woman in the role of deputy police commissioner.

Messerli noted that in her interviews, Barnes made "little attempt to place the celebrity in the context of his or her own history" (*I* 5); true, but this may point to her reliance on the savvy of her New York readership, who might have known more than she did about, say, the latest doings of the boxer Jack Dempsey. It may also point to her regard for privacy, surely a rare inhibition in a journalist. She guarded her own privacy, except among close friends, and seldom let her guard down otherwise; this courtesy she would have extended to celebrities, resisting the temptation to pry. If they were happy to speak openly of deeply held fears, concerns, and aspirations, that was another matter. Often she just let the celebrity speak or participate in interview dialogue. At other times she used her literary talents for creating or re-creating her impression of her subject in witty Barnesean prose. Yet even within these limits she displays quite a variety of skills and techniques.

Some of the *Interviews* articles were strictly show business dialogues with celebrities of the moment, such as Mimi Aguglia, who played Salomé on the stage; the dancers Vernon Castle and Irene Foote, "who occasionally tango past their home"; or the actor Charles Raun Kennedy and the French dancer Gabrielle Deslys, who are allowed to speak directly in response to questions posed.

The beautiful Lillian Russell told Barnes, "I could never be lonely without a husband," as long as her trinkets were about her (*I* 50). Barnes caricatured Russell as a sultry vamp in one drawing and, in another, portrayed Diamond Jim Brady, who probably wore more diamonds as part of his daily attire than anybody in history, as a fat face composed of diamond shapes. Barnes remarks: "If you are sharp you can catch glimpses of Brady between his jewelry" (*I* 62) and suggests that he hung "his underwear in his safe" (*I* 65).

Fortunately for her subjects, Barnes sometimes put words into their mouths, or so it seems, for few could have equaled her wit, and their natural mode of expression was probably too dull for the tabloids. According to Barnes, Flo Ziegfeld defined a vampire as "a woman who eats lightly of uncooked things; who walks out between tall avenues of spears to die, and doesn't, and finally spends the evening in an orgy of virtuous dreams. That's time wasted. A vampire is a good woman with a bad reputation, or rather a good woman who has had possibilities and wasted them" (*I* 73). This is pure Barnes, with its clever impenetrability and hint of decadence—the yellow nineties updated a few decades.

At other times there gleams a Wildean cleverness, which is still pure Barnes, as when she described the boxer Jess Willard: "His head, having been overlooked by Sargent, is reproduced in every forest where cutters have been—that gravely solemn thing, the stump of some huge tree staring in blunt Rodinesque mutilation from the ground" (*I* 137). Sometimes Barnes's observations are cleverly enigmatic, with finally no meaning perceivable beyond a certain stylishness, as when she said that the ballet dancer Alfred Bolm "sails a boat and drinks tea with graceful repugnance" (*I* 169), or that Wilson Mizner had "a laugh like a submerged French pastry shop" (*I* 175). Obscure phrases such as these foreshadow *Nightwood*.

Among the most memorable of Barnes's interviews is the one with the labor activist Mother Jones, in which she simply stood aside to allow her subject's rage to boil over in scalding tirades against oppression. Here the painter's eye notices every detail of Mary Jones's eighty-two-year-old figure: "A little ponderous below the belt, but sitting straightly in a high-backed chair, her hands folded in front of her—gnarled, crooked fingers, bent in a lifelong attempt to straighten things" (*I* 95).

Barnes also occasionally turned to aphorisms. In another interview, she said, "One can afford to be simple with life when one has acquired the knowledge of being simple with the past"; of course, one might object that much depends on a definition of "simplicity" (*I* 188). Of Mother Jones, she wrote: "In youth one may have been a peacock, in old age one is a sparrow. . . . Upon thinkers, death steals from the feet up; upon laymen, from the head down" (*I* 97). And sometimes she made the painterly detail aphoristic: "It is a flat, straight back, and broad. It has never had time to become individual. It is not a personal vertebra" (*I* 103). But mostly one is moved by Mother Jones's pithy phrase snapped in ferocious tone: "I haven't enough brains to be a suffragette—I'm too busy trying to locate the left side of the world where the heart is supposed to be" (*I* 99).

Sometimes Barnes's cleverness simply backfired, calling attention to a momentary clumsiness in the art of mystification, as when she said of Frank Harris (1856–1931): "His eyes were keen at once and kind; not overoften, but once now and again one could see that this man had not flung the harpoon alone" (*I* 202). The image is one of an Irish Queequeg teaming up to fling harpoons at some hapless whale who had mistakenly entered his editorial office.

Barnes's interview with Billy Sunday, the ex–baseball player who became one of the most famous show biz evangelists of his age, will remind Joyceans of the ending of the "Oxen of the Sun" episode of *Ulysses*, which parodied Sunday's muscular evangelism. Joyce called him "Alexander J. Christ Dowie, that's yanked to glory most half this planet from 'Frisco Beach to Vladivostok,"[22] and so combined qualities of two evangelists, giving Dowie, who founded the Zion, Illinois, commune, the oratorical style of Billy Sunday. Barnes noted that Sunday loved the multitude but not the individual; a cynic might have countered that he was one up on her.

Since on occasion Barnes interviewed celebrities who were friends, or became friends with celebrities she interviewed, as with Frank Harris, Alfred Stieglitz (1864–1946), Helen Westley (1879–1942) and James Joyce (1882–1941), she herself becomes part of the scene. She came to know Mabel Dodge Luhan (1879–1962) in the fall of 1914. The heiress who gave D. H. Lawrence his Taos ranch was generous with her sandwiches, and she thanked Carl Van Vechten for introducing Barnes to her (*I* 213), but she was lukewarm in her praise of the pictures Barnes had brought to show her. In this interview, published on 25 February 1917, Barnes reveals much about herself at this time in her life:

> Two or three of the older gentlemen paid some small attention to me, and I wondered at the time if it was because of my lack of *sang froid* or because they liked my drawings. I wondered a little, too, why old men have always had a peculiar liking for me where young men are entirely indifferent—and why at the same time for me there existed no man, young or old, who could draw the slightest, faintest word of interest from me apart from my drawing or some abstract thing connected with themselves. Perhaps it was because love had

been much discussed in my family circles, because all the old romances of man and maid had already been read to me. Perhaps it was because, and this surely was it, that art had been something that I felt and not saw, longed for and not possessed, to its outward fullness, hoped for and at last approached.

And yet I was in awe of no one; I attempted not to show the arrogance of my upper lip that would persist in an attempt to curl, probably because I wanted to cry and wouldn't. I felt cold because I wanted so dreadfully to feel warm and hopeful and one with them.

But all of this is entirely out of the way, except to give a small pen picture of myself at the time when Mr. Alfred Stieglitz first came into my life. Mabel Dodge was holding up a painting of mine, extraordinarily bad, too, and she was hesitating between approval and disapproval. "Anyway," she said, "go to 291 Fifth Avenue and ask for Mr. Stieglitz, and show him; perhaps he can help you." (*I* 214)

Even at this early age, depression had become for Djuna a more or less permanent condition,[23] but then the scars from her breakup with Putzi Hanfstaengl were still probably unhealed. The ferocity of the decadent drawings that accompanied her interviews may partly indicate this anguish. As she interviewed Stieglitz, the bitterness of these years when her own career seemed to be going nowhere was displayed in a surprisingly open way:

> From this place I have been standing eternally, looking out toward the world with my eyes and seeing men pass and look back at me. And I cold and lonesome and increasing steadily in mine own sorrow, which is caught like the plague of other men, until I am full and my mouth will hold no more, and my eyes will see no more, and my ears can stand nothing further. Then do I begin the steady, slow discharge which is called "wisdom." (*I* 220)[24]

Barnes may have been impatient for the fame she begrudged others, but that fame was less easily achieved than she probably imagined. In her interviews with two boxers, Jess Willard and Jack Dempsey, she brought the conversation around to women. Willard

thought that women would soon be boxing, so fast were things chang-
ing, while Dempsey characterized female boxing fans as a bit perverse
since, paradoxically, they like to watch a handsome face (which
Dempsey hadn't) and a "fetching smile" take a pounding. "The more
a guy's got to lose the louder they yell," Dempsey said (*I* 286).[25]

In her journalism, Barnes occasionally found the right moment to
celebrate her friendship with a talented artist. Helen Westley, twelve
years Barnes's senior, was a cofounder of the Washington Square Players and the Theatre Guild. Robert Sarlós notes that she "became the
first of the Guild to enter Hollywood films and debuted in *Moulin
Rouge*. She also appeared in *Bedtime Story*, *Rebecca of Sunnybrook
Farm*, and *Heidi*."[26] In a cameo appearance in Barnes's article "The
Washington Square Players," Westley narrates the players' beginnings
and success; then she sends Barnes to interview the financial backer.
The article's ending reflects Barnes's joy in her subject's slightly mad
company: "like a large crescent-stepping cat, Helen emerges with her
impossible spats and her trailing tailed muff from which protrudes a
large volume of Flaubert. And arm in arm we go together to search
out a soda fountain." Westley also appeared in Barnes's article "The
Old Theatre in New Attire," which is about stagecraft and set design.
Barnes's best portrait of Westley, though, is in "Three Days Out":

> And with me went Helen, the woman of mystery, who had been
> always a little something more than strange. A vampire type, with
> coarse black hair folded above the slanting slate gray eyes, as cold
> as ships of ice, the nose long and narrow with cruel dented nostrils,
> a large flexible mouth turning down at the corners without a sign
> of that deep melancholy that such a mouth should wear, and rows
> of splendid white teeth.[27]

In "Confessions of Helen Westley," Barnes comes across more
clearly and enjoys herself thoroughly. She describes how Westley, who
apparently requested the interview, appeared in a secondhand gown,
carrying a secondhand book, "showing her thirty-two perfect teeth,"
and, though it is 3:30 P.M., asks the waiter for oatmeal (*I* 251). The

dialogue that follows is the wittiest to be found among the Barnes interviews, and the written version must have greatly delighted both of them.

While reporting the cultural scene, Barnes encountered the lover of Dada artist Man Ray, Kiki of Montparnasse (this name was certainly more exotic than her real one, Alice Prin, and evoked a more exciting place than her native village in Burgundy). Kiki was a talented model and singer, whom Barnes described in a decadent mood that hints at delicious perversity:

> "Life," murmurs Kiki, "is, *au fond,* so limited, so robbed of new sins, so *diabolique*—," she raises her mandarin eyes, slanting with kohl, "—that one must have a mouse, a small white mouse, *n'est-ce pas?* To run about between cocktails and *thé.*"

Do you want to be a movie actress? D. W. Griffith advises aspiring stars. Is there a certain way that women in love should dress? Mary Garden insists that such women should dress with passion and describes how it is done. Should actors be married to each other? Lord Alfred Lunt and Lady Lynn Fontanne spell out the pros and cons. Barnes's interview with the cast of *The Green Pastures* makes for embarrassing reading today, filled as it is with black stereotypes, but "Nothing Amuses Coco Chanel After Midnight" is worth a perusal for what it tells us of the industrious founder of the House of Chanel.

To caution those American women waiting for titled foreigners to sweep them off their feet, Barnes wrote "American Wives and Titled Husbands." It seems that the transatlantic chemistry is not always good, as several American expatriates tell us. The "supremely unfaithful" Italian marries for manners: "it is good form to have a home and children" (*I* 316). Countess von Bernstorff, also an American, declares that Germans know too much and tend to be sentimental and bossy. This witty article encouraged the starry-eyed antecedents of Grace Kelly to trade the sword of foreign conquest for plows nearer the old homestead.

Rivaling the Stieglitz interview for authorial transparency is an angry one with the facile writer Donald Ogden Stewart, who got the breaks Barnes feared would never be hers in a country where talent is so seldom rewarded. " 'Do you,' we suddenly shouted, frenzied with blighted hopes, and maddened with years of living through the darkness before the dawn, 'do you ever think of those millions who have trained, and struggled, and wept, just to attain to a certain well-merited oblivion, while you, without so much as a smothered sob, roll over and find yourself famous . . .' " He asks Barnes if she needs money, and she responds, " 'Oh no, we interview successful people just to prevent ourselves from becoming groggy with rich port and caviar; to save ourselves from becoming blunted with idleness; to arm ourselves against doing murder to one or more of our slaves and out-runners!' " (*I* 337–38). Barnes says that she wouldn't mind dying at this point, a depressing and perhaps unprecedented note on which to end an interview (*I* 342).

Morbidity is the central theme of one of the few interviews Barnes herself gave, the last item in the *Interviews* collection. Here Guido Bruno summarizes her play *Three from the Earth*.[28] Although he excuses Barnes's pessimistic feeling that life is empty, meaningless, and cruel as uncharacteristic, the opposite was true, for this was a fairly consistent mood. Bruno notes disapprovingly the slovenliness of her self-portrait, rendering her in upbeat terms that describe the face she presented to an uncaring world:

Red cheeks. Auburn hair. Gray eyes, ever sparkling with delight and mischief. Fantastic earrings in her ears, picturesquely dressed, ever ready to live and to be merry: that's the real Djuna as she walks down Fifth Avenue, or sips her black coffee, a cigarette in hand, in the Café Lafayette.

So successful was Djuna Barnes with her articles and drawings evoking the New York scene that opportunity began regularly to stop at her door. It was *McCall's* magazine that in 1921 first sent Djuna to Europe, where she arrived with thirty dollars to her name. By late summer of 1921, she was in Berlin. When Chester Page asked her to describe Berlin in the 1920s, she replied: "Good heavens, do you think I remember? It was very nice, things so cheap for us that you felt almost ashamed to be there. Full of buggers from America who bought boys cheap. The only thing I bought was a blouse. You read my story, 'A Young Girl Tells a Story to a Lady.' "[29]

From *McCall's* she received fees of fifteen hundred dollars apiece for interviews with notables such as the duchess of Marlborough, who showed her around Blenheim Palace at a time when Djuna had a sore foot. When Djuna excused herself to go to the bathroom, the American-born duchess said, "This may be a palace, but there isn't one decent bathroom in the whole bloody place." Djuna also interviewed George Moore on his favorite subject, "women in love."

In October of 1921, Barnes tried unsuccessfully to catch the Belgian writer Maurice Maeterlinck (1862–1949) for an interview in the south of France. She finally caught up with him in February 1924. Since he spoke no English, Barnes took William Carlos Williams along to interpret. It was a wonder to her that despite their inability to understand each other, she managed to write ten pages. Maeterlinck, who had just married the much younger Renée Dahon, was interviewed on "can a young woman love an old man?" One can scarcely imagine him answering in the negative.[30]

When Djuna returned from Europe late in September of 1921 and was in need of money, *McCall's* commissioned her to write twelve illustrated articles on "swank New York cuisines," an assignment that took her three months and earned her a surprising seven thousand dollars. After this, Burton Rascoe agreed to send her back to Europe almost immediately, with a contract for a dozen more articles, for which *McCall's* paid her a thousand dollars apiece. She was to interview royalty on favored recipes and cuisine.[31] Unfortunately, the only royalty she would manage to reach was the king of Italy, who apparently did not object to his chef divulging culinary secrets. Barnes returned to America in March 1922; a reporter from *The Greenwich Villager* interviewed her on March 11.

Paris was to become Djuna Barnes's favorite city, for artists and thinkers seemed to reign supreme there, but in later years she realized that the New York editors on whom she depended for support were beginning to forget her. Eventually she had to work very hard just to get the editors' attention, but in the early twenties they were eager to publish her interviews with artists who were central to the Paris scene.

Barnes's famous interview with James Joyce came out in *Vanity Fair* a few months after the publication of *Ulysses* in 1922; then she continued her impressions of him in "Vagaries Malicieux," an unmalicious, if rambling, article describing her first trip to Paris.[32] Richard Ellmann used some of Barnes's details in his biography of Joyce.

When she met Joyce, Barnes was mostly known as the brilliant New York journalist who had arrived in Paris to observe the Left Bank scene. There were any number of mutual friends and connections: Barnes had met Helen Fleischman, Peggy Guggenheim's cousin and Joyce's son Giorgio's wife-to-be, in 1917. Joyce and Barnes were both friends of Robert McAlmon and, of course, Sylvia Beach, who may have arranged for them to meet at her bookstore. Their meetings took place at the Café des Deux Magots, across from the church of Saint-Germain-des-Prés and not far from Barnes's flat. Barnes said that during her four months in Paris, she talked with Joyce often.

With the keen eye of a portrait painter (a sketch accompanied her interview article), Barnes saw Joyce emerge from the fog sporting goatee, bluish-gray coat, and heirloom waistcoat. In the interview, she says that she had read *Dubliners* during World War I, recommended *Exiles* to theatrical committees, and perused *A Portrait of the Artist as a Young Man* shortly after its publication, but she only spotted the singer in Joyce when she read chapters of *Ulysses* in *The Little Review* (where some of her own stories had appeared). She attributed the experimentalism of Joyce's book to his musical interests.

Both had learned more from writers of the earlier periods of English literature than from modern ones, and Barnes must have listened closely when Joyce declared: "All great talkers have spoken in the language of Sterne, Swift, or the Restoration. Even Oscar Wilde. He studied the Restoration through a microscope in the morning and repeated it through a telescope in the evening" (*I* 293). Barnes wrote her late play *The Antiphon* in a style informed by Restoration drama.

She struggled to do her subject justice by penning observations that do not easily yield their meaning. Joyce evoked "the sadness of a man who has procured some medieval permission to sorrow out of time and in no place; it is the weariness of one self-subjected to the creation of an overabundance in the limited." His head seemed to be "turned farther away than disgust and not so far as death" (*I* 293). Despite the dubious brilliance of these aphoristic pearls, Barnes's interview of Joyce remains one of her best.

"Vagaries Malicieux" describes a different encounter with Joyce. It is quoted in full below, since it is comparatively unknown:

> Coming from the church [Saint-Germain-des-Prés] one evening I stopped a moment at the cafe of the "Deux Magots" and had a glass of wine, while Joyce, James Joyce, author of the suppressed "Ulysses," talked of the Greeks.
>
> A quiet man, this Joyce, with the back head of an African idol, long and flat. The back head of a man who had done away with the vulgar necessity of brain-room.
>
> He spoke, too, of Moore "The Playboy of the Western World," he said, sipping his Black and White.[33] He went on to speak of Yeats. "A good boy and a fine poet, but too proud in his clothes, and too fond of the aesthetic—as for the rest of them—Irish stew! They don't even know that Gaelic is not the tongue of Dublin!"
>
> At another time, walking under an umbrella, he mentioned Synge, but not before he had taken a smell of the damp air.
>
> "A great lump of a man who could not be argued with. It is said that he was a silent man, but he was not. I always disliked his 'Riders.' I was the first person he showed it to, and I told him, then, to make a lasting argument—or to make none.
>
> " 'But,' he [Synge] protested, 'it's a good play, as good as any one-act play can be.' And it was then that I [Joyce] said that Ireland needed less small talk and more irrefutable art; and that no one-act play, be it as good as its master, could be a knock-down argument."
>
> He smiled as he said this, showing those strangely spoiled and appropriate teeth.
>
> Joyce lives in a sort of accidental aloofness. He is pleased when friends call, and he will go anywhere, it is said, and drink anything.

He dislikes art-talk, and his friends are quite the common people.

His chief topic is Greek mythology, and he never tires of telling of the origin of Orion's name, information that would seem very shocking to the most scholastic mind, for he makes the Greeks "naughty boys," and leaves them shaking hands, across the gulf, with Rabelais.

He drifts from one subject to the other, making no definite division. Presently one finds that he has come from the origin of Greek names to a certain Baroness called by the French "La Sirène."[34]

"She had two islands off the Cretan coast, and there seven husbands were tearlessly buried, it is said, though she only admitted three to me. There was a rumor about that she had some very fine engravings illustrating the Odyssey, and I wrote her that I would like to see them. She came across the water herself, standing up in the little boat, her dog beside her, a great hat of straw on her head, and when she was within hailing distance she called out to me that I was no Englishman, and I called back 'No, Irish.' "

Here I stopped to think what the picture must have been, the Baroness coming across the water, standing straight on her two legs with her dog beside her, throwing defiance and observation at this sad tall Irishman who had come to see Ulysses.

"The pictures turned out badly after all," he said. "The sirens had never been in a wind at all, for their hair was as set as a German wig, and the sea was just appropriately watered. Only one of the lot was, to me, at all pleasing—one in which the artist had conceived Ulysses as being tired and so sitting down to draw bow."

My mind wandered a little, I looked out into the square and wondered if I would ever come to this cafe again.

Just how long it was before I realized that Joyce had been talking to me I do not know, but when I gave him my attention again he was in the middle of a sentence whose conclusion was—"and that is how I missed seeing Tagore; another one of the world's misconceptions of the mystic. Because I had no evening clothes."

"One of the world's misconceptions of the mystic!" This ran about in my head a while and got mixed in, some way or other, with Joyce's next observation, that opals in iron were very fine finger rings and that he liked heavy perfumes, but one in particular, though he never used scent, the name I think, was appopynax [i.e., opopanax[35]], and here I lost all connection with this man, sad, quiet, and eternally at work.

On the first page of Djuna Barnes's copy of "Vagaries Malicieux," she made a note in the margin next to "I lost all connection," which reads: "Why did I say this? Not so." There, too, she indicated her admiration for the Joyce section and her distaste for the rest of the article: "Junk. Save for Notes on Joyce," and, in the right margin: "See for note on Joyce—the rest, horrible junk." Though it came relatively easy to her, Barnes was not easy on her own journalism.

That Joyce admired Barnes and counted her among his friends is indicated by the fact that he gave her a bound copy of the proof sheets of *Ulysses*; the inscription, which simply reads "To Djuna Barnes, James Joyce, Paris 16 February 1922," was written two weeks to the day after his fortieth birthday, which was also the publication date of *Ulysses*. In September 1952, Barnes, in dire poverty, sold it to Harvard University's Houghton Library for $125.

Reading Joyce's *Ulysses* marked a turning point in Barnes's development as a writer, for Joyce's influence on her was ultimately unsurpassed by any other literary forebear. She found Joyce extraordinary with his variety of styles, which struck her as so awesome that she wondered how anybody could have the temerity to write novels after *Ulysses* had been published. Yet she did just that. Before Djuna Barnes read Joyce, she was essentially in the decadent tradition of Oscar Wilde and Aubrey Beardsley; afterward she was a modernist. The play of styles in Barnes's *Ryder* acknowledges her debt to Joyce, but the wit and bitterness were all her own.

Greenwich Village as It Was[1]

"I give praise to my sour grapes, they make exceeding excellent wine."[2]

The building at 86 Greenwich Avenue, where Djuna Barnes shared a newspaper-filled flat with Courtenay Lemon (1883–1933) and where Georges Clemenceau had once lived, housed an astounding collection of talented residents. Susan Light, editor of *All-Story Weekly*, where Barnes published eighteen stories between 1914 and 1919, and her husband, Jimmy, who acted and directed at the Provincetown Players, had leased this large residence and sublet rooms to various and sundry Villagers. The photographer Berenice Abbott (1898–1991) was there, and the literary critics Malcolm Cowley (1898–1989) and Kenneth Burke (1897–1993). To these Andrew Field adds the feminist-lawyer-actress Ida Rauh (1877–1970), who played Kate Moreley in Barnes's play *Three from the Earth*; the editor, biographer, and historian Matthew Josephson (1899–1978); the actor and painter Charles Ellis (1893–1976), who in 1921 married Norma Millay (1893–1986) and who did abstract paintings and set designs for the theater; and Dorothy Day (1897–1980), later of the Catholic Worker Movement. Regular visitors were often connected with the Provincetown Players: Floyd Dell (1887–1969), associate editor of *The Masses*; Mina Loy (1882–1966), one of the best and brightest poets of her generation and a lifelong friend of Barnes; and Eugene O'Neill (1888–1953), the dramatist who got his start in Village theater (Barnes called him "a boy who was too shy to speak"[3]). Then there were the photographer Alfred Stieglitz (1864–1946), the writer Edna St. Vincent Millay (1892–1950), possibly the critic Edmund Wilson (1895–1972), and the painter Marcel Duchamp (1887–1968). Burke remembered other tenants, such as one Sara Alice, and an Australian on the first floor who played Mozart on the piano and gave parties on Saturday nights.[4]

Wilson described 86 Greenwich Avenue:

> That *cavernous old house,* where Fitzy [Mary Eleanor Fitzgerald], Stark Young [theater critic], one Dorothea Nolan and Djuna Barnes once all lived at the same time—with its wastes and stretches of linoleum, its steep staircases and rambling halls, its balustrades, its broken skeleton hatrack in a marble-framed niche, its high square-topped radiators, its enormous vestibule doors, its mysterious inside windows covered over with cloths from within, the desolation of its corridors, the interminable and exhausting climbs of stairs, the yellow plaster and yellow woodwork, the smell of bathrooms, the sound of dripping bathtubs and defective toilets.[5]

Susan Light, who had been Berenice Abbott's roommate at Ohio State University, befriended Abbott when she arrived in New York in 1918. Abbott, who was six years younger than Barnes and didn't know her well then, remembered that the hallway went the length of the house and that there were many rooms (Field says seventeen).[6] Abbott, the youngest of the residents, had a room next to the kitchen, while Barnes and Lemon had one at the end of the hall. There were some riotous times and heated debates, but Lemon and Barnes were reputed to be among the quietest, most orderly tenants in the household. Djuna was the most elegant of the group in her fashionable clothes, often black. Abbott described Barnes as "romantic" in dress, frequently in a cape, always immaculate, brilliant, and extremely witty. Barnes and Lemon quarreled over her pendulous earrings and doubtless over other matters, but they were committed enough to speak of their arrangement as a common-law marriage. Their flat contained a tenant of equally colorful plumage: in his memoir, William Carlos Williams relates how Lemon almost got his nose bitten off playing with his parrot.[7]

Susan Light tried to persuade Berenice Abbott to become involved with Kenneth Burke, perhaps not realizing that Abbott would prefer women. Barnes overheard their conversation and advised Abbott not to "pay any attention to that stuff," so Burke joked that he never got a chance to flirt with Abbott. He lived on the third floor, which was also occupied by two old women with a retarded boy.

In later years, Burke would experience Barnes's wrath for an article he wrote on *Nightwood*,[8] which she thought was "all wound up in symbolic meanings. Disgraceful, and nearly perfectly incorrect."[9] Unable to stop its publication, she denied Burke permission to quote from her novel. He wrote to her, defending his article, in October 1966, and a few days later received a letter harking back to Greenwich Avenue days.[10]

Abbott spoke of an epidemic of Spanish flu early in 1919, which hit Villagers especially hard and killed several of her friends. Barnes came down with it and was nursed to health by Lemon not long before she left him. Abbott's flu required that she be hospitalized for six weeks; after her ordeal, she had to learn to walk again. In April 1921, she went to Paris to become a sculptor, but eventually she became the apprentice of Man Ray (1890–1976), and so made photography her artistic medium. Tension developed between Man Ray and Abbott when Peggy Guggenheim appeared at his studio to be photographed by Abbott, but soon Berenice had her own studio. In later years, Barnes would call Abbott "that little number" and say that she never liked her much, perhaps in part because Abbott preceded her as the lover of Thelma Wood.[11]

Barnes had already described Greenwich Village life in four articles of 1916, but several years later, the scene had shifted somewhat for residents of 86 Greenwich Avenue. Their favorite restaurant was Christine's, and their favorite creative outlet the Provincetown Players. Christine's Restaurant is colorfully described by Sarlós:

"Christine's" was a place where Players could retreat in solitude, or mingle with nonmembers; there images and philosophies were tested and argued. Aside from providing a congenial atmosphere and renowned homecooked meals, the "earth mother" Christine herself contributed greatly to the attraction of the club. She dispensed unsolicited solace and chastisement, and became the heroine of countless stories, some convivial, others hair-raising.[12]

Barnes described Christine as "a woman who, had she not been born in this century, would have been some great heavy goddess whose presence would have been justice without word of mouth" (*NY* 232).

Occasionally Djuna would send to the Huntington farm copies of newspaper articles she had written, such as the one describing the force-feeding stunt, but her hurt was deep and the grudge she bore her family enduring, so she kept her distance. The truth was, she did not wish to be plagued by the family problems, for the demands of her career and her social life were about all she could handle. On the other hand, news of the family came regularly to Barnes whether she wanted it or not. In May 1913, her grandfather, Henry Budington, sent a copy of his genealogy, *The Leyden Branch of the Budington Family*, which she faithfully kept.

Wald kept up his relentless optimism and artistic production (music, prose, poetry, painting), even when their garden rotted in 1914 because of too much rain. Though there was little to be optimistic about, Djuna's father charged her with needless pessimism in a verse that he sent to her on 25 January 1915. It is simply called "To Djuna":

> Not so long ago—we called you—baby-one!
> Felt that, bred of love. What we had done
> Was good: by naught transcended under sun!
> Hark you—daughter—use your keener sight
> Art-radiant-beckons: *leave your gloomy night!*
> Turn your genius to its nobler flight!
> Breast [Blest?] Beauty's Star![13]

Djuna's "gloomy night" was made cozier by a series of love affairs, which came in the aftermath of her breakup with Putzi Hanfstaengl, though their impermanence reinforced her pessimism. As a girl, she had imbibed the family's philosophy of sexual freedom; as a young woman in Greenwich Village, she had sexual liaisons with both men and women. On the other hand, she seemed to desire a monogamous permanent relationship, though not necessarily marriage, and certainly not children.

Barnes gossiped about the bed-hopping antics of Villagers, but she did not disapprove. For instance, she told her young pianist friend Chester Page a bit of Provincetown scandal to illustrate the easy morals of Village life. "One of the players had a brothel on the side. His daughter found out about it, visited it and fell in love with one of the trollops."[14] For Barnes and her circle, sex was essentially recreational, part of a lifestyle that they believed left them free for more important matters, such as art. Provincetown's high artistic standards, which implied a contempt for financial success, combined with sexual freedom, remained at the core of Djuna Barnes's philosophy of the artistic life.

In her voluminous 1930s correspondence with Emily Coleman, Barnes described her taste in lovers. If Emily liked "impossible men . . . I like devils myself (among others) they are so much more interesting."[15] She contradicted Coleman's notion that she was overly attracted to good looks; she admitted that Thelma Wood was "damned handsome," but generally she looked for distinction. She had a particular fondness for Latins and confessed to "two Italian lovers, and one Cuban!"[16] but she liked to keep the upper hand in any relationship. "I like weak people, I want to be the boss covered with treacle!"[17] She claimed that she liked her "tea strong," but obviously she didn't mind a little sweetness in the brew.[18] If they were to be "ugly, then ugly in an *important* way":

What about Jimmy Light? You dont call him good looking for God sake, nor very neat as far as that goes, and usually as drunk as a coot; well I liked him for a minute (he put his foot in the soup rather early in the game) and there was an hay-chewing number from Arizona, or such parts, who looked like a disappointed horse, and another who was no bigger than Tom Thum, and Courtenay Lemon wasnt handsome, neither was Putz, so why do you insist on it that I can only like something utterly ravishing? *Its the kind,* no man can know anothers kind, so there is little use discussing that point.[19]

The list was obviously not exhaustive, for there were many other lovers she fails to mention, but here she focuses on her Greenwich Village years.

Wald Barnes's letter of 1 July 1916 to the Romanian writer Konrad Bercovici advocating that they migrate to California suggests by implication that Djuna may have been having an affair with Bercovici (who was married), since Wald assumes that Konrad and Djuna will be a couple. Whether lover or friend, he was close to Djuna Barnes just after her breakup with Putzi Hanfstaengl. Bercovici knew the man Barnes often identified as her common-law husband, Courtenay Lemon, long before Barnes did, probably as early as 1912. In his book *It's the Gypsy in Me*, he says that he met Lemon at a gathering of socialists and anarchists, describing him as "a tall, broad-shouldered young man with a small head and a pale face"[20]; "six foot three, this side of thirty, and very handsome, he was a master of English, a fascinating talker, a mathematician, a critic, a theorist, a socialist, a philosopher, and with it all one of the most charming of men. But lazy . . . irresponsible, forever in debt, and borrowing from Peter to pay Paul."[21] Lemon and Barnes roamed the East Side of Manhattan, frequented socialist cafés, and talked excitedly of books and ideas.

Lemon and Barnes probably lived together from late 1916 or early 1917 until January of 1919, but they became acquainted a bit earlier. If Barnes knew Bercovici in the summer of 1916, as Wald's letter indicates, then she surely knew Lemon, for it was in December of that year that Lemon published his article "Free Speech" in *Pearson's Magazine*, which Frank Harris had recently bought and now edited.[22] We know that she was sexually involved with Lemon in March of 1917, because in a literary fragment she wrote of purging the horrifying images of Zadel's death (March 16) through passionate lovemaking with him. Perhaps writing helped the purgation as well.

Though he is not mentioned by name in Edmund Wilson's *The Twenties*, he is described there in the words of Djuna Barnes:

My husband was a scholar, he really had a fine mind. . . . He works on the *American* to earn a living—and uses his money to buy books. . . . He's writing a book on the philosophy of criticism—but it'll never be finished. He's been working on it seven years. . . . He had me absolutely stunned so that I didn't know whether I was coming or going. . . . Oh, you couldn't pry me away from him. . . . The amount that man knew was appalling: he knew about all sorts of different editions and things. . . . But he thought earrings were very foolish; he couldn't understand why I should want to wear earrings. . . . But I couldn't stand it any longer.[23]

Exceedingly attractive to women, and often involved in more than one affair at a time, Lemon found it difficult to balance his love life with his commitment to socialism. By the time he lived with Barnes, his drinking may have diminished his appeal, for she was attracted to his mind rather than his appearance. Lemon struggled with a project he never finished, "pegging away at his immortal book at the rate of ten words a week, dismiss[ing his friend's] anguish with quotations from Marx and Engels."[24]

Bercovici, on the other hand, was a prolific writer of similar political persuasion who soon began to make a good income from his writing, especially with memoirs of his early life in Romania. By the time Djuna Barnes became involved with Lemon, it was Bercovici who was winning fame and Lemon who saw life through the distortion of a gin bottle. The men's friendship continued for years and revolved around publishing; Lemon found a publisher for Bercovici's *Crimes of Charity* (1917).[25]

Bercovici valued Lemon's friendship but pitied his ineptitude, as seen in his description of Lemon at a party for Rebecca West given by Lawrence Langner (1890–1962), who founded the Washington Square Players in 1915, the Theatre Guild four years later, and, still later, the Shakespeare Festival in Stratford, Connecticut:

Poor Courtenay Lemon had been so eager to meet Rebecca West that he had come to the party ahead of all and was already drunk. . . . Poor Courtenay! What a far day from the day when we had first met, when he was everything and I nothing. I introduced him to Rebecca, said he was a most magnificent writer, and went overboard in my praise. But the more I praised him the somberer his face became. My praise was gall; for he knew he had done nothing yet to deserve the praise.[26]

And he would never merit such praise. His obituary says that he was "for many years dramatic critic of *The Call* and later assistant editor of *Pearson's*" under Frank Harris.[27] Between 1922 and 1930 he read plays for the Theatre Guild. For the next three years he lived with his wife, Alice, on a farm in Hillsdale, New York, then, at age fifty, he died of heart disease. His book was never finished.

Why was Barnes attracted to Lemon? Because he was an intellectual involved in the great debates of the day, who read voraciously in philosophy, political theory, and literature, a man with whom she could share ideas. Sometimes Barnes resisted Lemon's attempts to educate her, as when he made her read Bergson, but she later spoke often of how fascinated she once was with this intellectual dynamo. He seemed to have read everything, could speak at rallies, and was the darling of the socialist cafés. He seemed capable of any achievement, if he could only get his life together.[28]

A sample of Lemon's urbane intelligence may be seen in his omnibus book review for *Pearson's* in February 1917. Against the backdrop of the Great War, he is contemptuous of philosophers and scientists who have allowed the war to rob them of their reason and "respect for truth." Not wars, but the great thinkers, will shape the course of human events. Arrogance is discernible: "Loeb's experiments with lower organisms or Watson's studies of the behavior of white rats, with their sinister suggestions of universal automatism, are more appalling still, to the thoughtful mind, than the fate of Belgium. . . . Measured against such Himalayas of the human mind and soul as Darwin and Marx and Newton, Napoleon and Bismarck and Alexander are not even among the foothills of human significance."[29] After two pages of such finger-wagging, Lemon briefly reviewed books by Maeterlinck, Bernard Shaw, co-author of an essay with Romain

Rolland, H. G. Wells, Anatole France (he called him the greatest of living writers), Bertrand Russell, John Dewey, Max Eastman, and Louis Bondin. Of course, the socialist writers emerge as the enlightened ones.

Contrary to what was often said, Barnes never married Lemon; marriage records in New York State record no nuptial union between them. Barnes told Chester Page that she had a common-law marriage with Lemon, who "was a nice enough man, who got lost in the woods and died."[30] In May of 1919, they were still attached, though perhaps not cohabiting, when Barnes apparently became involved with the painter Maurice Sterne, onetime husband of Mabel Dodge Luhan (1889–1962). There is a letter of 12 May from Sterne in answer to an irate letter from Lemon accusing him of alienating the affection of his "wife." Sterne says Djuna probably left "due to your fierce and uncontrollable temper of which you sent me a sample this morning." Lemon's angry letter seems to have contained an anti-Semitic barb, which made it all the more unpleasant.

Virtually no correspondence between Barnes and Lemon survives, nor could there have been much, since they lived in the same city until they were past caring about each other's fate, but there is one undated letter from each that tells the other that the affair was ended. Barnes wrote: "You promised that you would not trouble me again— I have nothing to say & nothing which I want to listen to." For his part, Lemon mentions a misunderstanding, certain mitigating facts responsible for his recent behavior that she couldn't have known about, and asks her to forgive and forget. He no longer blames her for anything, and concludes: "I love & bless you & trust to yr strength of intellect to pull you through to the interesting, fruitful life that this false start should not be allowed to blight."

One possible reason for their breakup was differing work habits, for Barnes was busily writing plays, stories, and interviews in 1919; in later years, she found that she could work best alone. Then, too, it would have been her practice to ask him to read her work. Considering Lemon's politics and his preference for artists and thinkers who felt some commitment to the struggle for social justice, he may not have been very supportive of Barnes's literary endeavors. He may also have felt bitter because she was completing her writing projects and he was not.

Djuna Barnes was attracted to remarkable people in the world of arts and letters, and perhaps none was as remarkably original as the Baroness Elsa von Freytag Loringhoven (1874–1927). She makes a cameo appearance in Barnes's journalistic piece "How the Villagers Amuse Themselves," which proves that Barnes knew her at least as early as 1916. She alights from a cab

> with seventy black and purple anklets clanking about her secular feet, a foreign postage stamp—canceled—perched upon her cheek; a wig of purple and gold caught roguishly up with strands from a cable once used to moor importations from far Cathay; red trousers—and catch the subtle, dusty perfume blown back from her—an ancient human notebook on which has been written all the follies of a past generation. (*NY* 249)

Most artists were content to create art; Elsa tried to become art and so was admired by the *Little Review* circle, the Dada group in Paris, and later the Surrealists. Barnes became Elsa's main benefactor, even agreeing to become her biographer and literary executor. She had proposed to try to have published a volume of the baroness's poems and then made several attempts to write a biography from the disordered autobiographical fragments that Elsa composed for the imagined book's preface when she resided in a home for the down-and-out in Potsdam in 1924.[31] Wald Barnes would have been proud of his daughter's attempts in so many media.

Now that Paul Hjartarson and Douglas O. Spettigue have published Elsa von Freytag Loringhoven's autobiography, we know considerably more about her. She was born Else Hildegard Ploetz in 1874 in Swinemünde, a town on the Baltic. Her abusive German father was a master mason.[32] Elsa claimed that her mother was of Polish descent, but family surnames do not suggest this. Her unhappy childhood led Elsa into prostitution, venereal disease, endless affairs, and, after an interval as an art student in Munich, into marriage to an architect named August Endell in Berlin in 1901. Endell, who eventually became a professor at Breslau, turned out to be impotent. Her strong sexual needs unsatisfied, Elsa next fell in love with Felix Paul Greve (1872–1948), her husband's friend, who had important contacts in German literary circles. She eloped with him to Italy. (Greve occasionally signed hotel registers "Baron Volkbein," which is probably the origin of Felix Volkbein's name in *Nightwood*.[33]) After a stint in prison in Bonn, Greve faked his suicide, brought Elsa to Kentucky, farmed awhile, then abandoned her there in 1909. Elsa somehow made her way via Cincinnati to New York and then to Germany.

Unknown to Elsa (or Barnes), Greve went to western Canada, changed his name to Frederick Philip Grove, and became one of Canada's most successful novelists.[34] As Greve, he wrote novels based on Elsa's life: *Fanny Essler* (1905) and *Mauermeister Ihles Haus* (1906), translated as *The Master Mason's House*.

Fanny Essler, about Elsa's early life in Pomerania, amplifies the autobiography she wrote for Barnes. Many details of Elsa's remarkable life emerge—her mother's insanity and death from syphilis, which she contracted on her wedding night and for which she was too ashamed to seek medical attention; her father's remarriage to a woman Elsa hated; Elsa's running away at age eighteen to Berlin, where she had many lovers in artistic circles; and her own eventual contraction of syphilis, for which she was careful to find treatment.

After her abandonment by Greve, Elsa married Leopold Freiherr von Freytag Loringhoven in New York in 1913; he had been born in Berlin in 1885, had been dismissed from the army, and had little income.[35] The baron returned to Europe alone at the onset of the Great War and committed suicide in St. Gallen, Switzerland, in 1919, supposedly as an antiwar protest. Abandoned and destitute once more, Elsa drifted to Greenwich Village and became an artists' model, living from hand to mouth, often starving, until she returned to Germany in April 1923.[36]

Elsa was adopted, metaphorically speaking, by Jane Heap and Margaret Anderson of *The Little Review*, but she must have resented Anderson's stylish good looks; as Barnes put it to Hank O'Neal, Anderson "was always drinking perfume and toilet water, and that's why the Baroness put dogshit on her doorstep."[37]

Barnes may have met the baroness at *The Little Review*. The elegant, sardonic Barnes and the outrageous Elsa at first didn't care for each other, but need always brought out the maternal instinct in Barnes, and never would she encounter a needier person than Elsa, who had no source of income but charity.

Memoirs of life in the Village at this time invariably mention the baroness and her costumes. In one of her ledgers, Elsa records what she wore on a visit to the French consulate:

> wearing a large wide, sugarcoated birthday cake upon my head with 50 flaming candles lit—I felt *just so* spunky and affluent [sic]! In my ears I wore sugar plums or match boxes—I forget wich [sic]. Also I had put on several stamps as beauty marks on my emerald painted cheeks and my eyelashes were made of gilded porcupine quills—rustling coquettishly—at the consul—with several ropes of dried figs dangling round my neck to give him a suck once and again—to entrance him.

The baroness was arrested often, for her bizarre costumes or her violent behavior or for theft. She seemed to be a kleptomaniac, though most of her time was spent writing or producing art objects out of other people's rubbish. She had untrained dogs—the number varies between two and five—which kept her tenement flat a mess (two of them once copulated on her filthy bed while she spoke in courteous tones with the poet and physician William Carlos Williams).

She pursued Williams for years, even to his home in Rutherford, New Jersey, where she had an accomplice call the good doctor to see a sick baby. She waited for him in his car, slugging him on the neck when he refused to satisfy her. Margaret Anderson reported her explanation: "I thought we could have a real talk, she told us afterward—meaning a conversation of at least three hours."[38] Once she proposed that Dr. Williams contract syphilis from her so as to free his mind for art. She pursued many Villagers (Wallace Stevens was terrified of her), one of her passions being Marcel Duchamp, for whom she composed her short poem "Marcel, Marcel, I Love You Like Hell, Marcel."

The opera singer Marguerite d'Alvarez, who Andrew Field said had a dalliance with Djuna Barnes's father in Cornwall-on-Hudson (I've seen no evidence of this) and who is the model for Carmen La Tosca in Barnes's story "A Boy Asks a Question of a Lady," was once upstaged by the baroness after a concert.

> She [the baroness] wore a trailing blue-green dress and a peacock fan. One side of her face was decorated with a canceled postage stamp (two-cent American, pink). Her lips were painted black, her face powder was yellow. She wore the top of a coal scuttle for a hat, strapped on under her chin like a helmet. Two mustard spoons at the side gave the effect of feathers.[39]

In his unpublished memoirs, Louis Bouché remembered still more of Elsa's costumes: "a black dress with a bustle on which rested an electric battery tail light" and, another time, "a wooden bird cage around her neck housing a live canary." Bouché remembered her once inviting friends to tea and surprising them with her having "shaven her head entirely and painted it purple." On another occasion, Bouché brought Elsa a copy of Duchamp's *Nude Descending a Staircase*, and, to show her devotion to Duchamp, she "took the clipping and gave herself a rub down with it, missing no part of her anatomy."[40]

George Biddle writes of meeting the baroness in Philadelphia when she approached him in the spring of 1917 to inquire if he needed a model.

> With a royal gesture she swept apart the folds of a scarlet raincoat. She stood before me quite naked—or nearly so. Over the nipples of her breasts were two tin tomato cans, fastened with a green string about her back. Between the tomato cans hung a very small bird-cage and within it a crestfallen canary. One arm was covered from wrist to shoulder with celluloid curtain rings, which later she admitted to have pilfered from a furniture display in Wanamaker's.

She removed her hat, which had been tastefully but inconspicuously trimmed with gilded carrots, beets and other vegetables. Her hair was close cropped and dyed vermilion.[41]

The stories are endless and oft repeated, and they play upon a repetitious theme. Steven Watson says, "Unlike other artists associated with New York Dada, the Baroness did not keep herself at one remove from her art, and nothing she did was mediated by irony."[42] There may have been little irony, but who would doubt her sense of humor? Yet there was also a very serious side: Elsa had sold her body, and in old age it was unwanted.

Because of Elsa's antics, too few of her friends focused on the originality of her mind to attempt to save her from her own despair. Here Barnes was the exception. When Barnes was in France in 1924, Elsa wrote her interminable, repetitious letters asking for any kind of assistance: money, socks, underwear—anything that would help her tolerate the cold and hardship at the poorhouse in Potsdam. *The Little Review* and *transition* later published excerpts from the more poignant of these letters.

Barnes responded to the human need, but she also recognized Elsa's untutored genius and understood her German friend's fanatical commitment to the cause of art. This Biddle, too, understood when he wrote that of all the art collectors he had known, she "was the most sensitive, critically understanding and emotionally generous."[43] Essentially Elsa's total commitment to art implied a value system on which Barnes herself had been nourished as a child, a system that may produce a self-consuming artist. Barnes never forgave her brothers in later years for failing to offer her the unconditional support that she had offered Elsa in time of need.

Eventually Elsa made it to Paris, in 1926. Her tragic life came to an end on 14 December 1927, snuffed out by gas fumes from an oven, just months after Barnes had bought her new flat. Either it was suicide or it was the grim joke of a departing lover. In either case, it was an end to suffering.

Another lifelong friend (and, briefly, lover) of Barnes was Laurence Vail (1891–1968), who in 1922 became Peggy Guggenheim's first husband and in 1932 Kay Boyle's second.[44] An American citizen, Vail was born in Paris, attended Oxford, and wrote articles for various magazines. His surrealist play *What D'You Want* was staged in 1920 at the Provincetown, where he also played a minor part in *The Emperor Jones.* Boyle's biographer Joan Mellen described him as a red-faced man, "slender, and of medium height with streaky yellow hair and a beaklike Roman nose."[45] His sister, Clotilde, an adept singer of the blues, was later a friend of Barnes. Laurence Vail is perhaps best remembered for his surrealist painting and sculpture and for his novel *Murder! Murder!*

Barnes told Chester Page about first meeting Vail:

> She thought she had first met him many years ago in a pastry shop on the corner of 8th Street and Sixth Avenue, where a drugstore is now. She was having breakfast when this young man with blond hair and wearing a long white coat down to his ankles, came in, looked at her, came over and asked if he might join her. She said she thought, "what nerve," but said "certainly." He had a little money, was drunk most of the time, according to Djuna, and did paintings on bottles.[46]

Mellen noted the qualities of this frustrated artist who lived under the shadow of the very productive Kay Boyle and finally never accomplished much, which would have made Barnes sympathetic to him: "Laurence Vail was a veritable soul of wit. Constantly amazed at life's contradictions, he was forever alert to the absurd. He was worldly, ironic, sophisticated, mischievous, and no fool, although utterly impractical about money."[47]

Many of the friends Djuna knew and loved during her time in Greenwich Village were associated with the Provincetown Players, which was founded by George Cram Cook (1873–1924). Known to his friends as "Jig," Cook was described by Alfred Kreymborg as "a white-haired man with a youthful face and delicate manners."[48] His enthusiastic spirit and that of his third wife, Susan Glaspell (1882–1948), were this theater's inspiration and a lasting impetus to the little-theater movement in the United States.[49] Cook and Glaspell married in 1913 and made their way from Iowa to Provincetown, at the end of Cape Cod, where in 1915 they founded the Players. They staged plays in a fish house that sat on a wharf belonging to fellow socialist Mary Heaton Vorse. It was here that Barnes became friends with Charlie Chaplin.

Some of Eugene O'Neill's earliest plays originated in the old fish house: *Bound East for Cardiff*, *Suppressed Desires*, etc. Out of these amateur theatricals in Provincetown, a Greenwich Village theater evolved. Mary Pyne, at the time attached to Harry Kemp, was apparently there from the start.[50] Also essential to this enterprise was John "Jack" Reed (1887–1920), who later wrote *Ten Days That Shook the World* and was laid to rest in 1920 under the Kremlin wall. He was involved with Mabel Dodge (later Luhan). After their summer seasons on Cape Cod, the group all packed up and moved to New York. These years were some of the most important in the history of the American theater, which was finding its authentic voice. As for making that voice heard, Barnes wrote that "our destiny made us speak before we understood, write before we should and produce before we were able," and claimed that Greenwich Village's precarious Provincetown Theatre, which was housed in an erstwhile stable, "was always just about to be given back to the horses."[51] A common criticism was that Jig Cook and Susan Glaspell were too much the masterminds of the group, and it was only their sabbatical from the theater in 1919 that gave Barnes's friends James Light and Ida Rauh a chance to direct the Provincetown Players.

Of the playwrights, Barnes said:

> Eugene O'Neill wrote out of a dark suspicion that there was injustice in fatherly love. Floyd Dell wrote archly out of a conviction that he was Anatole France. I wrote out of a certitude that I was my father's daughter, and Jig directed because he was the pessimistic Blue Bird of Greece.[52]

O'Neill was a powerful presence from the earliest days, but other writers associated with the Players were also to achieve fame. Three years before Wallace Stevens published his first volume of poetry, *Harmonium*, his play *Three Travelers Watch a Sunrise* was performed (February 1920). In December of the next year, the Players put on Theodore Dreiser's already well-known play *Hand of the Potter*, but even in late 1919 Dreiser must have been associated with this group, as was Edmund Wilson. Mina Loy and William Carlos Williams acted the parts of lovers in Alfred Kreymborg's play *Lima Beans*.[53]

Players took turns directing, producing, acting, sweeping, writing plays, painting scenery, being stagehands, and business managers, and doing whatever odd jobs were required. Membership was by majority vote; their politics were anarchist, communist, socialist. Even under such broad collectivist banners, there was rarely unanimity of opinion about how the theater was to be run. As Sarlós says: "Floyd Dell, Max Eastman, and John Reed, who considered theatre as but one weapon in the class struggle—and Alfred Kreymborg and William Zorach, who saw in it an extension of the visual arts and poetry, were in turn disappointed when the Players proved unwilling to serve any cause except the theatre's."[54]

Opposed to show business commercialism, the mindlessness of Broadway plays, and a celebrity system that made plays subservient to the needs of stars, these thinkers were part of a radical movement in art, politics, and ideas that attracted the bright, the young, and the unconventional. It was "little theater" at its best, where success was measured only in artistic terms. Subscriptions paid the bills, not the box office. The Provincetown Players operated a mere seven years: on the wharf at Provincetown, during the summers of 1915 and 1916, then on MacDougal Street in the Village. The theater is still at this location, though not currently in use.

Although professionalism was anathema to the little theater movement in the Village, the lack of it finally did them in: in 1920, Eugene O'Neill's *The Emperor Jones* brought in so many customers, and so much cash, that the play had to be moved to a theater uptown, beyond the control of the Provincetown Players. Commercial success was not what they were about, but O'Neill was not averse to it. After this triumph, he had no need of an amateur theatrical group dedicated to promoting experimentation in the theater by homegrown American talent. Once a playwright graduated from amateur status, it was time to move on.

Barnes apparently had the respect of Eugene O'Neill, who was to send her an occasional friendly note and humored her by saying that she was the better playwright. Chester Page asked her "what sort of man Eugene O'Neill was." " 'A nice drunk,' she said. 'I saw him every night at dinner, at Polly's or whatever the name was. Edna Millay was there. Polly was drunk and served rather drunk dinners which we all ate.' "[55]

A major cohesive force in the Provincetown Players was Mary Eleanor Fitzgerald (1877–1955), known as "Fitzi." Like Cook, Glaspell, Dell, and other Players, she was a Midwesterner (from Hancock, Wisconsin). In recent years, she had worked for the anarchist magazines *Mother Earth* and *Blast*, had dedicated herself to freeing political prisoners, and had been secretary to the anarchist Emma Goldman (1869–1940).[56]

When Fitzi became the business manager of the Provincetown Players in the fall of 1918, she became its keystone. To be sure, it was rather strange to hire an anarchist to be the salaried manager in charge of keeping order, but no politically conventional person could have done better. What she had to offer fellow radicals, with whom she felt comfortable, was sweet reason, tenacity, long hours, and selfless dedication to a cooperative artistic venture that gave expression to new voices struggling to be heard in the theater.[57] Thinking back to *Uncle Tom's Cabin*, Barnes compared Fitzi to Eliza crossing the ice, the baby in her arms being the Provincetown Players.[58]

Helen Deutsch and Stella Hanau record an indelible impression of Fitzi at the Provincetown.

> Many remember that energetic figure, in tan covert, usually, with a little brown leather hat, mothering her three casts, interviewing new aspirants, endlessly signing little requisition slips in green ink. . . . She was everywhere, active and endlessly interested; she might be showing the scrubwoman an overlooked corner ten minutes be-

fore sitting down to work out a scheme for raising the entire year's budget. . . . Soon after she had taken over the bookkeeping, the records, the box office, and a few other odds and ends in her part-time job, Jig came to her, so the story goes, and said seriously: "The trouble with this place is that you're not here all the time." So she gave up her political work and was there, it seemed, literally all the time for ten years.[59]

Barnes's associates at the Provincetown formed the core of her circle of friends in Greenwich Village between 1913 and 1920, and few were closer than Fitzi, who is mentioned often in Djuna's letters to her mother in the 1920s.

Apparently Edna St. Vincent Millay had serious doubts about Barnes's friendship. In a letter of 18 March 1921, she wrote her sister Norma a warning not to let the Provincetown Players see Edna's Vassar play *Snow White and Rose Red*: "They would hate it, and make fun of it, and old Djuna Barnes would rag you about it, hoping it would get to me."[60]

If Millay didn't like Barnes, there were certainly those who did. It was about this time, through Guido Bruno, that Barnes met Charles Edison, the inventor's son, later governor of New Jersey, who moved to the Village in the summer of 1915 and gave generously to artists. Barnes claimed that he once proposed to her.

Barnes herself spent a considerable amount of her creative energy writing drama. She began to publish plays in Sunday newspaper magazines at the end of 1916, about the time when the Provincetown Players became established in Greenwich Village. Doubtless she was attracted to the players because of their bohemian values and their intense discussions about art. Her allegiance was to them, and their values inform the closet dramas she published in the *New York Morning Telegraph* magazine, short plays that were meant not to be acted but to be read as dialogue for singular effect. Though they take the form of dramatic dialogues, these closet dramas are not very distinct from her stories in theme or technique.

Barnes's early plays often have an aura of decadence, echoed in the accompanying drawings that Djuna did in the style of Aubrey Beardsley. That the most famous illustrator of the 1890s had been dead for nearly twenty years when Barnes decided to become his American avatar shows that she was at this time clearly looking backward rather than forward to literary modernism. She chafed under the twin yokes of commercial journalism and naive apprenticeship, and probably hoped that her association with the Provincetown Players might provide her with a signpost to the future.

Hidden behind her cloak of originality were two Irish playwrights, one of whom is immediately suggested by her drawings: the Oscar Wilde of the decadent play *Salomé*. The 1906 American edition of *Salomé*, which Barnes probably owned, was adorned with Beardsley's strange illustrations. The Wilde play bears an obvious intertextual relationship with Barnes's slight story "What Do You See, Madam?" (1915), in which Mamie Saloam has always wanted to dance Salomé and kiss the lips of the decapitated John the Baptist. Wilde's *Salomé* also inspired Barnes's "The Head of Babylon," about a sort of female John the Baptist, whose limbs are paralyzed but whose voice sounds biblical prophecy. These stories, the drawings, the decadent aura, and the curiously stilted dialogue of many of Barnes's plays point with certainty to the Wilde drama as a very important early influence on Djuna Barnes.

A second significant influence was John Millington Synge (1871–1909), of whom she may first have become aware in 1913, when Dublin's Abbey Players launched their second tour of the United States.[61] Synge captured her imagination as few writers did before she read *Ulysses*.[62] Despite the irritation of some Irish nationalists on both sides of the Atlantic, Synge's idiom had struck a blow at the "faith and begorra" stereotype of Irish stage dialogue, creating a beauty perhaps unsurpassed in any dialect of English. Barnes remained captivated by Synge's language for nearly a decade. Around 1919, Robert McAlmon wrote to *The Little Review* inquiring "how came it that Miss Barnes was both so Russian and so Synge-Irish."[63] Djuna probed James Joyce for reminiscences of Synge when she interviewed him in 1922.[64]

In February 1917, Barnes published "The Songs of Synge: The Man Who Shaped His Life as He Shaped His Plays," an essay illustrated by the inevitable, though scarcely relevant, Beardsleyan drawings. Disclaiming any special authority, she said: "I am not a critic; to me criticism is so often nothing more than the eye garrulously denouncing the shape of the peephole that gives access to hidden treasure."[65] Since she had not known him personally, the peephole through which she peered was of necessity shaped by the commentary of those who had.

Barnes said that she merely wished to celebrate the beauty of Synge's stage dialogue; there was "nothing in the English language that sets my whole heart to singing as his lines (also from *Deirdre of the Sorrows*): 'The dawn and the evening are a little while, the Winter and the Summer pass quickly, and what way would you and I, Naisi, have joy forever?' " With the exception of Joyce, never again would Barnes pay such tribute to a literary forebear.

Beyond language, what appealed to Barnes most about Synge was the frank pessimism of a playwright who eschewed happy endings as incongruous with the reality of Irish life and whose tragic vision embraced as well the ironic dimension of the human enterprise. This was essentially the mood of Barnes's own literary work, and the Irish-American Dr. O'Connor of *Nightwood* was to give most eloquent voice to it. Barnes wrote of Synge: "And he realized that grim brutality and frankness and love are one, the upper lip is romance, but the under is irony, and he knew 'There is no timber that has not strong roots among the clay and worms.' "

Barnes was hardly surprised at the outcry of bourgeois nationalist reaction to *The Playboy of the Western World*, which was thought to slander Irish country people. Art that caused no stir was quickly forgotten, and for Barnes, Synge was everything that an artist should be; indeed, his vision matched the unhappy reality she knew. "He was a harp on which the sorrows and the great strifes played . . . his music was torn from him with the pangs of travail." Barnes concluded on a wistful personal note:

And so, looking it over, I find that, after all, I have not violated my strict intention of remaining practically uncritical—and for this I am grimly happy. I give praise to my sour grapes, they make exceeding excellent wine. It is enough that, turning back to look on Synge, I have more courage to go forward—that I can read at least eight books without having to say that I was duped into fruitless hours of attention, or into the temporary anguish of undiscovering a discovery.

Her article, accompanied by her three illustrations of imagined scenes from Synge's plays, has never been reprinted.[66]

Reading Synge did not help Barnes learn how to write Irish plays worthy of the master, for there were several problems with such an apprenticeship. Although his *Riders to the Sea* was a great one-act play, and imitation of mastery was desirable if she was to learn the art of writing drama, Barnes had never been to Ireland, had never met Synge, and her knowledge of Irish people and their speech was limited to the Irish Americans in New York.

As Susan Clark has pointed out, several of Barnes's play titles are embarrassingly Syngean: *Kurzy of the Sea* (Synge wrote *Riders to the Sea*), *Maggie of the Saints* (Synge wrote *The Well of the Saints* and Stephen Crane wrote the novel *Maggie: A Girl of the Streets*). Then there is Barnes's *An Irish Triangle*.[67]

The Death of Life (published 17 December 1916), a tragedy of slum life, was the first sign of Barnes's growing passion for the haunting language of Synge.[68] Her next one-act play, *At the Root of the Stars* (11 February 1917), which was published a week before "The Songs of Synge" and in the same newspaper, is more definitely "Irish." It tells of Mageen, who has elected to be a recluse in her boardinghouse in Southampton since, a decade earlier, her son Ulan departed for the Great War "with the tommies trotting behind like a pinch of pollen that does be following the breeze." She mistakes the passing of a donkey for the return of her son.

From Mageen, Barnes moved on to *Maggie of the Saints* (28 October 1917), a closet drama about the charwoman of a (presumably) Irish church who lives for dreams and visions that will transfigure her from her lowly state to a royal one. At the play's end, she seems rewarded momentarily when her mother takes her for the living statue of the Blessed Virgin.

After these Synge imitations, Barnes returned to journalistic subjects before writing additional Irish dramas. *An Irish Triangle* presents a dialogue between Kathleen O'Rune, the wife of John, who scandalizes the village by his intimacy with the lady of the manor, and Sheila O'Hare, "a middle aged woman, thin, small and sad," who represents conventional reaction to the scandal that Kathleen accepts as an interesting means of learning how the gentry lives. If Sheila is drying up, Kathleen is allied with the forces of nature. Sheila says of her friend: "The sorrow has gone out of your eyes, and your smile that used to be crooked with sadness, is glad and straight, and does be 'sassing' the sun." John is changed as well: "Right fine he is, and growing leaner and losing the lines of the poacher and gaining the muscles of him that do what he will."

Kathleen is another of Barnes's powerful women (like Julie von Bartmann or Helena Hucksteppe and emanating in part from the concert singer Marguerite d'Alvarez), whose moral strength and intelligence transform men into chattering monkeys, but Kathleen is different in that this strength derives not from worldliness, fame, and savoir faire but from the conviction that the superior lifestyle of the gentry awaits her if she publicly rejects the reactionary moral conventions of her native village.

Not only does Kathleen approve of her husband's philandering, since it brings her news of the world of taste and fashion; she also plans to visit the lord of the manor herself in order to educate John as to a gentleman's preferences (he's dying to know how the master wraps his puttees), thus making this Irish triangle a *ménage à quatre*.

Kurzy of the Sea is in setting and feeling close to Synge's *The Playboy of the Western World* and *Riders to the Sea*, as well as Barnes's own *The Death of Life*, wherein Ragna refuses to compromise her dreams. As in Synge's plays, the source of vitality is the imagination, in its ability to expose deception and hypocrisy, and in the uncompromising aspirations hidden beneath rather unpromising exteriors. In

Kurzy of the Sea, Rory McRace has been conditioned by his love of Irish fairy tales to disdain the ordinary, showing no interest in a conventional wife or job, preferring "a Queen or a Saint or a Venus, or whatever it is comes in with the tide." His fisherman father takes him rather literally: he nets a barmaid swimming in the sea and presents her to the family as "a sea-going Venus." Uncertain what sort of creature she is, Rory throws her into the sea as a test; she declares her identity, then swims away, taunting him. At the play's end, he asks for a boat to follow her. The extraordinary is to be found in the life force of the everyday, and this is how the dreaming Irish youth meets a mer/barmaid, who will lead him a merry chase.

Barnes's Irish dialect is at times ludicrous in *Kurzy of the Sea*, as when Rory's mother says:

> The Lord be thanked, for its my prayers are answered, and now I'll be showing the young woman the shawl I have for her. . . . Here you are darlint, and may you enjoy it hugely of evenings, when the dew is falling and there's no arms about your neck at all, at all.

Though Djuna Barnes recognized great drama and moving poetic dialogue, she could not yet imitate it. Trying to write like Synge did her no harm—her Irish plays were little more than pastimes that would pay the bills; she obviously knew how bad they were and later would try to steer scholars away from her juvenilia, which she thought worthless. And she was mostly right—few admirers would wish to reprint these early one-act plays.

Barnes gradually outgrew Provincetown, just as Eugene O'Neill had, and this coincided with a specific literary event. Margaret Anderson and Jane Heap moved with their *Little Review* from Chicago to New York in 1918, and soon thereafter they began to publish short stories by their new friend Djuna: "Finale," "A Night Among the Horses," "The Valet," "Beyond the End," "Oscar," "Mother," "The Robin's House," and "Katrina Silverstaff," plus the play *Three from the Earth* and a couple of poems: "The Lament of Women" and "To ———." Between 1918 and 1921, when she went to Paris, *The Little Review* printed what was arguably the best of the early Barnes.[69] During the 1920s, perhaps Barnes wished to avoid Heap, or perhaps she was just more focused on collecting her stories and writing *Ryder*.

Like the Provincetown Players, the political orientation of *The Little Review* was radical—anarchist to be exact—and the sexual preference of the editors was distinctly lesbian. Despite the attachment of Anderson to Heap, Heap became Barnes's lover for a while, which apparently created some jealousy in the triad. Maurice Sterne described a scene at Polly's Restaurant: "She [Djuna] took me over to a table where a mousy girl was dining with some friends. Djuna began hissing, 'I hate you, I hate you, I hate you' over and over again. The tan mouse smiled sweetly but there was an electric spark in her smile and they had an ominously quiet, violent fight before Djuna stalked out with that long stride of hers."[70] The adversary has been identified as Margaret Anderson.

In later years, Barnes had little good to say about Heap. Their affair seems to have begun about the time they attended August Strindberg's play *The Dance of Death*, with Helen Westley in a lead role.[71] Barnes told Emily Coleman that as a lover, Heap wanted her to have affairs with others, and that she was "wicked." When *Nightwood* came out, Heap told mutual friends that T. S. Eliot "wasn't nearly so crazy about the book as he said he was," which was true but hardly loyal.[72]

Barnes's last words for *The Little Review* are in her snobbish reply to a questionnaire, appearing in May of 1929: "I am sorry but the list of questions does not interest me to answer. Nor have I that respect for the public." She may not have realized that it would be printed; if not, then what could have been a request for privacy was made by Jane Heap to backfire. If Barnes expected it to be printed, then the haughty pose called attention to a privacy she wished to protect, suggesting a brilliance that was easier to evoke than to demonstrate by taking up pen. But Barnes *was* haughty: once, she told Edmund Wilson that the dirt of Paris "was a relief after the *Little Review*, anyway. 'You know they always used to wash the soap before they used it.' "[73]

Anderson complained about this Barnesian snobbishness in *My Thirty Years' War*, saying that in fact:

Djuna would never talk, she would never allow herself to be talked to. She said it was because she was reserved about herself. She wasn't, in fact, reserved—she was unenlightened. . . . It embarrassed her to approach impersonal talk about the personal element. It embarrassed us to attempt a relationship with anyone who was not on speaking terms with her own psyche. Her mind has no abstract facets.[74]

In her Village days, Barnes also gravitated toward the Theatre Guild, which was the brainchild of Lawrence Langner, Philip Moeller, Helen Westley, Theresa Helburn, Lee Simonson, and Maurice Wertheim, who put it together at the end of 1918. The Liberal Club's dramatic group (1914) had given rise to the Washington Square Players, which stayed together until May of 1918; some of this group, which had helped establish the Provincetown Players, now formed the Theatre Guild, and Djuna Barnes was an original member. The Guild flourished for more than fifty years and featured some of the age's finest actors and plays from both sides of the Atlantic, striking a compromise between the radical collectivist orientation of the Provincetown Players and the commercialism of Broadway.

Djuna Barnes had minor, nonspeaking roles in two plays. On 19 January 1920, she appeared in Tolstoy's *The Power of Darkness*, a play about redemption; and on Christmas night of 1922, she played one of six nuns in Paul Claudel's *The Tidings Brought to Mary*, in which with an excess of ardor the saintly Violaine kisses a leper and becomes infected.[75] Of her role, Barnes said in an interview, "I was petrified. The worst was when the other five nuns missed their cue, leaving me all alone on the stage, one nun doing the work of six."[76]

By 1920, Djuna Barnes had lived eight years in Greenwich Village, during one of its liveliest decades. She had shared in the founding of America's little theater movement, and she had interviewed some of her country's most interesting artists, directors, and entertainers. With her wit, style, and beauty, but above all her very important connections in artistic circles, Barnes was the darling of several New York editors, who paid her well and gave her the opportunity to become one of America's observers of the European scene. Djuna was happy to accept her next assignment, for if New York was the best American city for a young writer to begin her career, Paris was the place to observe the artistic scene in the 1920s and to learn the literary techniques that would guarantee her a place in the pantheon of modernist writers.

"So This Is Paris!"

"I hope you will suffer prettily in Paris."[1]

Barnes was first sent to Paris by Burton Rascoe, who became associate editor of *McCall's* magazine in April of 1921.[2] (Forty years earlier, *McCall's* had sent her grandmother, Zadel, to London.) A socialist and a former literary editor of the *Chicago Tribune* (1912–20), Rascoe was hired by Harry Payne Burton, who edited both *McCall's* and *Cosmopolitan* and who, more than any editor of his time, studied publishing trends to discover what American women wanted to read. What they seemed to want was sophistication, a hint of illicit romance, a peek at fashion—all of which Barnes's journalism provided. Rascoe stayed with *McCall's* for a year, then moved on to the *New York Tribune*, which also published Barnes's journalism, much of it anonymous.

Harry Burton's magazines were profitable; within a year's time, according to Rascoe, he increased the circulation of *McCall's* from six hundred thousand to two million.[3] Burton's and Rascoe's leftist views were not allowed to affect their magazine's agenda, for Burton believed that the average small-town American woman was interested not in issues such as women's suffrage or in culture, but in soap operas, "in how to save money, pretty up her rented house, and hold her husband . . . her tastes were for romantic fiction in which she could identify herself as the heroine."[4] Apparently the far smaller group of women who were politically committed would do better to read the *New Republic*.

Burton was enthusiastic about Barnes's journalism and was prepared to pay her well. In 1923, for instance, he paid her the handsome sum of five hundred dollars for "Tertium Organum," a story (with pictures), which was written but may have remained unpublished.[5] *McCall's* paid Barnes better than any American magazine of its kind could have. Of her, Burton Rascoe wrote:

> Djuna Barnes, who was as subtle and as individualistic in her caricatures as she was in her short stories and pseudo-Elizabethan stories of bawdry, was one of the handsomest women I have ever seen and one of the most amusing. I never saw her wear anything except a tailored black broadcloth suit with a white ruffled shirtwaist, a tight-fitting black hat, and high-heeled black shoes; and I rarely saw her without a long shepherd's crook which she carried like a Watteau figure in a *fête galante.* Her story of the "Odyssey of the King of the Ostermoors," in which she, Jane Heap, Margaret Anderson, and Georgette Leblanc, Maeterlinck's first wife, figured hilariously, as Djuna told it, is one of the classical anecdotes of New York literary life which, unfortunately, I am not privileged to relate.[6]

In "Vagaries Malicieux," published in May 1922, which was written in the snobbish style of the world-weary columnist who has seen everything and enjoyed nothing, Barnes remembered her first trip to Paris. Her fellow passengers aboard ship were "chiefly disappointed teachers from the Middle West"; Barnes kept company with a forty-three-year-old Frenchman, a professor in the United States, who claimed to have seduced three hundred women and who obviously found her attractive. At the captain's table, Barnes's laugh was apparently commented upon: "After one laugh the entire dining room was speculating on me—after the second they had made up their minds—after the third they were leading my life." It could have been the wine.

Then came the landing and culture shock. The professor, who spoke to her of his conquests and lamented that in his absence so many French women had been deprived of his company, sat with her from Le Havre to the Gare Saint-Lazare. Apparently she went straight to the Hôtel Jacob (later called the Hôtel d'Angleterre), down the street from Natalie Barney's at 20, rue Jacob, and thereafter walked to Nôtre-Dame Cathedral. A few days later, she moved to a pension on the rue de Grenelle. According to Arlen Hansen, Barnes also stayed in a room at 2, rue Perronet shortly after coming to Paris,[7] perhaps following the pension; then, returning from a sojourn in Berlin, she took a flat at 173, boulevard Saint-Germain (two small rooms and a kitchen), near the Café des Deux Magots and the Café de Flore.

A skeptic as always, Barnes looked for authenticity amid unfamiliar surroundings, and for the first three weeks she disliked Paris.[8] As she was "a lonely creature by preference," Nôtre-Dame left her "comparatively untouched"; she preferred instead the "less aloof" church of Saint-Germain-des-Prés. The middle part of "Vagaries Malicieux" describes her meeting with Joyce, after which she returns to her views of Paris as seen through the jaded eyes of an unimpressed outsider.

Barnes records details all around her: she overhears a woman commenting, "we have underestimated American plumbing." "The French woman is small, high hipped and amusingly dark, her thoughts are local, and her husband is minute and physically fit, apparently, only in reminiscence." The croissants were better at New York's Hotel Brevoort. She was absolutely determined to be unimpressed, to keep her nose in the air, to see her surroundings only as a source for amusing observations. The mood did not last long, for Paris was destined to become Barnes's favorite city, a place that would generate intense nostalgia.

In "Vagaries," Barnes quibbles with the professor about Paris's proudest gardens and monuments like a woman fending off seduction. The Jardin de Luxembourg "was all that I had imagined, but not quite what I had hoped," while the Tuileries lacked any "association," presumably in her memory. The flower market left her cold, the theaters were dull, the Folies Bergères was unimpressive, poverty despoiled the beauty of the Seine, the best shops were "like our worst stores on a half-holiday." Barnes admitted that she did like the "perfumes, powders, rouges, cosmetics of all sorts . . . your cafés," plus the paintings and the way men walk, "with a certain respect for the way their legs are fastened on."

And when the professor takes her to a French surgeon's family, so that she can see how the locals live, she cannot contain her enthusiasm for the rooms she sees: the satin-covered walls, the porcelains, the lace petticoats, the hand-painted spinet, the white fur rug. The surgeon, his wife, and their teenage daughter are described at length, in words reflecting admiration for their taste and charm. The daughter was eerily prophetic in showing Barnes to the door with the remark: "I hope you will suffer prettily in Paris."

Barnes did suffer prettily, for the aloof expatriate never assimilated and remained essentially unconnected with the life of the city, even as she made a home there. She learned no more than a few words of French and formed few acquaintances with Parisians. Emily Coleman was on target when she wrote Barnes in 1936:

> . . . when you were in Paris all those years you lived among Americans, not French, or English, or Germans. Your "friends" were all Americans. . . . And all the "girls" you ever speak of are American—Margaret Anderson, Solita, Alice, Jane, etc. . . . But my point is your love for Paris is a romantic passion, having little connection with Paris's reality, i.e., as the French capital; you love it because it is the past, and your past. . . . You don't feel pressed upon in France because you are not in the least aware of French life that is going on around you.[9]

At the Hôtel Jacob, where many American writers stopped, the translator Lewis Galantière often made the bookings; there Barnes would have partied with Sherwood Anderson, Harold Loeb, Alfred Kreymborg, and Man Ray. Kreymborg mentions the newly arrived Barnes's quite audible comment in the lobby of this favorite hotel of American expatriates: "So this is Paris!"[10] Later in the year, Ernest Hemingway arrived at the Hôtel Jacob; he traveled in more distinguished circles than Barnes, and she may not have met him until Robert McAlmon came onto the Paris scene. Though she thought that his work was overrated, she followed his career with interest. The style of her story "Behind the Heart" seems derivative of Hemingway's *A Farewell to Arms*, as well as of Gertrude Stein.

Hemingway made reference to Barnes in an editorial column in Ford Madox Ford's *Transatlantic* (April 1924), saying that according to her publishers, a "legendary personality that has dominated the intellectual night-life of Europe for a century is in town. I have never met her, nor read her books, but she looks very nice." Apparently he was just trying to stir up controversy, but Barnes didn't forget the barb, for many years later she wrote Natalie Barney: "There's a boy who really got about to thinking that the Sun also Rose for Hemingway."[11] As an economical reference to the soul of the Lost Generation, the name Jake Barnes of Hemingway's *The Sun Also Rises* may have its origin in the confluence of Djuna Barnes and the Hôtel Jacob.

It wasn't long after she arrived in Paris that Djuna Barnes began to meet influential people in the expatriate community. She made friends with Mary Louise Reynolds, a war widow with a secure income who moved to Paris in 1920, took up the cause of Surrealism, and became the lover of Marcel Duchamp. Reynolds first had a house in the place de la Sorbonne, then moved to rue Hallé, where, in her salon, she entertained artists and writers. Once, Reynolds's cat ate some lovebirds she was taking care of for Djuna; she replaced them with others, hoping that the switch would not be noticed, but on her return, Barnes immediately saw that the birds were not hers.[12] At her death, in 1950, Reynolds left vital historical documents on the Surrealist movement to the Art Institute in Chicago, and to Barnes she left a stipend.

Edmund Wilson, who had come to Paris in June 1920, in pursuit of Edna St. Vincent Millay, remembered that during a dinner with her in Montmartre in the summer of 1921, he asked Barnes to go to Italy with him.

> She said that she had refused because of my dinner with her, when I had talked to her about Edith Wharton. At the end of my little lecture, she had said something like "If there's anybody I loathe

it's Edith Wharton." She now explained her refusal: "I thought *Ethan Frome:* no!"[13]

Barnes's disapproval of Edith Wharton was intensified by rejection; some months later, she was sent to interview the novelist and found her at the Crillon, "chewing a chop like a dog."[14] Barnes told Chester Page that Wharton, spying Djuna, snapped, "please leave at once." Page said, " 'See, the shoe is on the other foot now' [i.e., now it is you who are famous]. 'Well, I understand exactly how she felt,' said Djuna."[15]

A *Greenwich Villager* interview, published in March 1922, when Barnes was newly returned from her first trip to Paris, confirms her view that the city grew on her, though at first she was unimpressed. She remarked on the numbers of Americans there, some of whom she knew from New York, who congregated at La Rotonde, a café that resembled the Village's Brevoort. Man Ray, Arthur Morse, Jo David-son, Clara Wold, Edna St. Vincent Millay, Marsden Hartley, Berenice Abbott, Harold Stearns, Sinclair Lewis—these were the better-known visitors to La Rotonde. She told Chester Page about having lunch with William Butler Yeats and the New York lawyer and art patron John Quinn, and of Hart Crane, who once left her a note affixed by a dagger on her wall.[16] (On another occasion, in 1929, she got Crane out of jail.) She met Constantin Brancusi and interviewed James Joyce on this trip, but in general, the atmosphere of Paris was not conducive to work, though a few, like Millay, managed it. As few of them knew any French, they tended to order the one item on the menu that they recognized—omelets.

Barnes's flat in the boulevard Saint-Germain was just down the street from the Brasserie Lipp, where late-night meals of beer, sau-sage, and potato salad attracted the American crowd. In a few months Thelma Wood moved from the rue Delambre into Barnes's flat, where they stayed until 30 August 1927. They moved then into a flat in the rue Saint-Romain, purchased with royalties from *Ryder*. To Emily Coleman, Djuna would write: "You have forgotten the days of *real* starvation when I took Thelma in as she had *nothing*."[17]

Robert McAlmon (1895–1957), who later wrote *Being Geniuses Together*, an autobiographical account of these years of the "Lost Generation," was a frequent drinking partner of Barnes, as well as of Hemingway, Fitzgerald, Joyce, and other literary celebrities. A writer whose bright future was ruined by drink and easy living, he was, Barnes thought, one of the saddest people she had ever known; often she saw him weeping against a tree, ill from a hangover.[18]

McAlmon was nevertheless an unusually astute judge of literary talent. He met Barnes in New York before 1920, probably through Jane Heap:

> I had known Djuna only slightly in New York, because Djuna was a very haughty lady, quick on the uptake, and with a wisecracking tongue that I was far too discreet to try and rival. . . . Jane kept assuring her that McAlmon was not taken in by her cape-throwing gestures but understood her for the sentimentalist she was. In the end, Djuna had gathered the idea that I disliked her, and that I was a very sarcastic individual.[19]

McAlmon had in early 1921 married Bryher, the lesbian daughter of one of Britain's richest families, in part to give them both the front they needed for their actively gay lives.[20] To his surprise, he found himself with plenty of money to spend and supportive relatives who liked him. He had known Bryher and her circle since Village days. Although McAlmon quickly became unhappy with his wife, Barnes told Chester Page that he never said an unkind word about her. Allan Ross Macdougall called him "Robert McAlimony," for he suspected that McAlmon was interested in Bryher's money.[21] As it turned out, he received a divorce settlement of fourteen thousand pounds, which for a while enabled him to live well and publish the works of Parisian expatriates.

In *Being Geniuses Together*, McAlmon comments upon Barnes's disdainful attitude toward Sinclair Lewis on one occasion in the Gypsy Bar; on another, she saved the day by escorting Harriet Weaver out when Weaver was shocked by Ezra Pound's failed attempt at breezy humor at her expense.[22] McAlmon's creative work is all but forgotten, but his memoir remains one of the best chronicles of the Lost Generation.

American expatriates in the 1920s also migrated to Berlin, which was popular for both its nightlife and its shocking inflation rate, which made life extremely inexpensive for those with foreign income. Marsden Hartley (1877–1943) was one of the first of his generation to love Berlin and to advertise its easily purchased pleasures. Thelma Wood was in Berlin at this time, mostly in the company of Berenice Abbott and the English painters Lett Haines and Cedric Morris,[23] and one saw visiting celebrities such as Charlie Chaplin and Isadora Duncan, as well as Barnes's erstwhile lover Putzi Hanfstaengl. Tea at the Hotel Adlon was a daily event for the expatriates. McAlmon remembered "the Russian jewelry, the orchids, not to speak of the absinthe, at the Adlon."[24]

It was a rather amazing scene. As well as perhaps the most exotic nightlife in Europe, Berlin had fine theaters and movies, which Barnes preferred even to those of Paris. As for the locals, their economy was so devastated by the Great War and the consequent reparations that they were often forced into prostitution and the drug trade in order to survive. McAlmon described the scene: "Dopes, mainly cocaine, were to be had in profusion at most night places. A deck of 'snow,' enough cocaine for quite too much excitement, cost the equal of ten cents."[25]

While in Berlin, Barnes had lunch with Charlie Chaplin, her friend from Provincetown days, then accompanied him to a hospital to visit a friend. When a nurse confessed that she had no idea who Chaplin was, he was so delighted that he embraced her.[26] A stylish photo of 1921 shows Barnes strolling down what appears to be Unter den Linden with Chaplin.

Barnes absorbed enough of the atmosphere of Berlin nightlife to fill some early pages of *Nightwood* as well as a story called "Cassation." In a particularly exotic scene in the novel, circus performers gather at a party, then go on to sample the clubs. During her stay in Berlin, Barnes saw much of McAlmon, Harrison Dowd, and Marsden Hartley. Hartley was an intelligent, articulate landscape painter, who was first exhibited at Gallery "291" by Alfred Stieglitz in 1908. Alfred

Kreymborg wrote that Hartley had "the aloofness of Hamlet,"[27] though a comparison with Polonius might have been more apt. Because of his prominent proboscis, Barnes dubbed him "the eagle without his cliff."[28]

Townsend Ludington describes Hartley's gay life in Berlin:

> He went to immense costume balls where in exotic dress he was worshipped by young men; transvestite parties such as those he described to Matilde Rice; and homosexual bars where he might fawn over a young male pickup such as Robert McAlmon told of in his short stories. "Life in Berlin then was at the height of heights —that is to the highest pitch of sophistication and abandon," Hartley wrote in his memoir. "None of us had seen anything quite like the spectacle. The psychological themes were incredible."[29]

Hartley told a story of coaxing Barnes into bed, which may have been wishful thinking, for William Carlos Williams says dubiously: "[Hartley] told me how once he had made rather direct love to DB— offering his excellent physical equipment for her favors. . . . I can see old Marsden now, with his practical approach, explaining to Djuna what he could offer her. Djuna and her evasive ways. Marsden was very fond of her."[30] That Hartley, like nearly all the men who surrounded her, was gay would have made little difference to Barnes, but it is far from certain that she would have agreed to his proposition.[31]

Hartley could be a valuable friend in Berlin, since he had spent many months there before the war and had the right connections. He loved Germany, where he felt at home as few American expatriates did. Hartley and Barnes had much in common and may have met in Provincetown in the summer of 1916. Like Barnes, Hartley had studied at the Art Students League under Frank Vincent DuMond, and he had known the painter Albert Pinkham Ryder, whose name Barnes may have appropriated for the title of her first novel. In *Adventures in the Arts* (1921), Hartley included a chapter on Ryder, which Barnes may have read. He was close to Stieglitz, Kreymborg, and McAlmon, and knew Man Ray, Gertrude and Leo Stein, and Marcel Duchamp.

According to McAlmon, Barnes stayed in Berlin only a few weeks, which, given her letter to him of that time, must have been around September of 1921. She writes that she planned to remain in Europe until her money ran out but was determined to get to London and to the hotel in Southampton where, on a family trip, she had found a ruby horseshoe stickpin. For a nine-year-old, this must have been an astonishing find. Djuna Barnes was in no hurry to return to America; she was having too much fun.

Back in Paris, Barnes's Left Bank routine meant spending nearly every evening in cafés, restaurants, and nightclubs, which did not help her form ideal work habits. She was often seen alone in the Café de Flore, where Edouard Roditi remembered her, solitary and neurotic: "She used to sit by the hour at a table there with the little saucers piling up, very often alone, sometimes with other women."[32] It is a description familiar from Barnes's story "Dusie." A letter of 1936 describes a routine that must have been quite similar to that of her earlier years in Paris:

> . . . have all the time in the world, heaven knows, but I get up, start painting, its lunch before I know it, vaguely reach out for a bun or an egg, start writing and its six and I go out for a little walk, an aperitif, my manuscript under my arm, start writing more notes, dont want to see anyone, eat my dinner alone, and scramble back into the house about eight thirty or nine, write letters, or go to bed and read Proust, or go to sleep, and usually wake about three in the morning unable to sleep any longer, light the lamp, try to remember what I was dreaming, stare at the dark for a couple of hours and fall to sleep again, there's my life![33]

In *This Must Be the Place*, James Charters (Jimmie the Barman) tells a story of Paris nightlife worth retelling:

> Djuna Barnes, the writer, is one of my good friends who has brought me many clients. She is very much of a lady and well liked. She was the cause of what Hemingway calls my "greatest socking exploit" in Montparnasse.
>
> It happened one night at the Select. Miss Barnes, Thelma Wood and another girl were having some drinks on one side of the room,

and near them were Bob McAlmon and Ian Meyers. It was my night off, and I came in for a quick one before bed. I think the six of us must have been the sole occupants of the bar, but there may have been others.

And then came swinging into the bar an internationally known American newspaperman. He might not like me to give his name, so I will call him Frank. He was roaring drunk. Focusing on Djuna, he lunged towards her and without ceremony not only sat beside her, but began pawing and mauling her in a fashion no gentleman should use.

Thelma Wood came over to me.

"Jimmie," she said, "please do something about Frank. Hit him or move him or something, right now." I hesitated. Frank was one of my best clients. In the end I got him to another table, bought him a drink, and tried to turn his attention away from Miss Barnes. But it wouldn't be turned.

"Let's go on the *terrasse*," I said, "and pretend to fight. Just an imitation fight. We won't really hit each other." By doing that I thought the girls would feel better and I could get Frank away. But it didn't work that way. Djuna Barnes followed us out and let forth to Frank a piece of her mind. Then, in the twinkling of an eye, for Frank was fast, he knocked down Miss Barnes with a well-placed blow to the chin. In a few seconds the other two girls, Bob McAlmon and Ian Meyers were all sprawled on the sidewalk. But Bob jumped up at once, knocked Frank down and sat on him.

"Let me up!" said Frank. "Let me up! I'll behave." After solemn promises Bob let him up. But he had hardly gotten on his feet when he again let forth with both fists at the girls, at Bob and Ian. This must stop, I thought; so wading into the fight, I brought up all the force I had. Three times I knocked Frank down, leaving a gash that required three stitches later in his face. The third time he could hardly stand.[34]

Frank's identity has been a well-kept secret.

It was in January of 1927 that Ford Madox Ford wrote to his companion Stella Bowen about meeting the amazing Djuna Barnes;

the letter reflects an amusing combination of self-aggrandizement on Barnes's part and distortion for dramatic effect on Ford's:

> Djuna Barnes came into tea yesterday. She is a most amazing young woman, for, with half the publishers in New York clamoring for her novels she simply ignores them. She had a rich father who, after writing a book of philosophy for thirty years just threw it up—so she takes after him. I have just succeeded in forcing Boni's to take Asch's second book that no one else would publish—but Djuna won't even send them her [manuscript].[35]

The reality was somewhat different. In 1923, Barnes had published her collection of stories *A Book* with Boni & Liveright, publishers known to her from Village days and at the time a fortunate choice, since they printed some of the best contemporary American writers. Now she signed with the same publisher a contract to publish her first novel, *Ryder*, essentially an autobiographical family chronicle in experimental form. Barnes was apparently under the impression that Horace Liveright had offered an advance against royalties of $1,000, but when the editor Donald Friede read a version of *Ryder* in June 1927, he wrote that he "did not like it half as much" as he had expected and wished to reduce the amount of his own verbal offer from $500 to $250, to be paid only when the manuscript was accepted.[36]

This was a slippery business, as well Barnes knew, and she must have rejected the terms, for the contract she finally signed in August 1927 stipulated an advance of $500.[37] On 8 August, Liveright returned the corrected manuscript. The first galley proofs were sent the next February, and the book came out in August 1928, in an edition of 3,000 copies.

A colleague of Friede's, T. R. Smith, wrote Barnes that the "Prologue" and "Tale" at the beginning of *Ryder*, written in Chaucerian style, would harm sales, because readers would fail to understand and would read no further. He wanted these sections shifted to the end. (As it turned out, it was the United States Post Office that would fail to understand; in June 1928, postal inspectors in New York held up copies of *Ryder* on account of the Chaucerian verse.[38]) Smith also wanted to delete the illustrations, as being potentially harmful to sales: "an unadorned text is vastly superior . . ."[39] Barnes complained to Natalie Barney:

> They want *all* the charming possibilities removed—the drawings cleared of chamber pots—& the thing generally gilded! I have refused & hoped to get the contract broken in this way, but I am afraid they are not going to let me off so easily—Liveright says a private printing is out of the question for the reason that one must be simple etc.!!![40]

"Tale" became Chapter 10, "The Occupations of Wendell," but the illustrations stayed. They were inspired by *"L'Imagerie Populaire*, an anthology of illustrations compiled and published in Paris by Pierrie Louis Ducharte and René Saulnier in 1926."[41] Barnes freely acknowledged her debt to this book. In the first edition of *Ryder*, there were nine drawings; two additional ones, originally omitted as too risqué, were restored in the 1979 edition, published by St. Martin's Press.

Boni & Liveright seemed not to understand the sales potential of one of the first books by a woman author ever to challenge seriously American laws against obscenity, and they consequently failed to advertise *Ryder* with much conviction. If numbers of Americans were returning from Europe with copies of *Ulysses* in plain wrappers from Paris bookshops such as Shakespeare & Co. to decorate coffee tables, surely the same large clientele would have been pleased to display the bawdily illustrated book by Djuna Barnes.

Boni & Liveright missed on *Ryder* at a time when the firm was in financial trouble (owing in part to risky speculation in Broadway plays). Friede deemed sales "purely problematical. It may sell well, and on the other hand, the chances are that it will sell hardly at all."[42] Presumably he wished to reduce Boni & Liveright's risk to the minimum because of its financial instability, but if his judgment of the sales potential of their other books was similarly off the mark, it is little wonder that the firm went out of business. The *New York Times*

Book Review for 8 September 1928 listed *Ryder* as one of six current best-sellers, and sales were so strong that the first printing quickly sold out.[43] By the time Boni & Liveright could manage a second printing, interest had faded and the opportunity was lost.

In the next year, Barnes sought the help of the Authors League of America, hoping to disentangle herself from Boni & Liveright, who held the options on her next two books; and in 1933, she consulted the literary agent William Aspenwall Bradley. Bradley wrote her that the now foundering publisher had her bound hand and foot: they could allow *Ryder* to go out of print without invalidating their contract with her, and still had first-refusal rights on her next two books. Boni & Liveright advanced Barnes $1,200 in 1933, presumably for *Nightwood*, even as they were going under.[44]

At least the royalties allowed Barnes and Thelma Wood a geographical center in Paris. *Ryder* was dedicated to Wood, but only her initials appeared, because of Wood's nervousness about any publicity surrounding their relationship.

In August 1927, largely with royalties from *Ryder*, Barnes purchased an apartment at 9, rue Saint-Romain, in one of two new elegant brick buildings, set back from the street, around the corner from the rue Vaneau metro station.[45] She and Thelma moved in at the end of September, after having workmen remove a wall. The flat was on the fifth floor, up stairway D, in the building to the right. Barnes's new home had three rooms, a bath, a kitchen, and a maid's room, which served as a studio for Thelma and a guest room for visitors such as Charles Henri Ford. There were hardwood floors and two fireplaces in white marble.

Descriptions and inventories tell us how the Barnes-Wood apartment looked: The hallway was decorated with a large mirror, an African rug, and two red-and-gold chairs. The "grand salon" held a large oak provincial table, two heart-shaped mirrors, two oak bookcases, seven ecclesiastical pillows, and two pairs of white organdy curtains with red flowers. The bedroom, painted pink, contained sixty-seven pictures on the wall (one of them was of Saint Stephanus, painted on glass), church roses in tinsel, one church runner over the mantel, and one china Virgin. There were many books on Catholic philosophy. In the kitchen were Quimper dishes. Barnes was especially fond of a Spanish *poupée* and a griffin.[46]

In the same building lived Mina Loy (1882–1966), who, next to Thelma Wood, was probably Barnes's closest friend during the 1920s and arguably one of the most talented.[47] Primarily a poet, she wrote plays, painted, designed elegant lampshades, and occasionally acted. Born in England in 1882 (she was Jewish on her father's side), Mina Loy was a good-looking woman who attracted people wherever she went, and when her two daughters, Joella and Fabienne, were with her, the three beauties could cause all the heads on the boulevard to turn in their direction.[48]

Acclaim was essentially meaningless for Loy, however, and she never cared to promote herself as the talented poet and painter she was. What others thought was of little concern—privacy was what she valued, and the freedom to rattle the bourgeoisie with dramatic statements. Her radical antibourgeois *pro arte* values were precisely those of Barnes.

Loy had studied painting at various art schools; in 1899 she went to Munich to work with Angelo Jank, and in 1901–2 she studied with Augustus John in England. On the last day of 1903, she married the Englishman Stephen Haweis, whom Mabel Dodge Luhan described as "very fin-de-siècle and sad."[49] Loy lived with Haweis in Paris, where she came to know Gertrude Stein, then they moved to Florence in 1906. They separated in 1913. Loy mingled with the futurists in Florence and had affairs with Filippo Tommaso Martinetti (1876–1944) and Giovanni Papini (1881–1956). In November 1916, she moved to New York, where her reputation as a radical thinker, feminist, experimental poet, and spokeswoman for the avant garde preceded her.

By this time Djuna Barnes and Mina Loy had mutual friends, including Mabel Dodge and Carl Van Vechten; a bit later, the circle expanded to embrace Laurence Vail, Marcel Duchamp, and Man Ray. Barnes met Loy and Marcel Duchamp in Man Ray's studio. Loy linked up almost immediately with the "291" circle of Alfred Stieglitz, Walter Conrad Arensberg, and Alfred Kreymborg, and the circle of her fame

soon widened. On 17 February 1917, the *New York Evening Sun* selected Mina Loy as the epitome of the "Modern American Woman."[50]

Late in 1916, with William Carlos Williams, Mina Loy played a
lead part in Alfred Kreymborg's *Lima Beans* at the Provincetown Play-
house, where she would often have been in the company of Djuna
Barnes. In 1918, in Mexico City, when the divorce from Haweis was
final, she married Arthur Cravan (1887–1918?), a nephew of Oscar
Wilde, and a boxer hero of the Dadaists and Surrealists, who apparently disappeared in Mexico while she was pregnant with Fabienne.

Some say that his body was found in the Mexican desert, but of
Cravan's disappearance, William Carlos Williams wrote:

> he bought and rebuilt a seagoing craft of some sort. One evening,
> having triumphantly finished his job, he got into it to try it out in
> the bay before supper. He never returned. Pregnant on the shore,
> [Loy] watched the small ship move steadily away into the distance.
> For years she thought to see him again—that was, how long ago?
> What? Thirty-five years.[51]

By 1920, Loy was in Paris, seeing much of the expatriate crowd
—McAlmon, Barnes, etc.—and she settled there in 1923. In that
year, McAlmon published her first volume of poetry, *Lunar Baedecker*.
Loy had a workshop at 21, avenue du Maine, where, with her daugh-
ters and other employees, she made collage lampshades, which Peggy
Guggenheim sold in Loy's shop in the rue du Colisée. Mina and Fa-
bienne moved to New York in 1936; they were preceded there by
Joella, who married Julien Levy in 1927.

Mina Loy's daughters didn't care much for Thelma Wood, but they
liked Barnes for her sense of style: she was so dynamic, so sure of
herself, so jaunty, talented, and chic, an electrifying presence. They
also remember Barnes as being mostly alone; her rare companions
were Natalie Barney, Romaine Brooks, Peggy Guggenheim, Laurence
Vail, Jane Heap, Sylvia Beach, and Constantin Brancusi. Barnes often
accompanied Loy and the girls to a café, where Mina would sit and
work a crossword puzzle as the others chatted.

Once, in 1928, Barnes, Loy, and Fabi were walking along the rue

Saint-Romain when a woman, angered by their speaking English, hit Barnes on the head. When Barnes said that she would report the incident to the American embassy, the Frenchwoman excused herself, having supposed Barnes to be English. The franc was suffering against the pound at the time, and opportunistic British shoppers were less than welcome in Paris.

Mina Loy was wary of the Paris scene, for she wished her beautiful daughters to marry well and not become entangled in sexual relationships.[52] Joella, being of seduceable age, was not allowed to visit Natalie Barney, though Fabi, still a child, could do so. Though Barnes portrayed Loy as part of the Barney circle in *Ladies Almanack*, Loy was definitely not a lesbian.

Barnes was something of a disturbing influence in Loy's life. When Joella married Levy, it was falsely assumed that he was rich; Barnes kept asking Loy why she didn't ask Joella to buy her a house in the south of France, why her rich daughter didn't give her more money. This made for tension between Mina and her daughters. On one occasion, Levy walked into a room where Barnes had been and smelled marijuana, which Joella claims that Barnes and Wood occasionally smoked. This deepened their suspicion of Barnes.

In the summer of 1930, when Barnes was in New York, she wrote to Loy about various problems with her Paris apartment: one table was being devoured by worms, and she wondered whether she ought to sell or let the flat. The Wall Street crash was much on her mind: "I don't know if Wall St. crash ruined everyone, but everyone *thinks* they are ruined, so the effect is all the same."[53] She went on to say that advertising had dried up for magazines, and so consequently had income from journalism. She tried to get a part in the Broadway play *Elizabeth the Queen*, with Lunt and Fontanne, but to no avail. Even during the Depression, New York seemed three or four times as costly as Paris. Part-time work for the *Theatre Guild Magazine* would have to do for the time being.

Barnes told Chester Page of a particularly gruesome event associated with the Great Depression in New York. She was walking along a street to deliver an article to *Theatre Guild* when a man plunged to his death before her eyes, close enough so that his brains splattered her fur coat. In Page's words, "she was sickened, brushed off the gruesome pieces, thrust her article at the editor, went home and fainted dead away."[54]

Having a flat in Paris had become a burden to Barnes in 1930, stranded as she was in New York during the Depression, and part of this burden Mina Loy loyally assumed. She would look in from time to time, pay bills, and run errands. As much as Barnes loved Paris, she had begun to feel that her career as an artist had been adversely affected by her exile from New York. The adage "Out of sight, out of mind" was a difficult barrier in hard times. "Oh why did I ever buy a home? Why did I ever meet T. Wood, why did I ever put my face out of my own country . . ."[55]

By 1930, Barnes imagined that she could no longer live with anybody comfortably; like Loy, she preferred solitude. "I've gotten cranky & old-maid like—I don't even like to have an animal looking at me, & when I lay a thing down I want to find it exactly where I put it—its as bad as that!"[56]

Mina Loy, who never really recovered from the loss of Arthur Cravan, left Paris in 1936 for New York and relative obscurity, the consequence of her passion for privacy. Since she took little trouble to keep in contact with friends, Barnes and Loy drifted apart after their Paris days, though they did occasionally correspond. In New York, Loy wrote poetry and, in the tradition of Elsa von Freytag Loringhoven, created collages from scraps picked up from the streets. From 1953 until her death, in 1966, she lived near her daughters in Aspen, Colorado, difficult in her eccentricity, out of place in her talent.

Another important figure of Djuna Barnes's Paris years was Natalie Clifford Barney. Of English, Dutch, and Jewish extraction, Barney was born in 1876 in Dayton, Ohio, the daughter of an extremely wealthy father, who left Natalie and her sister, Laura, each some three and a half million dollars.[57] This was more than enough to enable Barney in 1909 to purchase a three-hundred-year-old house at 20, rue Jacob in Paris and to live there in great style for the rest of her life. Her house became the center of lesbian culture in Paris for half a century. Unlike Djuna Barnes, Natalie Barney had connections to Parisian cultural life and knew most of the major French writers of her day.

Barnes described Barney's salon to Chester Page: " 'A tree grew up in the center of the room. The ceiling was decorated with pictures of scantily clad females.' "[58] In her garden, she had built a "Temple à l'Amitié" (Barnes called it the Temple of Love at the end of *Ladies Almanack*), a Grecian structure that was the scene of concerts, readings, dances, and elegant parties. As Arlen Hansen says, Barney's Friday afternoon salons "rivaled Gertrude Stein's for the importance of their guests. Whereas Gertrude Stein promoted cubism and emphatically identified with modernism, Barney held to the fashions of La Belle Époque."[59] Both men and women were welcome at her salons, as long as they could display undisputed talent, for Barney was snobbish and selective.

Whereas Stein knew that she was a writer of great merit and looked for protégés who would reflect her influence, Barney was more interested in supporting the arts in general, and especially women of talent. Her book *Les Aventures de l'Esprit*, written to spread the word about her circle, contains impressionistic short chapters on various women writers and some men, such as Paul Valéry. In her chapter on Barnes, she quotes several pages of the story "Aller et Retour," plus a few poems, and includes remarks that are not always complimentary; for example: "I never introduced an author more gauche and more incapable of helping her own cause."[60]

A literary fragment in Barney's papers called "An Impression of Djuna Barnes & Her Book by the Amazon of Remy Gourmont" influenced the chapter on Barnes:

> She has wrung from raw material of life poems that are decompositions of its essence, dialogues that are duels . . . her physique is as original and as composed as her work—though perhaps more limited. The first thing one notices is the charming *tilt* of her features and everything about her slant up or down. Her up turned well-sharpened nose, meeting her sideways down-bent hat at right

angles (a strip of auburn hair completes the other hat-forsaken profile! The robin-egg look to her eyes . . . the large square teeth of a
3 year old thorough-bred (equal to 33 in women?) the angular, yet
feminine hang of her clothes . . . the broad palm of the hand (a
gathering in of many paths and many reins!) the fingers tapering
command of pen-and poison. A pen dipped in the blood of her
models . . . & creator.[61]

Barnes, in turn, was willing to play the role of literary agent for
Aventures while in New York. Barney expected loyalty and cooperation
from her circle and wanted to be celebrated by those she patronized.
Many years later, in an ungenerous mood, Barnes wrote that Natalie
Barney was "a cheap—well kept, smug, over fed, lion hunting
S.O.B."[62] But after some years in journalism, Barnes knew on which
side her bread was buttered and was willing to oblige her patron by
writing *Ladies Almanack*, a satire on the Barney circle (a "slight wig-
ging," as Djuna called it in a later preface), which Barney adored.

Ultimately this work may have earned Barnes even more money
than *Nightwood*, because it made Barney a lifelong devotee who could
be depended on in emergencies. Late in life, she would give Barnes
a monthly stipend; since the donor was not known for her generosity,
this stipend was a sign of great respect. Dolly Wilde, Oscar Wilde's
niece, was envious: " 'Why should *you* be the one with genius?' said
Dolly to Djuna. 'If anyone has it, it should be me.' 'But it's Djuna,'
said Natalie."[63]

Despite her occasional negative comments about Barney, it seems
that Barnes was genuinely fond of her. She became less tolerant of
her protégées:

> I can't any longer talk to "the Girls" Solita, Katie, Alice, Marga-
> ret—they have gone out of my life somehow—Natalie is, as
> you know, a "character" & thats a great deal, but her friends are
> too boring—& when she is not alone she loses 90 per cent of her
> charm for me—Dolly very hard to take—so damned conceited.[64]

Djuna Barnes probably met Natalie Barney in 1924. In 1927, she
offered Barney her maid, Berthe, who stayed with her until her death,

though Berthe did complain to Barnes about her treatment at 20, rue Jacob. Renée B. Lang said that Natalie Barney claimed to have been Djuna's lover; though Djuna denied this, it could well have been true. Barnes always said that she had been faithful to Thelma Wood, but Barney may have pressured Djuna into a brief affair soon after their first meeting.[65]

Barney knew at twelve that she was a lesbian, and she never wavered from her orientation. Once, she invited Lang and her nephew to lunch at rue Jacob. After the meal, she took her usual rest, leaving Lang and the nephew to twiddle their thumbs across the room. At one point, she said to the boy, "Come lie down with me," but he was shy. She then said, "Come lie down with me, and then you can say that you are the only man who ever went to bed with Barney."

Lang saw Barney as interested only in her own pleasure, caring little whom she hurt with her promiscuity. She deplored possessiveness and wished her friends to be sexually free and without conscience. Many, such as Renée Vivien, Romaine Brooks, and Dolly Wilde, were hurt by her infidelities, but since she was wealthy, she felt free to do as she liked. According to Lang, Barney was uninterested in politics, had no social principles, and didn't read much or take an interest in the arts except to promote the careers of her protégées. As lacking as she was in serious intellectual commitment, Barney did work hard to introduce her circle to the world via loosely conceived books such as *Les Aventures de l'Esprit* and *Nouvelle Aventure de l'Esprit*.

Lang believed that friendship for Natalie Barney implied the right to be manipulative. In the 1950s, she wanted Lang to sit at her side and write a book about her, even though Lang was already engaged in writing on another subject. Lang refused, saying that Barney was too insensitive and authoritarian for such an enterprise to be a success, which drove a wedge between them. One can well imagine the same pressure being applied on Djuna Barnes over the writing of *Ladies Almanack* or on Radclyffe Hall, who depicted Barney as Valerie Seymour in her 1928 novel *The Well of Loneliness*.

Barnes remembered with pleasure a trip to the Pyrenees with Natalie Barney in the 1920s:

> I remember you and Mina and that "mad chauffeur" of yours, and the car you shared with, I think it was your sister Mrs Dreyfus (?), and how frightened Mina was of the Pyrenees, or should I say the Alpes-Maritimes, and how you came into our rooms to shut out the night air (I don't know how Mina felt about it) which I liked, and which you, like all good Frenchmen, considered worse than death. . . . And now I am remembering that delightful Englishwoman, was it Lady Westmecott (?) and her bath tub-full of parrots, and of Honey Harris, and her sorrow with the person of the high Russian boots . . .[66]

Since Djuna Barnes's unsteady sources of income often failed to support her stylish tastes, her preference for restaurants as opposed to dining in (she could scarcely boil water), and the nightlife in cafés and pubs, she badly needed patrons to whom she could turn. Natalie Clifford Barney and Peggy Guggenheim appreciated Barnes's genius, wit, and good company, and they were, within reason, ready to help. In June 1933, when Barnes found that she was pregnant in Tangier, it was Barney she asked to wire her money so that she could return to Paris for an abortion. She never read Natalie Barney's books, which were written in French, but she was grateful for many favors.[67] As for Barney, she reread *Ladies Almanack* many times and often wrote Barnes letters expressing admiration and gratitude for this delicious satire. In many ways it has become Barney's monument, even though the likeness is not entirely flattering.

Djuna Barnes always claimed to have written *Ladies Almanack* for fun, as a lark, at Natalie Barney's suggestion, and most of it was penned in March or April of 1928, while Thelma Wood was convalescing in a Paris hospital.[68] It was Robert McAlmon who suggested publication, but *Ladies Almanack* was never copyrighted, something its author later regretted. Still, it paid the hospital bill and provided risqué entertainment on the Left Bank.

Barney was, of course, delighted at the suggestion that the work might be dedicated to her, since it was about her, but "Dolly Wilde let out a shriek, told her how her reputation would be ruined, and stopped" the dedication.[69] Barnes dedicated it to Thelma, and Barney had nothing to do with its publication. Robert McAlmon footed the bill for the printing at the Darantière Press in Dijon, which had printed Joyce's *Ulysses*, and Barnes paid for the reproduction of her drawings. William Bird saw the work through the printing and binding, and stored some of the copies. The first set of proofs was corrected at the end of June 1928 and the second around the first of August. Barnes herself colored the twenty-five illustrations in forty of the copies; others were done by her Polish friend Tylia Perlmutter and Mina Loy's daughter Fabienne.

Given the racy subject matter of *Ladies Almanack*, Barnes apparently thought it dangerous to have the page proofs sent to her own address, so she asked Sylvia Beach to receive them. Beach declined, wishing to avoid any official notice for Joyce's sake.[70] As the publisher of *Ulysses* in 1922, she was probably under scrutiny by the authorities. Fitzi Fitzgerald arrived toward the end of June and stayed with Djuna and Thelma until the middle of August; she could have been counted on to import copies into the United States, but they were not ready. In the meantime, Barnes, fearful of confiscation by postal authorities or other legal entanglements, was leery of advertising *Ladies Almanack* until she had smuggled a sufficient number into the United States. Copies were hawked on the streets of Paris, and when Barnes returned to America in the winter of 1928–29, she sold forty-seven copies at fifty dollars and three at twenty-five dollars (presumably all these were hand colored), and felt that she could sell another hundred uncolored copies for five dollars apiece.[71]

Edward W. Titus (the husband of Helena Rubinstein), who had a bookshop, the Black Manikin in the rue Delambre, persuaded Barnes to place his name on the title page, as if he were the publisher, in exchange for selling the book in his shop. When the copies arrived from the binder, he also tried to get Barnes to agree to giving him a large cut of the royalties in addition to the retail markup (even on those copies she sold on the street), which infuriated Barnes and re-inforced her disillusionment with the book trade. In September 1928, she instructed McAlmon to remove Titus's name and address from all title pages and circulars.[72] Barnes named the villain of her late play, *The Antiphon*, Titus Hobbs.

Because of legal uncertainties, Barnes declined to have her name on *Ladies Almanack*, preferring to attribute authorship to "A Lady of Fashion." Titus, who was frequently asked about its authorship, was instructed by Barnes to use "discretion." However, word got out rather quickly.

One can well believe Djuna Barnes's claim that *Ladies Almanack* was not written for the public eye, for it rivals Joyce's *Finnegans Wake* for both obscurity and bawdiness. It is not really an almanac but a satirical biography of one Evangeline Musset *(bien amusée)*, "as fine a Wench as ever wet Bed." Its twelve chapters correspond to months of the year. The story line is digressive, circuitous, and often more silly than amusing, but the bawdy illustrations—"baroque cher-ubs, medieval grotesques, parodic iconography, feminized zodiacs, sexual caricature, and other emblems archaic and arcane"[73]—are entertaining.

There are two interrelated and persistent themes, regarding sex-uality, in *Ryder* and *Ladies Almanack*. In *Ryder*, it is the irresponsi-bility of procreating when one cannot support the children; in *Ladies Almanack*, it is that in avoiding procreation and thus the problem of supporting offspring, lesbian sexuality is more responsible than het-erosexuality. Still, it is quite apparent that Barnes does not really approve of Evangeline's insatiable womanizing, which she pursues as if neither love nor fidelity were plausible goals, but conquest alone is the point of sexuality. Evangeline's search for "converts" is little more than this. Other themes in the book are the torments of love, the futility of wisdom, mortality, and the desire for transcendence.

Scholars have had problems agreeing on the implications of *Ladies Almanack*. Some think that Barnes's target is middle-class values, but this seems off base, since a lesbian world is here assumed. Others see the book as a celebration of lesbianism, which is hard to reconcile with much of the satire. Still others view it as a disloyal work by a woman who had doubts about her own sexual orientation. Certainly Barnes was not targeting either homo- or heterosexuality; she had nothing against responsible free love, but she valued fidelity rather more.

The picture becomes clearer when one compares *Ladies Almanack* with *Ryder* and the later works. Barnes always satirized what was closest to her—family, friends, and origins—often in a mean-spirited way that allowed the full play of her astonishing wit. Evangeline Musset resembles Wendell Ryder in her irresponsible, insatiable desire for conquest, but Barnes's attitude toward Musset seems more bemused than censorious. As with Dan Mahoney, the original of *Nightwood*'s Dr. O'Connor, Barnes would certainly not have found Natalie Barney interesting enough to write about if she had been conventional. For these reasons, it is beside the point to argue that *Ladies Almanack* is either pro- or antilesbian.

The one heterosexual in *Ladies Almanack* is Mina Loy, called Patience Scalpel. Also featured are Señorita Flyabout (Mimi Franchetti), Doll Furious (Dolly Wilde), Lady Buck & Balk (Lady Una Trowbridge), Lady Tilly Tweed-in-Blood (Radclyffe Hall), Bounding Bess (Esther Murphy), Cynic Sal (Romaine Brooks), and two page figures (Solita Solano and Janet Flanner).

When the almanac months end, in December, Evangeline dies at ninety-nine, and her death causes much grief among the converts. Forty women shave their heads, carry the corpse through Paris on a catafalque, seal her in a tomb for some days, then lay her upon a funeral pyre, where all is burned but the tongue. On this smoldering tongue many mourning women sit as in prayer, later taking it with the remaining ashes in an urn to the altar in the Temple of Love— Barney's Temple à l'Amitié.

When Djuna Barnes's mother told her that she "could never expect to live down that city," meaning Paris, she may have been thinking of *Ladies Almanack*.[74] But Barnes would not live Paris down for a rather different reason: her most important years were spent there, and when she left, the best part of her life was over. The name Djuna

Barnes is synonymous with Paris café life in the 1920s, which she brought to life in *Nightwood*.

These were the best years of Barnes's life: she was sought after, published, and thought brilliant by many whose judgment could be trusted. And except for the uncertainty about her relationship with Thelma Wood, she was as happy as she would ever be.

Thelma

"This night I've been one hour in Paradise;
There found a feather from the Cock that Crew—
There heard the echo of the Kiss that Slew,
And in the dark, about past agonies
Hummed little flies."[1]

The great love of Djuna Barnes's life was Thelma Ellen Wood (1901–70), a tall, handsome, hard-drinking woman from Saint Louis, whom she met at the Hôtel Jacob in Paris in 1921 or 1922.[2] At the time, Wood was the lover of the photographer Berenice Abbott and, according to Barnes, penniless.[3] Barnes told Hank O'Neal: " 'Well, I gave Berenice the extra *e* in her name and she gave me Thelma. I don't know who made out better' " (O'Neal 146). Ultimately it was Barnes who made out better, for if she had never suffered through her eight-year lesbian marriage to Thelma Wood, she would never have written *Nightwood*.

The intensity of Barnes's love for Wood has its origins in her own family, and the patterns are familiar. Barnes's first great love, her grandmother, Zadel, had betrayed her in ways that hurt her deeply. The result was not wholly negative, however, for Barnes re-created a broadly satirical story of Zadel and her progeny in *Ryder*. Although Barnes denied it, the spirit of revenge or satire—often both—motivated all her best work, which usually targeted her family.

Djuna often said that she came to love Thelma because she looked like Zadel, a very odd perception for one who specialized in portraits, for they looked nothing alike. In *Nightwood*, Nora repeats a similar observation: "For Robin is incest too; that is one of her powers"

(*N* 156). Thelma Wood was family to Barnes, and the kinship was somewhere between metaphor and psychology. When this new family member betrayed Djuna, all was not lost, for her grief at rejection was the autobiographical impetus of *Nightwood*. Of course, there is more to the novel than that, as we shall see, but as in *Ryder*, angry vengefulness spurred Barnes on to artistic creation. It does not diminish the great artistic achievement of the novel to say that revenge played a part, but the motive is undeniable: Robin (one of Djuna's pet names for Thelma was "Bird") is essentially an enticingly mysterious sensation-seeker who lacks direction, is torn between animal lust and spiritual longing, and seems indifferent to the pain that her infidelities cause others.

Having struck back in art for what troubled her in life, Djuna Barnes naturally sought justification. As if to defend herself against Emily Coleman's dim view of her capacity to judge character, Barnes wrote to her about Wood: "I must have been *very* young at twenty nine when I met her! Much younger than her nineteen, for her years were aged in sensuality and its consequent need of craft—I was a (truly) virgin yokel looking for lost sheep, and mistook her wolf's blood" (14 February 1937).

It was by the winter of 1922 that Thelma left her flat at 16, rue Delambre to live with Djuna, close to the Café des Deux Magots, a popular watering hole for writers. Like Abbott, Thelma Wood had come to Paris to be a sculptor, but Djuna persuaded her to take up silverpoint, which from then on was her artistic medium. Images of plants and animals predominated: a tiger, a giraffe or some other African animal, a bull, or a banana plant, or a hand with flowers.[4] An exhibition of her work in New York was reviewed in 1931:

> An artist with an exceedingly fresh point of view was presented in a collection of silver prints shown at the Milch Galleries. Miss Thelma Wood has apparently made a very far-reaching study of the animal world and its relation to all trees, shrubs and flowers. In the picture of hers that we have used as an illustration, there is a sense of jungle life rarely so well expressed except, perhaps, by the fa-

mous Rousseau. This is so very lightly and delicately presented, yet with a sureness of stroke and with a confidence that must always be related back to knowledge.[5]

Thelma Wood, the counterpart of Robin in *Nightwood*, was born in either Concordia or Beloit, Kansas, on 3 July 1901, the daughter of Maud and William Barg Wood.[6] She was a native Kansan, and he was from Illinois. With their live-in servant, the family moved to Saint Louis in 1909 and soon bought a fine house at 7651 Hiawatha Avenue, in the Richmond Heights district, where Thelma would have spent much of her girlhood. In 1918, they moved to 4018 Flad Avenue, next to Saint Louis's botanical gardens. Mr. Wood was a sales manager for the Warner-Jenkinson Company, which sold extracts, before he founded his own company in 1915. The William B. Wood Manufacturing Company imported extracts for ice cream makers, bottlers, bakers, and confectioners. After the 1929 stock market crash, the company disappeared from city directories.

Thelma claimed to be part Native American and looked it, with her dark hair and eyes, near six foot height, and muscular strength. As she grew older, her large boots hid thick ankles, her loose clothing a broad beam. While Djuna dressed fashionably, Thelma was rather a sloppy dresser, who usually wore casual men's clothes and a tam or beret. But in Paris, Thelma and Djuna often dressed, as Joella Loy Bayer remembers, in black capes and manly hats, and walked glued together along the boulevards of the Left Bank. It was an image that doubtless stuck in the minds of many an expatriate. They were an astonishing-looking couple.

Berenice Abbott remembered Thelma as sweet, tall, very handsome, a woman who attracted many admirers because of her beauty and youth.[7] She certainly made the rounds in Paris. In addition to Abbott, Thelma had an affair with Edna St. Vincent Millay in the early twenties,[8] and on her knees proposed sex to Peggy Guggenheim (*OC* 33). Andrew Field mentions her madly driving a red Bugatti, minus muffler, through the streets of Paris, but Djuna herself said that Thelma was destitute and starving when she took her in.[9] There is no real inconsistency; she may have received twenty-five dollars a month from home, but this would have run through her fingers in a matter of days. Thelma was incapable of managing money and in Paris was probably supported almost entirely by Djuna. In his *Autobiography*, William Carlos Williams mentions once meeting Djuna and Thelma in the south of France: Thelma "had lost all the cash Djuna had given her at Boule then borrowed from Floss and lost that also."[10]

Emily Coleman did not admire Thelma's mind, remarking to Djuna that "half-intellectuals like Thelma are *perfectly awful*,"[11] but Thelma could talk layman's philosophy, psychology, and theology. Letters reveal her reading Emil Ludwig's *The Son of Man*, Ernest Renan's *The Life of Christ*, Hermann Keyserling's *Europe*, Ernest Dimnet's *The Art of Thinking*, George Amos Dorsey's *Why We Behave Like Human Beings*, Raymond Pearl's *The Biology of Death*, and William James's *The Varieties of Religious Experience*. Such a reading list reflects an intense interest in metaphysical questions.

In one diary entry (8 December 1933), Coleman noted that Thelma Wood was "tiresomely sentimental . . . Loves Jung & Keyserling," but mostly she described her in terms of her sexual attraction. Here is an excerpt from August 1932, written at a time when Wood was visiting Paris:

Peggy [Guggenheim] said Thelma made her think of pale, dead flesh, but Djuna thought her paleness was of life. John [Holms] said the obvious thing about Thelma was sexual vitality, but that other people told him she was just a strapping, fucking wench. Djuna believes her to be a wonderful wild creature, with much evil in her, but all that evil is romanticized.

In December 1933, Coleman recorded her discussion with John Holms on the subject of Thelma's sexuality:

I said, "What gave one the feeling that she lives for sex?" He said the way her eyes were set, and said her face was coarse (which I couldnt see), and said she was made for fucking. I said, "But she has a damnably sweet and unaffected manner, something straightforward about her which, in someone with such a handsome face is most exciting physically." If I had met her at another time Id have taken pains to see her again. But as it was I was too divided, my vanity and curiosity were stimulated (I felt she was slightly attracted to me). . . . Ive never seen a more attractive woman, even on the stage, they dont often have such a compelling face as that. She makes one want to make love. But it isnt in obvious ways, thats what is moving. She *seems* to be interested only in what is going on. One feels that underneath that reserve there is a tremendous power. . . . She hardly opened her mouth the whole evening, her reticence and shyness of course adding to the charm of her handsome face and bent-down head. Next to Thelma (that name!) Djuna appears, to the ordinary eye, unattractive. But she has so much life in her face that the other hasnt got.[12]

Djuna was proud that Thelma captivated other people through sex appeal, but she wanted theirs to be a monogamous relationship and for many years was convinced that it was. God help the man or woman who tried to interfere. This Marsden Hartley found out when he came to the top of the stairs with amorous designs on Thelma, only to be hit on the head by Djuna with a large stick (O'Neal 151). How far down the stairs he fell is a matter of speculation, but it would have been in character for Djuna to help him up.

When Barnes could not have monogamy (and in the circles she frequented, fidelity was a concept found in dictionaries and practiced in the midwestern towns of their youth), she would for many years have nobody. She wrote Coleman on 22 November 1935: "I know from my experience with Thelma, that *no one* could have thrown me into any other arms, not even for the months when I had nothing whatsoever to do with her, not even after we had separated for a number of years, how many? two three? I simply had no room for any other 'terrible attractions.' "

Not so with Thelma. As Barnes went on to write, Wood wanted her "along with the rest of the world." One such evening at the Café Flore is described in a Coleman diary entry (19 December 1933):

Thelma got me between her legs and said I was the servant of art. . . . Djuna wept. I sat comforting Djuna. Thelma went up to another table, where negroes were, and sat down. Djuna was humiliated. John got her out by dancing with her. Poor Djuna said, "Thats her sex appeal." . . . When we met them at the Flore, Djuna looked pretty and lively, Thelma like an old greyhound. . . . John said Thelma looked like a polyp; then he said she was like a stuffed mushroom. I did think she was like an amoeba, feeling about with stumps. But I felt sorry for her Sunday night.

As Thelma slid deeper into alcoholism, she would comb the cafés, apparently looking for casual partners of either sex, while Djuna went from place to place in pursuit, often ending up as drunk as her quarry.[13] Djuna demanded honesty in their relationship as an absolute minimum, but this was impossible for Thelma, who had good intentions but no self-discipline. Years later, Djuna speculated that her mate could not confess her infidelities because of amnesia produced by alcohol.

If there is a key to the Djuna-Thelma relationship, it probably lies at least as much in domesticity as in sexuality. The furnishings of their apartment, their geographical center and a bond between them, are partially listed in *Nightwood* (55–56). Nora even fears that "if she disarranged anything Robin might become confused—might lose the scent of home" (*N* 56). Djuna gave Thelma a doll every Christmas, a symbol of their union, and New Year's Eve was a special day of the year when they thought of each other, a sentiment that must have persisted well beyond their eight years together. They doted on an orange cat named Dilly, taken as soon as she was weaned from her mother, who wore a three-bell collar and used to sit on Djuna's typewriter (O'Neal 176). Back home, Djuna had left a cat named Simonette with her mother. Simon was Thelma's pet name; Irene was Djuna's.

In many ways they were a good match: Thelma was an excellent cook (unlike Djuna), though by dinner she was often too drunk to dine (a favorite drink was rum and cola). She was a fine companion, who was serious about her art, and she was free to travel. Djuna, for her part, had real genius, style, important connections, and a good income from her writing.

Djuna provided Thelma with a safety net, a structure within which she could live, as any family would. If disaster happened, as it often did, Djuna was there to help. In 1924, when Thelma was hospitalized with spinal problems, Djuna wrote and illustrated *Ladies Almanack* to pay the bills. In a letter to Emily Coleman, Djuna said that Thelma "had to go to an hospital for an infected hand, take ether, came out thinking I was just leaving her, burnt her whole arm lighting the gas oven a few days later etc etc. I burst into tears, she's so utterly unable to look out for herself, moves about her life like a moth."[14]

In 1928, Thelma formed a liaison with Henriette McCrea Metcalf (1888–1981), a friend of the novelist Colette (1873–1954). Barnes savagely caricatured Metcalf as the "Squatter" Jenny Petherbridge in *Nightwood*:[15]

> Jenny Petherbridge was a widow, a middle-aged woman who had been married four times. Each husband had wasted away and died; she had been like a squirrel racing a wheel day and night in an endeavour to make them historical; they could not survive it.
>
> She had a beaked head and the body, small, feeble, and ferocious, that somehow made one associate her with Judy; they did not go together. Only severed could any part of her have been called "right." (*N* 65)

Although the caricature was recognizable, since she was small, birdlike, had a crossed eye, and talked incessantly—especially of actresses she had known, such as Sarah Bernhardt, Tallulah Bankhead, and Yvette Guilbert—Henriette Metcalf was nevertheless a much more formidable rival than *Nightwood* would suggest. Born into a wealthy Chicago family in 1888, she was taken to Paris at the age of six months; she began her schooling at the Parisian Convent of the Rule and continued it at Chevy Chase School in Maryland, with Teddy Roosevelt's daughter, Alice, and Mabel Dodge.

Henriette's mother died when she was ten and left her starved for affection. French was virtually her mother tongue, and she knew German and Italian as well. At eighteen, she went to Germany to study at a girls' school in Dessau, where she was unhappy, especially with classmates who asked if there were Indians in Chicago. She inherited

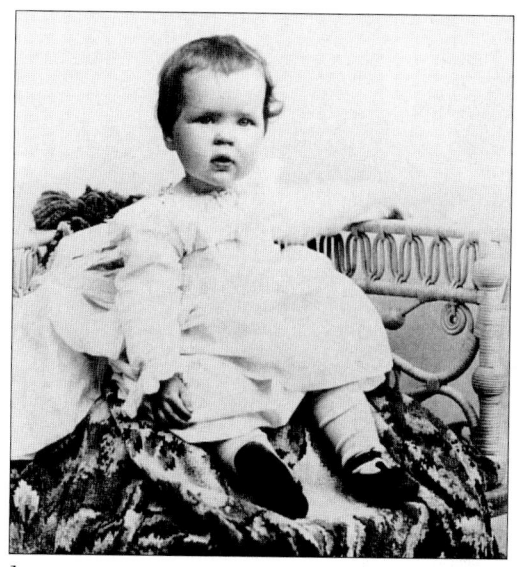

1

2

4

3

■ ■ ■

1. Djuna, aged one

2. Elizabeth Chappell
Barnes in 1892;
photograph taken when
she was pregnant
with Djuna

3. Wald Barnes

4. Djuna, about twelve
years old, and
Zadel

5

6

■ ■ ■

5. The children of Wald and Elizabeth: Saxon, Zendon, Charles (Shangar), Thurn, and Djuna, Morris Park, 1913 or 1915

6. Wald's second family: Duane, Muriel, Wald, Zadel, Buan, and Fanny, September 1916

7. Djuna in her early twenties

8. Djuna undergoing force feeding for her article "How It Feels to be Forcibly Fed," published in *New York World Magazine*, September 6, 1914

7

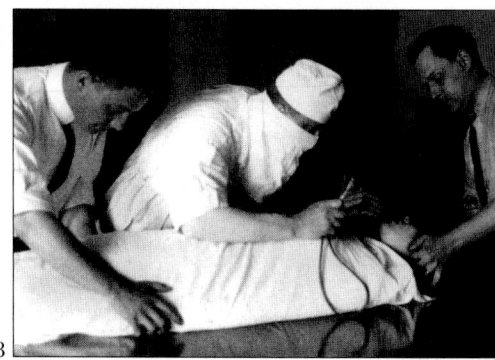

8

9

10

11

9. Mary Pyne

10. Ernst "Putzi" Hanfstaengl

11. Baroness Elsa von Freytag
   Loringhoven and Djuna

■ ■ ■

12

13

14

12. Djuna and Thelma
Wood, 1920s

13. Thelma, 1920s

14. Djuna, 1920s

15. Djuna, Paris, 1925. Photographer unknown,
although this was originally attributed
to Man Ray

■ ■ ■

■ ■ ■

16. Djuna and Mina Loy, Nice, France,
about 1930

17. Djuna and Natalie Barney, Nice,
France, about 1930

16

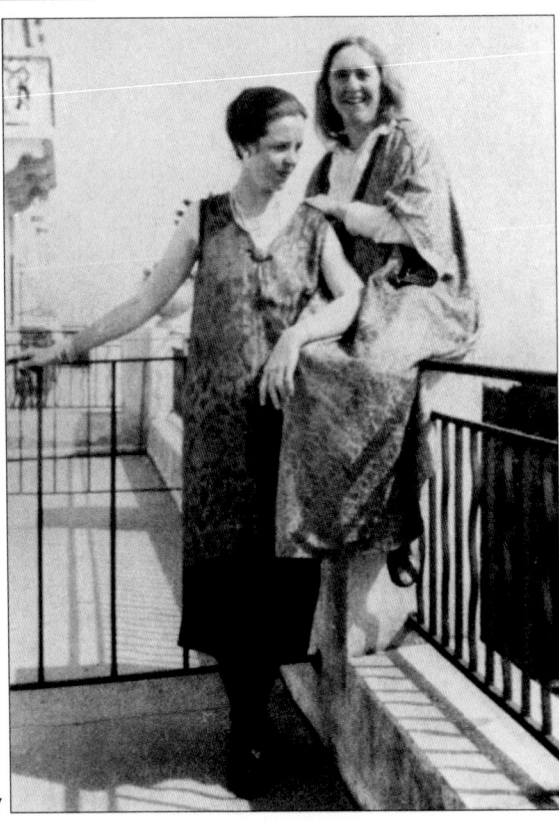

17

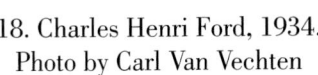

18. Charles Henri Ford, 1934.
Photo by Carl Van Vechten

19. Putzi, Djuna, and Charles Henri Ford,
Munich, 1931

20. John Holms, Djuna, Antonia White, and Peggy
Guggenheim at Hayford Hall, summer 1932 or 1933

21. Emily Coleman

22

23

. . .

22. Sif Ruud as Augusta in
the Stockholm production
of *The Antiphon*,
February 1961

23. Photo of painting of
Cordelia Coker Pearson by
Djuna Barnes, 1947; location
of original painting
unknown

24. Djuna outside Patchin
Place, April 1962. Photo by
Marion Morehouse a.k.a.
Mrs. e. e. cummings

24

both of her parents' considerable estates and was free with money. A bisexual, she was twice married, once to the landscape painter Willard Lloyd Metcalf (1858–1925), and for a short time to Marcus Aurelius Goodrich (1897–1991), nine years her junior, a drama critic and the author of the novel *Delilah* (1941).[16] She came to Paris with Goodrich in 1925 and did some translation for him; he stayed for a year, until their separation, while she stayed an additional three.[17] Henriette Metcalf translated into English the Alexandre Dumas *fils* play *La Dame aux Camélias* in 1931.

Unable to find a suitable outlet for her brilliance, Henriette seemed forever lonely, with a voracious appetite for affection that smothered its objects; she was quick to give presents so as to bind affection, and yet was so overpowering that many people fled her company in dizzy relief. Her knowledge of the theater was encyclopedic; her pursuit of theater people was inexhaustible, beginning as a girl with Bernhardt, whom she eventually succeeded in knowing. Alys Gregory, who later edited *The Dial*, dubbed Henriette at twenty "Fifirella."

Elizabeth de Veer remembered Henriette Metcalf in the years after her separation from Thelma:

> Her intellect was free and ranging but curiously hobbled by superstition. Often it was surprised out of consistency by a poet's words, by the occult or a prognostication in a horoscope, or by a sudden intuition. She was spirited, sweet, domineering, and loquacious. She believed in God, astrology, psychic phenomena, and, intermittently vegetarianism and vitamins.[18]

In middle age, Henriette was to make her house an asylum for orphans and sick and abandoned animals. It was clear that she was out to "rescue" Thelma as well. How they met, given their different social circles, remains a mystery. Henriette's friends were French, not the expatriates of café society, so they may simply have met by chance.

As Thelma began to spend more time with Henriette and less time at home, Djuna found the situation increasingly intolerable and broke with her wandering lover. Barnes first met Metcalf in 1928, when the three women met to discuss the terms of Thelma's separation from Djuna, and in that year Thelma moved to New York, shortly before Henriette. Thereafter Wood returned to Paris only to visit. In New York, the lovers took separate apartments at first, Thelma in the Village and Henriette in Gramercy Park, but they were together every day. The friends in their circle occupied the world of the arts and publishing, but included the wife of Vaslav Nijinsky, the dancer. Henriette had no real financial worries, but she did have two children to keep out of the way, so she sent them off to boarding school and took an editorial job at *Vanity Fair*.

Hedging her bets, Thelma sent an undated letter to Djuna that evoked their lost life together:

> Henriette is very sweet to me and it wouldn't be so easy without her—She insists on buying me clothes though and I don't quite know what to do—she is so insistent and says I am mean and give her no pleasure etc. . . . But I cant be rude as Henriette is such a silly little goodhearted female I feel so sorry for her. . . . Anyway I would rather be with you than have all the money in the world— and I wish we were in the country togeather [*sic*] with many fires and stacks of books—and then a big chicken dinner and we'd play cards and Ill take such good care of you—and be so sweet to you forever. . . .

Thelma wrote Djuna that she would stop drinking if Djuna would take her back, but this promise was clearly specious. Despite her experience with alcoholic lovers, Barnes did not develop a realistic attitude toward alcohol until she had to conquer her own alcoholism in 1950, but she knew enough not to believe Wood.

Another undated letter to Barnes explains Wood's sense of helplessness in the Metcalf affair:

> How could I feel as I did towards her—and in front of you? I have asked her not to come here but have gotten letter after letter saying it would be alright—and that I loved her—I became frantic—then hypnotized and resigned—like the measles. . . . As for the rest of

our eight years you seemed to have had a pretty rotten time—with my brutishness and I'm sorry—sorry—you say you know me now so terribly well. Something is undoubtedly wrong with me—I lack perhaps a conscience or sensibility or memory or logic or all—when I left France I felt as you say unfit for human dignity. . . . I did not mean to reject your friendship—that I took for granted in the course of events—as we loved each other—But perhaps it's grown so colossal in your mind you would not want that either—for after all why an untrustworthy and unmannerly friend?

Thelma said that *Nightwood* proved Djuna had never understood her, but privately she admitted that she understood only too well. Barnes felt guilty about her treatment of Wood in her novel, feeling that if it was a betrayal, the novel might find its justification in its immortality; that, like *Ryder*, it was, fundamentally, written out of love (except for the "Squatter" chapter).

Barnes continually paid a price for her novel. One instance, in the 1930s, illustrated Coleman's point about the falsity of Natalie Clifford Barney: At a party Barney gave not long after *Nightwood* was published, she announced that one of Thelma Wood's former lovers, Elaine, had not after all slept with Wood. Elaine retaliated by attacking Barnes, where it hurt most: " 'Your book has ruined Thelma's life, she is deadly ill & threatening suicide because of it.' " Barnes became dizzy, "dashed into the other room & burst into tears—after telling N. I thought it the most incredible & brutal half hour I'd ever spent. . . . She said 'the trouble with you is, you never know the real point of anything (?) [sic] if T. is going to kill herself, I thought you should know.' "[19] What else are friends for?

Wood didn't precisely ask Barnes to destroy the typescript, but she did hit Barnes in the mouth, knock her down twice, and throw a cup of tea at her when the novel was read aloud, so the author of *Nightwood* could hardly have been wide of the mark in creating Robin Vote. Barnes often stated that she had feared Wood; perhaps violence was one reason.

In the year that *Nightwood* was published, Djuna had nightmares while staying in her Paris flat:

Thelma is dead in them & being buried in a blue china coffin (queer that) as big only as a childs, but when she is laid in it, it becomes the right proportion. I am screaming, then crying with difficult sleeping tears, & in my sleep saying to myself 'You are over dramatizing this now—you know you are' & Henriette running out of the crowd of mourners at me as organ grinders move forward, sad but seeming to be asking me for a *pour bois*—my God![20]

To Natalie Barney, Djuna wrote that Thelma seemed sad and muted, and "turned more & more to the Catholic faith."[21] In a moving letter to Emily Coleman, she summed up her life with Thelma:

She stayed with me last night, Muffin [Peter Neagoe, Djuna's current lover] had been with me in the afternoon, and I lay in bed looking across at her lying in the other, and I had the strangest feelings. Muffin seemed, for the first time, to be *nobody and my lover* (the only reality, and the untouchable and now unclaimable) seemed to be her, sleeping in that other bed. Not that I could do anything about her anymore (or she about me) but she was that terrible past reality, over which any new life can only come, as a person marching up and over the high mound of a grave. . . . But I went over in my mind my feelings for him, and just the fact of her sleeping body across the room seemed to kill him like a powerful disinfectant. . . . I have *had* my great love, there will never be another.[22]

Thelma expressed similar intensity in a letter to Djuna:

. . . some thing will happen and I go to pieces—for instance I dream of you every night—and sometimes Djuna I dream we are lovers and I wake up the next day and nearly die of shame—taking advantage in my sleep of something I know so intimately—and something you do not wish me to have. . . . I'd cut my heart out and send it to you if you cared for it—[23]

Djuna Barnes gave up on fidelity, for neither she nor Thelma Wood, nor Henriette Metcalf, would ever find a lasting love. Thelma, though, was the great love of both these women and of one more whom we shall meet. Metcalf might well have echoed Barnes's often stated view: "I was never a lesbian—I only loved Thelma Wood" (O'Neal 137, 171).

In brilliant prose, Barnes mystifies Robin as an otherworldly creature:

> The perfume that her body exhaled was of the quality of that earth-flesh, fungi, which smells of captured dampness and yet is so dry, overcast with the odour of oil of amber, which is an inner malady of the sea, making her seem as if she had invaded a sleep incautious and entire. (*N* 34)

In the chapter called "Night Watch," the two women meet at a circus, where a lioness seems to recognize Robin as a kindred spirit: "she turned her furious great head with its yellow eyes afire and went down, her paws thrust through the bars and, as she regarded the girl, as if a river were falling behind impassable heat" (*N* 54). There begins the love affair that is *Nightwood*'s chief interest. Robin soon wanders, from café to café, drinking heavily. In "The Squatter," Robin leaves Nora for Jenny Petherbridge, which becomes Nora's great tragedy, an obsession that she attempts unsuccessfully to conquer during the rest of the novel. In the next three chapters ("Watchman, What of the Night?", "Where the Tree Falls," and "Go Down Matthew"), Dr. O'Connor provides what consolation he can for those who desire Robin: Felix, Nora, and Jenny. But Nora is inconsolable, saying to herself: "In the resurrection, when we come up looking backward at each other, I shall know you only of all that company." Robin responds: "Don't wait for me" (*N* 58–9).

Robin has been portrayed as "beast turning human" (*N* 37), drawn to Roman Catholicism perhaps as an antidote to animal lust (*N* 46). *Nightwood*'s bizarre last chapter, "The Possessed," where Nora's dog barks excitedly as the two of them walk down to the small chapel, reveals a mad Robin, worshiping before a "contrived altar" (*N* 169). She slides down before the dog in such a strange way that the dog seems maddened with fear.

The ending of *Nightwood* gave Djuna much grief, for despite her protests to the contrary, readers interpreted it sexually. Her friends did, and surely Thelma did. To suggest that one's former lover has become so unselective and deranged as to copulate with a dog before the rejected lover's very eyes would surely be one of the most savage attacks ever perpetrated by a novelist.

Whenever Barnes came to know anybody well, she eventually brought up this ending. To Chester Page, she insisted: "The dog is *not* being romantic towards Robin! It is furious at the mystery of her drunkenness, a kind of exorcism of what it does not understand."[24] The scene had been suggested by her friend Fitzi, who once, when drunk, playfully pretended that her dog, Buffy, was her sweetheart. Her strange behavior made Buffy highly nervous.[25]

Despite the denials, there is a pattern to be observed: Barnes had lodged the accusation of bestiality in an earlier work, *Ryder*, where it is implied that Wendell, whose counterpart is Barnes's own hated father, Wald, copulates with his farm animals. In *Nightwood*, Robin turns from altar to dog, suggesting an ambivalence Barnes probably felt to be characteristic of Thelma Wood, whose artistic subjects were often animals and whose nature seemed torn between good and evil. Then, too, Robin was the name of one of Peggy Guggenheim's dogs.[26] This clear message about the animality of Thelma Wood could be neither retrieved nor obscured by authorial interpretation.

Djuna also found a way to exorcise Wood when she cleaned out the storage room of their Paris apartment, as she described to Emily Coleman:

> . . . really what an *idiot* I was—her stock was so exactly what the young, budding St Louis homosexual would have, De Sade, Chanson de Bilitis, the poems of Wilde, the French texte for anything voluptuouse, the newest movement in German art, the surrealists, her drawings, worst of all her note books full of "lamb chops so much, candy for Djuna so much" . . . and sketches of butterflies!!!! . . . This sounds terrible, I really love her, but I know her now,—she should be damned glad for Nightwood, and to what I made her, instead she's sulking, and won't write.[27]

Whatever mysterious, otherworldly qualities Djuna Barnes might have imputed to Thelma Wood's fictional counterpart were now gone.

The spell was broken; no lioness would genuflect in recognition of her wild spirit. Still, Djuna felt that her terrible suffering had taught her much. Beyond the revenge motif, *Nightwood* was not simply an attack on an unfaithful lover but a protest against the conditions of life itself, in which the fulfillment of all desire seemed an impossible goal. Indeed, each woman had had her greatest love, and neither ever had another of the same intensity. Among the souvenirs of that one great love to be found in Djuna's New York apartment was a photo album of Thelma Wood and some of the books she left in the storage room, including Schopenhauer's *Studies in Pessimism.*

Thelma was attached to Henriette Metcalf in New York from 1928 until March of 1934, when they moved to a country house (Penny Royal) on forty acres in Sandy Hook, Connecticut.[28] The house deed was eventually amended to make Thelma co-owner. Whether or not the imminent publication of *Nightwood* was a factor in their decision to move to the country is a matter of speculation, for there are other factors to be considered: both women loved animals, Henriette had no need to be employed, and the seclusion must have appealed to them.

Tension would soon grow between them, for Henriette was like an obsessive schoolmarm and Thelma like an incorrigible pupil. The latter's drinking had been a source of constant dispute, as had the former's domineering attitude. Frustrated at Thelma's idleness, Henriette set her lover up in a gourmet catering business in Westport, which failed because of Wood's ineptitude in practical matters. Metcalf might have agreed with Barnes's point that "you can't re-work God, which is a womans eternal effort."[29]

Eventually Metcalf decided to help Thelma financially on the condition that she move out, which probably happened in 1942–43. Thelma wanted Penny Royal, but Metcalf wouldn't sell her half, which delayed the settlement. In September 1945, the house was finally sold, and on 22 August 1946, Thelma signed a will that left her estate to Margaret Behrens, her new partner; it was executed primarily as a slap in Henriette's face. The witnesses to the will were in fact Henriette's friends. The "marriage" of Thelma Wood and Henriette Metcalf had lasted for sixteen years, about twice as long as that of Wood and Barnes.

After the separation, Metcalf moved into nearby Newtown, Connecticut, and led a rather lonely life. She continually reached out to unfortunates and in 1952 adopted a war refugee, a Dutch boy, to whom she eventually willed most of her considerable estate. With her own children she had a troubled relationship, but her daughter, Rosalind, was fortunate enough to inherit her French books.

Thelma moved to Margaret Behrens's house in nearby Monroe perhaps in 1943. Behrens's father had been a grocer who became mayor of Bridgeport, and she was active first as a realtor in the area, then as the owner of an antique store. Henriette's friend Caroline Stokes remembers Behrens driving a jeep around Newtown, accompanied by Thelma, in beret, dangling a long, booted leg out the side.

Thelma spent her last years living quietly in Monroe, where in all seasons she wore a navy-blue tam and mannish clothes, still the *somnambule* but now much heavier, wandering the dusty roads with her companion, both with walking sticks. They sometimes attended town meetings, for Behrens was intensely interested in civic affairs. Their house at 515 Fan Hill Drive in Monroe was very old and beyond restoration; there Thelma would do some yardwork, always careful to ask Behrens what she should do next.[30] On 10 December 1970, Wood died, in Danbury Hospital, of breast cancer that spread to her spine and lungs; before her death she wished to see Metcalf one last time but was refused.[31] After the breakup, Wood simply ceased to exist for Metcalf. A Congregational pastor conducted services over a closed casket at a funeral home; three relatives and seven friends were present. The mourners then drove for dinner and drinks to the Yankee Drover Inn in Newtown. Thelma's ashes were interred in the Behrens plot in Bridgeport.

After Thelma's death, Behrens wrote grief-stricken letters to Barnes, whom she probably never met. In one letter, she asked for an interpretation of Thelma's confession that she, Thelma, would have been a great artist if she had not done "one thing." What that offense against the muses was, Barnes didn't know, or wouldn't say.

CHAPTER 8

Charles Impossible Ford

"She noticed that his eyes lay in the side of his head, not as human eyes that are lost in profile, but as the eyes of beasts . . ."[1]

D juna Barnes's love story "Behind the Heart," published only after her death, celebrates her transitory passion for the young writer Charles Henri Ford, whom she affectionately dubbed Charles Impossible Ford. The story takes place in Paris during a week in the late summer of 1931, when she was thirty-nine and he twenty-one.

When Jane Heap gave up on *The Little Review* in the spring of 1929, Ford saw a chance to establish a new journal for avant-garde literature. He called it *Blues: A Magazine of New Rhythms.* (In the 1940s, Ford would edit the important avant-garde magazine *View*.) That he published *Blues* from Columbus, Mississippi, a town remote from the centers of culture, was not seen by either him or his New York partner, Parker Tyler, as a serious impediment to success. Indeed, the two men kept the journal going from February 1929 until the fall of 1930 and in that short time managed to publish Gertrude Stein, H.D., Ezra Pound, Eugene Jolas, William Carlos Williams, Louis Zukofsky, Kay Boyle, and others. A fellow Mississippian, William Faulkner, submitted a story called "Death in Naples," with a nod to Thomas Mann, but *Blues* folded before it could appear.

In the spring of 1931, several months before "Behind the Heart" takes place, Barnes was living at 62 Washington Square South in Greenwich Village, briefly reunited with Thelma Wood. Ford had written a short notice about *A Night Among the Horses* (1929), Barnes's collection of poems and stories, for *Blues*: "In these stories of abnormality Miss Barnes reveals an astuteness of manufacture, and an intellectual tension verging at times on genius or insanity. Aside from the poetry, derivative in most cases, every piece in the book is almost too deeply disturbing." Ford and Tyler subsequently paid Djuna a social visit. Wood hated Ford on sight, spewing jealous invective.

Ford's boyish good looks attracted Barnes, and around April they went dancing at the Cotton Club in Harlem. They got rather drunk on whiskey and kissed in the taxi on the way back to the Village. A few kisses made it to Ford's long sideburns, where the lipstick wouldn't show. Barnes's famous beauty so captivated him that he saw her again on 29 May, on his way to embark on the *France* for Europe. She kissed him good-bye, saying, "I just wanted you to know that I could kiss you sober too." On 11 July, she also sailed for Europe, arriving in Paris a week later.

Ford's diary entries in *I Will Be What I Am* are very precise about these days. On 21 July, Ford went with a friend named Bart to see Barnes, whom they found suntanned, golden-haired, and appealing. They drank "vile" tea among cartons of clothes and talked. On 3 August, Ford and Barnes had drinks at the Dôme and dinner in a café near the Seine, where they dined on frog legs and omelets, then they went on to the Café Flore for coffee.

In early August, Barnes began having stomach pains, and on the thirteenth she was taken by the *New Yorker* journalist Janet Flanner and her companion Solita Solano to the American Hospital in Neuilly, where she was operated on for appendicitis. Ford visited her every day, and when she was released, on the nineteenth, he was invited to stay at her apartment until she recovered. Ford stayed in the *chambre de domestique* two flights up and brought her meals on a tray. Sometimes in the evening she hypnotized him with bedtime stories, for she was a great raconteur in the tradition of her grandmother, Zadel, whom Barnes imitated in bleating, goatlike, "Little Nell," the long-suffering character in Charles Dickens's *The Old Curiosity Shop*. On 26 August, Barnes was well enough to go out for a walk, so they strolled through the Luxembourg Gardens, then went to Shakespeare & Co., where she bought a book of poems by Gerard Manley Hopkins.

At this point, *Nightwood* was already more than a vindictive gleam in Barnes's eye but, still called "Bow Down," less than a polished typescript. Barnes had stopped thinking of Thelma Wood as her partner, perhaps, in 1929, though they visited each other occasionally for several years more, during which time there was still some hope of reconciliation. Their flat in Paris, at 9, rue Saint-Romain, is where "Behind the Heart" takes place. Though Wood would always be remembered as the great love of Barnes's life, Ford provided sweet companionship and solace in trying times.

As they huddled together in rainy, chilly Paris, Barnes told Ford that she wished to write a story about their time together, and for her it would be a new kind of story, which truly sprang from a region nearer the heart.[2] There is in that story sweetness, vulnerability, and none of the bitterness or irony characteristic of Barnes's earlier stories.

The lines from "Behind the Heart" that Ford always remembered were: "he slept many long hours like a child" and "she noticed that his eyes lay in the side of his head, not as human eyes that are lost in profile, but as the eyes of beasts." The animal imagery recalls that associated with *Nightwood*'s Robin Vote. Barnes used her experience as a portrait artist consistently and with telling effect: she was fascinated by the contours of the boyish Ford's features, as by his walk, even by his sleep. Although he is unnamed in the story, she calls her persona Hess, which is the name of her autobiographical persona in early drafts of *Nightwood*.

The narrative device of a story told to a third party, "Madame," is familiar from Barnes's stories of the 1920s, yet Barnes offers something more. This love story in the time of rain, with its echoes of death, told with painful honesty in simple yet carefully crafted phrases—a love story about convalescence from surgery and falling in love with one's nurse—suggests Ernest Hemingway's *A Farewell to Arms* (1929), which had recently been published. But the autobiographical impulse that prevails is as valid as Hemingway's.

Why was "Behind the Heart" not published during her lifetime? Barnes probably lent the typescript to Ford to read, but when their passion cooled she had second thoughts about celebrating in public yet another relationship gone dead. Readers might get the impression that she was a difficult person.

As for the very young Ford, he was "as loose as a cut jock strap," as he said, which seemed not to bother Barnes, who, after Wood, had about given up on fidelity. He was quite open about his promiscuity, and, according to him, his bisexuality was not a problem because their sexual orientation was identical: one fell in love with the person, not the gender.[3] His letters to Parker Tyler show that he loved Barnes, and an unpublished letter of 27 August 1931, written during her convalescence, reveals his joy in their life together. He praised the flat,

> with its two fireplaces with big heartshaped mirrors above the mantles [sic]. Her bedroom has lots of sweet pillows which she has had her head on for days but she is up now. . . . D—— likes Chaucer, Wuthering Heights, Dostoevsky and she likes me. . . . She said she'd rather have too much love than too little. It has been beautiful with her in a way that it has not been beautiful before with anybody else.[4]

Ford came to know Barnes's friends. One morning, Mina Loy came into the apartment, picked up a bottle of vinegar, and shook it all about, saying, "Did you have a night of love, did you have a night of love?" On another occasion, Ford remembered a grand reunion with Kay Boyle and Laurence Vail. Vail was still in love with Barnes and had been the subject of Thelma Wood's frequently jealous remarks some years earlier.

Ford had come to Paris hoping to persuade Gertrude Stein to back the publication of a homosexual novel, The Young and Evil (originally called "Love and Jump Back"), a veiled autobiography that he wrote with Parker Tyler.[5] Stein was very taken with the novel—she thought it showed her influence—and offered a blurb saying that the novel "creates this generation as This Side of Paradise by Fitzgerald created his generation." Her enthusiasm was shared by Carl Van Vechten, who, according to Barnes, thought Ford "the next great genius—crazy about his book—&, of course, could devour C.F. personally."[6]

As for Barnes, she read it straight through in one sitting, finding it quite amusing, not "arty," as she had expected. Still, it did not meet her high aesthetic standards. Her ungenerous comment, written for William Aspenwall Bradley, the Paris-based literary agent whom Barnes had contacted on 8 July 1932 about *The Young and Evil*, is noted on the back of the current edition:

> Never to my knowledge, has a certain type of homosexual been so "fixed" on paper. Their utter lack of emotional values—so entire that it is frightening; their loss of all Victorian victories: manners, custom, remorse, taste, dignity; their unresolved acceptance of any happening, is both evil and "pure" in the sense that it is unconscious. No one but a genius, or Mr. Ford and Mr. Tyler could have written it.[7]

Since he sometimes imitated Stein's style, Ford secured her patronage, though he sometimes referred to her as "Sitting Bull" and her companion, Alice B. Toklas, as "the Knitting Maniac." Stein's enthusiasm for Ford's novel may also have been the kiss of death for Barnes, because she intensely disliked Stein, who generally ignored her in favor of Ford when they visited. Barnes said that Stein thought that she herself was the world's greatest writer and Henry James was second (Ford 176). This animosity may have been flavored by an encounter with Stein's brother, Leo, who, more than a decade earlier, had said that Barnes's artwork had no weight; at the Dôme, she now asked him about the weight of his own painting, a question he must have found puzzling (Ford 176).

Years later, Barnes told James Scott that Stein

> couldn't write for beans! But she did write "A rose is a rose is a rose"—that was good. The only thing she ever wrote that was. D'you know what she said of me? Said I had beautiful legs! Now, what does that have to do with anything? She said I had beautiful legs! Now, I mean, what—what did she say *that* for? I mean if youre going to say something about a person . . . I couldn't *stand* her. She

had to be the center of everything—a monstrous ego. Her brother, what was his name? Leo Stein. Poor thing. He was a nice boy. She simply *ate him up!*[8]

Ford records one conversation in which Stein asks Barnes about *The Young and Evil*, but literary chitchat was not Barnes's style. "Well, it's not sentimental," she said, which infuriated Ford. Stein went on to praise the readability of *Blues*, hoping Barnes would endorse this opinion, but Barnes said that she had never read Ford's journal. Pursuing the matter, Stein asked Barnes: "Well does he show any feeling for words I mean do you think he is a born writer?" Barnes said that she did not know. At that point Ford realized that "what Stein was wanting to know was if the book showed her influence" (Ford 183).

In the middle 1930s, when it became obvious that Ford was not really a protégé of Stein—he had taken up with the Russian painter Pavel Tchelitchew (1898–1957) and the Sitwells—Stein would barely speak to Ford, as happened one evening at Natalie Barney's (Ford 331).[9] Barnes's predictable response was: "So Stein has done the turn on you? I knew she would. Why not, she has done it to everyone else" (Ford 346–47). In later years, Barnes found infuriating the general assumption that she had been a friend of Gertrude Stein's in their Paris days.

When Barnes recovered from surgery, she proposed to take Ford to Munich, Vienna, and Budapest, a trip they made in October—when the theater season began—of 1931. As it turned out, they spent four to five days in Munich, eleven days in Vienna, and, entering Hungary on 8 October, a week in Budapest.

In Budapest, they stayed at the Hotel Bristol, on the Danube, visited coffeehouses and night spots, and absorbed the atmosphere to the sound of Gypsy violins. Ford remembers that they liked Spolarich's best for the prostitutes, who were there to tempt the officers, with "swords clanking" (Ford 172). For a Hungarian theatrical magazine, Barnes posed with a famous actress for photos, but she hated them because they obscured her cheekbones and made her look like a "creampuff" (Ford 172). In Vienna, Ford remembers visiting the Spanish Riding School, going to hear Jeritza in Strauss's opera *Salome*, and seeing a play by Ferenc Molnár.

In Munich on 17 October, the couple had tea with Putzi Hanfstaengl and his friend Oswald Spengler, who gave them his views on the decline of the West. Barnes listened, though apparently she did not write up the interview for publication. On another occasion, Putzi introduced his visitors to the royal Wittelsbach family.[10] What Barnes really wanted was to interview Adolf Hitler. Around Christmas, *Cosmopolitan* cabled a warm response to her idea, but Putzi said that Hitler wanted the preposterous sum of two dollars a printed word, and so the interview never took place.

Ford's diary tells of their stay in Munich:

We visited the Theatre Museum, former villa of the (late) tragedy-actress Clara Ziegler; D—— loves the theatre: in there were miniature sets, photographs of stagepeople, costumes, prints, etc. But the night of our arrival not knowing what to do we stumbled into a huge café with balcony crowded with the lower middleclasses being entertained by an orchestra blaring forth German music and directed by a buxom lass in Bavarian costume; another night to the Prinzregententheater to see a play of Schnitzler's acted in German, we not understanding two words but it was well done, later we met the leading actor, Waldau, backstage for a short while, D—— having to collect material for her column. . . . The theatre itself was a doll place in the shape of a horseshoe with the boxes in red and gold all around the walls. Again, to a café where they had peasant plays and music, the audience singing and it all seemed amusing to those who knew the language. Munich you know is famous for its dark and light beers and there is the largest room I ever saw, the Hofbrauhaus, where most of the students and people go to listen to a blaring band. However, I haven't even had a beer since Sept. 1, D—— and I decided not to drink and haven't; it's so nice to wake up in the morning without a hangover! . . . Day before yesterday we went out to the tiergarten. . . . Yesterday we visited the former palace of the mad king Ludwig II. . . . We were accompanied by Herr Hanfstaengl. . . . Later he took us to tea at the house of a friend of his. [He] played the piano marvelously for us: Bach and Schubert and Chopin: another time we had photographs taken with the doves in the Odeonplatz (Putsy, D—— and I) and after that we ate white sausages made of young veal and pancakes stuffed with applesauce. The people on the street almost scream at D——'s French hat but you should see the way some of them look: . . . D is planning to stay over and finish her novel instead of returning to New York in November as she had planned. Of course I'm in love with her and think she is wonderful. (Ford 167–69)

On this journey, Barnes took notes for the background of *Nightwood*, which begins in Vienna with a history of the Volkbeins; she had also promised Hiram Motherwell, editor of the *Theatre Guild Magazine*, that she would send articles on Viennese theater for her "Wanton Playgoer" feature, at the time a principal source of income for Barnes.

Years later, Barnes said that she had not enjoyed Ford's company on this jaunt: "When I was there [in Munich] I was in the worst possible company, Charles, who was always ill and yawning and didn't want to look at anything."[11] On their return, Thelma Wood made scenes and was especially angry when Barnes gave Ford Wood's "long military cape," mentioned in "Behind the Heart." In the 1920s, the two women had turned the heads of Parisian café society by walking arm in arm in their capes.

Barnes invited Ford to stay with her for the winter, a welcome offer since he had spent his winter rent money on the trip and could ill afford his room at 9, rue Vanvin. He moved back into Barnes's upstairs room and slept long hours, appearing for breakfast at about one in the afternoon.

Ford wrote Tyler:

D—— and I wander quite a bit, one day have Welsh Rarebits on the terrace of the Café de la Paix, another night crème de menthe at a little bistro on the Seine . . . and look in antique shops which she loves like you do; and buy paper books for 2 francs and flowers for our buttonholes for one franc. (Ford 163)

Earlier temperance vows were now forgotten. On rainy days in Paris, one had breakfast at Lipp's in the early afternoon, washed it down with *bière* demiblonde, then went on to the Dôme or the Deux Magots for more beer, then to other cafés, perhaps ending up at Le Train Bleu for some late-night dancing. One evening at Le Boeuf-sur-le-Toit, Barnes asked the band to play "Saint Louis Blues," a request she could not have made without feeling deeply the loss of Thelma Wood, her Saint Louis woman.

Barnes and Ford generally declined to drink Pernod, which she wished to be stopped from ordering, for she spoke of once drinking three or four with James Joyce and Mina Loy, "and Joyce and Mina and she wandered all over Paris trying to find their way home and she woke up next morning home and Mina sleeping on the floor" (Ford 191–92). This was a time of late-night dancing and dissipation; on 9 December 1931, Ford wrote Parker that he had "been drunk for a week." They lived day by day; he remarked once to Barnes, "live fast, die young, and have a beautiful corpse."[12] At this pace, they seemed to be on their way.

The couple had to be careful about appearing at Natalie Barney's inebriated, because Barney disliked any sign of barbaric excess. Ford remembers the nudes on the ceiling panels, the portraits of Natalie at sixteen, the uncomfortable chairs, and Barnes, full of beer, having to make a sudden, hurried exit to the toilet.

A concert or a party or a visit to Natalie Barney or Gertrude Stein often broke the routine. So did going to the theater. Ford's diary entry of 23 January 1932 says that they saw Cocteau's film *Le Sang d'un Poète*, about which Barnes was enthusiastic. At other times, they went to the Comédie Française, to *Domino* at the Comédie Champs-Élysées, or saw movies: *Smart Money*, with Edward G. Robinson; *The Brothers Karamazov*; and the German film *M*.

Whether in New York, Paris, or Vienna, Barnes was in love with all aspects of the theater: not only the plays but the ambience, the costumes, the curtains—it was her spiritual home from Provincetown days onward, and even in old age she decorated her stage set in the text of *The Antiphon* with paraphernalia of the actors' troupe. In Paris,

Barnes attended Balinese dance, a performance by Sergei Prokofiev at the Salle Pleyel, and the Cirque Medrano, which gave her some ideas for the beginning of *Nightwood*, which features circus performers.[13]

Soon after their return to Paris, Ford asked Barnes to marry him, a proposal he would repeat in Tangier. She may have had reservations about wedding a bisexual man. Then, too, she didn't want children; she had suffered enough playing midwife and nursemaid during her girlhood to find childbearing odious. There were, of course, times in her life, before and after Thelma Wood, when she would have married a man just to be settled—until she remembered her need for privacy, independence, and the peace of mind necessary for creative work.

If Ford was fascinated by Barnes's beauty, he was also entertained by her astonishing, often cruelly acerbic wit. Her motto for Solita Solano (1888–1975) was "Solita, Solita, with the hungry hanging lip."[14] Of Carl Van Vechten's gap-toothed smile, she noted: "you were always expecting him to fall out between his two front teeth." She remarked about Sarah Bernhardt (1844–1923), long since dead, that "Somebody is always breaking into a light trot when they see [her] and she can't do a thing about it." Once, she described being hung over from a night of celebration: "We both felt like death's daughter dragged in backwards" (Ford 179). Of a friend with a hangover, she observed: "He looks like something in the morgue that came up to identify itself" (Ford 365). Ford once asked her: "how do chauffeurs' ears get so dreadful in Paris and she said, 'They *must* do the housework with them!' " (Ford 206). Of penury, she declared: "One cannot live on bird cries and cat calls" (Ford 341).

On Saint Gregoire's Day, 1932, Ford and Barnes went to a fair, played the wheel of fortune, and searched without success for traditional chamber pots with painted eye looking up from the base, as in *Ryder*. Barnes also wanted two merry-go-round horses "at the foot of her bed and the organ playing pipes and drums with the wood figures and painted rococo at the head of her bed!" (Ford 220).

Late in the spring of 1932, not long after finishing *The Young and Evil*, Ford went to Italy in the company of Tyler's friends Carmita

Mariño and her lover Pita Rodríguez. Ford took them around Paris first and introduced them to Barnes, who liked the Spanish-born Carmita, who had emigrated to Cuba. The sadness at the end of "Behind the Heart" seems to capture Djuna's emotions at this particular departure by Ford, though in the story the boy says that he will return in ten days. Instead of returning to Paris, the trio went to Madrid and, in November, continued on to Tangier at the invitation of the writer-composer Paul Bowles, recently seen in Paris, whom Ford had published in *Blues*.

When Mariño and Rodríguez left, Ford invited Barnes to join him in Tangier, and she traveled there from England (where she had also spent part of the preceding summer) in early April of 1933.[15] Despite her affection for Ford, Tangier had not really been her first choice: she was longing for Marrakech, for friends had invited her to stay with them there and, after three weeks, to house-sit. Somehow it didn't work out, and so she went to Tangier, by way of Paris, where she had tea with the Joyces; to Bob McAlmon she wrote that Joyce looked "old and shrunken and sad," apprehending yet another eye operation (22 April 1933).

Barnes's attraction to North Africa sprang largely from her trip there with Thelma Wood in 1927. She told Chester Page of "a funeral procession, in which everyone danced around down the road, and after the burial erected a kind of shrine to feed the birds. 'Wonderful!' she exclaimed. She loved the idea that they celebrated rather than mourned."[16] But her principal motives seem to have been her interest in Ford and the low cost of living Tangier promised.

Paul Bowles lent the couple his studio. In his biography of Bowles, Christopher Sawyer-Lauçanno describes Bowles's "little house on the Marshan, slightly on the outskirts of the city," with a rented piano.[17] Bowles stayed at a hotel in the medina, using the studio only for work. According to Ford, Bowles was an early riser, banging on their door at 7:00 A.M. to resume composing his sonatina.

The accommodations were so uncomfortable that the couple didn't mind vacating. Barnes wrote Mina Loy that Tangier was, after all, not inexpensive (a monthly stipend of forty dollars from Peggy Guggenheim would hardly do), and during the first eight days she slept with Ford on straw on the studio floor, without toilet, heat, water, electricity, or sufficient blankets.[18] To Natalie Barney she wrote that she had an abscessed tooth,[19] and she worried constantly about finding a suitable tenant for her Paris apartment. Disturbing news arrived: her old lover Courtenay Lemon had died on 2 April. In May, it was announced that Boni & Liveright had gone under, which meant that anyone interested in "Bow Down" would have to repay the publisher her twelve-hundred-dollar advance. Barnes took some pleasure in corresponding with friends: she wrote Bob McAlmon that Ezra Pound had recently written about her in *Il Mare*. Still, she was both worried and bored. The strong African sunlight was welcome, but there were limits to her patience.

Barnes complained to Natalie Barney that Thelma Wood wouldn't write: "Can T. intend never writing me again? Is she going to cut me when I see her—if I ever see her again? . . . She has too much to resent—B. Down—C. our lives—our time in Paris—me—."[20] She had seen Wood the previous November in Paris, where Wood was en route to Florence to attend an art school. It was probably on this occasion that Barnes had read to her from her typescript, only to receive a slap and a cup of tea in the face. When Wood did write, Barnes must have opened the envelope with trepidation, knowing that Wood was deeply offended by what she must have believed was the revenge of "Bow Down." Barnes wrote Barney:

> She says the book proves I never understood her—& that she does not much care to have it printed is clear—tho she does not directly ask me to destroy it—I admit the writing game is "dirty" but I hoped the book was good enough—I'm uncertain at the moment, as baby Charles has torn it to pieces as a work as a whole—says it has no plot (which does not so much matter) but has also no design—is written in different styles—does not hold together,—& is not as good as "Ryder" in spite of "splendid spots" about what John thought & Victor too. . . . Only you Lloyd Morris & Solita (in parts) really seemed to be pleased with it. I should not hesitate about it were I not uncertain in my own mind, which is because I

have seen so much of it, worked it over so often & heard so many opinions, that I am confused. I should put it away for a year (Charles says 100[?] years) & then see what I think of it. I am sure it will estrange T. even more than she now is, which I shall not like, but then what do I like just about now? . . . T[helma] is sailing about the 9th of June—no news here—one day like another—fine weather & sea & boats right under the window (am in Arab Quarter) hooting all day & night & I want to be on all of them![21]

After a week in Tangier, the couple found a flat in the Casbah (Babelhsah 63), with a balcony overlooking the bay and a courtyard shaded by a fig tree. It was one of three houses they occupied in Tangier. A local man ineptly cooked their meals and served them green tea. Barnes remembered this tea when she wrote a disturbing article called "Arab-Morocco," on Moroccan marriage customs and laws: "Green tea will be served, sweetened to sickening with large lumps of sugar and seasoned with fresh mint leaves."[22] (This very detailed essay describes plainly and without comment the appalling subjugation of Moroccan women.)

Charming though Tangier was, it was just not Barnes's scene: she felt isolated and would have moved on to Fez or Marrakech if there had been sufficient travel funds. What did Ford do all morning at the beach? she wondered, to which he replied: "I danced and picked flowers."[23] She wrestled with her memories of Thelma and the task of straightening out "Bow Down" so that Ford could help type it. During the days, she revised the typescript, while Ford swam or typed for her or worked on his poems.

Sawyer-Lauçanno says that in the evenings, Barnes, Ford, and Paul Bowles "would often rendezvous, usually in the Medina, near where Bowles was staying, to sit for hours in the Café Central, watching the crowds, gathering various others at their table." In Barnes's "outlandish makeup—blue, purple, and green—she was an object of curiosity to the Moroccans." Ordinarily Bowles was sensitive to such ostentation, but he did not mind this in Barnes because he respected her talent.[24] They drank virtually no alcohol in Tangier, and hangovers were not a problem as in Paris days.

Memories of Ford seemed to annoy Barnes in later years, as she indicated to Emily Coleman: "I really should have pushed him into the sea at Morocco—he is also reported to have told Miss Sitwell that I was a 'better writer than Virginia Woolf'—Miss S. drew herself up with 'she is my best friend & she's coming here this afternoon.' Allan Ross McDougall adds: 'No, Charles didn't leave; he stayed on for tea.' "[25] Part of Barnes's annoyance may have derived from his promotion of his poetry, which was not to her taste. On the verso of a volume of his poems, inscribed: "Please take me seriously, as I love you! Charles," Barnes wrote: "Hair mentioned *17* times—in 30 poems."

Barnes's romance with Ford came rather suddenly to an end. It was not just that the novelty of Morocco soon faded, for she knew virtually nobody and tired of the scene. It was not that she had no interest in the beach, where Ford spent his mornings, or that she was shocked one day to find that the Casbah rats had eaten holes in her stockings. Barnes left Ford because by June she realized that she had stopped menstruating; she was pregnant by the French painter Jean Oberlé, a friend of Peggy Guggenheim's with whom she had an affair that seemed to matter little to her.

On 9 June 1933, Barnes sent a telegram to Barney, asking her to wire sixteen hundred francs (as a loan) to Bankingles in Tangier, because she needed an operation in Paris. The funds came, and on the thirteenth she left for Paris, where Dan Mahoney—*Nightwood's* Dr. O'Connor—performed an abortion. Though he was no physician, Mahoney sometimes earned money as a *faiseur d'anges.* Ford had proposed to Barnes that they marry and keep the child, but to no avail; in a few days, he sailed for Gibraltar, where on 29 June he embarked for Toulon, thence to visit Stein at her country house near Belley. Stein's generosity was not to be despised. Djuna's romance with Ford had cooled for a second time, and now it was to be for good. It had been a love affair with symmetry, neatly framed by two medical emergencies, the later one hastening her return to her beloved Paris.[26]

CHAPTER 9

Hangover Hall

"Emily, you would make marvelous company slightly stunned."[1]

t is now time to introduce formally the most important benefactors of Djuna Barnes's life, Peggy Guggenheim (1898–1979) and Emily Coleman (1899–1974).

Peggy's father, Benjamin, went down with the *Titanic* and left his daughters great wealth, which allowed Peggy and her artistic friends to live in style. Peggy was introduced to Djuna by Laurence Vail in New York as early as 1917 and helped fund her first trip to Paris in 1920. In the next year, at twenty-three, Guggenheim lost her virginity rather casually to Vail, whom she then married, perhaps because married status afforded a gateway to a life of self-indulgence and bought pleasure. Increasingly in the next few decades, this pleasure was sexual, as one way of dealing with grief. Barnes told Chester Page that "Peggy Guggenheim once boasted she had had four hundred men. She thought of it along with the laundry. First she did the laundry in the morning, then turned to the men."[2]

Though often out of her depth among the intellectuals and artists with whom she surrounded herself, Guggenheim found in them the amusement she desired and the instruction she lacked. She kept them about so they could observe how she spent her wealth, but cared rather little if they strained against her short financial leash. Behind her back, and sometimes to her face, her entourage expressed resentment at her pettiness and callousness; like court jesters, they were given to know that they would be supported only so long as they pleased her ladyship. It was not a coterie that accepted largesse with much gratitude, but then few people do. Despite some jealous annoyance, Barnes benefited from Guggenheim's measured but astute generosity for most of her adult life, even after she alienated her benefactor. She had, in effect, a permanent Guggenheim fellowship.

Barnes was jealous of Guggenheim's money and bristled at the idea of charity, but both agreed that the very rich had a responsibility to support the arts. Still, there was frequent tension. Once Djuna told Peggy, "[You] can have a hall of stuffed Guggenheims too; cant you see Ma Guggenheim on a board, like a weatherbeaten moose?" Peggy asked Djuna, " 'All right, what would you do with my money if you had it?' I said: 'I'd be hog enough to have me a nice house, a servant or two, good food and wine for my friends (and myself) for only with a little luxury can one be social and have friends, and the rest I'd give to artists (if any) and to the nuns to give to the poor, to anyone in misery and distress."[3] Barnes especially resented Guggenheim's preference for spending money on paintings rather than on indigent artists.

In the summers of 1932 and 1933, Peggy Guggenheim rented Hayford Hall, an English country estate near Buckfastleigh in Devon. She invited several of her friends to stay there, including Djuna Barnes, who was still unhappy over her breakup with Thelma Wood. Taking refuge in Hayford Hall, Barnes found there a critical community that provided both intellectual stimulation and editorial input for her novel-in-progress. At Hayford Hall, much of the novel that would become *Nightwood* was written or revised.[4]

Guggenheim rented Hayford Hall to please her lover John Ferrar Holms (1897–1934), a brilliant, learned, but very alcoholic Englishman. Peggy had met both him and Emily Holmes Coleman, with whom he was then having an affair, in 1928 in Saint-Tropez. Peggy's marriage to Laurence Vail was nearly at an end when her love affair with Holms began during a skinny-dip in the moonlight.[5] Vail's drunken violence made life intolerable for Peggy; he habitually abused her physically, and once, in a fit of rage, he threw four bottles of wine against the wall of a Paris restaurant. He attacked Holms when he found him kissing Peggy.

Holms's common-law wife, Dorothy, overweight, depressed, and worried, tried to avoid noticing her husband's love affairs, though neither she nor Coleman gave Holms up easily to the carefree Peggy. Two years later, Guggenheim divorced Vail to be with Holms, but he could not reciprocate by cutting the knot with Dorothy. In fact, after considerable tearful harassment, he married her just to satisfy her need for legitimacy, then immediately returned to Peggy. Soon Coleman would also be divorced, but her chance to land Holms had been lost. It was all very confusing, especially for John Holms, pursued by at least three women. There was no end to the complexity of these entanglements: when Laurence Vail cooled down, he married Kay Boyle (1902–1992).

Holms attracted women with his athletic physique, his auburn hair and beard, and his intense brown eyes. His friend Lance Sieveking described him:

> He had an exceptionally well-shaped head with a magnificently broad, high forehead; his nose was straight, his mouth small, and his eyes were a hot brown and rather large. His hair was dark red and inclined to curl, but after that came the surprise. He was tall, just over six feet, with wide shoulders, small hips, and a magnificent chest. His physique was superb. All his movements had the smooth, easy suppleness of grace and strength that made me realise that he must be a remarkable athlete.[6]

A graduate of Sandhurst, John Holms, who would receive the Military Cross for bravery, had been captured by the Germans in the Great War. In prison camp, he met Hugh Kingsmill, who later wrote a book about him. The other close friends who visited him at Hayford Hall were the Chekhov scholar William Gerhardie (1895–1977), author of *The Polyglots* (1925), and the Scottish poet Edwin Muir, who would be Barnes's influential advocate for *Nightwood* and *The Antiphon*.

Perspectives varied on Holms. The novelist Antonia White's

daughter Susan Chitty called him "bearded and ethereal," while Barnes, irritated by his conceit, less charitably characterized him as "God come down for the weekend."[7] Holms was deservedly a legend, for he appeared to have read entire libraries, and even after many drinks could call to memory just about everything that he had read. He tended to lecture condescendingly rather than engage in a dialogue of equals, but his love for literature was deep and intense, and his critical integrity was severe and scrupulously honest. He lived for ideas, which he often discussed over drinks until dawn, though he seldom finished a sentence. Guggenheim said that he "held people spellbound for hours" (*OC* 98).

Sieveking remembers Holms discussing literature in prison camp:

> Holms had a way of producing some obscure fifteenth-century poet of whom neither Hughie nor anyone else had heard, and, in broken sentences, extolling his genius to the detriment of all other reputations. His method of argument was a process of removing other people's examples with a melancholy chuckle, as hardly worthy of serious consideration, until only his own obscure example remained in possession of the field, an easy victor, far, far ahead of the others in perception, penetration, technique, profundity, and truth. There were few of the more generally accepted names to which he would grant greatness. Among them were Donne, Blake, and Shakespeare, but even they had written much that was not worthy, a sad business.[8]

Despite his erudition, Holms suffered from a paralysis of the will to act, due to his drinking; by the time Guggenheim knew him, he could no longer write reviews or do much with his knowledge beyond impressing others with literary chitchat or giving a writer like Barnes an honest critique of her work.

At age thirty-seven, on 19 January 1934, John Holms died under anesthesia on Peggy Guggenheim's kitchen table, five months after falling from a horse at Hayford Hall and breaking his wrist. The anesthetic necessary to reset it after it failed to heal was too much for his system, damaged as it was by many years of heavy drinking. His heart stopped, and he could not be revived. Holms was the great love of Guggenheim's life; she could no more recover from her bereavement than Barnes could from the loss of Thelma Wood, which created a bond of sympathy between them.

Barnes mourned Holms as well. She wrote to Natalie Barney: "I feel it very badly—as I got, toward the end, to value him very much—he understood things people don't know much about"[9]; and to Emily Coleman: "I wept like one demented & could not stop."[10] Again, to Barney, she wrote: "My father (Wendel Ryder) died a few days ago. . . . I was surprised to find that I wept heavily and sadly for the death of John, but for my father only for death itself, and not for him."[11] Holms even came to haunt her dreams.

Barnes remembered the last time she saw John Holms, at the train station with Peggy. " 'When will we see Djuna again,' he said." Barnes kissed them both, seeming to intuit a final departure: "when I kissed John it did not seem to be anywhere, it might have been past, present, in the future, a sort of terrible Einstein farewell."[12]

When Guggenheim met John Holms and Emily Coleman, Coleman was still the secretary to Emma Goldman, who was writing her anarchist memoirs.[13] Born in Oakland, California, in 1899, the daughter of a Hartford insurance executive, Coleman was a 1920 graduate of Wellesley College. Her mother, who died when she was young, passed on to her a propensity for mental illness; after the birth of her son, John (1924–1990), Coleman spent two months at the Rochester (New York) State Hospital.

Emily came to Paris in 1925 with her husband, Lloyd Ring "Deak" Coleman, an American advertising executive whom she had married in 1921, and landed a job as society editor for the Paris edition of the *Chicago Tribune*. Soon thereafter she met Barnes at the Deux Magots. From 1929 through the early 1930s, Coleman lived mostly in London. Her excitable temper was famous. Arlen Hansen tells the story of how Coleman, when fired from the *Tribune*, slapped her drunken boss and according to some reports hit him on the head with a lexicon. In any case, she sued him for "back pay, plus severance," and won.[14]

At times Emily Coleman seemed brilliant, at other times just madly intense, but she shared with Barnes an uncompromising dedication to excellence in writing and all that was finest in literature. A phrase in the introduction to her skillful novel, *The Shutter of Snow* (1930), states the case: "She was possessed of the spontaneous combustion which is to be found in genius and, according to some, the saints."

Coleman's excitability led on occasion to irrational outbursts and violent deeds. (Barnes once said that she would "make marvelous company slightly stunned" [*OC* 140].) Besides *The Shutter of Snow*, which tells of her stay in the asylum, she wrote poems that appeared in *transition* and the *New Statesman*. Her enthusiasms and reckless affairs were often excessive and obnoxious, but her powers of analysis could be quite penetrating. No friend of Barnes ever discussed literature with more passion.

Djuna Barnes and Emily Coleman felt a closeness akin to love but were often at daggers drawn, for together they constituted an explosive chemical mixture that was stimulating but dangerous. For Coleman, Barnes was an acquired taste, as noted in her diary: "with scarlet lips and perched hat . . . Djuna talks through her nose like a sea-horn"; she felt caught between Barnes's "stupidity" and Guggenheim's "maliciousness."[15]

Coleman was arguably the most fiercely loyal friend that Barnes ever had, and the one who fought hardest both to influence *Nightwood* and to get it published; it was she who kept the pressure on Peggy Guggenheim not to stop Barnes's stipend regardless of her often insulting behavior. If one were to award laurels for the greatest contribution made to the artistic career of Djuna Barnes, it would have to go to Emily Coleman (second prize would go to T. S. Eliot.)[16] Her loyalty was rewarded in intimacy: Barnes revealed herself to this friend as to nobody else. After their friendship cooled, Barnes's letters were usually short, factual, and dry. She told one correspondent: "I can't write letters. Have not been able to for years now. I think the experience with those that I wrote to Emily stopped me. One really is a fool to write anything at all."[17] Coleman's long friendship with Barnes was a battle fought to the intellectual and artistic advantage of both women, with Coleman typically pushing to reveal truth and Barnes seeking to avoid self-knowledge.

Before Hayford Hall, Emily Coleman often traveled with John Holms and Peggy Guggenheim, and their times together were a foretaste of the summers at the Hall: there were intense literary conversations, from which Peggy would soon drift off to bed while Emily and John talked until early dawn. Coleman would retire sober, for her thirst was for knowledge, but Holms would drink right up until bedtime. He typically spent the entire day in bed with a hangover, to reemerge in the evening for more festivities.

In August of 1932, the Guggenheim contingent—including Holms, Barnes, and the cook—left Paris in two automobiles for southwestern England. Around the twenty-sixth, Coleman came to Hayford Hall from London, taking a brief respite from her current passion, Peter Hoare. Barnes promptly wrote Allan Ross Macdougall: "Look where I am! Smack in the middle of Hardy's moors & rooks! rain & sun, swimming & tennis, but *no* horse—I'm need I say with Peggy. Came by car (& luggage) to Havre, from Southampton here—almost dead when arrived—but tea was waiting in the Grand Hall so all was well. Thelma now uncertain about being able to come over—no money."[18] Though based in New York now, Thelma Wood was free to travel, but her new partner was not always free with funds for that purpose.

Barnes's decision to leave Paris for Hayford Hall was precipitated by a frightening attack of asthma at 5:00 A.M., which, as described to Natalie Barney, caused her hair to stand on end and her heart to pound in her chest. She took a taxi to her friend Victor Cunard, who got her coffee, held her hand, and sent his servant for their medical friend Dan Mahoney.[19] Apparently the attack was not serious, but Guggenheim suggested that Barnes pack a bag and go with her to England.

Guggenheim describes Hayford Hall:

It was a spacious, simply built, greystone structure about a hundred years old. The rooms centered around a large hall with a fireplace. This hall was well-proportioned, but its paneling was of an ugly new-looking wood and its furniture, though comfortable, was not attractive. The walls were covered with the usual ancestral portraits, shipbuilders from the Clyde. At the end of this room was a big cathedral-like window. All one could see through it were vast trees that kept out the sun. Apart from the eleven bedrooms, we never used any of the other rooms, except a very dreary dining-room, in which we ate our meals, adjourning immediately after to the hall. I am sure so much conversation was never made in this hall before or since. (*OC* 137)

The Guggenheim party found amusement in every incident. There was a flatulent black dog of Peggy's who hung about the dining room. Barnes said, "he effervesces at lunch," calling him the "wind-working wonder of Dartmoor" (Diaries 112).

In her diary, Coleman noted of Hayford Hall that the "grounds have been designed by someone most sympathetic. Half of it is wild and half laid out like [an] Italian garden, but not so formal. Great beeches *all* covered with moss, every twig. Beyond this semi-formal garden the moor" (Diaries 73). Barnes viewed the bleak beauty of Dartmoor, with its heather and marsh, with some apprehension: "Have you forgotten how the moors of Hayford Hall terrified me, because of the dead bones, horse skulls, and because the dog would dart at a rabbit & bring it (still warm & jerking) up to me or John or Peggy— finally I would *not go out at all* on the moor, because I simply could *not* endure it."[20]

Barnes's bedroom was in rococo style, which was deemed to fit her personality; in this room, it is said, during the summers of 1932 and 1933, much of *Nightwood* was written. Antonia White noted that "Djuna arranges herself very carefully, makes up meticulously and prefers to write in bed."[21]

Susan Chitty called Hayford Hall "a version of Boccaccio, written for an all-female cast."[22] Also present was Emily's son, John, as company for Peggy and Laurence Vail's children, Sindbad and Pegeen.[23]

Yet Peggy rented the estate as a love nest for Holms, who needed things to do besides talk, drink, or write and who was rather hard to please in the matter of residences. At Hayford Hall one could play tennis or swim or ride newly tamed ponies. Barnes herself spent little time outdoors, preferring to restrict her exercise to a short walk in the rose garden. Guggenheim says that she had no country clothes and wished to stay close to her manuscript of *Nightwood*, which Coleman had threatened to burn if Barnes revealed one of Coleman's secrets (*OC* 141), a real danger in their evening games.

Emily Coleman didn't like Barnes in the early days at the Hall. Barnes remembered how she once bought Emily candy, which was accepted "scornfully."[24] Emily was in fact a daily trial: she had shocking table manners and tended to gobble up all the edibles in sight; she could swoop down on a box of chocolates and make the contents magically disappear; she monopolized conversation with Holms, as if she were an investigative reporter; she frequently displayed a violent temper; and she often insisted on the best of everything for herself.

Susan Chitty describes the evening games at Hayford Hall:

> It was the custom for everyone to gather after dinner in the great hall, and there, beneath the cathedral window, engage in contests of wit. Djuna, fresh from a day in bed, spun her devastating aphorisms. Somehow Emily seemed often to be their butt. It was at Hangover Hall that Djuna described her as "a girl hiker with a primus in the realms of the infinite." When told that Emily had gone too far she replied "That is often her destination." The evening usually ended with paper games, and *Truth* was popular. Each player filled in anonymously a questionnaire about a selected member of the party, and these were then read aloud, usually by Djuna. Once more Emily received the most punishment. Djuna, coming back for something after the others had gone to bed, found Emily crouched over the wastepaper basket. She was putting together one of the questionnaires. "Garter see who gave me zero for sex appeal," she muttered.[25]

One evening, playing Truth, Coleman baited the group for a prescription: " 'Djuna, I cant help telling that you could say just one word to me and it would put me straight. What do you think I need?' Peggy said, 'A straight-jacket.' Djuna said 'Lydia Pinkham's Vegetable Compound. (Diaries 10)' "[26]

Coleman's diaries of late August 1932 record astute analyses of Barnes's mind and her reading, in which Djuna's taste revealed itself to be more antiquarian than contemporary. At Hayford Hall she read Henry Fielding's novel *Joseph Andrews* with great amusement. The next summer she read Dostoevsky—intensely, Coleman allowed, but without understanding a word. Coleman judged Barnes to have a shallow understanding of *The Brothers Karamazov*; noting that she "cannot say why she likes anything, so it is difficult, can only appreciate. But this is a good deal." (Diaries 78)

Coleman reported Holms's view that:

Djuna had no power of analysis, or logical reasoning, and had built up reserves against this knowledge, and hence was bored when books were talked about if they were analyzed. . . . John said Djuna was more sympathetic to him in some ways than I, in spite of stupidity, because she has a developed taste, while mine is still being formed. . . . Said Djuna had made superficial compromises with life, and lived on that, with people, but inside was a dreadful neurotic, and really felt like me. I said that I could endure Djuna's quips because I felt there was goodness beneath, but Peggy's malice I simply could not face. . . . I said, "What does Djuna think of me?" he said "She thinks youre mad, and very young, but she thinks you have a talent. . . ." He said Djuna was very conceited, and could not write without thinking she was a very great genius. Said this was due to very great inferiority complex underneath. (Diaries 79–83)

Holms was unsympathetic and unenlightened about women writers in general; he felt that in their insecurity they *needed* to be admired and were overly sensitive to negative criticism. He objected to Barnes's sensitivity about what others thought, citing Emily Brontë as a more desirably tough-minded woman writer. Still, he seemed genuinely to like Barnes and to believe that the sensitivity that made her weep so easily stemmed from having nobody to love (Diaries 90).

Coleman pushed Barnes on the subject of men, implying that her love for women meant that she was antimale. Barnes denied this but admitted that she could not stand men "weaker than she" (Diaries 85). She said she wanted them to be "gallant," like "troubadours." "We talked of the sizes of men's penises in an embarrassed sort of way. Djuna spoke of her father in a very vulgar way and terrified me" (Diaries 113).

One evening after Peggy had gone to bed, the other three stayed up to drink, read, and talk. Coleman recorded a typical scene at Hayford Hall:

[Barnes] drank a little, then got very tight, and began to attack John. She had my book of Renaissance Poetry, which she would read, pretending that absorbed her. Then she would intersperse a dig at John, while reading aloud the poetry. I laughed and laughed. I egged them on. John was quite tight, and wanted to say some truth. But he didn't get very far. The gist of their sentiments seemed to be that each thought the other was poor and miserable. They were amiable. Djuna said "I used to hate your guts, but now I think youre sweet." "What do you think he is?" I said. She said, "He's a poor little reed growing by the side of the river. So am I, but his reed is more gnawed than mine." "And much taller," said John. "How taller?" she cried. "Busy old fool, unruly son!" (Diaries 142)

Much of the discussion at Hayford Hall was of great writers. Emily Brontë, Barnes said, "was like God, like Shakespeare and the Bible," which infuriated Coleman, who thought such hyperbole typically American. Barnes said, "I think only two women have written books worth reading, Emily Brontë and myself" (Diaries 86). Besides Brontë, Barnes was enthusiastic about Chaucer, in whose style she wrote some of the best sections of *Ryder*. When pressed on this, she seemed unable to analyze this passion but could read from Chaucer to illustrate her literary taste. Holms thought her talent was indeed essentially Chaucerian ("nothing but people") but that the intuitiveness of this talent, unaccompanied by logic and personal insight, would be detrimental to her writing (Diaries 137). Barnes's defense was that "she couldnt write her life because she couldnt walk over people, that if she had been a man she could do it" (Diaries 139). This was hardly a perceptive insight, since, of course, both *Ryder* and *Nightwood* are in fact strongly autobiographical and the characters much trod on.

Discussions were hardheaded, extremely candid, and at times devastating. Everyone tried to provoke everyone else, but though cruel, they balked at dishonesty. Barnes expressed the view that talking about books was just party chitchat, mainly favored by those who do not write them. Peggy agreed with Barnes, instancing John Holms, whom she called "a washout." Djuna concurred, for she thought that he resembled another drunken intellectual who failed to live up to his early promise, Courtenay Lemon (Diaries 118). Coleman felt that Barnes was a poor judge of character ("she loves shoddy people") and was sentimentally unperceptive about dubious friends such as Laurence Vail, Thelma Wood, and Dan Mahoney. Another example of this vice was her longing for the company of Natalie Barney. " '*That* horror. Good God!' Djuna said she was one of her best friends. I said, 'Its definitely something bad in you that you call a woman like that one of your best friends.' 'What's the matter with her?' 'Shes a giddy gadder,' I said. 'Shes *false*, through and through' " (Diaries 119).

In her 23 July 1933 diary entry, Coleman saw similar examples of what she believed to be Barnes's intellectual dishonesty but that from a different perspective could be seen simply as loyalty: "she couldnt take Peggy's money knowing what Peggy is like, so she wont admit it to herself . . . just as she doesn't know what Dan is like, her whole book, and shes only found out now he is a shit" (Diaries 8–9). Holms agreed, noting that Emily's beloved game Truth was excellent medicine for Barnes, since she seemed a bit dishonest about herself: "she has never been emotionally honest about anything. Her courage is wonderful, in life, but in her art shes a coward" (Diaries 90).

On another occasion, Holms characterized Barnes as a "snob, a romantic innocent one. He said she was completely unconscious about herself . . . only an instinct for what she wants in people, and what she wants is social extroverts. . . . She had no feeling for natural beauty whatsoever" (Diaries 98). He and Coleman agreed that she lacked subtlety and that her "witticisms were always addressed to an imaginary audience, while Peggy's were unconscious, and therefore more genuine" (Diaries 100).

No psychiatrist could have been more probing than Coleman: Barnes was not "entirely honest, she pretended to think little of herself, and she really thought she was noble" (Diaries 129). Barnes admitted this but thought Coleman rather mad, though sweet, "goofy, but interesting" (Diaries 116). As for Holms, at first Barnes thought him an upstart who was only after Guggenheim's money.

Coleman's view of her own virtues relative to the others' is recorded in a 1936 notebook: "John was superior to me, and Djuna is my equal, if not my superior at certain points; but neither of them seem half so charming as my view of myself. Djuna is so much more witty and amusing, and better looking too; and dresses better. But not half so subtle or intelligent, or so happy-minded with the world" (Diary 228).[27]

At times Coleman found it trying to listen to Barnes: "Every word she says is dramatic, said for a reply. She cant help it. Peggy sits there flapping open and shut her jaws in agreement" (Diaries 234).[28] Although she didn't like to be read to, Coleman herself read sections of her diary to the group, which caused general hilarity.

Some time earlier, Holms had read Barnes's *A Book*: "I read Djuna's first book of stories & sketches etc. recently: the most *unbelievable* junk, so bad I thought that by now she'd know & laugh about them (written 10 years or so ago when she was 30) but she thinks they are very good. Nothing but haughty misunderstood women pointing to the door, mixed up with a lot of . . . geniuses & intense, in its own way, but . . . sentimental romanticism."[29] Coleman had criticized *Ryder* in a letter in 1929 as lacking in courage, but she hadn't read Barnes's stories, which Barnes admitted to her were not as good as she pretended. When cornered, Barnes said that she wrote only for herself (Diaries 131).

For July and August of 1933, Peggy rented Hayford Hall again. In the middle of July, Barnes appeared, newly arrived from Paris and Tangier, recovering from the abortion administered by Dan Mahoney.

Emily was again a permanent guest, but there were temporary ones as well: Wyn Henderson, Peter Hoare, Antonia White, and Barnes's New York friends the Bouchés—the painter, Louis, his wife, Marian, and their daughter, Jane.

In 1933, according to Barnes, a kinder mood prevailed at Hayford Hall; there seemed to be fewer insults, pecking parties, and forced confessions. Perhaps less needed to be proved, so guests were more relaxed. This was the gist of Barnes's July letter to Allan Ross Macdougall, but her main concern was to have him retrieve the death mask of Elsa von Freytag Loringhoven, which was made by Marc Vaux, the photographer for *Ryder*.[30] She was still serious about writing a biography of Elsa and wished to use a photo of the mask as an illustration.

She wrote again to commiserate with Macdougall over his apartment, lent to Charles Henri Ford, who had given a wild party there and left behind a mess. She said that in September she would sail to New York, a prospect that intrigued her. She felt positive about *Nightwood*, wrongly imagining that she had only two chapters to revise before having the manuscript retyped. Her daily routine, similar to that of the previous summer, was to write in bed until lunch, read, then take a walk on the moor or hit a few tennis balls.

Shortly after her arrival at Hayford Hall in 1933, she wrote an informative letter to Ford, who would do her the favor of obtaining the death mask and delivering it to Mary Reynolds. Several other matters were on her mind: She had been reading Herman Melville's *Typee*, which had "charm in spots." She discarded "Bow Down" as the title of her new novel. Occasionally she went motoring, but (she implied) after her recent abortion, she could not ride a horse. After-dinner games still included Truth, but she usually went to bed by eleven or twelve, for she continued to feel weak. She imagined that, with a bit of financial security at this time in her life, she could be reasonably happy. She parried Ford's notion that she resembled Mae West, presumably a reference to her buxom amplitude.

An important guest at the country estate that summer was Antonia White (1899–1979), who had just published *Frost in May*. Though the novel had received considerable attention, Barnes liked the author better than the book. White spent two weeks at Hayford Hall in 1933 and became close friends with Barnes, though not as lastingly close as with Emily Coleman. Emily thought them not entirely honest: "Djuna lusts for flattery to feed her ill opinion of herself, Tony wants it to make her feel in the swim. Djuna would die without flattery, but Tony would go rattling right along" (Diaries 6). Holms, considering *Nightwood*, felt that, at her best, Barnes was far superior to White as a writer.

One evening, Djuna began to flirt with Holms. Coleman noted:

> her hair was thick and very red, and she was loving. "This looks like a rape," said Peggy. She had been asleep on the couch. Djuna threw herself on John and kept hugging him. Peggy said, "He'll assert his lump." Then she made a comprehensive survey of her person and said, "Its all right." She said, "If you rise, the dollar will fall." Djuna said he had no technique. John said his technique was so varied he must get another bottle. . . . She flung herself on him perpetually, kissing him. She looked very pretty with her hair falling down. She kept twirling and untwirling a handkerchief. John told her she had written the best things of any woman in the last 50 years. She kissed him passionately on the neck. Then she began to pound Peggy in the bottom and Peggy shrieked, "My God, how this woman hates me" and Djuna kept pounding her, then she began to pound me. She hadnt hit me four times before I had an orgasm. (Diaries 7)

Coleman added details in a letter to Barnes: "do you remember when you washed your hair & we all loved you? You began the evening by saying you wanted to tell some truth to Peggy & she cried 'Come on, cutie! Come on, redcock!' You embraced & loved John & ended up by pounding me into an orgasm!!!!"[31] Barnes's marksmanship must have been extraordinary.

Coleman wondered about her sexuality a few years later:

> But what am I like sexually? I think of myself, with a man, as wholly feminine; and this has misled me greatly in my understanding of

[Peter] Hoare. I do not know in the least what I am like sexually —that is the truth. The only genuine sexual feelings I have ever had were the Lesbian affair I had in 1929 (and what about that? how much it showed!) my brief life with Bianchetti, and my life with Hoare. In the Lesbian thing I behaved exactly like a man. I wanted the woman terribly sexually, and took her, was bored with her afterwards. It was the first time I had felt sexual desire. I thought I was a Lesbian. But I kept on liking men, looking up to them, wanting their attention. . . . There are some people who seem to be *entirely homosexual*. They want *no one but their own sex.* (Diaries 146)

She resolved to consult Djuna Barnes on the subject of sexuality.

At times Coleman slept with Peggy and John in the same bed, an unsatisfactory ménage à trois, for John sat between them, drank, and talked to Emily, while Peggy complained about not being able to sleep. Apparently there was no more to it than that, but once Coleman's son, Johnny, walked in while Peggy and Emily were sleeping together. Chagrined, he said that his mother's posterior "looked like Norfolk and Suffolk," a pornotopographical insight of the first order (Diaries 96).

In late August of 1933, Djuna visited Victor Cunard in Venice and had a somewhat unhappy stay. As she sailed for New York on the *Augustus* in September, she could feel some sense of accomplishment in having secured the patronage of a millionairess who was convinced of her great artistic talent and believed that *Nightwood* was a truly important novel. In less than a decade, however, Guggenheim would be annoyed both by Barnes's drinking and by the nonchalance with which she accepted Peggy's financial aid. Barnes seemed to take for granted that the wealthy naturally owed a debt to artistic genius, which would be paid indefinitely and without resentment at bohemian irresponsibility. Emily Coleman was equally offended by Barnes's irresponsible attitude, but she was adamant and indefatigable in her support.

In later years, Barnes told stories of Peggy Guggenheim at her benefactor's expense, metaphorically speaking. To Chester Page she related the story of Guggenheim's wanting to buy a painting from a gentleman who told the intermediary that Peggy could go fuck herself. Guggenheim called up and asked if this was true: " 'did you say go fuck yourself or get yourself fucked.' He said that 'the first would be impossible and the second very expensive.' " Once, Coleman said that Guggenheim had lost her soul, to which Barnes replied: "Dear [Peggy] you are so saving you will find it again."[32] Guggeim reciprocated with stories about Barnes's selfishness: "It was about her refusing to bring Edward James to the gallery when I wanted to sell him a Tanguy. She said 'what have you ever done for me that I should do this for you?' . . . Finally she pulled herself together and said 'of course if he's your sweetie its a different matter and then I will.' This story is so typical of Djuna's selfishness, stupidity and denial of all I have done for her that I adore it."[33]

Late in April of 1940, Guggenheim wrote to Coleman:

The truth about Djuna first of all is that she is not a friend of 25 years but an acquaintance whom I helped since 1920—18 years ago—& only since John took her up did I become her friend. Incredibly John had no axe to grind & tried to stop me from taking on Djuna permanently, when she went back to America. He was wise enough to know I should not get entangled in people's lives & take on such responsibilities. I think Djuna the most ungrateful & spoilt person I have ever helped except Emma [Goldman]. She thinks everything I do for her is quite natural & every little thing any one else does wonderful. She hates me really at bottom because I help her. She has been nastier & nastier to me as time goes on & I finally felt that her dreadful collapse was due to her having too much money to live on. She was always complaining about not having enough. . . . Djuna has never in her life done one thing for me. . . . Djuna has written one beautiful book, for which I personally am according to you, to be . . . under eternal obligation to support her no matter how much destruction my $150 brings to her. I don't have any kind feeling towards her anymore.[34]

Here we see diametrically opposed views: Guggenheim's that Barnes's irresponsible behavior resulted from having too much, and

Barnes's that her increasing anxiety in the 1930s was owing to the precariousness of her financial situation. By 1930, she saw herself as an artist rather than a journalist, and she had nothing to live on but meager royalties, her Peggy Guggenheim fellowship or the odd stipend, and, in the early Depression years, a pittance from the "Playgoer's Almanac" column. But Barnes had something Guggenheim did not have. Antonia White identified it, as Coleman had before her, when she said: "Djuna has genius if anyone I know has genius."[35]

Creating the Misshapen Images
of *Nightwood*

"You have condensed your agony until its pure platinum . . ."[1]

ust as a grain of sand in an oyster shell may produce a fine pearl, Djuna Barnes's artistic genius, like that of many talented writers, normally required adversity to produce work of artistic merit. This is what her mother meant about *Nightwood* when she noted the alchemical process that produced not gold, but platinum, out of her daughter's agony over her loss of Thelma Wood.

Of course, agony alone is never enough: it lends narrative a poignancy that may capture a reader's interest, but it is craft that gives agony a shape, a purpose, a resolution. Craft was precisely Barnes's weakness, which is why *Nightwood* took so long to be written and published; her artistic strength combined the perceptive skills of the portrait painter or caricaturist with the dazzling sensibility of the poet. Together with a near-hysterical sense of loss, the platinum, Barnes infused into her novel a style so brilliant that it often overpowers sense, and a satirical thrust that has been known to distract readers from the essential tragedy of the plot, for *Nightwood* is essentially a tragic novel.

In diary entries during their stay at Hayford Hall, Emily Coleman recorded conversations with Barnes on the problems of shaping *Nightwood*. She objected to so much emphasis on Dan Mahoney (Dr. O'Connor), when the real subject of the novel was Thelma Wood. Barnes countered that she had written about Thelma, "and wept every time she read it, and could not face Thelma's reading it" (Diaries 86). She said that the heart was more important than the brain in artistic creation, and in some sense she had gone against her heart in putting Wood into *Nightwood*. At Hayford Hall, between drinks, she often read aloud passages from *Ryder* and *Nightwood*, sometimes breaking into tears when she thought of Thelma. Such behavior John Holms deemed "pathetic."

In December 1933, Holms made a dedicated effort to read *Nightwood*. Like Coleman, he found it very uneven. He thought it was "the darkest, saddest book he ever read," calling it a second *Anatomy of Melancholy*, a complimentary judgment since the great work by Robert Burton (1577–1640) was a favorite of Barnes's.[2] Aware of her sensitivity about negative criticism, they also knew that as an ungifted editor she could not always tell the good parts of her novel from the bad and so had to be guided, even if it added to the pain she felt regarding Thelma. Coleman's diary records their impressions:

> There were some sentences that were the absolute truth, come right out of genius. There was one about jealousy. Another wonderful one, watching the loved one waking up—"the smile of the hyena as she left that company." This gave me the most intense excitement. There were others too. Most of the book is sentimental shit of the worst kind (Thelma and Fitzie), then these sudden wonderful truths. I havent read it yet, but John read aloud the best things. Then he read 70 pages so bad that he didnt think hed ever see Djuna again. I told him it was his bounden duty to talk to her about the best and worst parts of her book. Another fine part in Djuna's book was about women acrobats, and another of a tiger passing in a circus. I have such a feeling for Djuna now, as if we had some deep bond Ive never felt before. Especially because of the sentence, "when she left that company." I wonder if she has the least idea what it means. I love her for that. . . . I want to see her now. John said he always knew she had it in her. You certainly couldnt know it from *Ryder*. (Diaries 236–37)[3]

Coleman may have had a Wellesley degree and greater powers of critical perception and analysis than Barnes, who had little formal education beyond art school, but Barnes had her own relationship to art, which her friend was honest enough to recognize: "She is much more gifted than I, I think—I used to have facility, but not like that, hers is much more varied. But I cant see how *any* artist can write more than a few scattered lines worth while if she cant free herself *intellectually* of wrong ideas. She thinks passion is the whole thing, its only three-quarters, really" (Diaries, 23 July 1933; p. 9).

In 1936, the year *Nightwood* was published, Coleman had further thoughts on the novel and Barnes: "No intelligence is evil, there is some (bad—before we're born) reason why genius like Djuna's should be left stranded without the clear light of the intelligence to give it patches of daylight in the darkness. . . . She lied for years pretending Thelma's evil was good, and her good evil. She got it right in this book. As a result, we know wonderful things about evil, we have never known" (Diaries 99).[4]

Emily Coleman loses her critical astuteness by applying what is essentially a Christian interpretation to *Nightwood*, for despite the minor theme of religious quest, Barnes's frame of reference is essentially larger and more complex than the battle of good versus evil. The novel begins at a deathbed, as Hedvig Volkbein dies giving birth to Felix, whose fate will not be a happy one. Guido, the father, dies soon after his son's birth; he is a Viennese Jew of Italian origin who calls himself "Baron," having invented a phony pedigree in "remorseless homage to nobility" (*N* 2). His whole life seems an absurd attempt to blot out his Jewish heritage in order to assimilate into an aristocracy that would have despised him.

Felix, the new Baron Volkbein, inherits his father's wealth but also his obsession with noble lineage, so that he comes to live in a world framed by historical allusion that has only an imagined reference to himself. Near the beginning of the novel, Felix has befriended circus performers in Berlin, who likewise falsify identities, preferring fabrication to authenticity. They, too, have phony titles, as well as ludicrous surnames: we meet a masculine Frau Mann, also called the Duchess of Broadback, whose "coquetries were muscular and localized," and Count Onatorio Altamonte, whose name suggests onanistic oratory on a high mountain (*N* 12). Felix becomes friends with Dr. Matthew O'Connor, who is not really a medical doctor and who sees himself as a woman, struggling to express herself in a man's shape.

Dr. O'Connor says, "only the scorned and ridiculous make good stories" (*N* 159), and Barnes seemed to agree. Nikka the Nigger is remembered, who used to wrestle a circus bear and whose tattooed body has become a highly allusive, erudite text (*N* 16–17); and then there is the legless beauty of the Pyrenees, Mademoiselle Basquette, who wheels through the mountains on a sort of skateboard (*N* 26). Much of *Nightwood*'s humor is an insensitive probing into the grotesque ways in which people deny nature and create themselves anew.

The marginal chimeras of *Nightwood* are really little more than humorous digressions; the novel's real interest lies in love entanglements and in Dr. O'Connor's brilliant, enigmatic, often hilarious commentary on them. Felix meets, woos, and weds the American Robin Vote, who has her origin in Thelma Wood, for "he wished a son who would feel as he felt about 'the great past' " (*N* 38). The couple move to Vienna, where Robin's behavior becomes stranger and more distant; she begins to wander, eventually leaving Vienna, Felix, and their baby, Guido, for the Paris life she once knew.

The first chapter's title is the novel's original title, "Bow Down," an act of obeisance impossible for Robin; the second chapter is titled "La Somnambule," with an ironic nod to the Bellini opera, suggesting Robin's nocturnal wandering and metaphysical hollowness.[5] In the chapter "Night Watch," Robin meets Nora Flood at a circus, and there begins the great love affair that is *Nightwood*'s chief interest. Inevitably Robin begins to wander again, from bed to bed and pub to pub, drinking heavily. In "The Squatter," she leaves Nora for Jenny Petherbridge, a tragic event for Nora, whose love for Robin is an obsession, which she attempts unsuccessfully to conquer during the rest of the novel. In the next three chapters ("Watchman, What of the Night?", "Where the Tree Falls," and "Go Down Matthew"), Dr. O'Connor becomes a clearinghouse of consolation for those who desire Robin: Felix, Nora, and Jenny. Robin's magnetism and what her loose behavior seems to reveal about human nature have a devastating effect on all concerned, not least of all the father confessor Matthew O'Connor. *Nightwood*'s bizarre last chapter, "The Possessed," takes us to a rural area (probably New York or Connecticut) where Nora has a house. When her dog barks excitedly, Nora finds the cause of his disturbance in a small chapel. There Robin, now seemingly derelict and insane, apparently worshiping before a "contrived altar" (*N* 169), slides down before the dog as if ready for another sexual conquest. On this strange note the novel ends.

Although Djuna Barnes incorporated many details and events from her life with Thelma Wood, it is on the level of metaphysics that *Nightwood* transcends the autobiographical, for it argues that regardless of sexual orientation, human nature is itself perverted and grotesque, which is why people seek to remake themselves. We are all God's jokes.

Barnes would seem to agree with Schopenhauer and Nietzsche that human existence is suffering. One of the central philosophical statements in the novel is: "No man needs curing of his individual sickness; his universal malady is what he should look to" (*N* 32). Yet in *Nightwood* only Matthew O'Connor, who, in the narrative style of his real-life counterpart, seems to represent Barnes's own worldview, can sufficiently transcend suffering to construct a metaphysics of pessimism, which, for all its rambling, does make a coherent statement about life. Other characters in the novel are so locked into their personal misfortunes that they scarcely make sense.

A more contemporary way to express the problem would be to say that at the core, *Nightwood*'s major characters are thwarted by desire: desire to change their own essence or that of Robin, whose problems energize the plot. Homosexuality seems hardly the issue, for *Nightwood* neither defends nor condemns it, except in one oblique way. Given that life is suffering, the greatest crime would be procreation, which seems to give homosexuality the edge as a preferred lifestyle, since it promotes the extinction of the human species.[6]

Everybody in the novel seems to be caught midway in some metamorphosis: Robin is "beast turning human" (*N* 37), and yet she converts to Roman Catholicism and aspires through religion to transcend her beastly limitations (*N* 46). Matthew O'Connor is a devout Catholic and an unrepentant homosexual, blaming the mistake in gender on God.

All desire in *Nightwood* is insatiable and ultimately narcissistic.[7] Barnes's point is surely about desire itself rather than homoeroticism, though this is her example. (Straight people, such as Felix and his son, Guido, or Mademoiselle Basquette, are no less frustrated.) The frustration of desire is aptly imaged in the symbolic positioning of Jenny and Robin:

> Jenny leaning far over the table, Robin far back, her legs thrust under her, to balance the whole backward incline of the body, and Jenny so far forward that she had to catch her small legs in the back rung of the chair, ankle out and toe in, not to pitch forward on the table—thus they presented the two halves of a movement that had, as in sculpture, the beauty and absurdity of a desire that is in flower but that can have no burgeoning, unable to execute its destiny; . . . eternally angry, eternally separated, in a cataleptic frozen gesture of abandon. (*N* 69)

Homoerotic desire in *Nightwood* is also narcissistic: Nora says, "Matthew . . . have you ever loved someone and it became yourself?" (*N* 152) and "a man is another person—a woman is yourself, caught as you turn in panic; on her mouth you kiss your own" (*N* 143).

The desire (especially of Robin and Dr. O'Connor) for religious transcendence in this fictional world of suffering seems the ultimate expression of narcissism. One sad, hilarious example is seen in O'Connor's talking to his penis while praying in a darkened church: "I was crying and striking my left hand against the *prie-dieu*, and all the while Tiny O'Toole was lying in a swoon. I said, 'I have tried to seek, and I only find.' I said, 'It is I, my Lord, who know there's beauty in any permanent mistake like me'" (*N* 132).

O'Connor's single obsession is his wish to be a woman. He says, "God, I never asked better than to boil some good man's potatoes and toss up a child for him every nine months by the calendar" (*N* 91).

Nora, seeing him in bed dressed in a woman's nightgown, awaiting a customer, thinks: "He dresses to lie beside himself" (*N* 80), as she has lain beside herself with Robin.

Felix longs for Robin and a son (*N* 38), and for the noble lineage he can never have. In part this impossible desire springs from the wish to shackle a homosexual to a heterosexual marriage: Barnes wrote Emily Coleman that she had wedded Robin to Felix to rebut the received opinion that lesbians would be heterosexuals if they had men to love. Robin had a husband and a child, yet returned to her earlier preference for women.[8] In an early draft of the novel, Nora was even the mother of two sons.

The theme of animality in *Nightwood* is related to questions of morality and religion, and here we return to the paradigm of nature. The central paradox of human existence as it is revealed in Barnes's novel is that we have lost our animal innocence and yet as humans cannot achieve transcendence, though we are doomed to pine for it in this vale of tears. Animal innocence means having no haunting conscience, no disturbing memories of the past, no guilt. This is the positive side of animal behavior, and the attraction of Robin. Dr. O'Connor says: "Have I been simple like an animal, God, or have I been thinking?" (*N* 133). It is consciousness that in Barnes's fiction alienates humans from the animal world.[9]

Yet for humans to act subhuman is both to deny their moral nature and to bring misery to others. Despite the trend to see Robin as a liberated woman and Nora as puritanical in wanting an exclusive relationship, a broader view of Barnes's work shows something different. To the extent that Robin is the prowling panther, insatiable in her animal appetites, she resembles the polygamist father, Wendell Ryder, hardly a positive model.

Though she loved to shock her readers by her portrayal of decadence, Barnes condemns Robin's unselective promiscuity as destructive. Nora, desirous of the exclusive relationship that most people want, regardless of sexual orientation, represents a norm in *Nightwood*; alas, it is left to Dr. O'Connor to smash her naive illusions, to show her the impossibility of stable human relationships in a world that seems designed to make us suffer. If Robin is to be pitied as "a beast turning human" (*N* 33), Nora is pitiful as the innocent romantic who believes that love is meant to last. Finally, it is Matthew O'Connor, Barnes's Tiresias figure, who, since he has lived as both man and woman, is condemned to see all and explain all in the terrible world that *Nightwood* evokes.

The Tiresias of *Nightwood* was in reality Daniel A. Mahoney, Barnes's close friend for many years and one of the most sadly entertaining "characters" in modern Left Bank history. Barnes would sit for hours listening to him, often taking copious notes, which became the basis for O'Connor's monologues in her novel. Sometimes the two of them would dance to a Louis Armstrong recording, for the good doctor was a fine dancer; more often they would just drink and talk. Of her solitary nature, he would say, "Djuna, you were the tree that was meant to stand alone."[10]

Although Barnes was neither the first nor the last to make use of Mahoney as a fictional persona (Robert McAlmon had preceded her), he made his Barnesian debut as a physician to the Ryder family.[11] In *Ryder*, Barnes tried (not very successfully) to capture the unique quality of his voice, without making him the bistro philosopher he is in *Nightwood*. McAlmon stated it a bit differently: he said Barnes "gave Dan a soul, when all he ever had was an ar-sole."[12]

Dan Mahoney, an Irish American, was born to a wealthy family in San Francisco around the late 1880s and died of cancer on the rue de Cels in perhaps early 1959.[13] He may have been a U.S. Navy hospital corpsman in World War I, and he later practiced medicine on the sly in Left Bank circles; his specialty was abortions, and his clientele included prostitutes. "Keep your pecker up, the Doctor said, and hang your shingle on it," says a note by Barnes, which could have been Mahoney's motto.[14] As an enemy alien and a homosexual, he was interned by the Germans at Chantilly during the Second World War, an experience he seems to have enjoyed. A note by Barnes says: "Dan: When I was taken prisoner in the war (Paris) I taught forty thieves the alphabet from the wrappers of chocolate bars, flattened on a cannon."[15]

Edouard Roditi, interviewed in 1971, remembered the good doctor well, recalling his fluttering hands, so apt to land on one's knee, and his excursions into the Paris night with the painter Lillian Fisk to pick up "somewhat frightening characters." Roditi was present when after World War II Mahoney debarked from a ship in New York carrying internees from German prison camps. Mahoney was "protesting viciously . . . against the absolute enormity of his having been shipped back to America against his will, and really furious at having left this internment camp in France, where apparently he had been able to establish a *modus vivendi* of the most agreeable kind with some of the German military guards and a few of the more sexually attractive internees."[16]

The writer John Glassco's description of Dan Mahoney is unforgettable, recalling Barnes's drawing of him in *Ryder*:

Height about 5'6"; short legs, broad shoulders, heavy build. Square face, ace-of-clubs nose, thin and very mobile lips always darkly lipsticked, massive jowls. Wore a small toothbrush moustache about ¼" long, and had stiff wiry hair cut *en brosse* [like a brush], both obviously dyed jet black though iron-grey at the roots. Eyes large, grey and protruding, heavy-lidded and artificially blued, eyelashes coated with mascara, his glance was always moving restlessly. His face was covered with deadwhite face powder through which a strong black beard showed. He always wore a white shirt with starched collar and cuffs, black four-in hand tie and black suit, without waistcoat, that seemed too large for him, its trousers too roomy in the seat and the jacket too long so that it gave the effect of a skirt. Small black pointed shoes; ugly, hairy hands. His gait was a kind of hip-swaying waddle; he always stood with his knees slightly bent and his arms held out in front of him, the wrists falling outward and down, like a dog walking on its hind legs (both Djuna Barnes and I made this comparison independently; the likeness was irresistibly suggested). He was a beautiful dancer, and very light on his feet. His voice was a light tenor, his accent a straight New York nasal twang, with "fairy" intonations and an artificial lisp. He was rumored to have been a professional boxer, and was in fact a redoubtable barroom fighter: I actually saw him break the wrist of a young American who had been gibing him in the Dingo bar on the rue Delambre. He was regarded as dangerous for his terrible temper.[17]

Mahoney was an inveterate fabricator, so that little faith is to be attached to the idea that he had been a professional boxer.

Charles Henri Ford remembered him as well:

> what he's always wanted to be: a big blond with a hundred children. But what he REALLY is he says is "just a shrinking violet under a load of cowshit." And his literary criticism is in this style: "James Joyce? Just a fart in a gale of wind." Everything he says is so grave and half of it heartbroken: D—— is writing a chapter about the night and wanted to know what he thought of it (the night) and what he thinks of it is: "the night is when you realize that you're all wet." (Ford 188)

Mahoney's wit was famous. Ford recalled his claim that he was "writing a new story entitled: 'According To Me, Everybody's a Kind of Son of a Bitch' " (Ford 191), which might have been an appropriate subtitle for *Nightwood*. Once, he compared the United States to a penis: "Well, its LARGE, but who cares?"[18] He remarked on "the slight swelling under the eyes of children, as tho they'd been slugged in Paradise."[19] To Laurence Vail, Barnes wrote: "Dan always clapped his hands when anyone died. When I asked why, he looked at me as tho I were mad."[20]

On one occasion, Barnes and Ford were buying him drinks when Glenway Wescott walked in. Mahoney greeted Wescott (1901–87), a gay writer perhaps best known for *Good-bye Wisconsin* (1928), with the insulting remark: "I thought you were beautiful in fact the last time I saw you you were goodlooking but how you've changed and D[juna] said WELL WHO HASN'T" (Ford 193). Another time, Ford recalls him saying: " 'The Irish may be as common as whale shit on the bottom of the ocean but *at least* they have a Creative Imagination.' . . . D—— calls him her *copy* and does turn his lines remembered from 20 years back into brilliant prose" (Ford 211).

Brilliant is indeed the word for Barnes's re-creation of Dan Mahoney's monologues in *Nightwood*: "The darkness is the closet in which your lover roosts her heart, and that night-fowl that caws against her spirit and yours, dropping between you and her the awful estrangement of his bowels" (*N* 89)—little consolation for the desolate Nora, seeking advice in the chapter "Watchman, What of the Night?" O'Connor's importance to the novel is vital: by raising to a fever pitch this good doctor's eloquence, Barnes managed to evade the finer points of plot, character, and some traditional problems of the novelist, exchanging them for the modernist form that it shares with *Ulysses* and *The Waste Land*.

Mahoney's self-hatred and general unhappiness were hidden beneath a witty volubility (Barnes called it "hilarious sorrow"[21]) that would become more marked the greater number of drinks he cadged. Once, he wrote Barnes: "I am always happier in rainy weather—less exposed somehow. When it is fine, I always feel like some poor old crustacean with its shell pulled off."[22]

Mahoney was proud to have been immortalized, but like that crustacean, he was not always pleased to be in the sunlight. Part of his displeasure came from Barnes's mentioning his unfeminine gunmetal chin, and her deletion from *Nightwood* of a story about an old lady and a peach that he used to tell. When Barnes once asked "how he felt about Nightwood & his fame, he looked all crumpled & sad fishing for a piece of sugar for the pigeons: 'I don't care,' he said—'is that all?' I demanded—I was so surprised—'Well, there are pretty awful things in it' he answered 'but I'd forgive you in case—I don't see you—if you would put my old lady back.' So there you are."[23]

Barnes saw a good deal of Mahoney even after the publication of *Nightwood*. She wrote Coleman that she was irritated by his unwillingness to pay his way. Returning from an excursion with Barnes to Cluny, he asked, "Got any tea, cakes, jam, butter?" Barnes said no. Then he said, "I've got to go to the can, so I may as well go home with you." He insisted that she pay for his bus ticket, and when she refused, he screamed, "everyone *knows* what a beast you are about money." Then there was his hideous personal hygiene. Barnes observed to Emily: "it made me sick every time he climbed into my tub—also he asked me to shove that awful cape of hair off his shoulders for him (I did it once & nearly chucked, as physically, he's so abhorrent to me)."[24]

As it turned out, Mahoney was storing up bitterness for the way Barnes had exposed him in *Nightwood*. Whatever pride he might have felt when the novel appeared seemed to evaporate at some point, perhaps because one of his friends, whom he'd insulted, bought a good many copies, marked the passages unflattering to Mahoney, and handed them out around the Left Bank.[25] Mahoney appeared at Barnes's flat at 1:15 A.M. in a dangerous mood one night and threatened her until 5 A.M. Barnes's 19 October 1937 letter to Natalie Barney is so descriptive of Mahoney at his worst that it deserves quotation at length.

> I was very ill & nervous any way, & in bare feet & nightgown & trying to figure out how I could get from the bed to the door & into the concierges loge to get help—I did try,—& Dan struck me in the face, knocking me down—I tried a second time & he struck me down again all the time using the most filthy language, & threatening to "knock the s—— out of me" & to slit my gizzard—really the most frightful experience I've ever gone through, & worst of all, was the knowledge that I was *too weak* to put him out—my heart began to pound so hard sweat, & faintness almost overcoming me. So I thought, really for a little while, that I was going to die there in bed listening to his filth, that I *had* to hear, because I could not stop it. Then he vomited—& in the end flung himself on me asking if I "loved him," or at least respected him!! I don't know how I had the courage to say no, I neither liked, loved nor respected him— in a way it's understandable, he *can't* endure it that I know him so well—what he hates in himself (& he *does* hate himself) he put on me—saying I was a filthy writer, could not put a sentence together—that he could not understand how I'd become a legend on *nothing*,—that I was a declassé bitch with lesbian friends no better—that I was a low form half-wit who had never "earned a cent in my life except by sleeping with dirty Jews" (poor innocent

H. Burton, who never so much as got near enough to me to put his arm around me—really!) then a tirade against everyone I know, including T[helma] of course—adding that considering what a worm I was, I had done quite well. It was really horrible—bully & beast that he is. Sitting there instead of loathing himself to such an extent as that—I knew, long since, that he was wicked & weak, & what a monster he is—*but* he did have something I wanted *enough* to face it—only, really, had I known what a last scene I was in for, I don't know if I'd have had the nerve to go through with it.

After he was ill, just before he left he said "Why didn't you beat me up—you could have"—I said "You know I'm too ill to fight a man now" "A man?" he laughed bitterly "a man—me—it's really me in all this world I loathe—hate—detest—I wish you had—I've no guts!" So pitiful—so horrible. And—next day—or the day after, I forget—he came to my home & rang the bell! I would not let him in—he said "Well, write to Dannie"!! I've been through a great deal with him, but that was the end—I shall never speak to him or see him again. I thought I had paid for "Nightwood" but perhaps the price goes on forever.

Barnes *did* see him again, and she *did* write to him, but things were never the same. Now two of the "characters" of *Nightwood* had assaulted her; although it never happened, it only remained for the counterpart of Jenny Petherbridge to have a go, for Barnes half expected to be knifed in the back for portraying Henriette Metcalf as the "Squatter" of *Nightwood*.

Another former associate of Barnes skewered in *Nightwood* was Guido Bruno, who had published Barnes's *The Book of Repulsive Women* in November 1915 from his garret on Washington Square, and who exhibited her drawings, those imitating Beardsley and the war drawings for *Trend*, the next year. He interviewed Barnes in 1919 and generally presented her as a risqué lesbian poet whom tourists would do well to read and gawk at, for he was primarily a promoter of bohemian Greenwich Village for commercial purposes (curiously enough, he was actually born in Bohemia). A complete charlatan, he also waged legitimate war against censorship; he published Marianne

Moore and was the first to publish Hart Crane. Through Barnes he came to know Frank Harris, to whom he was devoted. He was arrested by the vice squad for selling (and publishing) Alfred Kreymborg's *Edna: The Girl of the Streets* and used this incident to promote his own career. Eventually his various extortion schemes and sexual harassments of women began to catch up with him, and he left New York to campaign in Wisconsin for Senator Robert La Follette during his bid for the presidency in 1924. Barnes must have known of his unsavory side and may have had good reason (though she needed none) to caricature some of his faults.[26] He is described in detail by Andrew Field.[27]

The Guido Volkbeins of *Nightwood* (grandfather and grandson) were given Guido Bruno's first name, his obsession with disguising his Jewish background, and his habit of groveling before nobility, wealth, and fame. Bruno was the son of a rabbi, and his real name was Curt Kisch. Barnes's description of Felix Volkbein's physical features could fit Bruno: "Felix was heavier than his father and taller. His hair began too far back on his forehead. His face was a long stout oval, suffering a laborious melancholy. . . . The other features were a little heavy, the chin, the nose, and the lids. . . ." (*N* 8). Bruno had studied in Vienna (and elsewhere), as does Felix, and was reputed to know seven languages.

There is also a historical Felix in the background, who knew languages (his native tongue was German) and who occasionally signed into hotels as Baron Volkbein—it was Felix Paul Greve, the writer who abandoned Elsa von Freytag Loringhoven in Kentucky. His type is rather different—he was a very tall, blond, blue-eyed, immaculately dressed, non-Jewish North German—but he was there for her, described in great detail, in the autobiographical fragment Elsa left Barnes in the mid-1920s, to be used as the basis of the biography she never finished. Since Barnes never met Greve, one shouldn't make too much of this connection, but she combined him with Guido Bruno to form Felix Volkbein, whom she then superimposed on the Left Bank haunts Barnes knew and the Vienna she learned about on her trip there with Charles Henri Ford.

As for Nora Flood, the Barnes-like woman who agonizes over the loss of Robin, the general situation described is largely autobiographical, but some of her character was derived from Barnes's friend Fitzi, Mary Eleanor Fitzgerald.[28] Of course, Barnes's main interest in *Nightwood* was in coming to terms with the loss of Thelma Wood, whose surname occupies half of the novel's title. The recorded reactions of Felix Volkbein, Dr. O'Connor, and Jenny Petherbridge, as well as Nora, to their tragic sense of loss, and what this tells us about human nature—all this added depth, voice, and design to what came to be one of the great novels of the 1930s.

Barnes shed her sickness in art, as D. H. Lawrence would have said, experiencing purgation in the hope of artistic success. She said as much in a letter describing her deep attachment to the Parisian neighborhoods of *Nightwood*, which for a time after the novel's publication became her geographical center:

> I want to live . . . in the Hotel Recamier—where, in my book, Robin lived—tho Thelma never put her foot, in reality, over its steps—I haunt the Place St. Sulpice now, because I've made it in my book into my life—as if my life had really been there. . . . I love what I have invented as much as that which fate gave me—a great danger for the writer perhaps. . . . I come to love my invention more—so am able—perhaps—only so able—to put Thelma aside —because now she is not Robin.[29]

Emily and Tom:
The Practical Cats

"You make horror beautiful—it is your greatest gift."[1]

W hen Djuna Barnes returned to New York and Greenwich Village in the fall of 1933, after her last summer at Hayford Hall, she took a flat at 111 Waverly Place, across from her mother's, where she lived until moving to London in 1936. Her time was taken up with writing a few journalistic pieces, circulating "Bow Down" among the publishers, and trying without much success to revise the novel after rejections by Scribner, Simon & Schuster, Viking, and Covici. Emily Coleman had given the typescript to the publisher Ben Huebsch to consider, but he, too, was uninterested. Boni & Liveright sent a negative report, demanding a complete rewriting of her book.[2]

Since Barnes had no editorial skills and, being more attuned to the lyrical voices of her characters, had little clear sense of what was and was not digressive or irrelevant, she had tended to let the novel's Dr. O'Connor rattle on at will. Publishers wanted a tighter organization but left her with the task of deciding what was to be done. A good editor working full time on *Nightwood* might have shortened the publication history by at least two years. As it was, Barnes arranged the chapters on the floor, circling them, as she said, "like a murderess about the body."[3]

Letters to Emily Coleman and Charles Henri Ford tell of Barnes's life during these years of the Great Depression, which were to intensify her own great depression; those to Coleman, taken as a group, form the nucleus of what we know about Barnes in the 1930s and early 1940s.

Barnes's high-ceilinged flat on Waverly Place consisted of a large room and a bath; the rent was paid by her brother Saxon, who prospered as a banker even during these lean years and whose generosity was in equal proportion to Djuna's amiability. Saxon took her for rides in his red-wheeled racer, or to the beach with their mother. He was content for her to read, paint, and revise her novel, and in the early 1930s was not yet pressing her to get a regular job. At this time she enjoyed having him and her mother conveniently near, and privacy was less of an issue than it would become as the years passed and she began to drink more heavily and would have to bear their blame and her own guilt. On the whole, Barnes was content with her surroundings, except for a speakeasy next door, where the tumbling noise of drunken men during late hours disturbed her peace of mind.

Her reading at this time included William James's *The Varieties of Religious Experience*, Louis-Ferdinand Céline's *Journey to the End of the Night*, as well as Luther, Pascal, Montaigne, and her two lifelong favorites Robert Burton's *The Anatomy of Melancholy* (1621) and Sir Thomas Browne's *Religio Medici* (1643). In 1935, she read with great pleasure and excitement Alexis Carrel's *Man, the Unknown*, an anthropological study that she felt echoed her own understanding of human nature. Of Spinoza she wrote: "Theres a man who got into his own mind and ran around in it trying to find cover and a way out."[4] She never liked Kafka or Ibsen much, finding them too reliant on symbolism, but greatly admired Shakespeare, Isak Dinesen, Dostoevsky, Proust, and Goncharov's *Oblomov*.

In the evening, Barnes regularly saw plays or had dinner with a few friends—the Bouchés, the Langners, or Thelma Wood, whom she continued to meet as a friend.[5] At the end of 1933, she was frequently with Alice Rohrer, whom she would paint in oil on a five-foot canvas, completed in February 1934.[6] The painting was one of Barnes's favorites, though Alice didn't like it; it aged with Barnes and grew dark in her Patchin Place apartment. (Barnes claimed to have refused an offer of fifteen thousand dollars for it.) Painting occupied a good deal of her time while she tried to figure out what to do with her novel; she painted Emily Coleman in 1934 or 1935 and named the portrait Madame Majeska,[7] then painted her lover Scudder Middleton. She found this deeply satisfying; had she just started early enough and been persistent, she felt, she could have been a great painter.[8]

She undeniably had talent. Barnes's friend of later years Chester Page, a connoisseur of art, was impressed by her drawing of Jules Pascin (1885–1930) in pink collar, which must derive from the 1920s. Pascin was a Bulgarian-born painter of the Montmartre circle of Modigliani and Chagall.[9]

By 1934, mortality began to take its toll of loved ones. The death of John Holms affected Barnes very deeply, as it did Peter Neagoe, a sentiment that began to bind them together in melancholy. Her father's death in May (followed shortly after by Fanny's) affected her far less. She wept for mortality but not for Wald, she said. It was just "an added melancholia to the body of sad speculations and memories."[10]

But there was more to endure. As publisher after publisher rejected "Bow Down," Barnes began to imagine that only dark and bloody works such as Erskine Caldwell's *Tobacco Road* were being encouraged, for only they had sales potential. Her family gradually began to get on her nerves, but for a time things went well with Saxon (who bought a concert grand piano and rented a large beach house for the summer holidays).

Over the years, though, Saxon became less tolerant of what he perceived to be Barnes's indolence. He proposed that she move elsewhere in Manhattan and get an office job, so that at least she could support herself. This ongoing suggestion was a humiliation that Barnes had to bear in mind during the years to come, and one that she would avenge in her last play, *The Antiphon*. Saxon could be quite brutal in the interest of practicality: he scolded his mother because she let a roast burn; he threatened to move to the country, though he promised that Elizabeth Barnes could count on him for a corner somewhere.

Returning to Europe certainly had its appeal for Djuna, for Elizabeth's health seemed to be failing, and she was horrified at the idea of watching her mother die—and of being under her brother's thumb. She kept in touch with friends such as Charles Henri Ford, who wrote her of his life in Paris with Pavel Tchelitchew. Like many writers and artists in the 1930s, Ford had become a Marxist, which failed to impress Barnes. She had no use for political theories, saying that she was "a complete egoist . . . only interested in beauty, art and religion."[11] In passing, she asked Ford: "What is your idea of love? Have you chosen men only?"[12]

It seems Ford had, and so had she, for in 1934 she would begin affairs with both Peter Neagoe (1881–1963), nicknamed Muffin, and Scudder Middleton.[13] To Coleman, Barnes confessed that her sexual passion for Middleton derived from his resemblance to Thelma (who had reminded her of Zadel).[14] For the first time, Emily seemed to understand both her friend's preoccupation with her family and her need for privacy. Middleton repeated the pattern of Courtenay Lemon and Thelma Wood, for he was rather hopelessly alcoholic. He also seemed to have family problems; Barnes said that his brother hated him "because he is beautiful, witty, talented, poor and a drunk."[15]

Romance flowered in lonely self-deception. While Barnes loved Middleton, she was also enamored of Neagoe. She was convinced that Neagoe would leave his wife for her, but the affair dragged on without direction until perhaps March of 1936, followed by another brief interlude in 1937, when Neagoe visited Paris en route to his native Romania.[16] The Neagoes had lived in France for several years during the late 1920s and early 1930s, and had become friends with Eugene Jolas, Peggy Guggenheim, John Holms, Emily Coleman, and Emma Goldman. Peter Neagoe had edited *Americans Abroad* (1932), which included two of Barnes's stories, "Cassation" and "The Little Girl Continues," and he'd written many stories and novels, bringing to the world's attention the culture of the Romanian peasantry.[17] Neagoe later wrote a biography of his friend Constantin Brancusi (1876–1957) titled *The Saint of Montparnasse* (1965). He did some painting as well, but his wife, Anna, was far better known as a painter.[18] She was from Lithuania, the daughter of a rabbi.

A good deal of subterfuge accompanied the affair with Neagoe, which Barnes discussed openly with Coleman. Anna Neagoe probably knew about it but pretended not to, perhaps confident that her husband would not leave in the end. Barnes was simply the "other woman" in this triangle. When Neagoe's wife was around, he made excuses about the necessity of returning home, wrung his hands with helplessness, and expressed fear that he had ruined Anna's life. When Barnes was loving, he was indecisive; when she was cool, he was ardent (precisely the pattern that plagued Coleman). Elizabeth Barnes said he probably thought Djuna a whore, playing mousy with her only while the cat was away. To Djuna's consternation, Saxon agreed.

Although he meant well, Neagoe led Barnes on for years, which was not hard to do since love made her ever blind to harsh realities. Barnes loved him because "he is so good in a clear simple way, like no one I ever knew, nothing evil in him anywhere."[19] (He thought *Nightwood* should have been more cheerful.) Her mother "react[ed] to love in the damdest [*sic*] way," which meant with a pessimism that her daughter would soon adopt.[20]

During the previous December, T. R. Smith, of Boni & Liveright, had suggested that "Bow Down" be completely rewritten. His firm, which had published her short-story collection and *Ryder*, had first-refusal rights on her next book, so the news was particularly distressful. Now Smith sent another report, saying that the manuscript would not be considered further without additional revisions of a substantial nature. His letter of 29 August 1934 was to be a typical response to the novel:

> The theme in itself is obvious but it is all very difficult to extricate the story from the mass of brilliant and somewhat mad writing. The early part of the book is clear enough but it soon becomes obscured in nothing more than a welter of homosexuality, described and analyzed. It is obvious to me that you tried to do an honest study of perversion but I am afraid you got lost in your studies. There is so much brilliant writing, so much unusually broad observation of life and behavior, so much keen philosophy, that it is a pity that the book succeeds only in being a rambling, obscure complicated ac-

count of what the average reader will consider "God knows what." I wonder if it is humanly possible for you to revise this book again to the point where an ordinarily intelligent person will not have to read things into your subject but can understand the psychological manifestations as part of your main theme. And further, I think something should be done about O'Connor. He really is of course a brilliant commentator on life and manners but like so many brilliant commentators he frequently becomes a bore.

Barnes would have preferred an outright refusal, which would have allowed her to keep her twelve-hundred-dollar advance. And so the revision continued, but this letter would be taken as a refusal, which would allow Barnes to submit elsewhere. In June 1935, Barnes hit upon the title "Nightwood" for her novel: "it makes it sound like night-shade, poison and night and forest, and tough, in the meaty sense"[21]; the novel was a soliloquy, "it remains a soul talking to itself in the heart of the night."[22] But Scudder Middleton said that this new title sounded "like a local stop on the Long Island Railroad."[23] Many years later, Barnes told Hank O'Neal that the "title came from William Blake's 'Tyger, tyger, burning bright in the forests of the night . . .' " (O'Neal 104). T. S. Eliot rejected the alternative title "Anatomy of Night," preferring *Nightwood* because "he wanted 'something brief and mysterious, giving no clue whatever to the contents.' "[24] Andrew Field was wrong to suppose that Eliot invented the title *Nightwood*, for Barnes had thought up the title some four months before Coleman approached Eliot about the manuscript.[25] Eliot simply preferred this title to any other, and so it stayed.

By July, Barnes felt once again that she had finished her revisions, and she sent the typescript, now some 250 pages in length, to Clifton Fadiman (T. S. Eliot told her he was "an intelligent Jew"[26]), who read it for Simon & Schuster. Though he said that it was the wittiest book he had ever read, his general reaction was that it was too "written" and "inverted" for a standard publishing house, and he thought it rather anti-Semitic as well.[27]

Meanwhile, Emily Coleman took a copy of the typescript to London, where a groundswell of support for its publication occurred after Coleman received an enthusiastic reader's response from Edwin Muir.[28] Coleman had spent some time helping Barnes edit the novel in May, when she was in New York; toward the end of August, she sent Barnes a remarkable eight-page, single-spaced critique that was full of valuable insights, containing just the right mix of praise and careful advice.

Emily's long letter set in motion Barnes's final revisions of *Nightwood*, though other readers would take it to the cutting board after she had finished. Coleman told Barnes, and surely T. S. Eliot as well, that "There is no doubt that there are pages and pages in this book which are the best writing ever done by an American; to say nothing of profound human truths, for which you will be revered some day; which have not yet been said by any human soul, man or woman."[29] She thought that the writing surpassed that of Joyce, Lawrence, Hemingway, or Faulkner, and that of any woman writer but Emily Brontë. Only *Moby Dick* could match *Nightwood* in delving the depths of the human psyche. Coleman thought that the novel was essentially a great dramatic tragedy, with an unfortunately blurred focus; it shifted its center of attention among the major characters instead of concentrating on Nora's mad, Othello-like jealousy. Nor was there a coherent philosophy among all the deeply intuitive, valid insights into human suffering. What was evident was a "pathological introversion," as Coleman put it, which manifested itself as Barnes's inability to write good dialogue, for, Coleman said, except with John Holms, Barnes had almost never been able to communicate her feelings.

Barnes had described for Coleman the ending in its final form, with Robin falling down before Nora's dog, apparently seeing nothing puzzling about it: "Let the reader make up his own mind, if he's not an idiot he'll know."[30] Alas, nobody quite did. What amazed Emily was how little aware Barnes appeared to be of the implications in her own writing. She seemed to believe that Barnes had had no intention of making the ending of *Nightwood* in any way sexual, though everybody read it that way—Guggenheim, Muir, etc. Of course, Peggy was well acquainted with Fitzi and her dog, Buffy, the model Barnes had used for her ending, and she described Fitzi's curiously sexual feelings for her dog. In other words, Coleman and Guggenheim believed that Barnes had accurately depicted a magnetism she had not consciously perceived—yet it was Robin who was supposed to be the somnambule. Still, Coleman thought that the revisions had helped greatly, and Chapters 2 and 3 were about perfect, though some of Dr. O'Connor's monologues still had to be shortened.

Barnes responded in detail to Coleman's criticism, having revised according to her instructions, though she wished to leave off cutting the good doctor's monologues until later. She admitted faults: "I cant, I never have been able to plot or plan a book or give it, apparently any structure." She said she wrote from the heart, not the head, and pleaded guilty to introversion. As for her indictment of humanity, she had seen too much not to despise it intensely. Her preference was to be alone in her room, listening to classical music, reading, or painting. Half a dozen friends were company enough.[31]

Coleman devised a plan to submit Barnes's novel to T. S. Eliot at Faber & Faber. She imagined him to be one of the best critics in all of literary history—though it was a pity about the poetry—and greatly feared his judgment. Yet her determination to see *Nightwood* published was even greater than for her own current novel, which with trepidation would also be submitted to Faber. Support for *Nightwood's* publication could be expected from the poet George Barker, whose career Eliot had long supported, and Antonia White, who admired Barnes's writing. Barnes was not happy about Coleman's enthusiastic circulation of her unpublished novel among London friends, but there was little she could do about it. She was also uncomfortable about such frequent and revelatory correspondence with Coleman: "Darling, you pile up on top of me like a life-work! . . . If you had got hands on Proust he would never have written his great work, he would have written letters of the remembrance of things past."[32]

Edwin Muir read manuscripts for Faber & Faber and was thus a perfect conduit for Barnes, for as a poet he could recognize the brilliance of the novel's prose. Not satisfied to rely solely on Muir, Coleman wrote a careful letter to Eliot on 25 October 1935, mentioning

Nightwood's faults but also its virtues. Her strategy was to cut the ground out from under Eliot before he could reject the novel in a pro forma manner. She damned Barnes's early work ("to spike his guns" she told Barnes) as exhibiting "emotional falseness," a problem kept to a minimum in *Nightwood*. She perceived the lack of "organic structure" but praised the book as containing "as extraordinary writing as has been done in our time." Coleman requested an interview to discuss the excerpts from Barnes's novel Muir had read, then passed along to Eliot.

Eliot responded cautiously, for he was irritated by the book's style, comparing the work unfavorably with that of Kay Boyle, whom Faber had published. Emily cut out ten pages of Dr. O'Connor, and on 4 November she sent the entire typescript, marking the passages she thought Eliot would like. She still had serious misgivings about weaknesses she was sure that he would spot, principally the blurred focus from so much universal pain, which should have been foregrounded in the tragedy of Nora and Robin.

In any case, on 20 January 1936, Eliot committed himself to *Nightwood*, saying in a letter to Coleman that now that he had read the entire typescript, he was more favorably impressed. If Mr. Faber couldn't be persuaded, then he would certainly support publication by another press. He suggested some revision of *Nightwood*'s beginning and the deletion of the last chapter, but he read the novel differently from Coleman, seeing O'Connor as a central consciousness. He hoped for a final decision sometime soon. Emily Coleman was ecstatic, and wrote Barnes: "Faber & Faber are the best publishers for a serious writer *in the world*."[33] And she wasn't far wrong. Barnes was eternally in her debt, for Coleman had accomplished something of which Barnes herself seemed incapable—she had attracted someone as eminent as T. S. Eliot to *Nightwood*, and he would guarantee its publication.

Emily's diary of late April 1936 records details of her visit to Eliot to discuss *Nightwood*. She was terrified of the trip to the Faber offices in Bloomsbury and went early, dodging into the British Museum to muster courage.

As soon as I got in the tiny little room of Eliot (in which he has the mantelpiece covered with snapshots) everything, of course, changed. He was very affable, and whats more, is attractive. He has an odd face. He looks like a sea-lion. We had tea and American chocolate cake. . . . Most of the time we were laughing. We laughed about everything. I had a list (in my bag) of intense serious subjects. I was going to get down deep into Life and Lit. But we just laughed; he made rather good jokes about Barker and Djuna—what she might be like—about everything. He has the sweetest smile. . . . He said he didnt think he would have guessed Djunas book was written by a woman . . . he didnt think the Doctor seemed like a womans creation. . . . The problem was that the book might be taken up by the censor. I said I knew she would be amenable to small matters of omissions. . . . They are really enthusiastic about the book. [Eliot's] eyes deep and very moving, his smile wide, his face sad and miserable, hollow eyes, not a very good brow. He sounded like any intelligent intellectual. . . . He said he could not read new poetry because it upset him if it was good and bothered him if it was bad. Did not mind prose.[34]

Eliot called Emily Little Annie Oakley, perhaps on the basis of her inclination to shoot from the hip as much as her address. Her London flat at 7 Oakley Street was in a neat brick row house with black and white checkered stairs, just above that of Peter Hoare. The street was close to the Thames. She had met Hoare in 1929 at a party in Paris and was avidly pursuing him, but he showed little inclination to be caught. Susan Chitty gives a wonderful description of Hoare:

Emily was having one affair, writing a novel about her last one ["Tygon"] and planning a third. The current affair was with Sir Alexander S. [Peter Hoare] a man of extraordinary intelligence whom she had met at a Left Bank party in Paris. He was rather high up in the Foreign Office, a small middle-aged Scot, with a long inquisitive nose, and eyes as bright as a bird's. His private life was arid but when he got tight he liked to dance with a tall blonde whose breasts could rest on his balding head, while he breathed heavily into her rib cage. His life was divided into secret compartments. The compartment he failed to keep secret was the one immediately above his flat. Emily, with marriage in mind after a five-year siege, moved into it.

There can seldom have been a stranger coupling than that of Emily and Alex, "she so Bacchic, he so puritanical. He had no opinion of her mind and thought her interminable poems would have been best unwritten. (He himself had published a paper on Rilke.) As a lover he was reluctant."[35] Hoare became "head of the international division of the Home Office" and was friends with the poets George Barker, Dylan Thomas, and David Gascoyne.[36]

Hoare loved Emily in his way, but he surely suspected that her proximity could be disastrous to his peace of mind. Once he told Coleman, "If you would wear no clothes, had no temper and perfect social manners, I could stand you."[37] Hoare, exceedingly prudish about sex and a confirmed bachelor, felt guilty about satisfying Coleman's pressing sexual needs. Barnes wrote rather obscurely of this problem: "Can Peter Hoare help it that he sits on himself as if he were a door knob, instead of an egg?"[38]

At the same time, Emily was falling in love with George Barker, fifteen years her junior and a friend of Hoare's. "He regards me as an American older woman who likes literature, who has gobs of money, travels the globe, knows the world, and hence has to be somewhat kept up with."[39] At one point they had sex, but Barker felt physically ill afterward because his preference at that time was for men.[40] Coleman's lack of success with the men she pursued seems attributable either to her being attracted to men who were not attracted to her or to her pursuing them with a maniacal intensity that sent them scurrying. As for Barker, he claimed to be both bisexual and married to a lesbian, which put him rather in the closet with Robert McAlmon.

When it became quite clear that Faber & Faber would accept *Nightwood*, Barnes immediately arranged to go to Europe. In the meantime, to support herself in New York, Barnes had obtained a temporary federal sinecure for artists with the Works Progress Administration, writing a history of radio as part of a collective effort to produce a guide to New York City. The project required her to do research in the New York Public Library. She began work in February 1936, at a salary of twenty-two dollars per week, and may have worked until the end of April, when she prepared to sail for Europe. (Her brother Saxon asked her not to cash any WPA checks in *his* bank.) Like other writers, she hated the job, describing the WPA office as "one great morsoleum of misery and deferred life."[41] One reason her job was disagreeable was that she found it difficult to escape radical politics. "The communists are closing in on me, everyone of the W.P.A. (a few exceptions) give me talks on the mass consciousness (Muffin's new book to be about 'the people'!) and offer me massive tomes on the same subject."[42] Even Charles Henri Ford had become a dedicated Marxist, as she wrote to Barney:

> He got like that in New York—its the style now—everyone (in the literary & artistic world) has now a notion that any artistic manifestation is utterly worthless *unless* it is "in the Mass"—Filled with "Mass Consciousness"—whatever that is—I am, of course, being an Elizabethan—quite indifferent to the Mass, tho I do *not* doubt (much to my sorrow) that they will shortly be ruling the roost. What is the most annoying thing about Charles & all the others like him, is that they all take it as if it were something amazing & *new* a great big discovery—whereas its something the world has fought for 20 centuries, in one form or another—.[43]

She had planned to give up her job as soon as Peggy agreed to bring her to Europe, and was delighted to receive the news that *Nightwood* would be published. She sailed on 2 May 1936, taking the Norddeutscher Lloyd ship *Europa* to Cherbourg. Her departure was hastened by another item of news: her Paris apartment had been wrecked by the previous tenant. The good news did not quite cancel out the bad, for her Paris apartment was an extension of herself, so that she felt personal violation as much as financial loss. How would she afford the repairs necessary to rent it? Further bad news came when she heard that Dan Mahoney was destitute and suffering from stomach cancer, though his death did not seem imminent. Barnes cared deeply for the welfare of her friends, if not for humanity at large. Soon she would see for herself how things stood in Paris and London.

She went first to Paris, where, with her maid, she worked to straighten out the chaos in her apartment. On 16 May, she was off to London; over the next few years, she would travel between these two cities with some frequency. In June, she, Emily, and Peter Hoare drove to see Djuna's mother's town of Oakham, in County Rutland, an unusually exciting visit to Barnes's ancestral past. Oakham would provide the setting for *The Antiphon*. With excitement, she wrote to her mother of Oakham, and about her mother's sister, Susanna, who was living in dire poverty in London. Barnes enlisted her brothers—especially Charlie and Zendon—to help Aunt Sue financially.

By June, Barnes was negotiating with Faber & Faber over the contract for *Nightwood*. She wished to reserve the American rights and to have an advance, but Eliot could not agree. The firm was to retain a quarter of all profits and seemed inflexible.[44] Coleman pushed Barnes to be modest in negotiating the contract, to remember her publishing difficulties and just be thankful. Emily had given Eliot longer and shorter versions of the novel; as good publishers, he and F. V. Morley chose the shorter one, in part because Dr. O'Connor was not to be allowed to take over *Nightwood*, regardless of Eliot's approval of his monologues.[45] Beyond this, in a letter of 23 July 1945 to Barnes, Eliot says that he and Morley improved the novel by eliminating a good deal of material deemed irrelevant. Barnes seemed not to mind.

Eliot has been blamed for cutting too much from both *Nightwood* and *The Antiphon*, but Barnes wrote one Helene Hollander that "one cut was made by Mr. Eliot (an unnecessary story by the Doctor) and some few of his Eliot's objections smoothed out. As he said, I seemed to be able to justify my lines."[46] His editing was probably more extensive than Barnes remembered.

That Eliot stuck his neck out for Barnes is evident from a letter he wrote to Geoffrey Faber about *Nightwood*:

> I believe that this may be our last chance to do something remarkable in the way of imaginative literature. . . . This writer is some-

body to whom something has happened that happens to very few (because we don't want it): she has caught up with her own sorrow, identified it and tapped it on the shoulder. . . . It's a sorrow much deeper than personal vicissitudes, of course, but it is the sorrow of life, the worm unkillable by any of the agents of this world. And as for her style, it has what is for me the authentic evidence of power, in that I find myself having to struggle, directly after reading, not to ape it myself: and very few writers exercise that pull.[47]

When she was first in town, Djuna Barnes shared Emily's Chelsea flat at 7 Oakley Street, where she came to know the likable Peter Hoare. In early July of 1936, she went to Peggy Guggenheim's summer house, Yewtree Cottage.[48] Then it was back to Paris, where she wavered between selling the apartment and holding on for dear life. (With sadness and many misgivings, she would sell it in July 1937.) She wanted to visit Chartres with Dan Mahoney, who knew how to appreciate church architecture. Mahoney was getting used to the notoriety of being the original of Dr. Matthew O'Connor. Once, Barnes found him in bed dressed for a scene in *Nightwood*, "all bathed and perfumed and made up like a hussy, the clock was ticking, the radio going, the kitchen kettle steaming, and he was eating peppermints!" She pitied him his advancing age and illness but was at the same time rather horrified: "what he says is too much like a cornered rat, the granary is closing down, for that I am sad for him, but its a rather dreadful spectacle."[49]

Barnes found Englishmen "hard to take, they all seem to suffer from a highly sensitized inferiority and a shyness and lack of life that might be called educated erasure," for they appeared "to crawl out of the cradle with long whiskers and a coffin on their backs."[50] As for Frenchmen, she wrote Lady Ottoline Morrell that she found them "most displeasing."[51] Of course, she had nothing good to say about America or Americans either. But she would hear no criticism of Paris, for she had rediscovered her intense attraction to that city.

While in Paris, she tried to make some progress on the biography of Elsa von Freytag Loringhoven but found it all becoming poetry, which wouldn't do. She felt torn, wishing to write verse, while believing that the world had no use for the poetic muse; the novel was all the fashion. Eventually Eliot expressed the opinion that Elsa's life should be used solely as impetus, just to gather some momentum on a writing project, and if it turned into something different, that would be entirely satisfactory.[52]

While Barnes was struggling with Elsa in Paris, *Nightwood* was published in London around 15 October 1936, with a dedication to Peggy Guggenheim and John Ferrar Holms. To Barnes, Faber & Faber seemed a bit high-handed and ungenerous. For instance, they wished to keep advertising to a minimum, supposedly so as not to attract censorship; of course, this would also limit sales. When Barnes communicated her fury at the purple cover and annoying errata, Eliot sought to soothe her feelings on these and other issues.

Word certainly got out that an important novel had been published, for Lady Ottoline Morrell, the Hermione of D. H. Lawrence's *Women in Love*, began sending invitations to Barnes in early November. Barnes was wary of this patron of the arts who had invaded her privacy so far as to ask her if she was a lesbian. (Barnes responded "no.") Lady Ottoline sent her a volume of Keats letters and promoted *Nightwood* among friends such as Julian Huxley, who wished to meet the author. When Barnes knew her, Lady Ottoline was recovering from a stroke, but she wouldn't have been Barnes if she hadn't seen her ladyship's disability as essentially grotesque: "her hand laid across her throat clasping her pearls really alarming, looked as if someone behind her had a great paw on her for a mantlepiece rest."[53]

While Barnes was in Paris, her friend Emily was bouncing in and out of beds as if propelled by an unseen force. In an amazing letter to Barnes dated 12 October 1936, she announced that she was going to marry the poet Humphrey Jennings. Chitty says that Jennings "became a film director and died by walking backwards off a cliff in Japan while planning a take."[54] Perhaps he had a vision of Emily in pursuit. She had dallied with him innocently while waiting for Barker, then had quickly fallen in love. Nevertheless, she went on to seduce Barker, who was so unsuccessful in hiding his disgust that in anger she returned home and slept with Hoare. These encounters in turn convinced her that her amorous designs on Hoare and Barker were at an end and she was now free to pursue Jennings. As they walked together in Kew Gardens, she announced her wish to marry him.[55] As far as she was concerned, the matter was settled, but in the next month, when he kept putting her off, she quarreled with him, and the truth came out: he was already married and had two children. She wrote Barnes: "The colossal brutality of his behaviour is beyond belief."[56] By the middle of January, she would be hopping into bed with Dylan Thomas.

In Paris at the end of November, Barnes suffered several sleepless days and nights with an abscessed tooth. Since the age of twelve, she had experienced dental problems; once, Saxon Barnes had paid a seventeen-hundred-dollar dentist's bill for her. Barnes had little faith in medicine, dentists, or doctors, and delayed seeing them until matters became intolerable. In general, her health was declining: when others drank sherry, she drank gin or whiskey; she smoked heavily (Chesterfields), got no exercise, and was often depressed. Chitty says: "she seldom showed much respect for the medical profession. She referred to an expensive pill prescribed by a Harley Street specialist as 'powdered Christ.' "[57]

Then there was some good news: Harcourt, Brace had bought the American rights to *Nightwood* from Faber & Faber, had given Barnes an advance of fifty pounds, and would publish the novel in 1937. Furthermore, Eliot had written a 1,500-word preface, which made Barnes very proud, though a good deal of it consisted of posturing: No, *Nightwood* was not precisely a poetic novel, but readers of poetry would best appreciate it. No, it was not a psychopathic study. He found "the great achievement of a style, the beauty of phrasing, the brilliance of wit and characterization, and a quality of horror and doom very nearly related to Elizabethan tragedy" (*N* xvi). It was on the whole not a very helpful introduction, but it did attract attention as an apparent imprimatur by T. S. Eliot. In fact, it smacked of coercion. Barnes told James Scott that Eliot had "really missed the mark" in his introduction, that "the only two people who have got it right are Edwin Muir . . . and the literary critic Joseph Frank."[58]

Emily Coleman said that Barnes's "attitude to Eliot was that of a little girl *bringing an apple to Teacher*," a sentiment Barnes did not deny.[59] Not very flattering, but not far wrong, except that Barnes was certainly not diffident, for she delighted in baiting the poet. Eliot truly admired Barnes: he kept her photo on his office wall, between his wife and W. B. Yeats, and just above Paul Valéry and Groucho Marx. How does an American comedian enter this distinguished literary company? Peter Hoare wrote Barnes: "If you don't understand TSE's cultivation of Groucho Marx, you have forgotten his penchant for farting fruit (your phrase) and similar forms of fun."[60]

Eliot delighted in Barnes's company. She had met him at the Café de Flore in the early 1920s. At the end of October 1937, at a tea given by Lady Ottoline, she again met Eliot, who, though smothered with attention, wished to be with Barnes. As she left, he ran to put her into a cab, inquiring after her health. She expressed dismay that she couldn't write, for to friends she now expressed her fear that *Nightwood* might be her last book. Djuna Barnes came to love and deeply respect T. S. Eliot and would depend on his advice for many years to come.

Barnes was also flattered by Dylan Thomas's enthusiasm for her novel. Apparently he read passages of it at Cambridge University to admiring students and even derived the imagery of one his poems from Barnes's novel.[61] He thought *Nightwood* one of the three best novels by women. Years later, his melodious voice would be recorded reading *Nightwood* for Caedmon Records, perhaps a confirmation of Eliot's idea that it was a poetic novel.[62] In any case, Barnes felt pride and admiration for Thomas, believing that his voice was the best reading voice that she had ever heard (she also loved Eliot reading *The Waste Land*), and, perhaps in consequence, declined numerous requests to record her work herself.

Others were unenthusiastic about *Nightwood*. Eliot failed to persuade André Gide to write the introduction for the French translation; though he surely hadn't read it, he was loath to stick his neck out for a writer he scarcely knew.[63] Ezra Pound disliked *Nightwood*: it was all a "muddle"; he thought *Ladies Almanack* better, he told Natalie

Barney. In slurring Barnes's novel, he also disparaged Eliot as a critic. Pound once wrote a limerick about Djuna in a letter to Eliot's colleague F. V. Morley:

> There once wuzza lady named Djuna
> Who wrote rather like a baboon. Her
> Blubbery prose had no fingers or toes;
> And me wish Whale had found this out sooner.[64]

Barnes savored revenge against Pound in a letter to Coleman:

> He now thinks hes a sort of Caesar Borgia, and to that end has had collonades [sic] and what not painted on the walls of his three by two study. Olga Rudge (ex-lesbian poor dear, and mother of [or Homer—don't know which] Omar Shakespeare Pound) is kept with the goats on the hill, tho occasionally shes allowed to climb down the slippery stones of Rapallo to the meeting House to play her fiddle, Mrs Pound somewhere in the offing, darning his beard I presume! He writes in the local gazette, and talks like a hick, every time he opens his mouth a stalk of wheat falls out.[65]

Barnes was anxious to hear from Thelma Wood now that her novel was out, and Wood finally wrote, expressing her sense of pain and mystification as to what the grievance of *Nightwood* was all about. She said that she felt that "a truck had hit her," and had no notion why Barnes had decided "to ruin her life." Barnes cried many tears, but decided "shes sort of right after all, in that the writer is a bastard, take him how you like, for at least out of his miseries he makes a book, and she, out of hers?"[66]

Though she couldn't always practice it, Barnes believed in self-discipline and the daily struggle of writing. Chitty says:

> Djuna encouraged Antonia to write. She wrote, "It's getting the awful rust off the spirit that is almost insurmountable. It's why working every day is important—one may write the most lamentable balls but in the end one has a page or two that might not otherwise have been done. Keep on writing. It's a woman's only hope, except for lace making."[67]

Barnes was having some vivid dreams at this time, stimulated perhaps by her increased consumption of alcohol and/or depression. These dreams she pondered in a letter to Emily. "Because—dreams are unconscious, so there is something to be learned of them, like children possibly. The moment you put them to school, give them direction consciously, you are bound to love some of their secret code."[68]

Two dreams are especially remarkable, the one described in Chapter 7 about Thelma Wood in "a blue china coffin" and one that was aquatic:

Melancholia, melancholia, it rides me like a bucking mare—a seal woman came up out of my sleep and told me to feel her, she was almost like a human, but prickly when you touched her, and she had legs and a pelvis, but nothing else, and she said she could not talk much because she was fish, she smelled like a fish, briny, and her brothers were ferocious puppy seal animals with puppy hair, they came up out of a lake to fight me, and one of them ate my only weapon, a long brush, and my cain [sic], head and all, under the waters of the lake a red and white dog seemed to be floating, but not dead, shallow blue water, under a line of trees—how is that for a dream? Animals, always animals, its sickening, and those babies of my mother's, and now its fish.[69]

In the summer of 1937, Barnes moved into a large Chelsea flat over an antique shop at 60 Old Church Street, on the corner of King's Road, near where Peter Hoare and Emily Coleman lived. Rain leaked through an overhead skylight, but it was otherwise suitable.[70] It wasn't far from one of her favorite pubs, The Six Bells. Djuna also had a new passion, Antonia White's former lover Rudolph "Silas" Glossop (1902–), whom she introduced to Barnes in May 1937, when Glossop returned from the Gold Coast.[71] Susan Chitty, the daughter of Glossop and White, described the occasion:

That meeting was never forgotten by anyone who was present. Djuna was fascinated by Silas, declaring that he had "the smell of death." She said she would paint him as a white negro with his face upturned against a ground of tropical fruit (she had trained as a painter). When they left, Djuna said "Walk away. I want to see you leaving. Yes, you've got that gorgon look from behind. Take care you don't develop flying buttresses, the infirmity of the Gothic."[72]

Antonia White's diary (25 May 1937) records the first meeting:

Last night I had an unexpectedly delightful evening with Djuna, Emily and Silas. . . . Djuna who had been inspired for hours became a little drunk, noisy and repetitive. Apart from nervous anxiety that Djuna would be bored by Silas (he was obviously excited and de-lighted by her) and that Emily would be violent with him, it was an excellent party. I fairly swam in flattery—Djuna said she had never known I could look beautiful before—and far better, she likes the prose poems. . . . He and Djuna were in complete accord. I was delighted. [Emily] and Djuna both have the same obtuseness of not being interested in anything that is not *immediately* relevant to their concern of the moment.[73]

Glossop was a mining engineer from Derbyshire, who had spent several years prospecting in northern Canada and in Africa. His father had been a bank manager and his mother a Scottish Calvinist. He met Antonia White in 1928, when she was involved with another man, made her pregnant, then in the spring of 1929 was obliged to leave for Canada. Glossop, passionate about literature and music, was un-usually intelligent and knowledgeable, and thus an excellent compan-ion for Barnes, Hoare, and Coleman. Lyndall Hopkinson, White's daughter by Tom Hopkinson, described Glossop: "tall, firmly built and good looking, he was a contrast to the people of indeterminate sex with whom [White] usually mixed. . . . He had a sensitive, intuitive poet's mind which was often overshadowed by the logical scientist in him."[74]

Barnes delighted in Glossop, but, as in her other love affairs, she was unlucky. Though she was still attractive enough in spite of her obvious alcoholism, she felt that he was initially attracted to her be-cause *Nightwood* had recently been published; there was the aura of Eliot in the background.[75] She wanted to paint him as a bull heifer:

"when his hair is rumpled, full across his forehead & he's a little heated, he's *exactly* a baby bull—slightly negroid, a little Mongole—& a lot distempered!"[76]

Silas Glossop was a bit puritanical about sex, which put Barnes on a parallel course with Coleman. In both cases, the fault was considered to lie in a dour Scottish heritage, but from the viewpoints of Hoare and Glossop, any tendency to a romantic commitment was made difficult by the intensity and aggressiveness of the women who pursued them. By the next summer, Glossop seemed to Barnes a lost cause: "I keep finding myself pouring out energy in 'bright' remarks only to look into the roof of his [Silas's] mouth."[77] Glossop's sexual interest in Barnes faded by about March of 1938 (it usually lasted about six months, he said), but Barnes once claimed that he proposed to her (C. Page 277). Glossop wanted friendship; Barnes wanted a lover. Of course, she cherished his gentleness and sweet companionship, but she wanted it all, and if she demanded a total romantic commitment, he was inclined to want no part of Barnes. He seemed to struggle for air.

> He says he will never care for me again as a sweetheart, that something has gone completely out of it for him, tho he is fonder of me now than in the beginning, indeed that that is his reason, he tells me now that I repelled him as well as fascinated him in the beginning, because of my rough facade, and thats what he needs for sexual stimulus, repulsion and attraction!!! Now that he feels me to be (quoting) "sweet and kind, and good" he can't do a thing about it. Do you see why women have become bitches, and harpies and furies? Because men can go to bed with them only so.[78]

Glossop did not deceive her or himself, except perhaps about sexuality, for he pursued women he didn't love, then told Barnes about his unsatisfactory romantic adventures: "he comes to me with these girls like a dog that has stolen a bone and sorrowfully lays it on the mat before his mistress."[79]

In other words, what Glossop told her was that he wanted no sex precisely because he loved her, a position Barnes felt was immoral. Her own view of sex was recorded by Antonia White: "Djuna told me she had no feeling of guilt whatever about sex, about going to bed with any man or woman she wanted, but that she felt extremely guilty and ashamed of drinking."[80]

Glossop was generally depressed about the situation, for he must have seen not only how he hurt Barnes but how dependent she was becoming on alcohol in her daily struggles with love and writing. White had the right perspective: "So I must feel there is something unbelievably shameful in the *desire* to attract. . . . Djuna has done the same thing with Silas. And she goes on clinging to him although she *knows* it is the wrong thing to do." As Barnes told White, "No man can stand an ailing woman."[81]

Part of Barnes's problem with Silas Glossop may have been her complaining about age and illness, because she told Coleman, "Peggy said she thought the reason he had gotten over me (physically) was because I kept on saying what an old woman I am."[82] Glossop, who was ten years her junior, agreed, which infuriated Barnes.

Barnes was concerned that Antonia White would discover the details of her unsuccessful affair with Glossop and blow it all up into a major scandal, for she looked for opportunities to disparage him. To further complicate matters, according to Chitty, Barnes was also attracted to White during September of 1937:

Djuna at this time seemed almost to fall in love with Antonia. One night at the studio she put a naughty idea into Antonia's head. She said Antonia had the power for evil of a Borgia, and should use it. " 'You crash straight into other people's lives and wreck them. Look at Tom . . . I saw him in his boat the other day and that engine just kept right on stuttering, "Tony . . . Tony . . . Tony . . . Tony . . . Tony." ' As she said this she kept kissing me and pulling my hair, saying 'But you're wonderful darling, you're marvelous. I can paint you now. I never thought I would want to. There's something funny and Greek about the back of your head . . . But I'd rather be dead for a row of pins than in love with you.' "[83]

Nightwood seemed to grow on White, and Barnes, pleased, quoted back to her her view of the novel: " 'Heaven revealed only in negation,' certainly the tendency of the modern writer (American, at least) is to put bearable things in an unbearable form—so if mine is the reverse, I'm glad of it."[84]

At times, White infuriated Barnes:

> Had lunch with Tony, I really get to hate that woman, she is so spotty! One moment something you want in your life and the next someone you would like to see floating in the Arno—she is really a cat. I know that my protracted ill health is a bore to everyone (chiefly to myself) but when she said "What do you really want Djuna?" and I replied "To die," she snapped out, with as much venom as would stock the guts of ten adders, "Then die"! A little unnecessary from a "friend" what?[85]

In her unpublished diary of 1938, Marian Bouché recorded her observations about her friend Djuna Barnes's sense of futility: Barnes felt that *Nightwood* would be her last major publication, that the British were superior to her in education, and she seemed actually to prefer the company of equally gloomy people. But Bouché also remembered with pleasure the Barnesian wit. When offering whiskey, she inquired, "will you have milk or water with it?"[86]

Barnes desperately needed help during this time and continued to rely to some extent on Glossop. She told one Dr. Alsop, who examined her, that she "drank like a fish and smoked like a chimney," but he thought the problem was more "nerves."[87] The symptoms of her illness were "fainting, giddiness, melancholia," but also insomnia, vomiting, lack of regular diet and exercise, the inability to work, and, behind it all, a nervousness to the point of hysteria. She wondered how *Nightwood* ever got written, and whether she was now cursed, as though Thelma still had some power over her.[88] All this affected her interaction with others. She hated people she didn't know well, but she found she now regretted not marrying and having children, after a lifelong aversion to both.

When for a short time her brother Saxon entered a sanatorium because of extreme stress, she nearly went over the edge, pleading hysterically with Peggy Guggenheim for money to help pay his bills and promising to do anything in return. As payment, she began a portrait of Peggy at this time, to be called "The Unhappy Vixen," but the foxy subject refused to sit still for it. Much of Saxon's stress was traceable to problems with his mother, so with rest and quiet he soon recovered. Apparently Mrs. Barnes coughed constantly and made life generally miserable for herself, Saxon, and his bride, Eleanor.

Though Djuna resented Saxon's treatment of her in New York, he was her favorite brother, and she was always passionately loyal to those she loved. She feared that she, too, would end up in a nursing home, for it was more than once suggested that she should go to one to dry out. (This became a lifelong fear.) Worried friends talked among themselves about her condition and what might be done about it. Glossop said that she had become "violent in speech and action."[89]

If Barnes's condition made her highly irritable, it also brought out her most acerbic wit, giving one a preview of the famous Barnes of later years, when a visitor saw little else but spite. For instance, a letter of 18 June 1938 to Coleman mentions Peggy Guggenheim hiking off to Paris again in pursuit of Samuel Beckett. Eliot's friend John Hayward was "tight, AS USUAL," when they visited him. The importance of fixing one's teeth is emphasized, because "one has to have teeth to snarl with even [though] one has no prowling." Edith Sitwell was "looking like a fat . . . anteater that has just regurgitated the last ant." Lady Cunard had "nine million wrinkles all in the other place, a kittenish manner and a large flowered hat." "Going to see Pavlic's show, probably ghastly." "Janet Flanner and Solita for lunch, poor girls, Janny beginning to suspect that possibly being a contributor to N. Yorker not such great genius after all." Advised by Dr. Alsop to make a life, Barnes said, "I *had* made one, that was the trouble, and that it was just finishing off the last gizzard like a hyena." And so on—all this in a single letter. Too much drink, too little sex, illness, and no work accomplished. Meanwhile, Emily Coleman was in Montreal trying to make a life with yet another new lover, leaving Djuna "all alone bailing the beastly canoe trying to get to Lethe!"[90]

CHAPTER 12

Stop *Praying* for Me!

The poisoned tree that blooms
In the orchard of my dreams
Once grew the fairest blossom.
Now a twisted nigger lives
In the shadow of its leaves.
His swollen brain's a beehive.[1]

B y the late 1930s, Djuna Barnes was caught in a spiral downward into alcoholism, self-deception, and continual illness. Only years of struggle and near-superhuman willpower would enable her eventually to extract herself. Soon she would give up even the pretense of writing or painting or being sociable and just drink alone in her room. Silas Glossop noticed that while her friends drank to promote conviviality, Barnes drank to insulate herself from human contact. It was only in 1950 that she stopped drinking and turned her full attention to artistic creativity, chiefly Elsa's biography (which she would never finish), *The Antiphon*, which would be her last great achievement, and her poetry, which gave her such pleasure. When it came down to it, the immense task of wreaking vengeance against her family in the strange idiom of *The Antiphon* required a riveting sobriety of which she had not been capable in years. It was either alcohol or revenge, so she chose the latter.

Virtually all of Barnes's friends were discussing the impending conflagration in Europe in the late 1930s. What views Barnes herself had were a bit askew, mostly because she had little interest in contemporary events: "As for the political situation, it appears from this end, that the French, not the Germans want war, that is the Cabinet —not the people, something to do with moneys of course."[2] Two years later, it was as if she had heard nothing about impending war: "I'm such a fool never to read a paper, either Peggy or Marian Bouché, I forget which, told me there was a war scare! I had no notion of it until then!!"[3] Still, if she thought to be worried, it was concern for architecture that bothered her: "I do not so much lament the dead in Spain—if they want to kill each other—well enough—but when they lay hands on cathedrals etc—then I am blind with misery—."[4] Humans were expendable; art was another matter.

Barnes tried to keep up a dialogue by mail on literary matters with Emily Coleman, but her mind could scarcely concentrate for the daily illness. When Coleman asked her for a considered opinion of Henri Bergson's philosophy, she remembered that Courtenay Lemon had made her read his works when they lived together, but it had not sunk in. Now a new effort to read Bergson was quickly given up. Yet she usually spent part of each day reading. The writers who gave her greatest pleasure at this time were Chaucer, followed by Proust, Brontë, Donne, Blake, and Dante, but philosophy was too abstract.[5] Like James Joyce, she had very little patience with D. H. Lawrence.

In October 1938, she had tea with T. S. Eliot and showed him some of her verse. "We got on like a couple of priests with only one robe," she wrote Coleman.[6] Apparently he wasn't very impressed, for he encouraged her to stick to prose, saying that he wished he could write prose as well as she. He jokingly threatened to give her a black eye if she persisted in writing poetry. In the poems he noticed the "tough, strong quality" of her prose but disliked what he considered to be an old-fashioned dependence on iambic pentameter.

In the middle of the next month, Djuna was in Paris again, en route with Laurence Vail and Kay Boyle to their home in Megève. Several years earlier, they had bought a chalet in this lovely mountain village in the Haute-Savoie; they called it Les Cinq Enfants, after their children by various partners. Joan Mellen described the chalet as "all stone and wood, three stories, with a wooden balcony all around carved with hearts and other fanciful decorations, and a dining room big enough for a banquet."[7]

While in Paris, Barnes had lunch with Bob McAlmon, whose new book, *Being Geniuses Together* (1938), she felt was a flop, being all gossip. Barnes hoped that leaving Chelsea, Silas, and the London scene would be good for her health, but the family life she found in the Alpine village southeast of Geneva was irritating, and the daily two-mile walks, with spectacular views of Mont Blanc, did little to alleviate her misery. There were too many children, dogs, cats, too much noise, too little privacy (there was one bathroom), too much depression. She claimed to have reduced her smoking and drinking (though Peggy Guggenheim later said that she averaged a bottle of whiskey a day), and she read some—Count Hermann Keyserling's *South American Meditations*, Kay Boyle's *Monday Night*, Ezra Pound's *Guide to Kulchur*, poems by William Carlos Williams, part of William Faulkner's *Pylon*, but none of it suited her. As for Henry James, he was just a "homosexual old woman."[8]

Even when she was depressed, Djuna's wit was irrepressible. Vail was an avid mountain climber, and he frequently took Kay and the children along. Barnes would certainly have declined any invitation to participate. David Gascoyne was also in Megève, and years later he remembered Barnes's remark "Now whatever is it that makes people want to go climbing mountains? However do you manage if you want to relieve yourself while you're climbing a mountain?"[9]

She disagreed with Kay Boyle on nearly every subject and could find pleasure in neither solitude nor company. Having just had lunch with Robert McAlmon, Barnes would have been sure to disparage him and his new book, which would have infuriated Boyle. Boyle had been in platonic love with McAlmon and would one day reedit *Being Geniuses Together*, with extensive commentary of her own. Barnes had been Vail's lover in 1919–20 and was supported by Vail's first wife, Peggy Guggenheim, whom Boyle hated. Boyle was a very prolific and successful writer, and each would have despised the other as a female competitor for accolades and for Laurence. Barnes could do no work at this time, whereas Boyle could scarcely stop, except at meals. In a jeu d'esprit, Kay even wrote a poem called "Angels for Djuna Barnes." Djuna felt jealous that Kay had a husband and spent her days typing stories, while she drank and indulged in self-pity. A peaceful death was the most appealing thought she could muster. Even now there was still the old attraction between Barnes and Vail, which caused some further tension. Vail knew that Barnes was jealous of Boyle and that she looked for opportunities to disparage her. But Kay was already tired of Laurence and would soon begin an affair with the local ski instructor, Kurt Wick. When Wick was sent off to the Foreign Legion, she turned her attention to his friend, an Austrian baron named Joseph von und zu Franckenstein, who was a refugee from fascism. Barnes wrote Emily Coleman in 1941:

> She is pregnant by him, and the nastiest part of it, for Lawrence [sic], are her remarks to the effect that she has been "killing time" (along with bearing him three children). . . . The bloody fecundity of Kay is revolting. She should have been a rabbit and have written in lettuce. The trouble with that girl is, she's got condor blood, and looks it. There is really something wrong with her. . . . Her stuffing comes out in so many places that one wonders where she is bound.[10]

Barnes dreaded the prospect of returning to London alone in her condition, so the Vails took her to Paris in the middle of January 1939. She stayed at the Hôtel Madison with Peggy Guggenheim, who was involved with several men, including Samuel Beckett (whom she dubbed Oblomov because he spent most of the day in bed). Barnes planned to return to London about 1 February. She had been gone nearly three months and dreaded the meeting with Glossop: "oh God damn love anyway . . . its all so ugly in the end, and seems to serve no purpose except to get one to the grave with a little knowledge."[11] While in Paris, she was extremely ill: "I've wrestled with tigers until my nightdress was soaking wet, that is, struggling *not* to take a drink, which is the *only* thing that stops my fainting spells, and I think I have won out."[12]

She managed to go on the "water wagon" for five weeks and was relieved to find that she had no attacks of nerves, fainting spells, nausea, or depression, but on returning to London she had another confrontation with Silas Glossop, which caused a relapse. It became clear that he didn't want to be her lover, whether she was drunk or sober, but just her friend, which was a difficult enough role for anybody. Glossop would be the last important love of Djuna Barnes's life.

Around 10 February 1939, Barnes rented a room in a London hotel and tried to commit suicide by swallowing eighteen Veronal tablets. These she vomited, but the episode caused a nervous crisis, which resulted in several hospital visits. Hospitals and doctors invariably exacerbated Barnes's condition, for she had no faith in them or the "powdered Christ" they prescribed. Throughout her life she regarded them as simply an invasion of privacy:

> [Peggy] dragged in the two *most* awful female doctors I ever hope to see, tho I'd told her "never a woman doctor" then I was put through the most humiliating two days of my life, you know me and my privacy of feeling, and my inherent shyness and detestation of anyone I don't really like, and then to be stark naked before someone I mistrusted (rightly) and disliked like poison, my private quarters shoved at with rubber gloves (the can containing them opened like a sardine box) the horrible manner of the females treating me like a refractory idiot child, me making faces at Peggy to take them away, and Peggy doing nothing. I could have killed her, but was far too ill, and thats the degradation, to be too ill, thats why beasts, in their decency go off alone to die.[13]

Eventually Peggy sent Dr. McKeand, who had been John Holms's physician at his death; had Barnes been aware of who he was, this alone would have sent her into hysteria. Peggy was wise to keep it a secret.

By 7 July 1939, Barnes was back in Paris, staying at the Hôtel Récamier, of *Nightwood* fame, where she had long wished to live. She had left London in less than an hour, turning over her flat to Silas, leaving behind a dead-end love life. In early September, Guggenheim described Barnes as in a state of collapse, for the most part confined to her bed, outraged at her friends' concern. To Coleman, Barnes wrote: "Natalie Barney really got me down this time I *detest* her, you were quite right about her, fundamentally, she is a cheap—well kept, smug, over fed, lion hunting S.O.B." Barney had asked at her hotel if she "drank & if so, *what* & *how many* bottles! . . . as if she were *my* keeper she always has the air of one perched on Gods piss-pot."[14] Mary Reynolds, who nursed her, in reality hated her, she felt, and "rots with envy."[15] Everybody was jealous of her talent.

About five o'clock one morning, she reported that a bellboy at the Récamier tried to enter her room—to rape her, she thought. She grabbed him in the hall and called the concierge, but nobody would believe that the event wasn't a drunken hallucination. Unlucky things just seemed to happen to her: at one point she broke some teeth when her Paris taxi had an accident, which was especially unfortunate since her teeth were bad anyway.

Barnes was becoming so impossible that Peggy's patience was at an end; she longed for Emily Coleman to take Djuna off her hands, but Emily had left her lover in Montreal and eloped to Arizona with a cowboy named Jake Scarborough. Peggy complained of Barnes's remark that "champagne was cheaper than water," when once she found Barnes drinking with a hotel maid. When Peggy could stand no more, she had her cousin Helen Joyce and a male companion wrestle Barnes into a taxi, then put her on a train for Bordeaux. Peggy was so angry that she threw a pillow in Djuna's face at the station, an insult never forgotten.

On 12 October 1939, Barnes sailed for New York on the *Washington*. She would never live in Europe again and would make only one trip more, in 1950. Guggenheim's friend Yves Tanguy (1900–55), the Surrealist painter, happened to be aboard the *Washington*, for he was emigrating to the United States. As Barnes described it, the crossing was a horrible experience: she had bronchitis, there was danger of attacks from U-boats, the sea was rough, and it was all Peggy's fault for kidnapping her. In New York, she was met by Saxon and Eleanor, Charles Henri Ford, Marian Bouché, and her brother Charlie's new wife, Virginia. She had not expected anybody and descended the gangplank with downcast eyes. After an initial stay with Marian Bouché, she was installed in a single room at 349 East 54th Street with her mother, who coughed constantly at night. Elizabeth Barnes's conversion to Christian Science produced zealous sermons, which made matters worse for Djuna. She was not about to give up the bottle and embrace religion.

For the time being, Barnes would no longer enjoy her regular Guggenheim stipend. Peggy sent money for occasional needs but not the monthly sums of the good old days, so furious was she. She felt that Barnes could stop drinking, that her condition was not alcoholism but complete "moral collapse." She recommended that either the Barnes brothers put her into a sanatorium, so that she could dry out, or Emily move her to Arizona, in which case Peggy would help financially. She refused to continue to pay for Djuna's drinks.[16] "Between me & Djuna there is not a vestige of friendship remaining—she got more & more horrible to me & further & further removed from me, as time went on. I think she was jealous of all my activities & hated me because I supported her."[17] Peggy felt that her support had actually prevented Barnes from continuing to publish creative work after *Nightwood*.

Barnes was outraged at her treatment. She felt that it was unfair to harp on her drinking when she had other health problems as well. Peggy and Helen Joyce both had a "Hitler Complex," which caused them to bully others. Her brothers had carried on the outrage that Peggy initiated. Drinking had nothing to do with her breakdown, she wrote Emily; she'd been ill with bronchitis. Indignities had been heaped on her from all sides. She began to suspect that she would end up like Elsa—down-and-out, friendless, abandoned, forced to spend sleepless nights in a single room with her dying mother, a scenario that was for Barnes the ultimate horror.

Barnes received a commission from *Town & Country* to write an article about Paris, "Lament for the Left Bank," but in order to get through an interview with the editor she had felt it necessary to imbibe, which sent her again into agonies of shivering nervous attacks. When she gained enough composure to write the article, her hands shook so that she could barely type. Barnes made some efforts in her own behalf. She contacted Carl Van Doren and Harry Burton at *Cosmopolitan* to let them know that she was looking for work. She convinced her brother Charlie that she needed a room of her own for two months, because only she could conquer her illness. She asked Charles Henri Ford to take her to the Earle Hotel in the Village, where her friends often stayed. If not for Charles, Emily, Fitzi, and Marian Bouché, she might not have survived, for she needed constant care. Her former lover Peter Neagoe kept his distance.

Since her hands shook, Barnes couldn't even open a soup can. At the same time, she saw herself as engaged in a heroic battle against great odds, surrounded by traitors who conspired to put her away in a sanatorium. Her letters at this time thus constituted a campaign of vilification. "I tell you, the Americans are maniacs—a fierce sadistic race crouching behind radiators."[18]

Barnes took a room for a while in January of 1940 but complained about mice nesting on her neck and the lack of adequate heat. More visits to the dentist and a new dental plate were in the offing. She had new eyeglasses made. But what Djuna wanted was for her family to recognize that she could not work, split the cost of her upkeep among them, and leave her in peace to do as she pleased—approximately what Peggy had done. This they would not do, because they believed what she needed was a full-time nurse.

In March, at their wits' end, her family sent her to a sanatorium in upstate New York, thus perpetrating what Djuna Barnes considered to be yet another violation of her person. Zendon had led her to believe that she would be going to Arizona, then Saxon brought her to Tratelja, on Diamond Point, Lake George. Outrageous! To Thurn she was just a "drunkard" who must be made to come to her senses. Nobody seemed sympathetic. Djuna contemplated revenge in a family biography, but it would have to wait for *The Antiphon*.

The first week in the sanatorium, Barnes just stewed in her room, a room that had been occupied by the Scottish scholar and critic Sir Herbert Grierson (1866–1960), who was hospitalized for the same malady as Barnes but managed to acquire whiskey while there. She apparently gave the psychiatrists fits but made friends with the kitchen staff and maids, who gave her all the dirt on her predecessor. One psychiatrist told her that she was brilliant but was trapped unless she could make money. Since this was what her brothers had been telling her for years, the advice was especially galling. Barnes refused to discuss anything personal with the doctor, preferring subjects such as "Goethe, Bauer, Bachaus, Memling, Mozart, Beethoven and Proust."[19] As she prepared to leave in early April, her two wishes were to find a job and to avoid contact with her family.

Even so, she was forced to return to her mother's room, in preference to the Salvation Army, she had heard, where women were strip-searched, which must have reminded her of her ordeal with the doctors in London. Then Barnes and her mother had a quarrel, which must have resembled the ending of *The Antiphon*. Things were said that had been held in for many years; Djuna would have found herself on the street, had she not been able to stay at Thelma Wood's for a couple of weeks, while Wood was away.

Her mother's attitude toward her might be summed up in an earlier judgment: "I believe she [Djuna] is happiest when she is doing something that is rendering her destitute," she wrote to her sister Sue.[20] Barnes felt that Elizabeth, who had wanted to be a poet, was jealous of her talent. Her mother, Djuna thought, detested and at the same time was fascinated by the libertine life her daughter had known. Once, when Djuna tried to read *Nightwood* to her, she threw it down and said she did not wish her ears to be contaminated. Yet her counterpart in *The Antiphon* is thirsty for lurid details of her daughter's love life. So lonely and frustrated was Elizabeth Barnes that one can understand the simultaneous appeal of Christian Science and licentiousness, or whatever else seemed empowering.

Only Djuna Barnes and Emily Coleman together could have concocted the next episode, one of the most impractical ventures imaginable for an artist such as Barnes, used to Greenwich Village, Chelsea, and the Left Bank. Guggenheim had suggested that Emily bring Djuna to Arizona, and now Helen Westley sent the train fare. One really has to pause for a moment to contemplate the notion of Djuna Barnes—author of *Nightwood*, recovering alcoholic—living on a working ranch in eastern Arizona with Emily Coleman. Emily's lover Jake Scarborough was still married, though separated, and was supposedly afraid to ask his wife for a divorce. He could not stand

Barnes's continual baiting of him. This trio made one of the most volatile mixtures imaginable.

The ranch was near Concho, just south of a Zuni Indian reservation, and Barnes must have gone there in May of 1940 and stayed about two months. She had once written Emily: "Darling, I can't come to Arizona, even if I liked the idea of the west, & I don't, it personifies everything in my father that I hated—Mark Twain—Bret Hart—Walt Whitman sort of thing—Ezra Pound & his hick-prune-chewing prose."[21] In addition, she was used to a modicum of comfort, not an outhouse and rough living miles from any town. She described the ranch to Bob McAlmon, whose brothers lived in Arizona, as "dust, dirt . . . dreariness . . . thousands of miles for a pound of butter . . . dirty dogs, blind eyed horses, crooked shrubbery, and a shit house on a distant hill for glory and charm. I get lyrical when I think of the horror of that visit."[22] After a few rounds with Barnes and Coleman, poor Jake went off to lick his wounds for a couple of weeks. He must have found punching cattle mere child's play compared to dealing with these two eastern tinhorns.

Meanwhile, Peggy Guggenheim had been in France. She was lunching with Brancusi when the bombardment of Paris began, and had three days to leave before the Germans took the city. She went to Megève, sending her collection of paintings—about seventy of them—to Maria Jolas's château near Vichy. Even before Barnes had left Paris, Peggy had been thinking of opening a gallery there, an idea Barnes mightily opposed; she thought it outrageous that Peggy had paid six thousand dollars for a Picasso instead of supporting needy artists. The news of war affected Barnes deeply—not because it might result in vast numbers of people being killed, but because her friends in Europe were threatened. Both Barnes and Guggenheim were oblivious in their different ways to the tragic conflagration that impended.

Back in New York, the happiest news of these years in Djuna's life was that she found an apartment, upstairs at 5 Patchin Place, a private court with iron gate (usually open) near Greenwich Avenue and Tenth Street. Patchin Place, a picturesque reminder of what Greenwich Village once had been, contained fifty flats in two rows, built in 1848 as boardinghouses for the Basque waiters at the old Brevoort Hotel on Fifth Avenue.[23] Many famous writers and intellectuals had dwelled in the short cul-de-sac, including John Reed, Theodore Dreiser, Padraic Colum, and Jane Bowles. E. E. Cummings lived across the way from Djuna, downstairs at number 4.[24]

Djuna Barnes moved into the apartment in September 1940, and for the next forty-two years, until her death, she would live and work there, with a tiny kitchenette behind a curtain, a bath, and an open fireplace. She had managed to scrape together forty dollars for the initial rent and another thirty dollars for food, cigarettes, and other monthly expenses. Emily would try to send twenty dollars indefinitely. Soon Peggy and Mary Reynolds would send regular checks as well. It was in the Village that, after all, Barnes felt most at home, and if she could ever be happy, it was there.

Even with this new life, Djuna had still not given up drinking, which occasioned an angry exchange with Emily when she visited with her son, John, now a student at Columbia. Emily had been frantically trying to raise money for Djuna and had recently agreed to send a monthly stipend out of her own meager resources. She expected a friendlier reception, but Djuna became very drunk one evening, and the next day, when they had planned to attend an opera, her hangover was so intense that she rudely asked Emily to get out.

Back in Arizona, Emily wrote a long letter citing many examples of Barnes's obtuseness about other people's feelings, her egocentricity, her inability to appreciate the best in other people, her constant raging about being abused by those who tried to help her: "I *cannot* understand how someone with your intelligence can be so lacking in self analysis. . . . I think that you are not intellectually honest."[25] Djuna Barnes seemed not to love her friends, Emily said, but inspired their love and devotion, which she seemed to take for granted. She used her friends, always taking, never giving, seeing any opposition to her wishes as abusive and disloyal. The friendship between Barnes and Coleman had been cooling for some time and would never again be intense, but Emily still made a great effort and extracted from Peggy

Guggenheim a promise to send Barnes one hundred dollars a month, plus a lump sum to cover current debts.

In 1945, a long and rather unhappy business relationship began between Barnes and James Laughlin, when one Samuel Sloan suggested that Laughlin's New Directions publish *Nightwood*. The American rights had lapsed since the Harcourt, Brace edition was allowed to go out of print, and several other publishers—including Simon & Schuster, Random House, and Scribner—declined to reissue the novel.

Eliot was fond of Laughlin, though he thought him a disciple of Pound.[26] But Laughlin found Barnes to be approximately as difficult as Eliot did. She demanded that a deluxe edition of *Nightwood* be published on paper that would last a thousand years. She was suspicious of everything Laughlin proposed, even lunch: once, he invited her to lunch with him, but instead of responding she simply sat there, glowering silently.

In the summer of 1945, Barnes signed a contract with Laughlin for the American rights to *Nightwood*, which gave her an advance of three hundred dollars and a ten percent royalty. New Directions printed the novel in 1946 in their New Classics series, in an edition of five thousand copies. (In November 1960, the rights to *Nightwood* were transferred by Harcourt to Barnes.) Laughlin tried to help Barnes in various ways, offering her a chance to translate Jean Genet, until it became embarrassingly apparent that despite all those years in Paris (and the French phrases in *Nightwood*), she knew only a few words of French. On occasion, Laughlin simply gave her money, which, under the right circumstances, she would accept.[27]

Barnes's financial situation improved in the last half of 1946, when the poet Allen Tate got her a job reading manuscripts for Henry Holt publishers, but by the end of the year she had been fired. From the caustic, negative reports she submitted, one can see why she might have been unsuitable for this position, for she seemed to admire nothing she read.[28]

Back in Concho, Arizona (Rafter Three Ranch, Mesa Redondo

Basin), Emily had participated in the branding of thirty-five head of cattle; she sat on their heads, crying her eyes out, while Jake branded their flanks. If Djuna had been there, she could have given them a hand, for her father had taught her to throw a lasso. In her present mood, though, she would likely have branded the cowhands and let the cattle go free.

Emily's main interest now was not Jake or the ranch but Catholicism, for the religious life was beginning to mean more to her even than art. Barnes was envious of her faith but not tempted by it: "Everything is *true* because people believe it," she wrote.[29] Emily had made friends with Jacques Maritain and his wife and was receiving instruction from them in the faith. Of course, Coleman, who could never do anything in moderation, would become the most zealous of Catholic zealots. She even wrote to a Passionist monk to enlist him in converting Barnes. When she wrote a passionately "Catholic" interpretation of *Nightwood* for Charles Henri Ford's new magazine, *View*, she was outraged that he and Barnes refused to accept it unedited and demanded that it be withdrawn. Ford sent a detailed critique of the article, in which Coleman called *Nightwood* the religious book of their generation, a Catholic sermon, in fact. Coleman set out to convert the world, beginning with Djuna Barnes. "Stop *praying* for me," Barnes said.[30]

Another result of Emily's conversion was that she had to leave Arizona and her common-law husband, Jake Scarborough, for according to Church law she was still married to Deak Coleman. She might have been ready to leave Concho anyway, but she seemed to love Jake.

Soon Emily would try to avoid Barnes when she came to New York. The same was true of Peggy, who nevertheless wanted to show Barnes's portrait of Alice Rohrer at the Museum of Modern Art (which eventually rejected the idea). Barnes was now even more distant from her old friends; reclusive, she was satisfied to read, sketch, and brood on injustice:

> I find myself (ask Johnny) cynical, somewhat bitter & correct—in that cool French manner—absolutely anti your type. I started out

grimly sentimental—which is silly. Now I would wish nothing better then to write logically & without emotion. Quite impossible for me of course. I even find in Shakespeare too great a sweetness. I know of no writer as mean as I would be! Proust, amid his icicles, drips sentimentality. John Holms said my book was the darkest, saddest book he ever read. If I ever finish (doubtful) another, I'd like it to be unmitigated & cruel, as cruel as fact.[31]

For approximately the last forty years of her life, Barnes feared being classified as a "lesbian writer," preferring a larger pool of authorship. She might have wished to be known as a "modernist," in the company of Joyce and Eliot, if she had been familiar with that term. To many of those whom Barnes came to know in her later years, she insisted that she was never a lesbian—she had only loved Thelma Wood. By this she probably meant that she was not to be tossed into a category with, say, Natalie Barney, but she could hardly deny that she had been bisexual—more so in earlier years, as she was more heterosexual in later years.

In later years, Barnes could be misogynistic as well as homophobic, but sometimes it was just a question of privacy. In 1961, she refused a request to include a section of *Nightwood* in a volume called *The Lesbian in Literature*. In 1972, she rejected similar requests for a book called *Women and Madness* and one to be published by the Feminist Press. She responded: "Talk about, teach, preach—etc. *writers.* Why *women* writers?"[32] She rejected the idea of women translating *Nightwood* into French and German: "I must admit to a certain distemper in regard to the intelligence of women in general. I'd rather have a man do the translating."[33]

This bitterly unjust attitude was surely exacerbated by her entanglement with Cordelia Coker Pearson of Gastonia, North Carolina. One of the most curious episodes of the postwar years for Barnes, it was an event that could explain the intensity of her subsequent homophobia. Having read about Barnes in a *Time* magazine feature article (18 January 1943), Pearson had written to Peggy Guggenheim in August, asking if Barnes would paint her in riding habit, preferably with a violin, with or without horses.[34] Peggy forwarded the letter. Barnes was angry that her privacy had been invaded but saw a chance to earn some money. When Barnes said that she couldn't get a horse into her room, the poet Allen Tate offered to paint the violin if his wife, Caroline Gordon, could paint the horse. In fact, he was so amused by Pearson's request that on 22 October 1946, he wrote her a letter in the guise of Barnes's secretary, a Miss Pamela Pickle.

> I write to say that Miss Barnes would be willing to undertake your portrait under certain conditions. Miss Barnes feels that perhaps she could not do all the detail of the picture, although she would consider doing that part of it which would be a direct portrait of you. Perhaps it would be possible to persuade Mr. E. E. Cummings, the poet, and Miss Caroline Gordon, the novelist, both very gifted painters, to do some of the background features. I need not say to you that the collaboration of these distinguished persons with Miss Barnes would add greatly to the historical interest of the portrait.[35]

Barnes was distressed by the Pamela Pickle letter, and when she next wrote to Eliot, she seemed convinced that the wariness she had always felt toward Tate had been justified. Tate wrote Pearson an apology, and Barnes sent a respectful letter to her, which encouraged this sad woman at just the wrong moment. A tipsy Cordelia arrived on Barnes's doorstep and soon made her intentions known: she was in love with the author of *Nightwood* and wanted the portrait as a way of becoming intimate with her. Barnes stood all she could, then demanded that she go home. On 28 November 1946, Pearson wrote Barnes: "Surely you cannot hate me as much as it would seem. If you do, it can only be because of my speaking of love. I am positive of doing nothing else in the least manner questionable. How strange that you should condemn me for something which you have interpreted so beautifully in your book."

Her mother came up with a thousand dollars for the portrait, which Cordelia offered as a token of her love, but Barnes was furious at this proposition. Presumably to discourage her, Barnes kept her waiting on the steps at Patchin Place for four hours. Then, trying to be civilized, she allowed Pearson to pose several times for her portrait and even took her to a Mozart opera, but she found her potential patron impossible. Once, in rage, she threatened to call the police.

In a letter dated Christmas Eve, 1946, Barnes stated her terms: $750 immediately and $750 on completion of the portrait, a princely sum for someone whose rent was forty dollars a month. She would arrange for a photographer and would paint from photos, undisturbed. In her own letter, also dated Christmas Eve, Pearson offered Barnes $1,500 to paint her portrait; later she upped the ante to $2,500 for a portrait done from life if Barnes would throw in her portrait of Alice Rohrer and an inscribed copy of *Ladies Almanack*.

Cordelia insisted on returning to New York in April. On her pleading letter Barnes made a note: "To order a painting of herself done by me executed for $15 hundred—spoilt by her drunken 'insistence of immediate shellac.' " In November, Barnes offered again to engage a photographer and said that Cordelia could bring her riding habit. On this letter Barnes wrote: "She orders a painting of herself (in habit-riding). Did not allow it to be finished & insisted on having it varnished while still wet (a crazy drunken girl—a nuisance)."

After the portrait was finished, the letters kept coming.[36] In May 1948, Pearson sent a note and a lock of her hair. In December, she wrote: "I have loved you more than I have loved my own life." She asked for fifty dollars to come to New York. A footnote to another letter says: "For Christ's sake, wake up. I am in love with you. You have driven me mad because you do not seem to be able to bring yourself to the point of doing anything. *Please do it.* I have earned your love."[37] Barnes saved the letters, perhaps expecting legal trouble. One letter says: "Are you really The Red Fox? Do you know how the cub loves the vixen? I know."[38] The most remarkable letter from Cordelia Pearson is the following:

> I swear by name, that if you do not face this thing now, I will climb up out of the depths of Hell—where I have been—to snatch off

your Madonna's robe, and rape you in Heaven! . . . What about those three red-headed babies? You will have to have triplets the first time. If you don't really want the babies, I'll be careful. . . . I mean it would be nice being married!!!!!

Cordelia's cousin Grady Pearson remembers her well. Her father died while she was in college; she had studied violin in Europe; her mother, of southern gentry, worried constantly about her alcoholic daughter, who would go on binges and run off to Greenwich Village. All their money spent, the mother died, then Cordelia ended up in a nursing home, where she died an alcoholic.

The episode with Cordelia Pearson exemplifies Barnes's troubles as the author of *Nightwood*. In 1948, Oscar Baron of the Alicat Book Shop proposed to republish Barnes's *Book of Repulsive Women*. Although she denied her permission, he went ahead with publication, asserting that he hadn't received the refusal. When he could no longer dodge her, he swore that he would put the books in storage, then sold copies anyway. There was little Barnes could do, since the poems had never been copyrighted, but it intensified her distaste for publishers, whom, with the exception of Eliot, she thought dishonest.

The downward spiral of Djuna Barnes was effectively halted in 1950 by her recognition that alcohol was destroying her life and her ability to work. As she told Irwin Cohen and Francesca Belanger years later, "she was tired of waking up in strange places with bits of her clothing missing."[39] She was tough enough to conquer her addiction, and astute enough to recognize that such an illness could not simply be erased but had to be dominated by will, that every battle of desire had to be won, or the war was lost. Even sober, though, she had the problem of intense feelings of anger at real and imagined grievances: publishers, her family, intruders, and basically anybody who requested anything of her. When she realized that only sober and only with her pen could she pay off old scores, she turned her attention away from the bottle and toward her family.

Prussic Acid in Dramatic Form:
The Antiphon

"I know of no writer as mean as I would be!"[1]

Richard Ellmann once wrote that James Joyce "waged literature like a battle," by which he meant that Joyce paid off old scores in his writing.[2] Joyce used the name of his legal adversary in Zurich, a Mr. Carr, for an English boxer who is soundly beaten by an Irishman like Joyce; he gave the surname of Carr's superior, Sir Horace Rumbold, to a professional hangman who writes an illiterate letter of application to perform a public hanging. Djuna Barnes was cut from the same cloth as her friend Joyce: she loved words and knew how to express through them her sense of bitterness and betrayal. In his review of *The Antiphon* (1958), Eugenio Montale called Barnes a sponge of prussic acid; so was the play, and the target was her family.[3]

The Antiphon is set in England in 1939. Jeremy, disguised as Jack Blow, has invited his mother, Augusta, to Burley Hall, her ancestral home, perhaps calculating that she would be brought by her evil brothers, Dudley and Elisha. His motivation is a bit obscure: in assembling the family in this ancient place, he may hope to patch up old wounds, or bring about a reconciliation, through some ultimate confrontation that will purge them all of bitterness toward each other. Maybe this is why he has had built a replica of their American farmhouse, together with tiny dolls resembling family members to inhabit it. This return to some primal scene as yet to be named, or perhaps even envisioned, seems calculated to force both Augusta and her daughter, Miranda, to confront the evil that has wrecked their family. But the cards have been stacked against the women. Since Jack-Jeremy's brothers have been brainwashed by their allegiance to commerce, and his father, Titus, whose schemes have brought the family disaster, is dead, only the women are left to challenge and harass.

Act I provides family history through dialogue among Miranda, Jack, and their uncle, Jonathan Burley. The brothers then state their grievances against the women, who they imagine threaten their financial security. Since Dudley says: "We'll never have so good a chance again;/Never, never such a barren spot" (*SW* 101), apparently murder is a real possibility.[4]

Augusta first appears in Act II, rather dazed and disoriented; she does not quite recognize family members, nor is she sure why everyone is at Burley Hall. The highly complex relationship of mother and daughter becomes apparent. Augusta seems to have admired Miranda when she appeared to be successful as an artist, and to have withdrawn affection whenever she faltered. We see how cheated in life Augusta has been, how she allowed herself to be manipulated out of her inheritance by her husband and his mother, Victoria. Much of this family history is familiar from Djuna Barnes's *Ryder*. The crucial conflict here involves materialism (American) versus culture (English) and the system of loyalties each lifestyle implies.

Elisha and Dudley cavort about the stage at times like intimidating rustics or barnyard animals, interrupting their mother and sister and generally behaving as obnoxiously as possible. When Jack and Burley leave, they become truly vicious, donning masks to hide both guilt and malevolence as they seize and rough up the women, whirling Augusta about and threatening Miranda. Dudley says to his aging mother: "Hi! I love to see a sway-back on the run" (*SW* 77).

Then Jack enters with the dollhouse, saying: "I give you Hobb's Ark, beast-box, doll's house— / That little alchemy unhems a man./ Madam, your contagion," to which Elisha responds: "The House that Jack Built:/ Feed her to the toy!" (*SW* 181) The horrid toy immediately resurrects the past, which Augusta persistently evades. Jack joins in the harassment to make her see that in failing to prevent the sexual violation of Miranda, she has made herself "a *madam* by submission/With, no doubt, your apron over head" (*SW* 185). Miranda takes her mother in to dinner, but one senses that Act II is but one skirmish in a family conflict that will lead to tragedy.

As Act III begins, all the characters are asleep except Augusta, who awakens Miranda, curled up on a gryphon (or griffin) car, apparently a relic of some carnival merry-go-round. Unable to sleep, Augusta wishes to playact, to imagine that she is young again, that none of the events which have wasted her life have happened. The only other woman's life she seems to be able to imagine, though, is Miranda's, a life she disapproves of as wanton yet envies, since at least it has been lived with intensity. Miranda sees all this and pities her mother: "O delayed and waiting creature!" (*SW* 199). To know with finality that life has passed one by is a great horror, though this knowledge, avoided by Augusta, is also Miranda's triumph. Miranda has made mistakes, has failed to make money, but at least she has known passion and some measure of artistic success.

Exasperated that Augusta will not recognize the bond between them or the conspiracy that threatens them both, Miranda says: "Is it really possible that you don't know/That your sons have come to hunt you down?" (*SW* 220). But the sons are by now determined to abandon the women rather than murder them; Miranda begs her mother to forget Elisha and Dudley and stay with her. In effect, she urges her to choose England over America, art over commerce, the daughter over the evil brothers.[5] Here Miranda speaks some of the play's most beautiful lines:

> Then stay with me and uncle Jonathan
> And do as I.
> Caught in the utmost meridian and parallel—
> As of a moor-hen, watching a hawk heel in,—
> Draw 'round in dust the broken wing
> Its last veronica.

But Augusta blames Miranda for her abandonment and, in consummate rage, smashes her daughter's skull with a curfew bell, falling dead at her side on the gryphon from the effort of murdering her only loyal offspring.[6]

There is a self-reflexive quality about the plot of *The Antiphon*, which, in effect, continually reminds the audience that they are watching a drama onstage. Miranda has been a successful actress and writer; Jack Blow seems to be a Shakespearean actor who finds himself on the wrong stage set. The deliberately dramatic atmosphere of the play not only is a reflection of Barnes's lifelong love of the theater and her reading of Renaissance drama but implies her disdain for the practical world of commerce to which her brothers have clung, which pales beside the richness of the theater.

In writing *The Antiphon*, Barnes combined satire with tragedy, as she had done in *Nightwood* and *Ryder*. Although at first glance the play's idiom suggests Jacobean tragedy, *The Antiphon* is really a family tragedy recalling O'Neill's *Long Day's Journey into Night*, Ibsen's *Doll's House*, and the Strindberg of *The Father* and *Miss Julie*. The idea for Barnes's play could, however, have come from a source nearer in time: T. S. Eliot's play *The Family Reunion* was published in the year *The Antiphon* takes place—1939. Barnes had seen it performed that year.[7]

Since Djuna Barnes's family was intent on living down the family history written of in *Ryder*, they must have been especially embarrassed that Barnes now hit them a second time with a public exposé. In both *Ryder* and *The Antiphon*, one may tease out the family history to reveal the invention: both hark back to Huntington days and the history that preceded them, but there is an added layer, which is downright wicked.

The tragic beauty of *The Antiphon* need not blind us to satirical precedents, for by this point in her career Barnes had plenty of experience in roasting loved ones and friends. She satirized the Natalie Barney circle in *Ladies Almanack*, re-created Thelma Wood and Dan Mahoney in unflattering terms in *Nightwood*, and at the end of *Nightwood* portrayed the drunken Thelma figure falling down before Nora's dog in a scene that Barnes's friends immediately recognized as explicitly sexual. In each case, the author couldn't imagine what all the fuss was about: she claimed that these literary counterparts were created out of love, but if so, her love was shockingly harsh. Little wonder that in *The Antiphon*, Augusta says to Miranda: "May God protect us! I wonder what you'll write/When I am dead and gone!" (*SW* 209), a sure sign that, whether by words or palette, Barnes knew exactly what she was doing. In *The Antiphon*, Augusta asks Miranda: "Why don't you love us any more?" to which she replies: "The question is, why do I" (*SW* 215). It is a very good question. It probably is fortunate that Elizabeth Barnes, who died in 1945, did not live to read this play.

An insight into the way Barnes's mind operated to justify her satirical pen and brush appears in a letter to Emily Coleman, in which she discusses her elitist views on privacy, her "dislike of parading, or 'telling on' the innermost secret, feeling that it should only be exposed in art, and then only by the best artist—when it is done for money, it becomes (for me) a brothel of the spirit. In exposing it in art, it is lifted back into its own place again, given back to itself, tho also given to the reader, the eye. Only the best reader will understand it, like initiation."[8] Certainly only the most dedicated readers of Djuna Barnes can become initiates to *The Antiphon*.

Perhaps the most convincing piece of evidence for the revenge motive is to be found in another letter to Coleman, in which Barnes threatens to get back at her family for putting her in a sanatorium; the imagined vehicle at that time was biography, but it would turn out to be drama.[9] The confrontational ending of *The Antiphon*, in which the lid comes off emotions suppressed for years and things are said for which there is no forgiveness, seems to be based on the fight Barnes had with her mother soon after she returned from the sanatorium. Following this battle, she found herself penniless and on the street, forced to ask charity of Thelma Wood, whom she had recently immortalized as the alcoholic somnambule of *Nightwood*. The rage of that time remained at the boiling point for many years, until Barnes poured it into *The Antiphon*. To Willa Muir, Barnes said: "I wrote the Antiphon with clenched teeth, and I noted that my handwriting was as savage as a dagger."[10]

The idiom of *The Antiphon* takes us back to the time when Flore House first came into the family of Djuna's mother, the Chappells. Although the play is set in 1939, Barnes wrote it in vaguely Jacobean verse form, strongly flavored with Shakespearean drama. Obviously nobody spoke this way in 1939; it is as if the characters conspired to select an idiom from an earlier century that would best express their emotions. Nineteen thirty-nine was the year in which Barnes was forced by Peggy Guggenheim to return to New York from Paris, and a year before she was sent to the sanatorium. In the play, Miranda and Jack have just arrived from Paris, fleeing the war.

The setting is a composite of two houses. The first is the one in which Barnes's mother was raised, Flore House, in the English town of Oakham (in England's smallest county, Rutland, which in 1974 became Leicestershire); in the play, it is called "Burley Hall, in the township of Beewick, formerly a college of chantry priests, in the Burley family since the late seventeenth century." Flore House was originally a Benedictine monastery built in the thirteenth century. The doors are peaked as in a church; upstairs was a child's footprint carved in stone, and over the door, the family name.

A map of the Oakham area reveals the village of Burley just to the northeast, beside the old manor house of Burley-on-the-Hill, the other house that inspired the setting. When Barnes visited Oakham, this country house was in ruins (it has since been restored), as is, metaphorically speaking, Miranda's family. Burley-on-the-Hill pro-vided the manorial and family name, plus the general setting for the play, while Flore House contributed the interior detail and historical background.

There appears to be no Beewick in England (although in Oscar Wilde's play *Lady Windermere's Fan* there is a Duchess of Berwick), but to the west of Oakham and northeast of Leicester is the village of Beeby. Barnes took geographical elements from here and there, then placed Beewick near the southeast coast, for the convenience of trav-elers from Paris.

The impetus for the play's setting was Barnes's visit to Oakham with Emily Coleman and Peter Hoare in June of 1936. A page of notes describes what she remembered (Djuna's later additions are in brackets):

> I have, in motoring through Rutland County, Oakham, just seen for the first time that eleventh century (monastery) [College of chanting Priests] which was taken over by my great great grandfather and turned into the Chappell home. From my mother I had all that I knew of it, and the few facts seem to have been well founded, as I later discovered by remarks dropped by a very old man [one Smith], gate keeper to the Palace, or court of assizes, who remembered my mother and her brothers from having gone to the same school, remembered the "pear tree" in which my mother was roosting when the prince on the white horse rode into the yard. The aviaries, the peacocks, the stables where the nobility rested their horses, the great antlered heads in the hall above the holy water stoop, or was it the granite basin, with two carved heads at either corner, where the monks washed their hands. thoughts of the past stelactites [sic] in the mind.[11]

For the dramatis personae, Barnes turned for names to family history and Shakespeare. Two of the characters in *The Antiphon* have ancestral names. Elizabeth Barnes had a brother named Jack; in the play, he is Jack Blow. The Elizabeth Barnes figure is Augusta; one of Djuna's notes mentions "Lord Gainsborough was landlord of Oakham house, sold it to his sister Lady Augusta Noël." A Shakespearean influence is present as well: Jack also resembles three disguised characters from *King Lear*—Edgar, a Tom o' Bedlam type; Kent (banished by the king but too loyal to leave); and the wise Fool. Miranda is the name of a character in *The Tempest*, though the resemblance between the two Mirandas is not striking. In an early draft of *The Antiphon*, she knows who Jack is and shares this information with the audience.

Jonathan Burley is Augusta's brother, a gentle, sensible fellow. The villainous Dudley and Elisha have the allegedly sinister bourgeois value system of Barnes's own brothers, against which Djuna raged.[12] Miranda repeatedly says that she fears merchants.

Miranda's father, Titus Hobbs, never makes an appearance in *The Antiphon*, but he is essentially the Wendell of *Ryder*, whose motto might have been "for polygamy is the only bed a man rolls out of, conditioned to meet the world" (*R* 167). In the play, these vitalistic views are the root of all the evil that has befallen the Burley family. When Barnes ended *Ryder* with a view of Wendell (Wald Barnes) alone at night in a field with his farm animals, his image battered by an authorial voice that says: "And whom should he disappoint now?" bitterness was set to overtake the book's comic muse.

The name Titus resonates for several reasons: Charles Titus was a member of the school board in Halfway Hollow Hills, Huntington, Long Island, and the Barnes's next-door neighbor. The Paris bookseller Edward W. Titus swindled Barnes, she felt, over *Ladies Almanack*. Finally, as Andrew Field points out, Titus Oates of Oakham was "one of the vilest characters in all of English history . . . the seventeenth-century imposter and fabricator of the story that there was a popish plot to burn London, assassinate the king, and massacre Protestants."[13] Hobbs was suggested by Wald Barnes's dubbing a house the family had lived in "Hobbs Ark." He liked to think of himself as the new Noah, or Adam. No matter who he thought he was, Titus Hobbs is the ultimate source of all the family conflict, a sort of original sin for which there is no baptism.

The autobiographical source of Miranda's dispute with her brothers over their callous materialism is clear. In a letter of 30 March–1 April 1940 to Emily Coleman, Djuna Barnes says: "I detest and despise what my brothers live for and by. . . . They are like hyenas creeping closer and closer waiting for me to be the necessary carrion. . . . Cant you see that . . . nothing on earth means anything but SUCCESS . . . the moment you are down they pounce on you."

Dudley and Elisha are vicious and conniving little-traveled dolts who have elected to go into business despite their mother's aristocratic heritage. Dudley's philosophy is "Down with sentiment and up by God with trade!" (*SW* 134). In reality, the Barnes brothers loved the arts but had been frightened by their artist father's irresponsible dilettantism, which had brought them to starvation's door. Fearful that anything but independence could again bring disaster, they were unsympathetic to their sister's determination to depend on patrons to allow her to write and paint.

Augusta shares her sons' concern with financial solvency, for of her daughter, Miranda, she says: "She's that part of me I can't afford" (*SW* 131). Barnes felt most deeply that her mother wronged her in siding with her brothers and in valuing them more highly for their steady income. Miranda says: "Of that sprawl, three sons she leaned to fairly: / On me she cast the privy look of dogs/Who turn to quiz their droppings" (*SW* 87). Ungenerous herself, Augusta nonetheless expects generosity of her daughter: having lost her own inheritance to her mother-in-law, Victoria (*SW* 152–54), the Zadel figure, Augusta takes Miranda's rings, then her shoes, then her hat, and finally her life (*SW* 141; 198; 203).

A second theme courses through *The Antiphon*—Augusta's envy of her daughter's sexually free life. She asks: "Is it true that you had forty lovers?" (*SW* 204). In one letter, Barnes mentions "this same mother tho, nevertheless, tries to live the life she thinks her daughter led, in order to have had a life, vicariously, even tho she would pretend, and think she meant, it quite frightful."[14] This is precisely Barnes's accusation against her own mother, who had wanted to be a poet and was now a Christian Scientist.

The play re-creates a number of autobiographical incidents already set forth in *Ryder*: Victoria's career in London, Titus's polygamy, his many mistresses, how he burned his polygamist credo, and how Augusta was defrauded of her inheritance to buy the farm in New York State. There are a few new ones, which have no autobiographical authority: for instance, how Titus was forced to leave England for his beliefs. But the real questions of the play have to do not so much with Titus but with Augusta's complicity in the disaster he engineered. Miranda is essentially a guiltless Joan of Arc, charged with little more than occasionally drinking too much, some promiscuity, and failing to earn her keep. She has been martyred to a philosophy of free love.

In *The Antiphon*'s autobiographical context, Barnes's comments on the play and on her early life became very entangled when the subject was as emotionally charged a one as rape. It is difficult to keep them separate, since, in Barnes's mind, the real-life impetus for the play was usually not clearly distinguished from the play's plot. In addition to her comments to friends, the context for understanding Barnes's complaint about her father's conspiracy to take her virginity as a girl is spread over several literary works, forming, in effect, an antiphonic response of art to life.[15]

The autobiographical circumstances she related to friends are generally consistent, with one apparent exception: her remark to George Barker that her father had raped her as a young girl. Usually she claimed that Wald brought in an older man to take her virginity. One might argue that many incest victims try to shield the perpetrator when he is a family member, but such was Barnes's desire to present her father in the worst possible light in both *Ryder* and *The Antiphon* that it is hard to believe that she would have absolved him of rape if the guilt was there; but perhaps it was.

When James Scott interviewed Barnes in 1971, she seemed straightforward. What she told him was most likely what happened to her, while in fictional form the events take on the horror that Barnes actually felt. She said to Scott that she had loved her father, though they didn't get along, and, like other family members, she had accepted his philosophy of sexual freedom and vitalism. Convinced that sex was beautiful, Djuna allowed herself to be manipulated into a humiliating sexual encounter when Wald arranged for a man down the road to take her virginity (was this Charles Titus?). Barnes implies that she was astonished that the pain, the humiliation, the sense of violation, were not what her father had promised her. Wald enjoyed this encounter vicariously, which could account for his callous satisfaction at breakfast the next morning, when, in some accounts, he rubbed his hands together with satisfaction that Djuna had now become sexually initiated.

One might easily conclude that in Barnes's own life the man was Percy Faulkner, Fanny's brother, but Faulkner apparently claimed that there was no blood on their "wedding night,"[16] which supports the theory that another man (either Wald or his surrogate) earlier took her virginity. Despite the confusion, Barnes seems to be saying that whether her father enjoyed incest directly or vicariously, he bears equal moral blame. It would be hard to disagree. The experience was one of the most terrible of Djuna Barnes's life, so painful and humiliating that she never forgave her father for this violation. A psychiatrist who specializes in such cases once convincingly stated that the psychological profile of Djuna Barnes was that of the sexually abused child.

Although the taking of Barnes's virginity was clearly a violation, what is one to do with all the evidence that Barnes was attracted to incest? There is the letter from Emily Coleman that says: "Why did you say he [Scudder] was a relative; does relative mean *sex?* If not why should you have felt such a sex-passion for Scudder, and also for Thelma, who was also 'your family.' Family means *sex*. I suddenly knew it."[17] When Nora's comment in *Nightwood* that Robin is incest (*N* 156) is added into the calculation, perhaps a reasonable conclusion would be that having accepted her father's philosophy of sexual freedom, she was indeed sexually attracted to both him and perhaps Zadel but felt deeply betrayed and hurt by what she came to recognize as rape.

One odd factor in any theory of *The Antiphon* as a family revenge play is the absence of the grandmother in all the accusations and counteraccusations. Barnes obviously wished to nail her mother as coconspirator, when in fact it would have made more sense to indict Zadel, who, as the family matriarch, could easily have stopped the rape of Djuna by instructing Wald to leave her alone. Elizabeth was a far less powerful influence. That Djuna chose to indict her mother suggests that her vengeance derives more from the sanatorium days than from her early life on the farm.

It is helpful to examine the autobiographical implications of Barnes's pre-*Antiphon* writings for elements of consistency and invention. The circumstances of rape in the "Rape and Repining!" chapter of *Ryder* are suppressed by a voice that cannot decide between wit and indignation and is therefore of little help to those searching for the truth about the rape of Djuna Barnes. However, in the early unpublished play "Ann Portuguise" (about 1920), Ann speaks to Anthony of her girlhood in Act II, Scene 1, and how she "knew a man," a friend of her father's:

> One night on passing the threshold of my door, I saw that my father had moved in a double bed—an enormous thing (She is in a kind of excitement bearing on hysteria). . . . Well, I wept for a long time, but after that I thought of all the trouble they must have gone to, to bring that thing down from the garret—I'm a Christian, you see —and of all my father must have expected. . . . In the morning I observed that my father had a great appetite, and he kept rubbing his hands together, but I could eat nothing—I kept sending him sidelong glances—I never forgave him for these glances. . . . And after, my father asked me. . . . I never told him.

In this ambiguous narrative, either the father brought in the double bed for his friend or, after she lost her virginity to the other man, the father moved in the bed to sleep with Ann himself.

Wald was hardly a seething Cencian monster, marauding among the womenfolks, but more likely a profoundly silly man who believed that Djuna would somehow enjoy this violation as a prelude to a rich and varied sex life. Still, he betrayed Djuna's love for him and caused psychological scars that never healed.

When discussing *The Antiphon*, though, Barnes was anxious to counter the notion that Titus has raped Miranda[18]: when she explained what happened to both her and Miranda, she was usually consistent about their being taken in by the family belief in sexual freedom, which could imply seduction. But again, she seemed to confuse life with art, for in *Ryder* and *The Antiphon*, the dirty deed clearly means rape, depicted as the most horrible violation imaginable and presented as if Miranda had been unwilling all along. The Djuna character is clearly raped rather than seduced and begs to be spared this painful humiliation, imagining the event as punishment for some indefinable transgression. So in effect, as with the ending of *Nightwood*, Barnes wished to deny the sexual implications of what her texts clearly suggest.

One could speculate about Barnes's reasons for obfuscation in these matters: perhaps in middle age she actually began to confuse certain events of her early life with her artistic rendering of them; perhaps she was protecting herself from inquiries into the lurid details of her rape; or —and this would be the least charitable view—Barnes was just deflecting attention from a consistent strategy of revenge in her literary work.

The notes that Barnes sent to Karl Gierow for the first staging of *The Antiphon* say that Miranda was not raped, even though it is clear, certainly in the play's earlier drafts, that she is, as punishment for her resistance to Titus. Barnes insists that Miranda

> *believed* [Barnes's emphasis] in her father (there are suspicions that Augusta did not), precisely because being a child she was walled off from the world, "like the wall of China." The whole family had been brought up on the faith: Titus had written a book about it. He tore it up later, in a cowardly fashion, when he was threatened by the law. (See *SW* 159)[19]

Ultimately Barnes's revenge against Wald for this early violation is her conversion of the evil deed into an even more horrifying one in fictional form than she ever suggests happened to her personally. Lynda Curry shows how this takes on clarity in the fourth draft, where Dudley describes Titus's rage at his inability to subdue and perhaps rape Miranda:

> She's been knocked into the stubborn ever since
> The hour she drove between our father and the gate,
> Where he tried to make her mutton at sixteen—
> Initiated vestal to his "cause"!
> Self-anointed Titus, Little Corporal,
> Horn mad after false gods; madder still
> For her wild teeth and even wilder kicking.
> And having failed in that, what did he then?
> Hauled her, in an hay-hook to the barn;
> Left her dangling; while in the field below
> He offered to exchange her for a goat
> With that old farm-hand Jacobsen.

Curry notes that "in the second draft of this hayhook speech two lines are added at the end . . . 'He offered to give her, to the farm-hand, for a goat,—/You know, I've seen heifers dangling from an halter/Just like that, while he charged the rape-blade in.' "[20] Deleted pages from *The Antiphon* clarify Barnes's version of the rape of Miranda, where Burleigh [*sic*] says lines finally apportioned among several characters:

> Crawling, with the instep, upside down;
> Dragging small blood, and her fathers laughter.
> Who, having failed to make her mutton to himself,
> That impious, and unhallowed man,
> Tossed her a Cockney, thrice her age . . .[21]

In an earlier draft of the play, Jack queries Miranda: "I understand he offered his daughter, later, for a goat?" Miranda responds: "He did. It was his idea of country equity."

This subtle play is, of course, much more than just a cry for vengeance. As the title suggests, it is a choral response to a dominant voice, the daughter's answer to disastrous patriarchal doctrine, the artist's answer to the demands of both family and society to earn a living, to be a success, to agree that wealth rather than art is the measure, finally, of success. Miranda, the Djuna figure, is brilliant in her defense of artistic integrity, demolishing her family's materialistic arguments. Threatened even with death, she maintains a lofty dignity, wishing what is best for her beloved but misguided mother, Augusta.

T. S. Eliot would not have recommended *The Antiphon* to the editorial board of his publishing house, Faber & Faber, solely on his own authority, but he had the very strong support of Edwin Muir, who proved as effective an intermediary as he had been with *Nightwood*. Barnes asked Eliot to enlist Muir as a reader for her new play. Eliot, deeply troubled by its obscurity, nevertheless did so, writing Muir that *The Antiphon* was "a work of genius and unutterably absurd."[22] For Eliot there was no inconsistency in that, and even in the blurb he wrote for the play he refused to gloss over his conflicted opinion: Barnes was a genius but was impossible and had little talent as a writer. Barnes's response was that she was "abused by praise."[23]

On the personal level there was similar tension: he and Barnes loved each other dearly as friends (in correspondence, their salutation was "Dearest"), yet found each other impossibly exasperating, especially in their roles as difficult writer negotiating with demanding editor. Barnes worked on *The Antiphon* steadily beginning in about 1952, finishing what she hoped would be her final draft in midsummer of 1954. Letters to Emily Coleman reveal that she had begun a play of some sort in 1949 but couldn't get on with the plot.[24] When she sent the play to Eliot, he hesitated to respond because he found it so difficult to comprehend—and if the author of *The Waste Land* found it difficult, how could general readers or theater audiences respond with anything but total mystification? One cannot easily ignore Eliot's considered opinion of *The Antiphon*. This 1948 Nobel Prize–winner had, after all, written a book on the Jacobean dramatists, *The Sacred Wood* (1920), as well as the plays *Murder in the Cathedral* (1935) and *The Elder Statesman* (1958) and a number of others, some of which he knew could never be very popular. But none of his plays approached the obscurity of *The Antiphon*. This posed a dilemma. When he finally responded on 24 August 1954, it was with his usual caution.

Just before Christmas, Eliot wrote again to Barnes to explain the delay in either accepting or rejecting the play: seven readers had now perused *The Antiphon*, and their reactions ranged from enthusiasm to mystification. He himself did not know quite what to think: the first two acts seemed puzzling, while the last one was like a nuclear explosion, "in which language disintegrates into some sort of primitive constituents of violent energy," a comment that Barnes particularly relished though it was not necessarily laudatory or even very illuminating.[25]

In the summer of 1955, Muir agreed to read *The Antiphon*. He had a fine poetic sensibility, was well disposed toward Barnes, and once again seemed the ideal arbiter. During the following year, which he spent at Harvard as the Charles Eliot Norton Professor, Muir visited Barnes more than once to discuss her new play. He studied the text very carefully and made a great many notes, and confident in his support, Barnes acted on his suggestions.

Barnes's respiratory problems were acute when Muir went to see her in early January of 1956. Muir wrote Eliot that

> she has great spirit and was surprised but not greatly offended by the extensive excisions I had marked on the margin of the first act. I hope she was not dejected by them after I left. After all she took four years to write the play, and is living now what seems to be a lonely comfortless life in a street and house which would cast most people (I know they would cast me) into hopeless depression.

Muir went on to say that the play was "one of the greatest things that have been written in our time, and it would be a disaster if it were never to be known."[26] After recommending that the second and third acts be left more or less intact, he went after the first act with a vengeance—it was simply "impossible," and numerous "brilliant" but digressive passages should be deleted since they did not further the action and would confuse readers. Whether or not Eliot and Muir went too far in cutting into *The Antiphon*, only a careful reediting of the play will tell, but they agreed that Jack Blow engaged in too much "speechifying" in Act I. Muir was concerned that the play would be neither published nor staged unless it was shorter, that it was "too much of a good thing," but Lynda Curry has shown how the cutting in some instances made the text even more obscure.[27]

Since Muir was spending a year at Harvard, Eliot's alma mater, and knew that Eliot would be in the United States, he arranged for the Poets' Theatre Company to give a reading performance of *The Antiphon* on 21 May 1956 at Phillips Brooks House, on the north side of Harvard Yard, to which he, Eliot, and Barnes could react. Djuna sat between Muir and Eliot, near Robert Lowell, and in front of I. A. Richards. As she reported to Solita Solano, nothing went right: Augusta was fat rather than stylishly thin like Edith Sitwell, whose dignified demeanor Barnes associated with Augusta; unrehearsed lines were mouthed without comprehension; the entire event was a disaster.[28] At the performance, Eliot's head sank into his hand; Muir became rigid. Barnes was furious that she was questioned in public about the meaning of certain words—but what they saw was, after all, the reading of an extremely difficult play by an amateur theatrical group, which didn't understand what it was all about. Still, it cured Barnes of the desire to see *The Antiphon* staged, and this she was mercifully spared. In fact, she thought that the Harvard reading had ruined the play's chances of ever being produced.

The night after the reading, Muir knocked on her door to return Barnes's cigarette lighter; before leaving, he "rose up on tip-toes, leaned forward, kissed me on the forehead and said: 'I wish I wrote poetry like that!' "[29]

In the end, certain lines were probably clarified by the Harvard reading, and so Barnes sent Eliot still another pruned typescript, but she continued to fume, and in truth she had much to be angry about: the reading had gone badly, recommended cuttings of her play seemed interminable, and publication seemed very far off indeed. There was no end of disagreements. Eliot objected to Jack's calling Burley "nuncle," since at this point in the play the audience was not meant to know Jack's identity. Barnes patiently explained to him that "nuncle" was Shakespearean for "uncle," to which he responded that of course he knew this usage, but nobody expects actors in 1939 to speak the idiom of 1589, and furthermore, Burley *was* Jack's uncle, which the audience was not yet supposed to know, which was the point of his objection in the first place![30]

Finally, on 8 November 1956, Eliot reported that the editorial board at Faber & Faber had accepted *The Antiphon*, offering a ten percent royalty. Still, Eliot wished to delay publication until early 1958, to leave time for further revision. In all, from first submission, it took three and a half years, at least five drafts, and a great deal of cutting for the play to see print.

Editing *The Antiphon* occupied a great deal of Eliot's time in those years. At one point, Eliot surrounded himself with three dictionaries in order to deal with lexical obscurities. He asked Barnes, "Why do you use foreign words [like Burgomeister] when purely local ones will do?" She countered, "Why do you inscribe me a book, dated in numerals Greek?" He gave no answer.[31]

When it came time to write a blurb for the play, Eliot let his irritation with Barnes show through.

We are firmly persuaded that in 1936 when we published Miss Djuna Barnes's novel NIGHTWOOD, there was no other publishing house, on either side of the Atlantic, which would not have rejected that book out of hand. To people of conventional manners NIGHT-WOOD was shocking, to people of conventional taste in fiction it was tedious and incomprehensible. Yet NIGHTWOOD, though it never captured a wide public, is now recognised by critics of discrimination as a classic of its period. After many years of silence the author has given us THE ANTIPHON, a Verse Tragedy. From the point of view of the conventionally minded, THE ANTIPHON will be still more shocking—or would be if they could understand it—and still more tedious—because they will not understand it—than NIGHT-WOOD.

It might be said of Miss Barnes, who is incontestably one of the most original writers of our time, that never has so much genius been combined with so little talent. Her writing shatters the normal structure of the English (or of the American) language. Neverthe-less, THE ANTIPHON is the nearest thing written in our time, to the grimmer and grislier masterpieces of Jacobean tragedy: the author has more in common with Middleton, Ford and Tourneur, than with any living writer.[32]

Eliot hated squabbles (he once told Peter du Sautoy, his colleague at Faber & Faber, never to have anything to do with Ezra Pound and family, who were so troublesome), and so it will remain a mystery why he could not foresee that he was swatting a beehive with this blurb. On 9 January 1957, Barnes protested: how could Eliot recommend the play to readers in such damning tones, in effect creating a "shroud" for a play that he was obliged to promote?[33] When Eliot came to his senses, in early February, he of course squelched the blurb, but Barnes had her copy and didn't forget his "malicious" lines: one of her notes says "he squirmed and said he was only quoting," presumably meaning that he was referring to what a critic, Isobel

Patterson, had said of *Ryder*, that Barnes had "genius but no talent."[34] As mean-spirited as the blurb sounds, Eliot did, after all, represent a commercial publishing house, which had spent an inordinate amount of time on a play that few could appreciate. Faber & Faber stood to lose money, though Eliot's seemingly hostile blurb would have ensured a greater loss, since his endorsement would be crucial to sales; whatever consequences accrued were on Eliot's head.

The reactions of Barnes's friends to *The Antiphon* were as mixed as the readers' reports. Peter Hoare thought it brilliant, while Emily Coleman, in a lengthy, detailed report typical of her honesty and thoroughness, said that the first two acts were "empty" and "artificial," without a "vestige of life." Coleman did admire some beautiful passages, but her general reaction was approximately that of Stanislaus Joyce when he first read passages from his brother's experimental work *Finnegans Wake*—a strong sense of disapproval. The last act was richer in conflict, Coleman felt, but *The Antiphon* was simply not a play.[35] If Coleman was generally right about *Nightwood*, she was a bit too harsh with *The Antiphon*, even to the point of suggesting that Barnes rewrite it without the Elizabethan-Jacobean idiom. Peggy Guggenheim didn't even pretend to understand the play, and she knew the Barnes family history quite well.

A reviewer in *Die Welt* thought *The Antiphon* "will not fall into oblivion, it was written for oblivion" (June 1967). In the *Times Literary Supplement* (4 April 1958), a review appeared that Barnes found so intelligent and intuitive that she thought Muir had written it, but it turned out to have been written by one James Burns Singer, who said that Barnes was the greatest poet among women who had written in English.[36]

Although Eliot said *The Antiphon* might be staged in fifty years, the world premiere occurred in three years, and not in Britain or America, as one might have expected, but in Sweden. Perhaps this was not so surprising, since the first translation of *Nightwood* had been into Swedish, but this first public performance was to signal a trend: in the decades to come, Djuna Barnes would command more respect on the European continent than in English-speaking countries.[37] A skeptic might say that her works improved in translation, but this is unlikely.

One irony of the foreign adulation was that Djuna Barnes, who had always regretted not having learned a foreign language, was unable to judge the accuracy of translations of her work. Still, she sprinkled her texts with flavorful foreign words, many of which she got from dictionaries, to lend an unearned authenticity to her international characters. Sometimes this strategy caught up with her, as when a Swedish translator, Reidar Ekner, asked her about the German word *prachtvoll* in her story "Cassation." She thought it was Swedish and had no idea what it meant. Her never taking the trouble to learn French was avenged in 1949 when she stumbled over a French dictionary, broke several ribs, and wrenched her back. It was a high price to pay for sloth.

Edwin Muir had something to do with Barnes's continental reputation, for in his enthusiasm for *The Antiphon*, he convinced Dag Hammarskjöld, the United Nations secretary-general, to read the play. Hammarskjöld, in turn, communicated his favorable impression to his friend Karl Ragnar Gierow, director of Sweden's Royal Dramatic Theatre, known as "Dramaten," where Greta Garbo had begun her career.[38] Gierow, best known for his productions of Eugene O'Neill's plays, had directed the premiere of *Long Day's Journey into Night*. He persuaded Majken Johansson to do a basic translation into Swedish, but it was decided that her text left too many problems for the actors, so he and Hammarskjöld retranslated the play.

Barnes followed the production of her play in Sweden with intense interest. At Hammarskjöld's urging, she sent a four-page summary to Gierow, answering his questions in detail. By the end of 1960, they were satisfied that most of the obscurity had been ironed out, and on 17 February 1961, *The Antiphon* premiered in Stockholm.

In appreciation of Swedish interest in her work, Barnes consented, in May 1959, to a rare interview.[39] She told Sven Åhman her years in Paris, dropping names of the literati she had known: T. S. Eliot, Edmund Wilson, Sinclair Lewis, Ernest Hemingway, Dylan Thomas, Jean Giraudoux, and James Joyce. She spoke of her resentment that Anaïs Nin had used the name Djuna in her books, a name invented by her father and not in the public domain. "Now there is even a circus horse called Djuna, how about that," she said, laughing. Barnes informed Åhman that she had written *The Antiphon*, which she valued more highly than *Nightwood*, because a doctor had given her no more than six months to live if she did not enter a hospital immediately, and she refused admission until she had written her play. She went on to say that during the years that she worked on *The Antiphon*, she concentrated as never before, refusing to open the door or answer the telephone.[40]

If Barnes seldom received visitors, she did consent to go out, for she was not quite the recluse she pretended to be. One page of her notes records a dinner on 5 June 1960 at Hammarskjöld's home in New York, at which Gierow was present. The Swedish diplomat invited her to dinner at least three times, once with the poet W. H. Auden, who edited Hammarskjöld's autobiographical *Markings*.[41]

Hammarskjöld told her that he and Gierow liked *The Antiphon* even more than when they first read it, calling the play "Himalayan" and *Nightwood* only a slightly lower peak. The praise was a bit too effusive for Barnes's taste, but she was obviously pleased, and she told the publisher Robert Giroux that Hammarskjöld was "one of the most perceptive and sensitive men she had ever met."[42]

Barnes must have deeply regretted missing *The Antiphon*'s premiere. Afterward Gierow and Hammarskjöld sent her flowers and treated her like the celebrity she was in Stockholm. In truth, it is amazing that a play which would have caused much head-scratching if done in English in London or New York should have been so well received in Stockholm in a Swedish translation. Perhaps the distinction of the translators and the quality of the production had much to do with the play's successful premiere.

Hammarskjöld sent Barnes translations of several reviews from Swedish papers: the play was called interesting, even fascinating, though generally puzzling. The reviewer in the *Expressen* (18 February 1961) said that the audience gradually caught on to this difficult play and called it "one of Dramaten's great performances."[43]

In the end, what did Barnes accomplish with this extremely problematical play? Miranda's identification with her mother is one key to *The Antiphon* and what it meant to Barnes. If Augusta was swindled out of her inheritance, so was Miranda, and so, Barnes felt, was she. If Augusta is abandoned at the end by her sons, Barnes saw herself as having been abandoned by her brothers. Her fury at her family sprang from the sense that she was perceived as a burden and a shame, one who had never married, never had children, and never made a steady income. They viewed her as an alcoholic, bad-tempered recluse. Barnes threw all this back in her family's face, saying, essentially: I have become what I am because of the ravishing of my youth. We may trace everything back to that.

A counterargument to the vengeful thrust of *The Antiphon* was made by Emily Coleman much earlier:

> You are not objective about your family. You are sentimental about them, alternating with bouts of hatred. . . . What you don't realize is how strange you are to *any* family. . . . You have never handled them with delicacy, or even *intelligence*. You told them about lesbian things . . . *you do not understand them.* You have never seen the point of view of anyone who was not half mad, or an artist . . . you simply do not know how 90% of the world's population live and what they think. . . . But what I blame you for is not seeing that your family unalterably must feel that way [about security]. Of course what is horrible about some of your family is their brutality & selfishness. One simply can't excuse that.[44]

Djuna's brother Thurn, on reading *The Antiphon*, wrote her a letter that could probably stand for the family's collective response to the play. His view attempts to minimize the importance of a violation that to Djuna was unforgivable:

> I am reading your play for the second time to try and understand what seems to me to be a fixation or sort of revenge for something

long dead and to be forgotten. The writing itself is tremendous but after that I can only wish the subject could have been different. One which could live as a monument to the genius of your mind.[45]

Next to the word "revenge" Barnes noted: "Justice not [revenge]," and next to "for something long dead," she wrote: "not dead." In writing *The Antiphon*, a play she considered autobiographical, Barnes indeed believed she sought justice more than revenge, when she evoked familial sexual abuse, a subject not dead for her and not to be forgotten. But which was the greater violation, which the greater impetus for writing the play—the first rape, when her virginity was taken, or the second, when she was forced into a sanatorium? And what anger remained from her being coerced into a common-law marriage with Percy Faulkner?

Art was Djuna Barnes's only refuge and her only means of striking back, whether out of the desire for justice or for vengeance. In a letter of 20 August 1962 to Willa Muir, Barnes said of her play: "If ever a thing were truly written for the writer this is it. This may be what is objectionable. If so it has to be so." And yet it was also a beginning, because she required bitterness as the fuel of her art, and in that sense posterity owes some gratitude to the Barnes family (and Thelma Wood) for making Djuna Barnes angry enough to produce her finest work.

CHAPTER 14

Obsequies and Meeting
the New Mrs. Eliot

"She's always pissing on the parade."[1]

The solace of advancing age for Djuna Barnes would be found not in her family but in her small circle of friends. T. S. Eliot took pains to keep in touch with her, encouraging her to think positively and to get on with her writing even when faced with an indifferent world. In the late 1940s and early 1950s, when there was rationing in Britain, Barnes sent Eliot cartons of Kools cigarettes, tins of beef or ham, liver pâté, rice, spaghetti—foodstuffs she could ill afford to send. He, in turn, paid the storage bills on her furniture from her Chelsea flat and later bought her British books or magazine subscriptions.

Eliot's letters to Barnes are invariably witty, and when she was in a good mood, hers rivaled his for wit. In 1948, Eliot had his teeth out just before a trip to France and wrote Barnes that he was hoarse because of the awkwardness of speaking French with false teeth. In the same year, Charles Henri Ford introduced Barnes to Osbert and Edith Sitwell, who were visiting New York. To Eliot, Barnes reported that Edith Sitwell "looked astonishingly like a sun-dial at court."[2] No matter how she suffered in her later years, Djuna Barnes's acerbic wit was legendary.

Even after the difficulties surrounding the publication of *The Antiphon*, T. S. Eliot continued to take Barnes to lunch when he came to New York, usually at a French restaurant near Patchin Place called the Charles. He seemed different in his native land: Willa Muir wrote that "Tom Eliot is much more human here than in England. He was less cautious, smiling more easily, spontaneous in repartee, enjoying the teasing he was getting from Djuna. . . . In her company he seemed to have shed some English drilling and become more American."[3]

According to Valerie Eliot, "Where he [Eliot] was concerned there was an element of needling in her banter as though she hoped to provoke him."[4] Barnes's wittiest line about her friend was "Poor Eliot, he kept his organ in the Church."[5] Eliot used to needle Barnes with "She's always pissing on the parade."[6]

But Djuna Barnes felt that there was a subtle hostility behind Eliot's affectionate manner and bantering tone, an attitude she did not quite understand even as she tweaked his nose. Once, she gloomily told Eliot that she had wasted her life. As she reported, he countered: " 'Yes, but think what you did when you weren't wasting it!' (one of the few spontaneous kind remarks, without that always hidden rancor, that I had from him.) He added 'I have wasted *my* life.' "[7]

What Eliot must have meant by this morose verdict on his past was that despite his international fame as a poet, he had known little happiness. This would soon change. A new, well-spent life began when he married Valerie Fletcher, his secretary of eight years at Faber & Faber. Jaws dropped to record levels on both sides of the Atlantic at the news that in his late sixties Eliot had remarried. As it turns out, he knew precisely what he was doing when he proposed to Valerie around Christmas of 1956.

Deeply moved by Eliot's poetry since the age of fourteen, when she had heard a recording of "The Journey of the Magi," Valerie Fletcher had come to London specifically to meet him and ended up employed as his secretary.[8] So dedicated was she, so knowledgeable about his poetry and career, that in retrospect it does not seem so unlikely that a man who felt so unfulfilled should, near the end of his life, propose to a woman who knew him thoroughly, could put up with his moods and remain so loyal. She made Eliot happier, for the last eight years of his life, than he had probably ever been. His poem "A Dedication to My Wife" expressed his feelings.

Nowhere was the surprise at Eliot's marriage greater than at Faber & Faber. Eliot asked Peter du Sautoy to cover for him while he was away and to find him a new secretary. Two days later, on 10 January 1957, Eliot married Valerie Fletcher at Saint Barnabas Church, Kensington. The groom was sixty-eight and the bride thirty. He told Djuna Barnes that he felt as "spry as a spider."[9]

Barnes was introduced to the new Mrs. Eliot a year later, in the spring, at a cocktail party in New York given by Marguerite Cohn of the House of Books.[10] Once, when Valerie was out of the room, Eliot turned to Barnes, "threw his head up, and almost shouting cried: 'I'm the luckiest, the very luckiest man on earth.' "[11] If Barnes had satisfied the masochist in Eliot, in his professional role, Valerie satisfied his need for love and companionship. At parties, they usually held hands.

Valerie Eliot seemed to take to Djuna Barnes immediately and confide in her, which may have been a mistake, since Djuna took notes afterward. Once, Valerie said: "For God sake, guess what he brought on his wedding trip." Just above this note is "Tom, [married,] taking Royal Jelly (!)"—a cautionary prescription to ensure potency, thus explaining, perhaps, his spryness when he leaped from the editor's chair to the marriage bed.[12]

Barnes liked Valerie Eliot's friendly openness and wit, but as with all she encountered, her satirical, painterly eye pinned Valerie wriggling to the wall. She was called "a great big girl from Lancaster [she was actually from Yorkshire]—mouth too small (3 cornered, as if a beak had been pulled off—)—flesh too feathery almost imperceptible eyebrows—will grow fat."[13] Ever the caricaturist, Barnes was probing the physical, but though the note is insensitive, she did not mean to express an attitude. There was nobody to whom she would not have applied the same scrutiny, examining the head closely from various sides and making remarks that were as often disparaging as complimentary. It probably all went back to the life drawing classes of her youth.

John Hayward, Eliot's housemate of many years, who suffered from muscular dystrophy, felt extremely upset when he found out about Eliot's impending marriage. James Stern reported that Hayward learned of the event from a note left on his pillow.[14] Eliot's housemate expressed his bitterness to many of their mutual friends, and chafing under her strict editor's yoke, Barnes recorded the gossip with obvious delight:

There was dire trouble in the house of Tom and Hayward when Tom left to get married, some of it appears to have been on which one should get a large chair "slumped in the seat" "like a fallen lap" — One fury of Tom's was that Hayward "farmed him out for favours" (done to Hayward, by others). Peter du Sautoy says Tom was as "one demented" just before marriage, taking care of "legal matters" (I know he had promised Hayward he'd pay a years rent if he left first, the same for Hayward to Tom). [Valerie] . . . has *"biddy" hero* worship—capable—in small matters. . . . Valerie recounted how Hayward (theres a rancorous and spiteful man!) had Tom in tears, saying he'd never write another word, after the lashing Hayward gave him on his "The Elder Statesman," (which indeed is awful). Talking of it just before he married, Tom told me that it gave him "shivers down his spine" thinking of it, if he could get it into the shape he wanted.[15]

Barnes left behind more notes for posterity on the subject of T. S. Eliot than on almost any other subject. Feeling perhaps deprived, Eliot told her that as a boy he had never had a dog, or a Noah's Ark (presumably a toy), a comment for which Valerie Eliot provided a useful gloss when she noted: "There was . . . a little boy in him that had never been released."[16]

Inevitably, much of Barnes's conversation with Eliot turned on publishing protocol, for first Eliot and then Peter du Sautoy labored as her unpaid literary agents, advising her on contracts and translation rights. In 1958, when Faber published *The Antiphon* in Britain, Eliot sent the typescript to his friend Robert Giroux of Farrar, Straus & Cudahy, who in the same year imported sheets and published the American edition. Two years later, the New York firm requested permission to print a volume of Barnes's selected works, which would mean purchasing from New Directions the right to include *Nightwood*, and Eliot advised Barnes on that matter. He thought that an omnibus volume was a good idea for the United States, but obviously he did not wish to publish a similar volume in Britain: it would have meant endless hassles with the difficult Miss Barnes.

Robert Giroux was the object of the same attitude Barnes maintained toward all publishers—except Eliot—or printers, as she called them: she detested him. Indeed, she would have preferred New Directions to do separate editions of her works, which would mean their purchasing *The Antiphon* from Farrar, Straus. Eventually the *Selected Works* would be done, but Barnes's suspicions of publishers were not disarmed by Giroux, who attempted to include *Nightwood* in the *Selected Works* on the basis of an exploratory conversation with James Laughlin of New Directions, even though no fee had been settled upon. Laughlin protested strongly; Giroux countered rather slickly that he had not realized that New Directions might want payment.

Barnes recorded her irritation with both Eliot and Giroux on a sheet of notes: it was enough that they were both publishers, but that they were also friends smelled to Barnes of collusion. She told Eliot that Giroux had treated her "shamefully" in regard to the *Selected Works*. Eliot replied: "You like people so long as they are valuable to you, you like people for the advantages you get out of them." But he then confessed to the same vice when she asked why he liked Giroux: "He is useful," in that he set up lectures for Eliot in the United States.[17]

Barnes surmised that Giroux did not approve of the new Mrs. Eliot and condescended to her, so she recorded with relish her friend Valerie's resentment. Barnes believed Giroux had tried to turn Eliot against her by telling him of her irritation that *The Antiphon*'s publication had been delayed for so long.[18] Once, when Giroux had stopped by to ask her to autograph newly published copies of the *Selected Works*, she threw him out; when she saw that he had left the books behind, she threw them down the stairs after him. She knew her signature had value and granted it as a rare gift to trusted friends, which didn't include publishers. In the final analysis, Robert Giroux probably walked the minefield of negotiation with Barnes as deftly as any publisher could have, but doubtless there were lasting wounds.

What Djuna Barnes really needed in her last years was a literary agent, for she often got matters confused and gave offense when none was intended. Peter du Sautoy of Faber & Faber, who acted as Barnes's agent in matters of foreign rights and translations, was always questioned down to the last penny. He found Djuna Barnes no less thorny than did Giroux.

Not having an agent led Barnes into amazing tangles, for instance with the German translation of *The Antiphon*. Christine Koschel and Inge von Weidenbaum made a translation, which Klaus Reichert corrected and sent to Barnes's German publisher, Suhrkamp Verlag. When the poet and translator Michael Hamburger eventually found the newly published translation of her play to be faulty, Barnes instructed Faber & Faber to have the German edition withdrawn. The problem was that Siegfried Unseld, the publisher, had contracted with Faber to translate the British edition, but the translators were sent the revised American edition, which incorporated 327 changes. When the German translation was compared with the Faber version, it was of course found to be inaccurate.[19]

This episode was important because, outside the English-speaking world, German readers of Barnes were the most appreciative. In part, this was due to the writer Wolfgang Hildesheimer, academic Klaus Reichert, Siegfried Unseld, translators Koschel and von Weidenbaum, the playwright Rolf Hochhuth, and the critic Brigitte Siebrasse, who was the first to write about her in Germany.[20] Barnes the portrait painter was interested in Unseld's profile; her verdict was that he "has the look of a man about to jump off into space."[21] Although she liked Unseld, she was not pleased when he wrote a letter to the *Frankfurter Allgemeine* in 1970, describing her circumstances as particularly desperate.

To a well-heeled Frankfurt publisher, Barnes's shabby little flat may have looked like skid row, but she wasn't doing too badly. The old Barnes fear of starvation prevented her living better. Then, too, thirty years' accumulation of books, letters, and manuscripts could not easily be stashed away. As it turned out, Barnes's true enemy was time, not poverty; she was too tough to be allowed a graceful exit.

Time continued to ravage the friends of Djuna Barnes, striking them with infirmity and death. One bond between Eliot and Barnes was their deep sense of loss at the death of Edwin Muir; she had dedicated *The Antiphon* to him. An Orkneyman, Muir was one of Scotland's finest poets and critics. He and his wife, Willa, a Shetlander, were a team of expert German translators. Before the Muirs, Franz Kafka was virtually unknown in the English-speaking world. When Muir died on 3 January 1959, Barnes was bereft of a distinguished supporter as well as a steadfast friend. As for Eliot, when the London *Times* published Muir's obituary, he responded by letter the next day to observe that in his view Muir's poetry and literary criticism were some of the finest of our time.[22] Eliot, Muir, and Dag Hammarskjöld would be those friends whom Barnes was proudest of knowing.

Muir's death also forged a bond of sympathy between Barnes and Willa Muir, who wrote one of the most perceptive and sensitive letters Barnes ever received, one that cuts to the heart of her life and work. She might have been describing the poet Arthur Rimbaud:

> You have entered imaginatively into *every* kind of human distortion, you have "imaged" them all with deep understanding; you have a genius for imaginative empathy, and that is why your language wells up with a force that is relatively primitive. But how can you have stood it all? Shaping it all with words has been, I can tell, your passion; you do that indescribably well; but none the less my heart is heavy for you, because the richness of the vocabulary, the aptness of the imagery, bring out into stronger relief the stark dreadfulness of the experiences you have made yourself undergo.[23]

Hammarskjöld was the next close friend to go. He admired Barnes the writer and cherished her company. Barnes thought him one of the most sensitive and perceptive men she had ever met, and would deeply regret her refusal of the tour of the United Nations buildings that he offered to give her, for she could see from his face that he was hurt. She later told friends, "What a terrible mistake that was."[24] That the secretary-general of the United Nations would esteem her play, translate it, promote her career, invite her to dinner, send her flowers to celebrate the Stockholm premiere of *The Antiphon*, and send her summaries of the Swedish reviews—such attention by a world leader inspired Barnes with both awe and the conviction that what she had written did, after all, matter.

Hammarskjöld's death in a plane crash in Zambia in September of 1961 devastated Barnes as had no death since those of John Holms and Edwin Muir. In his article " 'The Most Famous Unknown in the World'—Remembering Djuna Barnes," Robert Giroux tells of bringing Barnes some galley proofs to Patchin Place on the morning after she had received the news of Hammarskjöld's death. Standing by a banister, pale and distracted, in a transparent nightgown of "pleated muslin, longer than floor length, with a ruffed collar tied with a black ribbon up to her chin," completely unaware of her appearance, Barnes invited him up to her flat.[25] " 'I haven't slept a wink,' she said, 'I had ears glued to the radio all night. They've murdered him!' " Barnes called Hammarskjöld a saint, saying that "his death is one of the worst crimes against civilization ever committed. Dag Hammarskjöld did nothing but good, and look what they've done to him. And he really believed in the goodness of man. Well, *not I!*"[26] She took careful notes on the funeral, which she observed on television.

Barnes's grief over Hammarskjöld's death haunted her for months. She wrote Emily Coleman: "I repeat again the words of that remarkable Catholic writer Josef Pieper . . . Hammarskjöld was a man who 'dared to walk straight up to fearfulness'—A dedicated, able, monkish man, who 'had a vision' . . . and who was unafraid . . . and most modest."[27]

Valerie Eliot recorded a day on which Barnes saw Ezra Pound for the last time, which was also the first time in many years. Barnes first met Pound when Margaret Anderson sent her to interview him, and she had visited him when he was interned in Saint Elizabeth Hospital in Washington (O'Neal 48, 140). She had thought Pound charming as a young man in the 1920s, when she drew his portrait for *Vanity Fair* (which the magazine apparently lost). Barnes told Chester Page that she remembered the young Pound "with red, curly hair and flowing capes" (C. Page 228). She had resisted his attempt at seduction.

Now in New York in 1969 Barnes saw Pound old and feeble, and was appalled. "He seemed so [s]mall, his eyes no longer his own sort of eye."[28] Valerie Eliot records the meeting:

On 12th June 1969 I was in the New York Public Library transcribing *The Waste Land* when the telephone rang with an invitation to dine that evening with Ezra Pound and Olga Rudge, who had arrived unexpectedly from Italy some days earlier. (This was his first visit to America since being released from St. Elizabeth's Hospital in 1958, and he had wept at the sight of the manuscript.) I explained that Djuna and I were going to celebrate her 77th birthday at her favorite restaurant, Charles, in Greenwich Village and they urged me to bring her for drinks afterwards as they were staying nearby. Djuna received the news in silence but began to eat very slowly, paused lengthily between courses and talked inordinately about Dolly Wilde, Oscar's niece. I knew Ezra did not admire her work, but they had always liked each other, so finally I asked why she did not want to see him again. "I am frightened because it is almost 40 years since we last met," she answered.

It was approaching midnight when we left and feeling that I should apologize to Olga, I ran up the steps to their door, which was opened before I reached it by Ezra's grandson, Walter. "We're waiting!" he called. There was no escape. As Djuna climbed painfully behind me, I suggested that she should reminisce about their Paris days. This she did superbly. An occasional chuckle came from Ezra who sat with folded arms as she recalled people they had both known. When Peggy Guggenheim was mentioned, Olga nudged Ezra and said, "You never liked her, did you?" Djuna stopped and I feared the spell was broken. Fortunately Olga continued, "You always thought she had poor legs!" As Ezra laughed and nodded vigorously Djuna resumed her narrative.

When we rose to leave, to everyone's astonishment he jumped up in his slippers to accompany us in Walter's car. On reaching Djuna's courtyard, she said peremptorily, "Come in a moment Valerie, I want to speak to you," so the two men waited while I obeyed. "I never thought I would see Ezra in this condition," she said almost accusingly, obviously distressed. But as we continued our journey to the East Side where I was staying, I could feel delight in revived memories.[29]

At their last lunch together in New York, in about January of 1962, T. S. Eliot complained to Djuna Barnes that she had never done anything for him. He was presumably peevish because she said that she would "think" about acceding to his earlier request that she leave the Eliot-Barnes letters to Valerie (though in her 1957 will she had already done so). Eliot died in January of 1965 at the age of seventy-six, after years of suffering from emphysema with related heart disease. Valerie Eliot said that his "death was gentle and he bore his sufferings beforehand with great patience and sweetness."[30] After a private funeral in London, his ashes were scattered at East Coker; then there was a memorial service at Westminster Abbey on 4 February. Eliot's will requests his wife not to cooperate with his biographers.

The deaths of Eliot and Hammarskjöld came on top of reports of the deaths of still other friends, one after the other: Allan Ross Macdougall (1956), Dan Mahoney (1959), Victor Cunard (1960), Jean Oberlé (1961), Laurence Vail (1968), Romaine Brooks (1970), Thelma Wood (1970), Natalie Clifford Barney (1972), Margaret Anderson (1973), Emily Coleman (1974), and Solita Solano (1975).

One of Djuna Barnes's best poems, "Quarry," was written as a memorial to the artist Louis Bouché (*The New Yorker*, 27 December 1969). Barnes felt love and deep friendship for Louis and Marian Bouché, whose loyalty and understanding she had depended on for many decades. Bouché, born in New York of French parents in 1896, a friend of Man Ray, was a muralist and painter of country scenes. In 1954, he painted the murals for the Eisenhower Foundation Museum in Abilene, Kansas, and in Washington he painted murals for the Department of the Interior building. Louis Bouché was a large, jolly fellow with an Edwardian mustache. He had employed the Baroness Elsa von Freytag Loringhoven as a model, made his mark with a picture called *Celestine & Nana* at the 1917 Penguin Exhibition, and was written about by Carl Van Vechten as early as 1922.[31]

Barnes met the Bouchés at a party given by Norma Millay in 1920. They had been close to most of the Barnes inner circle, including Peggy Guggenheim, Peter Hoare, John Holms, and Silas Glossop. They lived around the corner from Barnes, at 20 West 10th Street, and Barnes also spent time with them at their country home in Old Chatham, New York. When Marian Bouché died on 26 April 1975, at age seventy-nine, her daughter Jane Strong continued the friendship.

Emily Coleman came to visit Barnes for the last time in 1970. Since leaving Arizona and Jake Scarborough, she had acquired a fanatical, obsessive, aggressive Catholicism, which caused others to flee in droves. In 1954, Peggy Guggenheim wrote that Coleman was up all night, partying, then went off to masses during the day; she generally gave everyone endless grief with her confrontational scenes.[32] When Coleman's friend Father Victor was dying, his one last wish was to be spared a visit by Emily.[33] In 1964, Guggenheim reported that Coleman had grown obese and developed a crooked grin, as if she had had a stroke.[34] Later in that year, she was operated on for a benign brain tumor, then given shock treatments for hysteria. Of Emily Coleman's last visit to Patchin Place, Barnes wrote Peter Hoare:

The last time I saw her, the first time in twenty odd years, she seemed erased. I dare say I seemed the same to her. I said would you have known me? She answered "No, except for the eyes." I don't think, had I passed her on the street, that I would have known her at all. She was colour dun, carrying a Rip Van Winkle staff, a fur pelt, in *baret* style on her head, her hair lank and to the turn of her cheek, the coat, capsized wool, the feet well apart. She said since her head operation she found it difficult to balance. How can I say this? How can I tell anyone about anything anymore: She was cheerful, seemed obscurely amused, and only Emily like when I put a bowl of excellent chicken soup before her. She did not seem mournful, but neither did she seem to have listed (in her mind) the passing of her life. She spoke of nursing (pushing about in a cart I take it), a cancer case. I asked her how could she stand it? She answered "God had intended it." Simple, like that.[35]

Emily Coleman died on 13 June 1974 at the Catholic Workers' Farm in Tivoli, New York, cared for by her devoted friend (and now literary executor) Joseph Geraci. On 31 March 1976, Peter Hoare died after increasing problems with aphasia and disorientation. Being knocked down by a fire engine as he wandered in the street hastened his demise.

Only one of Barnes's brothers survived her, and that was Saxon, who died in January of 1991. Although she didn't see them much, she said, "like a damned tapestry all their threads and all mine intermingle in the family pattern."[36] What the brothers had in common was that they all went into business and they were all unusually handsome men. They tended to be discreetly mute about their childhood on the Huntington farm and their father's bigamy and second family. They were proud of Djuna's artistic accomplishments but wary of close involvement with her.

Of the four sons of Elizabeth and Wald, only two kept the surname Barnes. The youngest, Shangar, who renamed himself Charles Chappell, developed meningitis in 1965, which left him disabled and unable to speak.[37] Charlie went to school only through the eighth grade, then worked to put himself through art school. During his career in advertising, he was responsible for the label of the Old Grand-dad whiskey bottle and the slogan "Wouldn't you really rather have a Buick." When he died, in Florida, on 16 December 1966, he left behind a great number of charcoal drawings, paintings, and sculptures.

Zendon Barnes died in March 1977, following a stroke. In his suffering, he told his son, Nicholas, "I am paying for my father's sins," a reminder that Wald's belief in polygamy had long-lasting consequences. By all accounts, Zendon was a successful advertising executive and a solid citizen.[38] He was closest to Thurn, and, like his brothers, he inherited the artistic urge. He enjoyed sculpting, woodwork, and drawing.[39]

Thurn, who in 1942 changed his last name to Budington, his grandfather's name, also worked in advertising, and wrote for the *Farm Journal.* He smoked cigars and wrote poetry, but apparently he didn't persevere with his trombone. He lived in Greenwich, Connecticut, and died in 1978 at the age of eighty-seven.

Saxon Barnes is the brother who figures most prominently in the life of his sister, Djuna, for he was the one she cared for and fought with most. He went to high school in East Orange, then moved on to Wall Street and a series of jobs that culminated with a thirty-six-year career at Citibank. Eventually he became vice president at the Rockefeller Center branch of Citibank on Fifth Avenue and was successful in securing some enormous accounts, such as those of Shell Oil and Sinclair.

An avid golfer, Saxon retired in the mid 1960s to an old Dutch farmhouse with a five-car garage on a four-acre estate in Bethlehem, Pennsylvania, with his wife, Eleanor. He took up sculpting and was apparently gifted, but he did a head of Djuna that infuriated her: she said he had made her look like a boy. When Andrew Field's biography of Djuna Barnes appeared, Saxon was extremely distraught, assuming that everybody at his country club was talking about his sister's being a lesbian.

Of course, Djuna pinned him to the wall on every occasion. In a letter to Silas Glossop, she mentioned Saxon's retirement: "I see that he is not happy, but indeed failing, fray, bending slightly forward, in that deprecatory stance of someone who has lost something he hopes you haven't found, and hoping that you have heard about something he would give his life to know."[40] Still, he outlived her by nine years. Thurn's assessment of Saxon was most astute: "Saxon is very generous but abusive as a coverup for his deep sentimentality."[41] Every inch the banker, he hid his feelings behind a tough exterior.

When Djuna Barnes died, no family member was bequeathed money, and none would be invited by friends to the spreading of her ashes. The harsh judgment of *The Antiphon* was never to be undone.

Madame Vitriol: The Century's
Most Famous Unknown[1]

"True death is wealth tremendous, but it must be earned with life; that is why still I live."[2]

D juna Barnes was aging with as much dignity as was possible, given that she lived with nearly constant pain and physical adversity during her last years. When walking around Greenwich Village, though, she seemed her usual elegant, witty self. Valerie Eliot remembered her "tall, spare figure, held very erect, in a neat black costume with a polka-dot blouse, a fur hat on her head and carrying a silver-headed ebony walking stick. An inquiry about her health was met with the words: " 'Breaking up nicely, thank you!' "[3] But the breaking up of her health would not be complete for many years.

Given Barnes's misanthropic view of the human enterprise, evident even in her earliest literary works, living to be ninety was hardly a goal until she was actually near to it. She managed to hold out, then died a week after her birthday. Some said that it was pure rage that kept her alive. As Barnes wrote Natalie Barney some twenty years earlier: "I have suffered shock, betrayal, disenchantment, outrage, the perpetual anxiety of small and uncertain money, and ill health."[4] Friends recorded her two favorite aphorisms: "Our first mistake was being born" and "The wish to be good is the wish to be destroyed" (C. Page 277, 294).

The longevity of the Barnes family was for Djuna an inherited curse. She had tried to end her life in London in 1939; in the late

1970s, she tried again, undertaking to swallow all the pills on her night table, though somehow she missed the sleeping pills. Barnes told Jane Strong that she woke up the next morning feeling better than she had for years.

But daily life and simple tasks became increasingly difficult. Her apartment was deteriorating and desperately needed remodeling. Roaches "ran races up the kitchen wall and danced at night under her bed," because her emphysema would not permit strong pesticides to be used (O'Neal 185–88). But the alternative to staying in Patchin Place drove Barnes to even more intense anxiety: a nursing home would be a fate far worse than death itself, for it would mean the end of creativity.

During these last forty years in Greenwich Village, Barnes was highly suspicious of most people with whom she came in contact; unless they were trusted friends, those who were invited past the threshold would probably be humiliated as in a trial by fire, to see whether or not they were worthy. She assumed that they were up to no good—robbery, fraud, or murder, likely enough, unless they proved otherwise. Nosy people invaded her privacy, wished to pump her for intimate memoirs, "wanted her on Forty-second Street standing on her head with her underwear showing."[5] She was actually less a hermit than she pretended, though, and her telephone gave her access to the world on even her most difficult days, enabling her to communicate with friends and terrorize the shopkeepers of Greenwich Village.

If a visitor managed to avoid the impulse to flee, he or she might be privileged to hear one of the most brilliant, witty raconteurs of the century. Nobody left unimpressed or unintimidated, and many observed Djuna Barnes's underlying warmth, dignity, loyalty, absolute honesty, and sense of uncompromising integrity as an artist. Chester Page's friend Louise Crane must have judged her abrasive even by New York standards when she dubbed Barnes "Madame Vitriol" (C. Page 240), but one simply had to brave the tirade long enough to see her relax.[6]

A short dramatization, courtesy of Douglas Messerli, will give an impression of what it was like to knock on Djuna Barnes's door.

Knock, knock. "Who's there?" Barnes peered through a crack in the door. "Its Douglas Messerli." "Who?" "Its Douglas Messerli. I've an appointment with you to discuss the bibliography that I'm compiling of your work." "What did you say your name was?" "Messerli." "God, that's an awful name, you should change it. You'll never amount to anything with a hideous name like that. Messerli. Ugh. What kind of name is Messerli?" "Its Swiss." "*Swiss!* Good God! No wonder you're a bibliographer—Swiss! O.K., I suppose you can come in, but I warn you it smells like old lady in here." The voice was theatrical, slightly British.

Although Barnes was often flattered by the right sort of attention, she was annoyed when approached even by artists. Carson McCullers and other writers tried without success to know her. Some writers were admitted to her apartment: Malcolm Lowry, who wrote her two letters, was brought by Barnes's journalist friend Jimmy Stern to meet her on 27 February 1947. Women writers might have knocked on her door with some encouragement, but her judgments of them were as harsh as her manners: she was contemptuous of Amy Lowell and thought Colette was a "cat" (C. Page 229), but she was distressed about Sylvia Plath and thought Ted Hughes should have put *his* head into the oven. She admired Isak Dinesen but was annoyed by Anaïs Nin, whose fawning attitude she found offensive: "Something of a pathological 'little girl' lost—sometimes a bit 'sticky,' she sees too much, she knows too much, it is intolerable."[7]

Barnes admired women writers when they met a certain critical standard, but her moods frightened away writers who would have interested her, including Susan Sontag, who sent her a copy of *Against Interpretation* in 1966. Barnes was one of her favorite writers, and Nathanael West was another; the two formed a matched pair. Barnes wrote Sontag: "I have been informed that seeing me on the village streets, you have refrained from addressing me, because someone has told you that I am a Demon, of some violence and invective. Please do me the pleasure of speaking with me the next time?"[8] Because of their mutual formality, they never met (O'Neal 33).

Marianne Moore was a poet whose craft Barnes particularly admired, but the feeling was not precisely mutual: Moore once said that "reading Djuna Barnes is like reading a foreign language which you understand."[9] Very much a Greenwich Village poet, Moore lived near Patchin Place, and the two encountered each other on occasion and were friendly; Barnes even made a point of attending her funeral in 1972. She referred to Moore occasionally in letters: "Do not know if you know Marianne Moore, the very famous American poetess? Met her on the street too, delicate, very determined, with the bright eyes of a wood creature, loaded down with green bananas, rolling grapefruit, and wistful after Dr. Brown's Celery Tonic, not heard of since grandmother's day, not at least here."[10] To Peggy Guggenheim, Barnes wrote of Moore: "I liked some thing lodging in her spirit" (undated letter).

Although Samuel Beckett had sent her part of his royalties for *Waiting for Godot* (O'Neal 140) and they had corresponded actively, Barnes had little to say about him or his work beyond that he looked wild but was a "lovely man."[11] Barnes never knew Beckett well but sometimes teased friends with the remark that she knew things about him that she would never tell.[12]

Despite the pain and fury, Djuna Barnes's astonishing wit never left her. Irwin Cohen, whose wife, Francesca Belanger, designed Barnes's bestiary, *Creatures in an Alphabet*, once asked Barnes if she knew who Bob Dylan was. Not wishing to appear uninformed, she answered, "Isn't he the best at what he does?" Once, apropos of nothing, she wrote: "No fortitude like the Prussians of an earlier caste, who buggered with clenched teeth keeping their monocle firmly graspt in the winched up eye."[13] Of some unnamed person, she noted: "she treats tradition as if it were a comfort station."[14]

Her painterly eye remained as astute as ever, even when veiled by cataracts: at a meeting of writers, she saw Carl Van Vechten, age eighty-four, in the year that he died, and found him "very bent, absolutely impeccable, creeping softly, with bright & canny eye (but now the eye must raise the falling head) to spy out the most likely fellow, (who happened to be Mr. Updike) as target for his camera."[15]

Though Djuna Barnes valued her privacy, her literary work was there to admire, and she had no doubt of its ultimate importance. *Nightwood* continued to influence important writers, such as McCullers, William Faulkner, John Hawkes, and others who admired her style and her sense of the grotesque. Tom Stoppard once wrote asking if he might quote one of her lines in a play; he must have explained the context to her satisfaction, because she granted permission (C. Page 286).

All requests for movie rights to her works (eventually there were some seven requests) underwent intense scrutiny, for Barnes wanted to know everything down to the smallest detail before she would allow a filmmaker to proceed; but of course, her permission would have been necessary before much planning for a movie could have taken place, so the reasoning was circular. Paul Sylbert, who represented Paramount Pictures, wrote to New Directions on 1 August 1969, expressing interest in the screen rights to *The Antiphon*. A few days later, Susan Blair of New Directions wrote Barnes that Paramount had been on the phone and it was apparent that Djuna Barnes could name her own terms, including the right to veto the screenplay, but Barnes wanted to see an elaborate plan, right down to who the minor actors were to be. Paramount responded that such questions were premature, and their representatives must have concluded that Barnes was more trouble than she was worth, for they broke off negotiations. Barnes seemed not to mind. She greatly enjoyed the company of the Zurich filmmaker Erwin Leiser, who advised her on European stage productions of *The Antiphon*; he knew her work and grew to know her mind. Ingmar Bergman and John Oppé were both interested in *Nightwood*. It is said that Barnes might have given the nod to Bergman if he could have persuaded Greta Garbo to play Robin. A less uncompromising attitude toward film rights might have made Djuna Barnes a wealthy woman in her last years.

Her views on artistic perfection were repeated often to friends: What one did had to be "marvelous," or why bother? It was better to write one good line of poetry than to make love all night. Her suspicion of virtually everyone interested in her writing resulted in her denying an Oxford student, Alida Greydanus, the right to quote from her literary works in a doctoral dissertation unless Barnes first approved the ideas, nor would she give her permission to have photocopies made of manuscripts and letters. What if the student did shoddy work or had an unacceptable thesis that might damage Barnes's reputation?

One could not be too careful, for Djuna Barnes imagined herself to be under siege by dissertation students, hippies, hoppies (her term), flower children, and potential thieves. There was some truth to the latter fear: on 27 July 1975, she confronted a mugger in her courtyard: "just now, a circling set of maneuvers around and around my court yard, fending off a purse snatcher (tall, thin, young, black) . . ."[16] When they were inside Patchin Place, she turned to face him, saying, "Now what do you want you s.o.b.?" Intimidated and amazed, the man fled (C. Page 235). Another thief climbed her fire escape and entered a window. In Chester Page's words:

> Instead of lying there quietly, she flew at him and slapped his face. "How dare you come into my room!" she exclaimed. Then, seeing his astonishment, she said, "I guess you have a tough time of it. Come, I'll let you out by the door." His response was, "I'll shoot you!" She ran for the door, had to unlock two locks, ran to the sidewalk screaming for help. "I could feel that bullet in my back," she said. Snow was falling, and though her neighbors looked out, no one moved to do anything. The man, standing on her fire escape, suddenly jumped and ran. (C. Page 235)

Darryl Pinckney, the author of the autobiographical novel *High Cotton*, was recommended to Barnes by Frances McCullough, an editor at Dial Press. He describes working for her during his days as an aspiring writer with a sparse income, noting the "one tiny, robin's egg-blue room with white molding," the night table with radio, telephone, medicine bottles, the envelopes labeled "Notes on Mr. Joyce" or "Notes on Mr. Eliot." Barnes once received Pinckney in "Moroccan robe trimmed in gold, white opaque stockings, and red patent-leather heels. Her eyes glistened like opals in a shallow pond and her skin was pale as moonlight." Between coughing fits, she gave him stern cautionary advice: "See that you don't grow old. The longer you're around the more trouble you're in." He was also to avoid marriage, blindness, surgery, and any dietary restrictions. In the meantime, he could refill the humidifier.[17]

Pinckney and other volunteers who went shopping for Barnes were given lists, which inevitably included ginger ale and Häagen-Dazs coffee ice cream, which she ate with her favorite silver teaspoons. If Irwin Cohen brought her tasty dishes, she was suspicious: "Mr. Cohen, *what* is this?" she said of an almond that appeared unannounced in her dish, as if she had unmasked a murderous intent in Cohen's kindness.

When medical problems threatened to overwhelm Djuna Barnes, friends sent emissaries to help. In the spring of 1970, when Marianne Moore was especially concerned about Barnes's failing health, she asked her young pianist friend Chester Page to telephone. He was invited to tea on 19 May, and a very close friendship was formed. Page took her to see physicians, helped paint her apartment, even shopped for her on occasion, but once he had seen Barnes's bad moods, he refused to allow her to become dependent on him, foreseeing the inevitable conflicts.

That eventually brought Hank O'Neal into the picture. He came to know Barnes through his association with Berenice Abbott, who urged him to contact Barnes when she was feeling particularly despondent about her health and personal affairs. O'Neal was a successful concert promoter, photographer, and record producer, but over a three-year period Djuna Barnes became his principal avocation. He helped with finances, persuaded her not to refuse reasonable offers to reprint her work, wrote an introduction to a new edition of *Ryder* (for which St. Martin's Press paid Barnes an advance of three thousand dollars), corresponded as her agent, negotiated copyrights for her literary works, and made up a chart listing the current status of all her literary copyrights.

Eventually Barnes became furious with O'Neal because, with a career that absorbed much of his time, he was not around enough to suit her. When a complex of electric plugs came out of the wall one night, she was sure that there was a citywide blackout and summoned him from New Jersey. With increasing age, Barnes became less and less able to attend to her own affairs; the more disabled she became, the more autonomy O'Neal assumed in making decisions. This presumption infuriated Barnes, who was used to running her own life. She really needed a full-time nurse and secretary, and although she had some $180,000 in various banks (O'Neal 184), she was unwilling to hire such help, convinced that she lived in poverty, as indeed her drab surroundings suggested. When O'Neal refused to be provoked by her angry taunts, she called him "plateface." Eventually, about a year before her death, Barnes fired him from his voluntary service, and the literary agent Irene Skolnick took over as her representative and adviser.

O'Neal records the brilliant, witty discourse of Djuna Barnes with considerable admiration, but he also notes her constant negativity. Some themes were repeated almost daily: she preferred the company of men to women, because women were "mushy" and sentimental. A gay sexual orientation always subjected a person to vituperation, a curious reaction for a bisexual woman living in Greenwich Village. Barnes was outraged that lesbians thought her one of them and, by wooing her with flowers and gushy praise, sought to bind her to a sisterhood of which she was contemptuous. Barnes's most frequent theme was that she had never been a lesbian—she had only loved Thelma Wood. She didn't want to create lesbians with *Nightwood*, and if she had known how the novel would be received, she insisted, she would never have written it.

James B. Scott had a theory about Barnes's derogatory comments on modern women: "Her mind simply refused to consider the possibility that *all* women could not be as smart as she was. She did not oppose women's *rights*, or, certainly, women finding fulfillment. Quite the contrary; she wanted women to do a great deal more than they ever had. But a 'movement' by its very nature sought to raise unearned the conditions of its adherents."[18]

Scott, an academic at the University of Bridgeport, wrote a book on Djuna Barnes and visited her twice in 1971.[19] Although she encouraged him, readily told him anything he wished to know, and read through three or four of the drafts for his book, she was furious when he attempted to publish material from the interviews, and she tried to force his publisher to stop publication. Barnes wanted Scott to write one of the great books of literary criticism, when what he mainly wished to do was get the facts straight about her life and work, which convinced Barnes that he was really a biographer in disguise. Scott, of course, felt angry and betrayed as well.

Though Djuna Barnes has been called "the Garbo of literature," her irritable reclusiveness did not mean that she wanted *no* company; it was just that she valued her privacy and found it uncomfortable to receive visitors in her small apartment. As she aged, privacy became less and less of an option.

Despite her lifestyle, Barnes was not as poor as she and others imagined.[20] Her rent was probably still less than $130 per month in the late 1970s; since she needed to pay only for food, medicine, and some medical care, she could manage on her income. There were occasional royalty checks. In 1981, thanks to Fran McCullough of Dial Press, who encouraged Barnes to write a bestiary, *Creatures in an Alphabet*, Barnes received a National Endowment for the Arts fellowship of $15,000 for creative writing and, along with other fellows, was invited to the White House, an opportunity Barnes had to miss due to her failing health. Because Barnes seldom knew precisely what her financial situation was, she often worried needlessly in her later years.

Any real financial precariousness came to an end when, in December of 1972, Djuna Barnes sold her papers to the McKeldin Library at the University of Maryland for about $48,000.[21] In her apartment were stacks of letters, manuscripts, inscribed first editions of most of the major modernist writers, and other valuable literary material. Various universities previously interested in the papers had seemed to expect a donation.[22]

As early as 1964, Barnes had in effect agreed in a will to give her papers to the Beinecke Library at Yale and had corresponded with Norman Holmes Pearson there about her estate, but by 1970 she had become convinced that the papers were too valuable to donate.

Fran McCullough, then at Harper & Row, arranged for an appraiser to visit Barnes's apartment so that her papers could be evaluated, but Barnes complained about being forced to observe his large posterior whenever he bent over.[23] McCullough had the papers moved to the Harper document room to be appraised.

Barnes was still nervous about her privacy and wished to prohibit access by scholars to family papers or anything of a personal nature until after her death, but her wishes went largely unheeded. Not only did she oppose the publication of James Scott's book, but she also asked her brother Saxon to see that Andrew Field, who wrote her first biography, did not gain access to her papers at the University of Maryland, which forced Field to send an emissary to do the research. On the other hand, she talked incessantly about her life and work as long as it was clear that the listener was not prying into personal matters. As O'Neal points out:

> There were certain things she didn't want anyone to know, drafts she didn't want anyone to see, notebooks of ideas that were hers alone, but in the end she made certain all this material would fall into public hands. She covered her secrets and lived a mysterious life, but she made certain all her secrets were written down and preserved or revealed over and over in conversations with me. (O'Neal 175)

Since the major work of Djuna Barnes is highly autobiographical, it is difficult to imagine what she wished to hide. Many sheets of notes, which Saxon Barnes eventually inherited, reveal the same ideas his sister communicated to O'Neal and were obviously written for posterity. Djuna Barnes probably shared Oscar Wilde's view that the only thing worse than being talked about was not being talked about, but she definitely wished to control what was said. O'Neal says:

> She bragged that she had been offered millions for her memoirs but never accepted any offers: She was disinclined, she said, to tell stories about her friends. She meant she didn't want to tell stories about them in print, but she could talk about them from morning to night and she did so. (O'Neal 126)

One consequence of the sale of her papers to the University of Maryland was that Barnes needed a new will. Originally she had meant to leave everything to Thelma Wood (C. Page 280). A 1957 will divided her literary papers between Harvard and Yale. Her attorney, Osmond Fraenkel, drafted another one in 1964, in which Barnes left to Yale University her papers, pen-and-ink drawings for *Ryder* and *Ladies Almanack*, her portrait of Alice Rohrer, two heads, and the letters and manuscripts of Elsa von Freytag Loringhoven. To Faber & Faber she left her copyrights. After deducting legal fees, she wanted the rest to go to the Dag Hammarskjöld Foundation. No letters were to be published, except those to Eliot, Muir, and Hammarskjöld. Her body was to be cremated.

Her final will was signed by John W. Shroyer, Doreen F. Dixson, and Edith H. Brownman on 4 March 1982. Shroyer, a friend of Saxon Barnes, said that Djuna Barnes asked the young Doreen Dixson—who had come as a witness—what her name was. Always interested in names, Barnes remarked, "Doreen, Doreen, sounds like a soap cleanser." Barnes's last will leaves her copyrights in equal proportion to the Authors League Fund and the Historical Churches Preservation Trust of London for the benefit of Saint Bride's Church of Fleet Street, London. Designed by Christopher Wren, it is known as the printers' church, and many of the great English poets have been inspired by its great beauty.[24]

If for some it was a house of prayer, Barnes would have had no objection. She was deeply respectful of religion and envied those who had religious faith, but she never tried to deceive herself: for her, religion was essentially a mystery. "We condemn God, saying why has he planted evil in the world, if he is all powerful and all perfection, but what do we know of his design, it is His, and for that we should be a little reverent."[25] "Fall-out Over Heaven," a poem she conceived in 1936, was revised to commemorate Eliot's seventieth birthday, despite his advice that she write only prose. It is framed by quotes from *The Waste Land* and biblical passages from Isaiah 65:25 and John 20: 15. The poem is rather obscure and disjointed, but the last few lines are memorable:

To Moses' empty gorge, like smoke
Rush backward all the words he spoke.
Lucifer roars up from earth.
Down falls Christ into his death.[26]

After *The Antiphon* was published, Barnes felt that her career as
a writer was about finished. To Willa Muir she wrote: "I think I have
now 'lost my occupation,' as I said to Edwin, when I had put down
the last line of that play. It kills one to write like that, quite literally
the heart fails, but it should not make your heart heavy."[27] There is
some truth to her view if by "writer" one means "published writer,"
for after *Nightwood*—that is to say, during the last forty-seven years
of her life—Barnes published very little original work beyond *The
Antiphon*.[28]

Barnes hated her notorious 1915 chapbook, *The Book of Repulsive
Women*: "My first book of poems is a disgusting little item. At one
time in the 1920s I collected as many copies as I could find and
burned them in my mother's backyard" (O'Neal 98). But in her last
years she wrote poems that rival those early ones for horrible images,
so the desire to shock was, in effect, a consistent impulse, reflecting
her innate pessimism.

Though discouraged by her friend T. S. Eliot from doing so,
Barnes labored steadily at her poetry during the final years. She hoped
to write a long poem—perhaps cantos—but the drafts accumulated,
the editing became impossibly complex, and the stacks of partially
completed poems rose higher and higher. O'Neal says that lines from
a draft of one poem were used in other poems; titles shifted; and each
day, if she had the stamina to work, she would begin anew to attack
the steadily rising mountain of drafts.

Still, there was an amusing side to her creative effort: if a thought
or line came to her as she compiled her grocery list, it was jotted
down with the other items, which must have confused the grocer no
end: "qt. Milk. Half pound smelts. (Of that balanced beast, the Uni-
corn.) . . ." or "1 Natracan. Large (Mint) Milk of Magnesia. (crenelated
roof, holes for shooting through.) (Kyrie eleison. Lord have mercy.)"
(O'Neal 75–76).

The startling images of many of Barnes's poems hark back to *The Book of Repulsive Women*, but they are also indebted to the Metaphysical poets, for she compiled images yoked together by violence to show the desperate plight of those who cling to life while slipping ever so perceptibly, and with much pain, into a yawning grave. "The Walking-mort" (1971) begins: "Call her walking-mort; say where she goes / She squalls her bush with blood. I slam a gate. / Report her axis bone it gigs the rose."

"The Marian Year," hitherto unpublished, is powerful in an esoteric way, but the interest seems more in the iconography of Italian Renaissance painting than in religion per se:

> How should one mourn who never yet has been,
> In any trampled list at Umbria?
> Nor yet in any Tuscan village seen
> The Unicorn thrust in his dousing beam,
> Nor Mary, from the manger of her gown,
> Ride Jesus down.

Barnes wrote poetry mostly for her own amusement, in the hope that flashes of brilliance would yet emerge, but it was, finally, her natural medium. In the end, only two of her poems satisfied her, "Quarry" and "The Walking-mort," which were both published in *The New Yorker*. Despite the echoes of Dylan Thomas, she was justifiably proud of "Quarry":

> While I unwind duration from the tongue-tied tree,
> Send carbon fourteen down for time's address.
> The old revengeful without memory
> Stand by—
> I come, I come that path and there look in
> And see the capsized eye of sleep and wrath
> And hear the beaters' "Gone to earth!"
> Then do I sowl the soul and slap its face
> That it fetch breath.

Her last poem, "Rite of Spring," appeared in *Grand Street* and contains the Yeatsean echo, in his Byzantium poems, of gyres and final things: "Man cannot purge his body of its theme/As can the silkworm on a running thread/Spin a shroud to re-consider in."

The last collection of Barnes's poems, *Creatures in an Alphabet*, published by Dial Press, did not require the effort of concentration or revision that, say, *The Antiphon* did, but there were nevertheless many drafts of each poem—"about fifty pages for each letter" of the alphabet, O'Neal says (41). The poems lay about in countless versions in many piles, for she couldn't simply revise yesterday's poem; it had to be reconceived from the beginning each day. Although *Creatures in an Alphabet* is an uneven bestiary, as Barnes well knew, a few verses stand out:

> Horrid hunger is the cause,
> That opens up the Lion's jaws;
> Yet what it tears apart for meat
> Is merely what its victims ate.

And another:

> The Hippo is a wading junk,
> A sort of Saratoga trunk
> With all its trappings on its back,
> Through which the birds of passage peck.

Even as life slipped away, the famous Barnes wit was at work on the jungle figures Thelma Wood had drawn and been inspired by.

As Barnes's health deteriorated, she told O'Neal of "seven operations, three broken ribs, a broken shoulder . . . a pinched nerve in her spine that causes constant pain, a weak heart, crippling arthritis, lungs filled with emphysema, dreadful dietary restrictions, and oncoming blindness caused by cataracts" (37).[29] She probably forgot a few afflictions.

Barnes wrote Mary Reynolds in 1949 that she had fallen in traffic four times, that her ankles and knees had worsened, and that she was developing asthma.[30] In October of that year, she broke several ribs and wrenched her back when she fell over a French dictionary. She slipped a disk in 1950 and in the next year fractured her spine in two places. Dental problems persisted, for her false teeth fitted badly.

In 1952, she fell and broke her shoulder. She crawled to her telephone and called on her neighbor E. E. Cummings, who climbed the fire escape, let himself in, and telephoned for the ambulance that took her to the French Hospital. Thereafter he would occasionally raise his window and shout, "Are you still alive, Djuna?" She outlasted Cummings by twenty years, but most of the time she wished she hadn't, for she was in persistent pain, particularly in the last three or four years of her life.

Though Barnes feared death, wit sustained her even in the presence of physicians: she quoted with approval one medical doctor's view that "any one dead is in the very best of health."[31] She wrote her friend Phyllis Jones: "As for me? So long as one can sit down and write, and stand up and hold ones water, one is considered to be in sterling condition."[32] Besides her wit, she retained her stern dignity, for Barnes detested the familiarity of most doctors' bedside manner. One physician patted her knee and said that "Ziegfeld would have liked legs like those," to which she later responded that Ziegfeld had, in fact, admired them (C. Page 243). Another doctor patted her on the back and called her "Djuna baby," which so mortified her that she was speechless for hours: even her first name was reserved for only a very privileged few.

In May 1968, Barnes had surgery for a double hernia of the groin. Her description of her ward stay is characteristic:

> I was surrounded by whimpering women, by ancient crones lamenting their lost youth, mothers showing photographs of babies, one darling in the corner, as blunt as a Jane Austin [sic], and as Kate Greenaway as you can imagine, passing angry at razors that took her fair hairs away (apendix) . . . and me, with my running ironic sense of humour, keeping the room in laughter.[33]

In December 1969, she underwent surgery for gallstones. The following February, she had part of her large intestine and her gallbladder removed, then recuperated at the home of her niece Leigh Ponvert for a month. After surgery in 1971, Barnes told James Scott that she had been informed by her doctor that she had already been dead. "So now you know what it's like to be dead," she said he told her. She continued: "Old people should be killed; you know that? There should be a law. This business of keeping them alive—its inhuman! I'm already dead. Do you know that? I've already died, and they brought me back. Now I have to go through the whole horrid business again!"[34] In February 1979, Hank O'Neal wrote to Mina Loy's daughter Fabi Benedict that cataracts had shut down Barnes's eyesight in one eye and were closing the other.[35] On 2 April, Barnes had the cataract in the left eye removed, which caused colors to appear as intolerably brilliant; on 26 November, the cataract from the right eye was removed.

Barnes's night table was covered with medicine bottles: there was Darvon for pain and nitroglycerin pills for the heart. She maintained a salt-free diet. Opium suppositories, though available in only one or two New York pharmacies, gave her what little comfort was possible, but the result, of course, was addiction. Still, the narcotic may have taken her mind off her extremely painful hemorrhoids. O'Neal describes one source of her discomfort:

> As a young girl Barnes had been advised by her grandmother that proper ladies always made use of a warm water enema to empty their bowels, and so the natural elasticity and functioning of her bowels was a memory. This, of course, added to the pain brought on by arthritis and, not surprisingly, her concern about cancer of the rectum.

Barnes had a series of well-meaning nurses to care for her, but most of them either were fired or quit when their tolerance for insults was at an end. Finally, in late March of 1982, when Barnes told her brother Saxon that she could no longer stand living alone in her apartment with constant pain, he arranged for her to be transferred to the Pine Run Nursing Home in Doylestown, Pennsylvania, a town roughly between Philadelphia and his home near Bethlehem.

Fran McCullough arranged for a limousine, the essentials were packed, and Barnes was driven to the nursing home, an institution she had greatly feared since her family had consigned her to a sanatorium for alcoholism. Soon Barnes felt even more imprisoned in the nursing home than she had in her apartment; she screamed in anguish and wrote her friends desperate notes, asking to be rescued. Used as she was to the darkness of her apartment and the dimness caused by cataracts, she was blinded by the bright light of her uncurtained room. Her opium suppositories were taken away; her respirator was stolen.

A month later, she was back in Patchin Place, though emotionally she never recovered from the nursing home ordeal. Page said that she seemed like a "confused, frightened child." Her constant refrain was "Now what shall I do?" (C. Page 291–92). There were times when she surprised her friends, even when apparently in a coma. Francesca Belanger, now finished with the book jacket for *Creatures in an Alphabet*, told her how happy she was that Barnes liked the design. Barnes opened her eyes long enough to say, "Make sure they pay you!"[36] Even near death, she had not abated her fierce distrust of publishers.

A haunting refrain in the last decade of Djuna Barnes's life could well have been Baroness Elsa's remark on mortality: "God is so slow with me." Although the suffering of Barnes's last days was particularly intense, her knowledge of her impending death seemed to Chester Page to bring out a sweeter disposition than was usually observed by the friends who came by to comfort her. Madame Vitriol became a saintly, loving friend, willing to hold hands and be embraced.

Throughout her life, Djuna Barnes often made cavalier remarks about death. Once, she wrote Natalie Barney: "I'll probably scream my lungs out and hang on like a cat on a curtain,"[37] but now she hadn't the strength. Neither did her death fit any of the patterns in her early piece "What Is Good Form in Dying?" (1923). She had often spoken of her deep horror of dying in the same bed her mother died in, and that is precisely what happened. Her ninetieth birthday came on 12 June 1982, and she died on the nineteenth at 7:00 P.M., accompanied only by a nurse.

According to her wishes, Barnes was cremated and her ashes were taken to her birthplace on Storm King Mountain, just south of Cornwall-on-Hudson. Not long after her death, Jussi Korzeniowski, who for many years had come to tidy her apartment, planted dogwood trees near the old schoolhouse, where months later there was a final ceremony. He said a few words in tribute and scattered the ashes among the dogwoods. Also present were Fran and David McCullough, Adam Shirey, Irwin Cohen, Francesca Belanger, and Chester Page, who laid a yellow sweetheart rose at every tree. Page saw a gentle rain begin to fall on Storm King Mountain, on the yellow roses, on the Hudson River below, and on the departing pilgrims.

In contemplating the relief that Djuna Barnes must have felt as the pain began to depart for the last time, one remembers her lovely poem, perhaps written in mourning for Mary Pyne, that celebrates that imagined final moment.

Finis

For you, for me? Why then the striking hour,
The wind among the curtains, and the tread
Of some late gardener pulling at the flower
They'll lay between our hearts when we are dead.

Notes

■ ■ ■

INTRODUCTION

1. DB to Emily Coleman, 14 December 1935.
2. *Theatre Guild Magazine*, 1931.
3. DB to Emily Coleman, 22 August 1936.
4. DB to Emily Coleman, 30 October 1935.
5. DB to Emily Coleman, 10 January 1936.
6. Elizabeth Barnes to DB, 1 December 1936.
7. Emily Coleman to DB, 27 August 1935, p. 7.
8. *SW* 87.
9. Emily Coleman to DB, 27 October 1935.

CHAPTER 1: ZADEL

1. Djuna Barnes, "The Songs of Synge: The Man Who Shaped His Life as He Shaped His Plays," *New York Morning Telegraph Sunday Magazine*, 18 February 1917, 8.

2. Djuna Barnes, *Ryder* (New York: Boni & Liveright, 1928; St. Martin's, 1979; 1981; Elmwood Park, Il.: Dalkey Archive, 1990, p. 35). (All references to *Ryder* are to the Dalkey Archive edition.) Djuna Barnes told James Scott and others that her novel *Ryder* was completely autobiographical. In a letter of 5 June 1934 to Natalie Clifford Barney, Barnes even refers to her father as the Wendell of *Ryder*. There are virtually no facts in the novel that do not correlate with details of her early life, and so I take the liberty of drawing on

Ryder for biographical information, a strategy that would indeed be suspect in most biographies.

3. This statement appears in a fragmentary note by Djuna Barnes (p. 9) beginning: "who was socially beneath her," owned by Peter Barnes.

4. Information on the Barnes family comes in part from a privately printed genealogy by the Reverend George Barnes, located in the New York Public Library (courtesy of Peter Barnes).

5. When Zadel's mother died, in 1867, Duane was a widower for two years, then on 22 September 1869 he married Frances Tibbals, a Connecticut woman living in Wilmington, Delaware. Their children's names were even more unusual: Urlan (1870–88), Niar (b. 1873), and Unade (b. 1884; anagram of Duane).

6. Page of DB's notes beginning "1826, Father born," owned by Peter Barnes.

7. Her son Justin Llewellyn combined the name of two of Zadel's siblings. In *Nightwood*, Nora remembers in a dream her grandmother's wall with a faded portrait of Llewellyn (62).

8. From page 9, beginning: "who was socially beneath her."

9. Wilbraham-Monson Academy has no record of Zadel's attendance, but entries in *Who's Who* mention it. Her sisters Marilla and Hinda were in the class of 1857. In 1856, the school's Old Boarding House, where students were lodged, was burned to the ground.

10. Henry's petition to remarry, filed in Springfield, Mass., in September 1879, shows that he and Zadel had also lived in Washington, D.C., for one year; in Leyden, Mass., for six months; in Chicopee Falls, Mass., for six months; in Bound Brook, N.J., for two years; in Berlin, Conn., for a year; in Greenfield, Mass., for eleven years, and in Springfield from 1873 to July of 1876.

11. *Appleton's Cyclopaedia* (vol. 3) says that for two years Zadel was political editor of a Massachusetts journal, which may just mean the *Franklin County Times*, but it hints at the distinguished *Springfield Republican*.

12. Henry's birth certificate in Greenfield spells his surname with two *d*'s.

13. In 1894, he published an article "On Symptomatic Heterophoria" (*New York Medical Journal*, 1894, lix). On 28 December 1881, Justin married Ida Berth Van Aken (b. 3 February 1861). Their children were Harold F. (b. 13 August 1887) and Justin L. Budington (b. 26 September 1889).

14. I am indebted to Janet Dempsey, the town historian of Cornwall, for this information.

15. Marilla married Derwin De Forest (1863), then Norman Harriman Bruce in 1870; he died in 1895 and five months later she married Malcolm Cameron. Hinda married a Boston man and Wesleyan graduate, George Litch

Roberts, who in 1870 became counselor of the United States Supreme Court.

16. On 12 September 1881, Henry married Sophia Steele Billings, age 57.

17. Budington's spiritualist pamphlets include the following titles: *Death Is Birth, or the Outcome of Transition* (1897); *History of the New England Spiritualist Campmeeting Association at Lake Pleasant, Mass.* (1907); *Man Makes His Body: or the Ascent of Ego Through Matter* (20 pp.) All were printed in Springfield, Mass., at the Star Publishing Co. Budington also published *The Origin of Life and How the Spirit Body Grows* (Faraday pamphlets, no. 2). (See also spiritualist writings of Thomas Cushman Buddington, Henry's brother.)

18. *Harper's*, April 1872.

19. Ibid., October 1880.

20. Ibid., March 1879.

21. The photographers were Elliott and Fry.

22. This appears in Chester Page's "Memories of Djuna Barnes," p. 251. All references to this unpublished memoir are indicated by "C. Page."

23. These testimonials were published in *The Magazine of Poetry*, July 1891, pp. 303–4. Zadel never dramatized "Karin."

24. J. R. Osgood published Zadel Barnes's *Can the Old Love?* in 1871 and Henry James's first volume of tales, *A Passionate Pilgrim* (1875), his *The American* (1877), and *The Europeans* (1878). In 1882, Osgood published Zadel's biography *Genevieve Ward*, and he was to have published James's *The Bostonians* as well, before he went bankrupt in 1885.

25. Henry James, *The Bostonians* (New York: New American Library, 1979), 26.

26. Joseph Cummings of the Methodist-Episcopal Church in Middletown officiated.

27. On a sheet of Djuna's notes from her last years, in Peter Barnes's possession, is the phrase "Grandmothers third child Emmanuel, died a baby." Emmanuel was named after Axel Gustafson's father.

28. At one point Gustafson observes that "The custom of greeting women by kissing on the mouth is said to . . . have been adopted in order to discover if they had tasted wine" (22). Of this book's success, *The Magazine of Poetry* (July 1891) says: "Its sales in England and in South Africa, India, the far East and Australia, have been unprecedented for a work of this character" (304).

29. Edwin Hodder, *The Life of Samuel Morley* (New York: Randolph, 1888), 419–20.

30. Beginning in 1882, the Gustafsons lived at 14 Brunswick Square, W.C.; they moved in 1884 to 45 Upper Gloucester Place, Portman Square,

N.W.; their final London address was 30 Cromwell Grove, W1. Djuna always recalled them living in Grosvenor Square.

31. Djuna kept a pamphlet of Zadel's called "Remember Trafalgar Square: Tory Terrorism in 1887," now in the DB Collection, University of Maryland, Series V, Box 1.

32. *The Magazine of Poetry*, July 1891, 304.

33. Oddly enough, Lady Wilde at one point lived at 146 Oakley Street (the street has since been renumbered), the same street in Chelsea where Djuna's friend Emily Coleman was to live (at 105 and 107). Another curious connection between the Wildes and Djuna Barnes is that her friend Natalie Clifford Barney had, in her youth, been engaged to Lord Alfred Douglas, whose homosexual liaison with Oscar Wilde led to Wilde's trial and imprisonment.

34. Richard Ellmann, *Oscar Wilde* (New York: Alfred A. Knopf, 1988), 9.

35. Horace Wyndham, *Speranza: A Biography of Lady Wilde* (New York: Philosophical Library, 1951), 69.

36. Ibid., 115.

37. Ibid., 119.

38. Ellmann, *Oscar Wilde*, 124–25.

39. "The Biography of Julie von Bartmann," unpublished play, 1924 (Manuscript at University of Maryland), 11.

40. Djuna Barnes wrote to Natalie Clifford Barney on 10 September 1967: "And I recall my grandmother, and *her* salon, and *her* Willie Wilde, Browning, Elizabeth Cady Stanton, the scandals of Stead and God knows what."

41. In *Children's Lore in* Finnegans Wake (Syracuse University Press, 1985), Stead is Grace Eckley's candidate for HCE in James Joyce's novel.

42. C. Page 258.

43. DB Collection, University of Maryland, Series II, Box 1.

44. Yvonne Kapp, *Eleanor Marx*, 2 vols. (London: Lawrence & Wishart, 1972; 1976), I, 236.

45. Steven Watson defines free love as follows: "According to this doctrine, sexual relationships (or *free unions*) should not be restricted to married couples but enjoyed by any mutually consenting partners no matter what their marital state. Free love advocates distinguished their activity from promiscuity, describing the sexual impulse as a form of spiritual enhancement." *Strange Bedfellows: The First American Avant-Garde* (New York: Abbeville, 1991), 144.

46. Theodore Stanton and Harriet Stanton Blatch, eds., *Elizabeth Cady Stanton as Revealed in Her Letters, Diary and Reminiscences* (New York: Harper, 1922), 410.

47. In a letter of 26 May 1941, Djuna apparently supplied information about Zadel for *Woman's Who's Who*, saying, among other things, that Zadel worked with Harriet Beecher Stowe for women's suffrage.

48. Page of DB's notes beginning: "better memory of her memories," owned by Peter Barnes.

49. *The Antiphon* says of Axel's fictional counterpart: "He left her later for a Cheapside Strumpet" (*SW* 153).

50. Fragment for "Oscar," DB Collection, University of Maryland, Series II, Box 4.

51. Letter from G. N. Swan of 30 August 1923 to the Newberry Library.

52. One project of this patriotic organization was to raise funds for a memorial for Theodore Ruggles Timbly, the inventor of the revolving gun turret on the USS *Monitor*. This was late in 1909.

53. In *Ryder*, Wendell, at the age of two, sets the barn and house on fire (*R* 17).

54. Irwin Cohen and Francesca Belanger told me that they were told by Djuna Barnes that Zadel was a bridesmaid in a royal wedding in Sweden, on which occasion she was given an onyx ring by the royal family, which Djuna still had in the 1970s.

55. Draft of *The Antiphon*, DB Collection, University of Maryland, Series II, Box 1, Act III, 13.

CHAPTER 2: STORM KING

1. This gloomy aphorism appears on a page of DB's notes beginning: "Undoubtedly the reason why uniforms," owned by Peter Barnes.

2. Five years later, he published a newspaper article called "The Barnes Air-Ship."

3. Herr Gustave is described in *Ryder*, 165–66. The certificate lists the Gustafsons' address as 915 E St., N.W., Washington, D.C.

4. Several lines in *The Antiphon* parody Wald's dilettantism: "A farm he never farmed—A House he couldn't keep—But to his credit, built the thing himself" (*SW* 128).

5. Accompanying DB's letter of 15 April 1971 to Scott.

6. DB Collection, University of Maryland, Series II, Box 1.

7. Interview with Saxon Barnes, 27 May 1989.

8. James Stern's notes from *Time* interview with DB, 18 January 1943. Hereafter "*Time* Morgue."

9. In 1936, Djuna began to write an unfinished narrative, called "The Beggar's Comedy," about her mother's background. Only a page or two survive, but I have exploited them for details such as these.

10. Besides Elizabeth, the Chappells' children were named John, Daniel, Susannah, Thomas, William, and Arthur. However, in "The Beggar's Comedy," Barnes mentions eleven children.

11. Page of DB's notes beginning: "1826 Father born," owned by Peter Barnes.

12. Elizabeth Barnes to DB, 23 November 1943.

13. Zadel, Axel, and Wald lived at 30 Cromwell Grove, near Shepherd's Bush Road, and Elizabeth Chappell next door at 33.

14. On 22 November 1901, Zadel made out her will, leaving her estate to Wald, listing her address as 39 W. 47th St., New York, N.Y.

15. The letter is dated only "Sunday."

16. Witnesses were Justin Barnes, M.D., Ida B. Barnes, Henry Mills Alden, and Zadel Barnes.

17. On two occasions Djuna Barnes told Chester Page that Zadel and Alden had been lovers.

18. H. L. Mallalieu, *The Dictionary of British Watercolour Artists Up to 1920* (Woodbridge, Suffolk, England, 1976).

19.   A thin little fellow had such a fat wife,
        Fat wife, fat wife, God bless her!
        She looked like a drum and he looked like a fife,
        And it took all his money to dress her.
        God bless her!
        To dress her!
        God bless her!
        To dress her!

        To wrap up her body and warm up her toes,
        Fat toes, fat toes, God keep her!
        For bonnets and bows and silken clothes,
        To eat her, and drink her, and sleep her,
        God keep her!
        To sleep her!
        God keep her!
        To sleep her!

        She grew like a target, he grew like a sword,
        A sword, a sword, God spare her!
        She took all the bed and she took all the board,
        And it took a whole sofa to bear her,
        God spare her!
        To bear her!
        God spare her!
        To bear her!

She spread like a turtle, he shrank like a pike,
A pike, a pike, God save him!
And nobody ever beheld the like,
For they had to wear glasses to shave him,
God save him!
To shave him!
God save him!
To shave him!

She fattened away till she burst one day,
Exploded, blew up, God take her!
And all the people that saw it say
She covered over an acre!
God take her!
An acre!
God take her!
An acre!

20. DB Collection, University of Maryland, Series II, Box 1.

21. The fragment by DB is called "The Sparrows," owned by Peter Barnes.

22. In *The Antiphon*, it is said that Titus believed in Brigham Young (*SW* 89).

23. Thurn changed his surname to Budington on 21 October 1942 and recorded it in Cornwall-on-Hudson. Thurn's birth was recorded, but not Djuna's, for whatever reason.

24. In a letter of 1 February 1967 to Yolanda Hendricks, who had named her daughter "Djuna," Barnes wrote of her name: "It is a name *made up by my father* . . . there was no other Djuna only me. Then my niece got it, and now your daughter. How nice! If the name means anything, it means *the light of the moon*, because my eldest brother, when an infant called the moon 'nuna.' My father, at that time, reading the novel 'The Wandering Jew,' by Eugene Sue (?), liking the Prince therein, called *Djalma* (Indian) (I think) put the Dj on to the *una*, and there you are, and blessings on her." University of Maryland.

25. DB to Emily Coleman, 30 October 1938.

26. DB to James B. Scott, 15 April 1971.

27. Djuna Barnes, "The Dear Dead Days," *Theatre Guild Magazine* VI (February 1929), 43.

28. DB to Emily Coleman, 7 August 1938.

29. DB to Emily Coleman, 14 February 1937.

30. Charles Henri Ford, "I Will Be What I Am" (unpublished manuscript), 258. Hereafter "Ford." Djuna Barnes told Ford this story.

31. Telephone interview with Saxon Barnes, 27 February 1990.

32. Janet Flanner, *Paris Was Yesterday* (New York: Viking, 1972), xvii.

33. *Theatre Guild Magazine*, April 1931, 30.

34. Peter Barnes kindly provided a copy of Thurn's travel notebook, which was recorded in his father Saxon's handwriting, faithful to Thurn's poor spelling. Apparently they left New York on December 10.

35. The deeds here show some curious patterns: On 2 November 1892, Theodore and Ellen Brown sold Wald and Elizabeth Barnes 4.09 acres of land for $500. On 21 January 1894, they sold this to August Klug, who had an estate named Abendroth, for the same price. (Abendröte is mentioned in a note for *The Antiphon*.) On 19 May 1894, Ellen Brown sold 3.73 acres to Zadel for $281.25, which Zadel sold to Wald and Elizabeth on 14 March 1896 for $350. On 25 March 1897, Wald and Elizabeth sold this to Klug for the same price. On 2 June 1897, the Browns sold 5.52 acres to Wald for $300, which he then sold to Klug for the same price nine days later. Either Brown wouldn't sell to Klug, or Wald was a fool at land speculation, for Klug (which means "wise" in German) seems to have done very well with Wald as his agent. The buying and selling patterns of the Huntington property were similarly curious.

36. The current address is 361 Half Hollow Road, near the Long Island Expressway's Exit 50. Due to the efforts of the Huntington Historic Preservation Commission, on 6 June 1989 the Barnes house was named a historic building; but the developer who had previously bought it, wishing to destroy it and build condominiums, eventually succeeded.

37. "The Biography of Julie von Bartmann," 72.

38. DB to Elizabeth Barnes, 25 June 1939.

39. Dated 6 February 1961.

40. Wald enjoyed reading Tennyson aloud, but when Djuna turned against Wald, she hated Tennyson as well.

41. "Playgoer's Almanac," *Theatre Guild Magazine*, November 1930, 35.

42. Some of the material for the hearing comes from "Julie von Bartmann."

43. Mary Lynn Broe, ed., *Silence and Power: A Reevaluation of Djuna Barnes* (Carbondale: Southern Illinois University Press, 1991), 365.

44. Wald to Elizabeth Barnes, 14 November 1912.

45. DB to Wald, 23 September 1921. Djuna had recently returned from Europe, disappointed with life abroad.

46. Djuna Barnes, *Nightwood* (New York: New Directions, 1946), 62.

47. DB to Emily Coleman, 3 March 1941.

48. Diaries of Emily Holmes Coleman (unpublished manuscript, University of Delaware Library), 137. Hereafter "Diaries."

49. DB fragment "The Sparrows."

50. Bercovici, who had come to the U.S. from Romania via France in 1904, met Lemon at socialist meetings. By 1916, Bercovici was having considerable success as a short-story writer, and in the next year he joined the *New York World* as a sports reporter. In the following years, he wrote many books on travel, history, and, especially, Gypsy life.

51. Buan died on 21 June 1960, Muriel on 24 December 1982, and Duane on 5 June 1990.

52. Elizabeth Barnes to DB, 27 January 1925.

53. In a letter of 23 May 1934 to Natalie Clifford Barney, written from 111 Waverly Place, New York, Djuna Barnes wrote: "My father died on the 21st of a heart stroke; quick and merciful, less than two minutes. He was 69 and had always had a bad heart. Effect on mother: she thinks of death." On 5 June 1934, she wrote Barney again, this time linking her father with Wendell of *Ryder*: "Things here in a bit of a flurry with me. My father (Wendell Ryder) died a few days ago. . . . She [mother] has not seen him in over twenty years, and one does forget even when one has had five children. I was surprised to find that I wept heavily and sadly for the death of John [Holms], but for my father only for death itself, and not for him."

54. One bitter poem is simply entitled "Life."

> Life is the dust
> From the bowels
> Of a giant's
> Burnt out hist.
>
> Life is the dregs
> From heated water,
> Spumed from the mouth
> Of Lilith's daughter.
>
> Life is the atom
> Detached and lost
> From a light
> As white as frost.

55. Elizabeth Barnes to DB, 29 March 1928.

CHAPTER 3 : DEAR SNICKERBITS

1. DB to Emily Coleman, 21 May 1938.

2. C. Page 252.

3. Page of DB's notes, owned by Peter Barnes, beginning with the quoted phrase.

4. George Barker letter to the author, 5 July 1990.

5. DB to Emily Coleman, 30 October 1938.

6. Zadel Barnes Gustafson to DB, 20 February 1906.

7. Zadel Barnes Gustafson to DB, 18 February 1909.

8. C. Page 287.

9. Mary Lynn Broe, "My Art Belongs to Daddy: Incest as Exile, The Textual Economics of Hayford Hall." In Broe and Angela Ingram, eds., *Women Writers in Exile* (Chapel Hill: University of North Carolina Press, 1989), 53.

10. Ibid., 56.

11. As we shall see, the "barter" of Djuna—presumably this means to Percy Faulkner rather than the violation of Djuna by Wald or his agent when she was sixteen—was engineered by Zadel, who, according to Eleanor Barnes, was very fond of Percy. She was happy that Djuna had developed "qualities I have hoped & prayed for *with all my soul. Love, sympathy, & trust.*" She encourages Djuna to keep on loving Percy.

12. Emily Coleman to DB, 27 October 1935.

13. C. Page 287.

14. The State of New York has no record of marriage between Djuna Barnes and Percy Faulkner.

15. Zadel used stationery with a letterhead and a message urging a memorial for Theodore Ruggles Timby, inventor of the revolving turret used on the USS *Monitor*, and began "Dear Madam." Apparently she was working for a patriotic women's organization soliciting funds for various causes.

16. See the photo of Djuna and her doll in Hank O'Neal, *Life is painful, nasty and short* (New York: Paragon House, 1990), 196. Hereafter "O'Neal."

17. Fragment of a draft of *Nightwood*, University of Maryland.

18. "She Tells Her Daughter," *Smart Set* LXIII (November 1923), 78.

19. Ibid., 77.

20. Ibid., 80.

21. Djuna's diary of 1912 records the following submissions: July 9: "Tomorrow Is Coming" sent to *Smart Set*; July 12: "My Solitude" sent to *Harper's*; July 26: "My Solitude" sent to *Smart Set*; August 6: "Tomorrow's Coming" sent to *Harper's*; August 10: "Tomorrow's Coming" sent to RHD; August 26: "Tomorrow's Coming" sent to Whiting; September 12: "A Cancelled Misdemeanor" sent to *Smart Set*; September 20: several pictures left at *Life*: "Beneath the Cameo," "A Warm Breeze," and "The Gold ?Dish"; October 30: "A Cancelled Misdemeanor" sent to Davis; November 30: "A Cancelled Misdemeanor" sent to *Harper's*.

22. Relevant letters from Reon Barnes are those of 16 August and 3 October 1912.

23. Barnes's address at this time is listed as 1320 Ward Street, Morris Park, N.Y. She was staying with her mother.

24. Lawrence Campbell to the author, 3 May 1990.

25. DB to Emily Coleman, 20–23 March 1936.

26. "Putzi" means "little fellow" in Bavarian dialect. I am indebted to Hanfstaengl's autobiographies and especially to Philip Metcalfe's *1933* (Sag Harbor, N.Y.: Permanent Press, 1988), which is recommended to readers who wish to know more about Hanfstaengl.

27. O'Neal 129. See photo of Putzi dated February 1915.

28. Metcalfe, *1933*, 37.

29. Ernst Hanfstaengl, *Unheard Witness* (Philadelphia and New York: Lippincott, 1957), 14.

30. Ibid., 33.

31. Ibid.

32. Ibid., 38.

33. *Time* Morgue.

34. There is a photo of Djuna Barnes, Inez Mulholland, and Putzi Hanfstaengl dated February 1915, University of Maryland.

35. C. Page 239.

36. O'Neal 129.

37. Hanfstaengl, *Unheard Witness*, 29.

38. Konrad Bercovici, *It's the Gypsy in Me* (New York: Prentice-Hall, 1941), 102.

39. Ibid., 294.

40. DB to Emily Coleman, 21 May 1938.

41. O'Neal 41; 129–30.

42. O'Neal 130.

43. ". . . und so zog mich auch dieser Gedanke zurück in die Heimat, da ich mir als Frau nur eine Deutsche vorstellen konnte" ("and this thought too drew me back to the fatherland, that I could only imagine having a German wife"): Ernst Hanfstaengl, *Zwischen Weissem und Braunem Haus* (Munich: Piper, 1970), 23.

44. Harold E. Stearns, *The Street I Know* (New York: Lee Furman, 1935), 96–98.

45. Maurice Sterne, *Shadow and Light* (New York: Harcourt, Brace & World, 1966), 155–56.

46. Interview with Joella Bayer.

CHAPTER 4: ''I COULD NEVER BE LONELY WITHOUT A HUSBAND''

1. "Monsieur Ampee" was a newspaper story by Barnes published in 1917. Three excellent sources of information on the journalism of Barnes are

Cheryl J. Plumb, *Fancy's Craft: Art and Identity in the Early Works of Djuna Barnes* (Selinsgrove, Pa.: Susquehanna University Press, 1986), 19–33; Carl Herzig, "Roots of Night: Emerging Style and Vision in the Early Journalism of Djuna Barnes," *Centennial Review* XXXI (Summer 1987), 255–69; and Nancy J. Levine, " 'Bringing Milkshakes to Bulldogs': The Early Journalism of Djuna Barnes," in Broe, ed., *Silence and Power*, 27–34.

2. C. Page 232.

3. *Time* Morgue.

4. Levine, " 'Bringing Milkshakes to Bulldogs,' " 28.

5. DB to Emily Coleman, 30 October 1935.

6. The distinction soon became blurred, however, since she did not totally abandon the "Djuna Barnes" byline for journalism.

7. Emily Coleman to DB, 27 August 1935, 7.

8. Djuna Barnes, "What Is Good Form in Dying?" *Vanity Fair* XX (June 1923), 73.

9. Ibid., 102.

10. Hiram Motherwell to DB, 14 May 1930.

11. Levine, " 'Bringing Milkshakes to Bulldogs.' "

12. DB to Willa Muir, 11 April 1968.

13. Such is the case in her interview with Jacques Copeau, the cofounder of *Nouvelle Revue Française*, who was briefly on tour in the United States as a theatrical manager. He extolled the virtues of high art, admiring Flaubert, Rimbaud, Mallarmé, Ibsen, and Molière. Barnes obviously admired his brilliance, good taste, and devotion to quality. She ends with an observation ostensibly quoted: "He will do for America what has never been done. He will shame her into becoming beautiful, into caring for her mind, in cultivating herself, lifting herself out of the bourgeois class." "Introducing Monsieur Copeau," *New York Morning Telegraph Sunday Magazine*, 3 June 1917, 4.

14. Margaret Anderson, *My Thirty Years War* (New York: Horizon, 1970), 182.

15. Since a footnote says that Bruno's article will be continued under the title "Greenwich Village as It Is," and the first of Barnes's four articles on the Village appeared in *Bruno's Weekly* on 29 April 1916, it is likely that Bruno handed over to Barnes the task of writing a series of articles on the Village.

16. Barnes told Hank O'Neal that Hartmann, who had children with several women, wanted to have one with her (O'Neal 44).

17. O'Neal 176.

18. Andrew Field, *Djuna: The Formidable Miss Barnes* (Austin: University of Texas Press, 1985), 53.

19. See the photo of Djuna and Dinah in O'Neal 167.

20. A print of this photo is owned by Chester Page.

21. Some of Barnes's interviews were presumably never published. For instance, she reportedly interviewed F. Scott Fitzgerald, who flattered her with the remark "*I* ought to be interviewing *you!*" (C. Page 270).

22. James Joyce, *Ulysses* (The Corrected Text) (New York: Vintage, 1986), 349.

23. A letter from Zadel Barnes to DB echoes her comment that life wasn't worth living.

24. Stieglitz's studio at 291 Fifth Avenue was *the* meeting place in New York for those interested in photography. He apparently solicited Barnes's comment on the studio for publication, for on 10 December 1914 she wrote him: "291 is the Attic near the Roof. It is nearer the roof than any other attic in the world. There insomnia is not a malady—it is an ideal." Stieglitz quoted Barnes in an issue of *Photographic Quarterly* called "What Is 291?" (p. 30).

25. Barnes told Hank O'Neal that she had interviewed Jack Johnson, who pinched her bottom, but she may have been referring to Jess Willard (O'Neal 44).

26. Sarlós 198.

27. *New York Morning Telegraph Sunday Magazine*, 12 August 1917, 4.

28. The introduction to the interview notes that she had introduced Bruno to Frank Harris in late 1916 or early 1917, an important event for Bruno. Barnes's play premiered at the Provincetown Players in 1919, and Bruno interviewed her shortly thereafter.

29. C. Page 248.

30. *Time* Morgue.

31. C. Page 225.

32. *Vanity Fair* XVIII (April 1922), 65; 104. "Vagaries Malicieux" appeared in *Double Dealer* III (May 1922), 249–60. The following section on Joyce appears in similar form in my article "Djuna Barnes Remembers James Joyce," in *James Joyce Quarterly* 30 (Fall 1992), 113–17.

33. Presumably Joyce meant that George Moore was a playboy, not that he was the subject of Synge's play.

34. This is the Baroness St. Leger, who lived on the isle of Brissago in the Lago Maggiore, not "off the Cretan coast."

35. Opopanax is "an odorous gum resin formerly used in medicine and believed to be obtained from Hercules' allheal" (*Webster's Third New International Dictionary*).

1. In this chapter I have relied to some extent on the following sources: Robert Károly Sarlós, *Jig Cook and the Provincetown Players* (Amherst: University of Massachusetts Press, 1982); Susan F. Clark, "Misalliance: Djuna Barnes and the American Theatre" (Ph.D. dissertation, Tufts University, 1989); Cheryl J. Plumb, *Fancy's Craft: Art and Identity in the Early Works of Djuna Barnes*; and Andrew Field, *Djuna: The Formidable Miss Barnes*.

2. Djuna Barnes, "The Songs of Synge."

3. Djuna Barnes, "The Days of Jig Cook," *Theatre Guild Magazine*, VI (January 1929), 31.

4. Telephone interview with Kenneth Burke, April 1990.

5. Edmund Wilson, *The Twenties* (New York: Farrar, Straus & Giroux, 1975), 369.

6. Telephone interview with Berenice Abbott, March 1990.

7. William Carlos Williams, *Autobiography* (New York: New Directions, 1967), 170–71.

8. Kenneth Burke, "Version, Con-, Per-, and In- (Thoughts on Djuna Barnes' Novel *Nightwood*)," *Southern Review* II (Spring 1966), 329–46. Also in his *Language as Symbolic Action* (Berkeley: University of California Press, 1968), 240–53.

9. DB to Natalie Barney, 9 October 1966.

10. DB to Kenneth Burke, 8 October 1966.

11. Barnes told Chester Page: "We don't really like each other very much, but she is like family. I've known her since she was fifteen" (C. Page 242). Hank O'Neal asked Berenice Abbott to write an introduction to his book on Barnes, but she refused: "Djuna bores me to death and she was a literary snob as well. I have no interest in writing about her" (O'Neal xiii).

12. Sarlós, *Jig Cook*, 64–65.

13. Wald sent a similar warning to abandon her deep pessimism to Barnes at *The Little Review* (May–June 1920): "Your longing to be 'original,' strange, compelling, is only too crudely evident in your prose work. . . . There is a *big better self*—the *real Djuna*—asleep now, but to awaken, sometime" (73). It was a judgment others would make as well.

14. C. Page 243.

15. DB to Emily Coleman, 3 August 1936.

16. DB to Emily Coleman, 10 March 1937.

17. DB to Emily Coleman, 4 February 1939.

18. DB to Emily Coleman, 6 June 1939.

19. DB to Emily Coleman, 3 March 1939.

20. Bercovici. *It's the Gypsy in Me*, 44.

21. Ibid., 53.

22. "Frank Harris Finds Success More Easily Won Here in America Than in England." *New York Morning Telegraph Sunday Magazine*, 4 February 1917, 8. (In *Interviews*.)

23. Wilson, *The Twenties*, 85–86.

24. Bercovici, *It's the Gypsy in Me*, 106.

25. Bercovici's article "Roumania" appeared in *Pearson's Magazine* in November 1916; in the next issue, Lemon's " 'Free Speech' in the United States" was published.

26. Bercovici, *It's the Gypsy in Me*, 163.

27. *New York Times*, 3 April 1933, 15. Djuna received the news in May in Tangier, apparently with little emotion, for in a letter of 8 May 1933 to Natalie Barney she says that she "got a notice one of my past sweethearts died April 2."

28. DB to Emily Coleman, 30 October 1938.

29. Courtenay Lemon, "The War and the Men of Thought," 184–86.

30. C. Page 282.

31. An unpublished draft called "Baroness Elsa" is dated 12 November 1932, 9, rue St. Romain, Paris. A fictional version of Elsa's life was begun in London in 1937, at various times called "The Living Statues," "Elsa," and "The Beggar's Comedy."

32. Elsa signed herself "Else," the proper German spelling, but her name has through time become anglicized.

33. Lynn DeVore, "The Backgrounds of *Nightwood*: Robin, Felix, and Nora," *Journal of Modern Literature* 10 (1983), 81.

34. See Paul Hjartarson, ed., *A Stranger to My Time: Essays by and About Frederick Philip Grove*, especially his essay "Of Greve, Grove, and Other Strangers"; and DeVore's "The Backgrounds of *Nightwood*, 71–90. I am also indebted to D. O. Spettigue's essay "Fanny Essler and the Master" in the Hjartarson volume.

35. Paul Hjartarson and Douglas O. Spettigue, eds., *Baroness Elsa* (Ottawa: Oberon, 1992), 26.

36. Elsa is described at length in Margaret Anderson's *My Thirty Years War*, William Carlos Williams's *Autobiography*, Steven Watson's *Strange Bedfellows*, Harold Loeb's *The Way It Was*, and George Biddle's *An American Artist's Story*.

37. O'Neal 139.

38. Anderson, *My Thirty Years War*, 211.

39. Ibid., 194.

40. Unpublished memoir of Louis Bouché in the Archives of American Art, Washington, D.C.

41. George Biddle, *An American Artist's Story* (Boston: Little, Brown, 1939), 137.

42. Steven Watson, *Strange Bedfellows: The First American Avant-Garde* (New York: Abbeville Press, 1991), 269.

43. Biddle, *American Artist's Story*, 141.

44. In a letter to Barnes of 6 February 1967, Vail mentioned their "very short" love affair more than fifty years previously.

45. Joan Mellen, *Kay Boyle: Author of Herself* (New York: Farrar, Straus & Giroux, 1994), 130.

46. C. Page 263.

47. Mellen, *Kay Boyle*, 132.

48. Alfred Kreymborg, *Troubadour*, 241.

49. Cook had been the author of *Roderick Taliaferro* (1903), about Montezuma, and *The Chasm* (1911), a socialist novel.

50. Mary Heaton Vorse, *Time and the Town*, 121.

51. Barnes, "The Days of Jig Cook," 31–32.

52. Ibid., 32.

53. Williams, *Autobiography*, 138.

54. Sárlos, *Jig Cook*, 154. In *Ten Days That Shook the World*, John Silas "Jack" Reed described the Russian Revolution; he was one of the founders of the Communist Party in the United States.

55. C. Page 271.

56. Sárlos, *Jig Cook*, 187.

57. Here, for instance, Edna St. Vincent Millay made her stage debut in Floyd Dell's *The Angel Intrudes*.

58. Barnes, "The Days of Jig Cook," p. 32.

59. Helen Deutsch and Stella Hanau, *The Provincetown: A Story of the Theatre* (New York: Farrar & Rinehart, 1931), 80–82.

60. Allan Ross Macdougall, ed., *The Letters of Edna St. Vincent Millay* (New York: Harper, 1952), 116.

61. Sarlós, *Jig Cook*, 3. The following section on Synge appeared in rather different form as my article "Djuna Barnes and the Songs of Synge," *Éire-Ireland* 2:28 (Summer 1993), 157–62.

62. At the end of one article she paraphrased Maurya of *Riders to the Sea* (without mentioning her), who said: "No man can be living for ever and we must be satisfied" (*NY* 252). On Barnes's visit to the Bronx, she gathered courage and wrote for a full page in the style of Synge (*NY* 353–54). Barnes's article "The Songs of Synge" appeared in the *Morning Telegraph Sunday Magazine* on 18 February 1917. As late as 1945, Barnes mentioned Synge in a review article of Gertrude Stein's *Wars I Have Seen* in *Contemporary Jewish Record*.

63. Robert McAlmon, *Being Geniuses Together: 1920–1930* (New York: Doubleday, 1968), 34.

64. Djuna Barnes, "James Joyce: A Portrait of the Man Who Is, at Present, One of the More Significant Figures in Literature," *Vanity Fair* XVIII (April 1922), 65; 104. Reprinted in Djuna Barnes, *Interviews*, ed. Alyce Barry (Washington, D.C.: Sun & Moon Press, 1985).

65. *New York Morning Telegraph Sunday Magazine*, 18 February 1917, 8.

66. Barnes's desire to imitate both Synge *and* Beardsley (and later Joyce) is obviously a measure of her relative immaturity as an artist.

67. Clark, "Misalliance," 74.

68. "The Death of Life: Death Is the Poor Man's Purse—Baudelaire," *New York Morning Telegraph Sunday Magazine*, 17 December 1916, 8.

69. Except for "Finale" and the poems, all of the *Little Review* work appeared in Djuna Barnes's *A Book* (New York: Boni & Liveright, 1923).

70. Sterne, *Shadow and Light*, 155.

71. DB to Emily Coleman, 14 December 1935.

72. DB to Emily Coleman, 3 March 1939; 16 May 1936.

73. Wilson, *The Twenties*, 85.

74. Anderson, *My Thirty Years War*, 181.

75. Norman Nadel, *A Pictorial History of the Theatre Guild* (New York: Crown, 1969), 21.

76. *Time* Morgue.

CHAPTER 6: ''SO THIS IS PARIS!''

1. Barnes, "Vagaries Malicieux."

2. Leo Fleishman borrowed $100 for Djuna Barnes's fare from his cousin Peggy Guggenheim. Zadel Barnes had earlier been sent to London by *McCall's*.

3. Burton Rascoe, *We Were Interrupted* (New York: Doubleday, 1947), 85.

4. Ibid., 95.

5. In a letter to Barnes of 21 September 1923, Burton says that he has received the story, together with pictures, and sent her $500 for it. This was probably a review of Peter Ouspensky's *Tertium Organum* (1920).

6. Rascoe, *We Were Interrupted*, 135. Perhaps Rascoe meant that this presumably racy anecdote could not be printed.

7. Arlen J. Hansen, *Expatriate Paris: A Cultural and Literary Guide to Paris of the 1920s* (New York: Arcade, 1990), 74.

8. DB to Charles Henri Ford, 4 August 1936.

9. Emily Coleman to DB, 3 August 1936.

10. Alfred Kreymborg, *Troubadour: An Autobiography* (New York: Boni & Liveright, 1925), 288.

11. DB to Natalie Barney, 31 May 1964.

12. C. Page 258.

13. Barnes seems not to have admired Wharton's *Ethan Frome* (1911). Edmund Wilson, *The Fifties* (New York: Farrar, Straus & Giroux, 1986), 555. Wilson did not respect Barnes's literary work.

14. Diaries 117.

15. C. Page 255.

16. C. Page 259.

17. DB to Emily Coleman, 5 February 1940.

18. C. Page 273–74.

19. McAlmon, *Being Geniuses Together*, 34.

20. Bryher's real name was Winifred Ellerman, and she is best known today as the companion of the American poet H.D. (Hilda Doolittle).

21. Interview with Charles Henri Ford, 14 October 1990.

22. McAlmon, *Being Geniuses Together*, 36; 100.

23. Ibid., 109.

24. Robert McAlmon to DB, 2 September 1952.

25. McAlmon, *Being Geniuses Together*, 107.

26. For a photo of Barnes and Chaplin together in Berlin, see Broe, *Silence and Power*, photo no. 44.

27. Kreymborg, *Troubadour*, 127.

28. DB to Robert McAlmon, 7 September 1921 (Yale).

29. Townsend Ludington, *Marsden Hartley: The Biography of an American Artist* (Boston: Little, Brown, 1992), 160.

30. Williams, *Autobiography*, 170–71.

31. See Field, *Djuna*, 61.

32. Edouard Roditi was interviewed by Daniel Halpern for *Antaeus* 2:99 (Spring 1971), 104–6.

33. DB to Emily Coleman, 22 August 1936.

34. James Charters, *This Must Be the Place* (London: Herbert Joseph, 1934), 118–19.

35. Ford Madox Ford to Stella Bowen, 15 January 1927 (Olin Library, Cornell University). Presumably the reference is to Sholem Asch.

36. Donald Friede to DB, 23 June 1927.

37. An offer for *Ryder* with Boni & Liveright, to be signed by Barnes and Horace Liveright, was dated 25 January 1923 and stipulated an advance of $200 (O'Neal 103).

38. Presumably this is what Barnes means by "Ryder is not out for

another three weeks, held up by the N.Y. post office on account of my long poem!" Barnes to Robert McAlmon, 14 June 1928 (Yale).

39. T. R. Smith to DB, 9 February 1928.

40. DB to Natalie Barney, 21 December 1926(?) (Fonds Jacques Doucet).

41. Hank O'Neal, *Life is painful*, 214–15.

42. Donald Friede to DB, 23 June 1927.

43. DB to Robert McAlmon, 25 September 1928 (Yale).

44. See the letters of May 1933 from DB to William Aspenwall Bradley in the Harry Ransom Humanities Research Center, University of Texas at Austin.

45. Barnes made her last payment on the $5,000 flat on 15 February 1929. Part of the money for the flat came from a $2,000 settlement from *McCall's*.

46. DB to Natalie Clifford Barney, 15 April 1933, 23 May 1934 (Fonds Jacques Doucet). The centerpiece of the stage set in Barnes's play *The Antiphon* is a griffin.

47. For a fine general introduction to Loy and her poetry, see Carolyn Burke, "Mina Loy (1882–1966)," in Broe and Ingram, *Women Writers in Exile*, 230–37. Roger L. Conover has edited the most important single volume of Loy's work: *The Last Lunar Baedeker* (Highlands, N.C.: Jargon Society, 1982). Other collections of poetry are *Lunar Baedecker* and *Lunar Baedeker & Time-Tables*.

48. With Stephen Haweis, Loy had three children: Oda Janet Haweis (1903–4); Joella Synara Haweis (b. 1907), who married Julien Levy and later Herbert Bayer; and John Giles Stephen Musgrove Haweis (1909–23). With Cravan she had Jemima Fabienne Cravan (b. 1919), who married Frederic Benedict.

49. Mina Loy, *Lunar Baedecker*, ed. Conover; photo of Haweis.

50. Loy, *The Last Lunar Baedeker*, lxix.

51. Williams, *Autobiography*, 141.

52. Interview with Joella Bayer. Much of this section on Mina Loy derives from interviews with her daughters.

53. DB to Mina Loy, 5 July 1930 (Roger Conover).

54. C. Page 278.

55. DB to Mina Loy, 5 July 1930.

56. Ibid.

57. Karla Jay, *The Amazon and the Page: Natalie Clifford Barney and Renée Vivien* (Bloomington: Indiana University Press, 1988), 2.

58. C. Page 276.

59. Hansen, *Expatriate Paris*, 49.

60. Natalie Clifford Barney, *Adventures of the Mind* (New York: New York University Press, 1992), 166.

61. Fonds Jacques Doucet.

62. DB to Emily Coleman, 11 July 1939.

63. C. Page 273.

64. DB to Emily Coleman, 24 May 1936.

65. I am obliged to Renée Lang, professor emeritus at Marquette University, for several of the following paragraphs about Barney, which derive from our discussions.

66. DB to Natalie Barney, 25 September 1964 (Fonds Jacques Doucet). The question marks are Barnes's.

67. DB to Louis F. Kannenstine, 27 October 1978.

68. O'Neal 34.

69. DB to Emily Coleman, 20 September 1936.

70. DB to Robert McAlmon, 14 June 1928 (Yale).

71. DB to Natalie Barney, 8 January 1929 (Fonds Jacques Doucet).

72. DB to Robert McAlmon, 25 September 1928 (Yale).

73. Susan Sniader Lanser, "Speaking in Tongues: *Ladies Almanack* and the Discourse of Desire," in Broe, *Silence and Power*, 157.

74. Barnes, "The Days of Jig Cook," 31.

CHAPTER 7: THELMA

1. Djuna Barnes, "Paradise."

2. The date is hard to establish: in one letter Djuna said that she was twenty-nine and Thelma nineteen, which indicates 1920–21, but Berenice Abbott believed that it was early 1922. Barnes always said that she and Thelma were together for eight years. Thelma and Abbott met in the fall of 1921.

3. DB to Emily Coleman, 5 February 1940.

4. In a letter from Wood to Barnes from Bermuda, simply dated "April 30," Wood says that she is bringing home "twenty lizards," chameleons, for their cat's entertainment. Wood had gone to Bermuda to paint in about 1927–28.

5. Mary Fanlon Roberts, "Speaking of Art," *Arts & Decoration* 34 (January 1931), 70.

6. Other children were Wilma, four years older, and Dick, two years younger, and a sister, Florence, about fifteen years younger. Thelma's mother was born in 1880 in Kansas, and her father in 1867 in Illinois (apparently his date of death was 1936, but I was unable to find her mother's). The Wood

family lived on West Ninth Street in Concordia, Kansas, when the 1900 census was taken. Margaret Behrens believed Thelma was born in nearby Beloit (Margaret Behrens to DB, 10 October 1973). Apparently there is no record.

7. Rosalind Metcalf didn't find Wood very attractive, saying that she had thick ankles, unattractive legs, heavy hips, and small breasts (telephone interview).

8. Wilson, *The Fifties*, 556.

9. Field, *Djuna*, 116.

10. Williams, *Autobiography*, 206.

11. Fragment of a letter (1935?), Emily Coleman to DB.

12. Diaries 209–10.

13. Henriette Metcalf's daughter disputes the common perception that Thelma was obsessed with sex. She points out that Thelma looked for drinking companions, or a lively party, and if she often ended up in strange beds, it was because she was too drunk to care.

14. DB to Emily Coleman, 22 August 1936.

15. Barnes saw Thelma and Henriette Metcalf walking together in 1940 and wrote Emily Coleman (10 September 1940) that "Henriette looked like Mona Lisa with no longer any reason to smile."

16. My knowledge of Henriette Metcalf mostly derives from Elizabeth de Veer and Richard J. Boyle, *Sunlight and Shadow: The Life and Art of Willard L. Metcalf* (New York: Abbeville Press, 1987) and from conversations with Mrs. de Veer, Caroline Stokes, Jay Arnoldus, Agnes Kobin, and Rosalind, the daughter of Henriette Metcalf. Although Barnes met Henriette Metcalf in 1928 when they became rivals, they had many friends in common: Eugene O'Neill, Carl Van Vechten, Frank Crowninshield, and doubtless others. Willard Metcalf's best friend was Frank DuMond, who was Barnes's teacher at the Art Students League of New York in 1915–16.

17. A journalist, Goodrich once interviewed Thomas Mann while Henriette translated; she balked at asking Mann whether or not *Death in Venice* was autobiographical.

18. De Veer and Boyle, *Sunlight and Shadow*, 259, n. 5. De Veer described Metcalf further:

> Loneliness was familiar, but did not diminish her need to dominate those with whom she came in contact. If a sense of guilt at her imperious ways was learned at the convent, although imperfectly, so also were endurance and courage. No matter how headlong her desires or unpredictable their consequences, she remained ebullient and gallant, bursting with energy, ready to take on the next challenge to her manifold abilities with verve.

But her need for tenderness went unfulfilled. A partial answer to that need was eventually found in lavishing loving care upon small, helpless creatures, birds and animals, and later, infants. (382)

19. DB to Emily Coleman, 7 April 1937.

20. DB to Emily Coleman, 24 May 1936.

21. DB to Natalie Barney, 5 December 1933. Thelma Wood was probably raised a Roman Catholic, for that was her younger sister Florence's faith. Henriette Metcalf gave up Catholicism in 1911 when she married the Protestant Willard Metcalf and thereafter belonged to no church. Although she spoke often of her Catholic upbringing, she would hardly have wished to influence Thelma Wood to become religious. On the other hand, she kept candles lit before a madonna in her house.

22. DB to Emily Coleman, 10 January 1936.

23. Thelma Wood to DB, 5 August, no year given.

24. In Broe, *Silence and Power*, 362.

25. A photo of Fitzi and Buffy appears in ibid., photo no. 42.

26. Field, *Djuna*, 160. *Nightwood*'s ending also evokes the mysticism that attracted Thelma and Henriette (who often held séances in New York) and reinforces the connection between Thelma and Djuna's grandmother, Zadel, who was a spiritualist medium. Then, too, church objects decorated the Paris flat of Barnes and Wood.

27. DB to Emily Coleman, 14 February 1937.

28. Julius Sherman Halleck wrote a book on Penny Royal: *Broken Notes from a Grey Nunnery*.

29. DB to Emily Coleman, 3 March 1939.

30. For the above details I am indebted to Jean Loveland, Vivian Capoccitti, and E. Eleanor Smith.

31. Metcalf would die in the same hospital in July 1981.

CHAPTER 8: CHARLES
IMPOSSIBLE FORD

1. This chapter is heavily indebted to Charles Henri Ford, through interviews and his unpublished memoir, "I Will Be What I Am." All citations to "Ford" are to the latter work. Part of the chapter appeared in *Library Chronicle* with my introduction to Barnes's story "Behind the Heart" (Summer 1993), whence comes the epigraph.

2. Not long before Barnes's surgery, Ford had also been in the hospital, afflicted by a bad case of gonorrhea, which doubled the size of a testicle. The relationship was then understandably platonic.

3. Interview with Charles Henri Ford, 14 October 1990.

4. Ford 161.

5. Sylvia Beach recommended the Obelisk Press, which in 1933 published Radclyffe Hall's lesbian novel, *The Well of Loneliness*. In August of that year, Obelisk published *The Young and Evil* in an edition of 2,500 copies, 500 of which were burned by British customs authorities.

6. DB to Natalie Barney, 5 December 1933 (Fonds Jacques Doucet).

7. Bradley placed the novel with Jack Kahane of Obelisk Press.

8. James Scott's unpublished interview with DB, 2 April 1971.

9. Jane Heap introduced Barnes to Tchelitchew in 1923. See Parker Tyler, *The Divine Comedy of Pavel Tchelitchew* (New York: Fleet, 1967; London: Weidenfeld, 1969).

10. Chester Page, in Broe, *Silence and Power*, 363.

11. DB to Emily Coleman, 22 August 1936.

12. Interview with Ford, 14 October 1990.

13. On 22 January 1932, Barnes went to the Cirque Medrano with Charles Henri Ford. In "I Will Be What I Am," Ford says: "We had ring seats and during the entr'acte saw the horses and photographs of lots of circus people including Barbette who has just had another fall in South America. What we went mainly for was Calleano the greatest tightrope walker du monde. D—— had told me about Calleano whom she saw at the Palace and rushed backstage to interview because she got a crush on him but lost it when she saw him in Broadway clothes and there were drawings of him by Tchelitchew at the Galerie Vignon" (Ford 203–4).

14. Some of these quips derive from interviews with Ford, and others from his memoirs.

15. Barnes's passport reveals that she arrived at Marseilles on 1 April on her way to Tangier, obtained a French visa for her return to France on 3 June, and left Tangier on 13 June, arriving in Marseille again on 15 June. On 1 July she was at Le Havre on her way to England and Hayford Hall.

16. C. Page 284.

17. Christopher Sawyer-Lauçanno, *An Invisible Spectator: A Biography of Paul Bowles* (New York: Weidenfeld & Nicolson, 1989), 145.

18. DB to Mina Loy, 20 April 1933.

19. DB to Natalie Barney, 15 April 1933.

20. DB to Natalie Barney, 8 May 1933.

21. DB to Natalie Barney, 30 May 1933.

22. *Hearst's International Cosmopolitan*, July 1934, 175–76.

23. Charles Henri Ford to the author, 23 November 1992.

24. Sawyer-Lauçanno. *Invisible Spectator*, 146.

25. DB to Emily Coleman, 10 January 1937.

26. As for Ford, by the middle 1930s he would be in the arms of Pavel

Tchelitchew, who had previously been attached to Allen Tanner. Barnes had met the Russian painter in 1923, introduced by Jane Heap, and Ford had met him at a party at Stein's nearly a decade later. In Paris, Barnes burned a portrait Tchelitchew did of Ford, "because it looked like the 'death of the opium-eater' " (Ford 331). Ford saw less of Barnes in subsequent years but went to her for advice on literary matters. His sister, Ruth Ford Scott, relished her friendship with Barnes (see her memoir in Broe, *Silence and Power*). Once, in later years, Ruth Scott called an ambulance to her New York apartment when Barnes drank herself to unconsciousness.

CHAPTER 9: HANGOVER HALL

1. Peggy Guggenheim quoted this quip by Barnes in *Out of This Century* (New York: Dial, 1946), 140. "Hangover Hall" as a nickname for Hayford Hall is from Susan Chitty, *Now to My Mother: A Very Personal Memoir of Antonia White* (London: Weidenfeld & Nicolson, 1985), 62.

2. C. Page 261.

3. DB to Emily Coleman, 20 March 1939.

4. Barnes seems to have arrived at Hayford Hall for the first time in the second week of August 1932, returning a month later to Paris. In 1933, she went to Hayford Hall in the third week of July, leaving for Paris at the end of August.

5. This web of confusing entanglements and partner swapping is recounted in Guggenheim's *Out of This Century*. Hereafter *OC*.

6. Lance Sieveking, "Hugh Kingsmill and John Holms," *The Listener*, 31 January 1957, 188.

7. Chitty, *Now to My Mother*, 60–61.

8. Sieveking, "Kingsmill and Holms," 187–88.

9. DB to Natalie Barney, 25 January 1934.

10. DB to Emily Coleman, 8 February 1934.

11. DB to Natalie Barney, 5 June 1934.

12. DB to Emily Coleman, 1–3 April 1936.

13. Many of the following biographical details concerning Emily Holmes Coleman are from Carmen Callil and Mary Siepmann, Introduction to Coleman's novel *The Shutter of Snow* (London: Virago, 1981).

14. Hansen, *Expatriate Paris*, 56.

15. Diaries, 1933, 10; 72–73.

16. In the financial category, the prize would go to Peggy Guggenheim, with second prize going to Natalie Barney.

17. DB to Silas Glossop, 24 November 1959.

18. DB to Allan Ross Macdougall, 15 August 1932.

19. DB to Natalie Barney, 31 August 1932.

20. DB to Emily Coleman, 17 February 1940.

21. Susan Chitty, ed., *Antonia White: Diaries, 1926–1957*, vol. I (New York: Viking, 1992), 92. A preliminary version of *Nightwood*, typed by Charles Henri Ford in Tangier in the spring of 1933, was in turn revised during the following summer by Barnes at this Devon estate.

22. Chitty, *Now to My Mother*, 61.

23. Sindbad (age 10) accompanied Barnes and his father back to Paris at the end of the summer.

24. DB to Emily Coleman, 1–3 April 1936.

25. Chitty, *Now to My Mother*, 61.

26. 21 July 1933.

27. 1 April–30 June 1936.

28. 14 December 1933.

29. John Holms to Emily Coleman, 2 May 1932.

30. DB to Allan Ross Macdougall, 19 July 1933.

31. Emily Coleman to DB, 14 November, no year.

32. Peggy Guggenheim to Emily Coleman, 27 April 1942 (Delaware).

33. Peggy Guggenheim to Emily Coleman, 24 January 1945 (Delaware). A version of this story appears in *OC*.

34. Delaware.

35. Emily Coleman diary entry of 28 June 1937 in Chitty, ed., *Diaries*, 92–93.

CHAPTER 10: CREATING THE MISSHAPEN IMAGES OF *NIGHTWOOD*

1. Elizabeth Barnes to DB, 1 December 1936. Some of the following chapter derives from my article "Djuna Barnes and the Narrative of Violation," in Reingard Nischik and Barbara Korte, eds., *Modes of Narrative: Approaches to British, American, and Canadian Fiction* (Würzburg: Königshausen & Neumann, 1990), 100–9.

2. DB to Emily Coleman, 28 October 1942; 19 August 1935.

3. 15 December 1933.

4. 2 March 1936.

5. The source of the chapter title "La Somnambule" may be found in a letter from Barnes to Natalie Barney, 23 May 1934: Thelma was "dreadfully bored I think, so bored that she is continually in a state of sleep."

6. See James B. Scott, *Djuna Barnes* (Boston: Twayne, 1976), 24, on Barnes's view of procreation.

7. This is essentially Alan Singer's point in "The Horse Who Knew Too Much: Metaphor and the Narrative of Discontinuity in *Nightwood*," *Contemporary Literature* 25 (1984), 70.

8. DB to Emily Coleman, 30 October 1935.

9. Scott, *Djuna Barnes*, 70. A Freudian might say that the minds of Robin Vote and Wendell Ryder are dominated by the id, which only desires satisfaction for instinctual needs.

10. Interview with Charles Henri Ford.

11. See Robert McAlmon's *Distinguished Air* (Paris: Contact Editions, 1925), which includes "Miss Knight."

12. DB to Emily Coleman, 8 July 1937.

13. There is a letter from Mahoney to Barnes dated 14 November 1958 from Paris. On 11 February 1959, Barnes wrote Solita Solano, who had recently written with news of Mahoney's death. On 20 August 1959, Barnes wrote Wolfgang Hildesheimer that he had died at seventy, "only a little while back." He would then have been born in 1888 or 1889; in 1933, Charles Henri Ford guessed his age at forty-six. Field, in *Djuna*, says that he was of the 1914 class of St. Ignatius High School in San Francisco, which would make him younger than Barnes and Ford imagined.

14. Page of DB's notes beginning "Tom," owned by Peter Barnes.

15. Ibid.

16. Roditi interview in *Antaeus*, 104–6.

17. Quoted in Field, *Djuna*, 144–45.

18. DB to Emily Coleman, 25 February 1936.

19. Page of DB's notes beginning "Were Midas ill," owned by Peter Barnes.

20. DB to Laurence Vail, 14 May 1966.

21. DB to Dan Mahoney, 14 November 1958.

22. Dan Mahoney to DB, 8 September 1950.

23. DB to Emily Coleman, 25 July 1936.

24. DB to Emily Coleman, 29 July 1936.

25. A letter from Mahoney to Barnes, simply dated 9 June (probably 1937) mentions this incident.

26. Some of the details regarding Guido Bruno derive from Marshall Brooks's 1975 article on him in *Newsart* (no date given).

27. Field, *Djuna*, 65–78.

28. Emily Coleman to DB, 27 August 1935.

29. DB to Emily Coleman, 22 July 1936.

1. Emily Coleman to DB, 27 August 1935, 7.

2. In December, Barnes received a letter from T. R. Smith at Boni & Liveright, advising her to rewrite the manuscript completely. Emily Coleman mentions Barnes's anguish over this letter in a diary entry of 19 December 1933.

3. DB to Emily Coleman, 17 May 1935.

4. DB to Emily Coleman, 26 June 1935.

5. Among other plays, Barnes saw *In Pursuit of Happiness*, Cocteau's *Blood of a Poet*, *School for Husbands*, *Ah, Wilderness*, *Queen Christina*, with Greta Garbo.

6. For a photo of this portrait, see Broe, *Silence and Power*, photo no. 26. In 1943, Peggy Guggenheim exhibited the portrait in a show of the women artists at her Art of This Century Gallery in New York. Barnes described Alice Rohrer as "a woman from the Allegheny Mountains who spoke French with a strange kind of accent and who 'loved blackamoors and negresses' " (C. Page 232).

7. Andrew Field identified the subject as Madame Modjeska, an acquaintance of Zadel Barnes in London (*Djuna*, 207).

8. DB to Emily Coleman, 14 December 1935. To Irwin Cohen and Francesca Belanger, Barnes spoke of her favorite painting, Van Eyck's wedding portrait of Giovanni Arnolfini, in London's National Gallery, a copy of which she kept on her mantel (interview with Cohen and Belanger). In Silas Glossop's possession is a painting by Barnes of a man on a sofa, not further identified.

9. The drawing was part of Scofield Thayer's Dial Collection, now at New York's Metropolitan Museum (C. Page 294).

10. DB to Charles Henri Ford, 15 June 1934.

11. DB to Emily Coleman, 10 January 1936.

12. DB to Charles Henri Ford, 23 November 1933.

13. Each vowel of Neagoe's surname is pronounced.

14. DB to Emily Coleman, 10 March 1937.

15. DB to Emily Coleman, 22 August 1936.

16. Neagoe was born at Odorhei, in what was then Hungarian Transylvania, but he was a Romanian of Christian Orthodox background. See Denise-Claude Le Goff, *Peter Neagoe: L'homme et l'oeuvre* (New York: Peter Lang, 1988).

17. Neagoe first wrote Barnes to request permission to publish something of her work on 27 July 1931.

18. The Neagoe papers are at Syracuse University. He published popular stories and novels: *Storm* (stories; 1932), *Easter Sun* (1934), *Winning a Wife*

(stories; 1935), *There Is My Heart* (1936), and *No Time for Tears* (1958). See Le Goff.

19. DB to Emily Coleman, 10 January 1936.

20. DB to Emily Coleman, 23 June 1935.

21. Ibid.

22. DB to Emily Coleman, 30 October 1935.

23. DB to Emily Coleman, 30 August 1935.

24. Valerie Eliot, review of Djuna Barnes, "I Could Never Be Lonely Without a Husband," *Financial Times*, 1 August 1987.

25. Field, *Djuna*, 212.

26. T. S. Eliot to DB, 23 March 1937.

27. DB to Charles Henri Ford, 15 August 1935; Emily Coleman to DB, 27 August 1935; DB to Emily Coleman, 30 October 1935.

28. Barnes first met Muir at a dinner party at Peter Hoare's in 1936–37. Barnes said little, while Hoare and Muir held forth on psychoanalysis, dreams, and poetry (DB to Willa Muir, 21 February 1968). Barnes wrote Helene Hollander that it was Coleman who took the typescript of *Nightwood* from New York to London (DB to Helene Hollander, 22 October 1967).

29. Emily Coleman to DB, 27 August 1935.

30. DB to Emily Coleman, 11 July 1935.

31. DB to Emily Coleman, 20 September 1935. Despite her preference for exclusivity, she wouldn't have minded if Mr. Eustace (Seligman?), her wealthy patron (not further identified), continued his stipend. When he didn't, Peggy stepped in toward the beginning of 1936 with a fairly steady monthly stipend, for in the past her support had been intermittent.

32. DB to Emily Coleman, 14 December 1935.

33. Emily Coleman to DB, 26 January 1936.

34. Diaries 254–55.

35. Chitty, *Now to My Mother*, 81.

36. Ibid., 333.

37. Emily Coleman to DB, 1 August 1935.

38. DB to Emily Coleman, 14 December 1935.

39. Emily Coleman to DB, 27 October 1935.

40. Diaries, 22 March 1936.

41. DB to Emily Coleman, 27 March 1936.

42. DB to Emily Coleman, 30 March 1936.

43. DB to Natalie Barney, 24 August 1936.

44. Andrew Field says that "the first half-yearly royalty statement to Miss Barnes from England was for £43-0-8; from America, $350.23" (*Djuna*, 215).

45. T. S. Eliot to DB, 12 August 1936.

46. DB to Helene Hollander, 10 February 1969.

47. Valerie Eliot, review of "I Could Never Be Lonely."

48. Hurst, near Petersfield, in Hampshire.

49. DB to Emily Coleman, 13 August 1936.

50. DB to Charles Henri Ford, 22 June 1936; DB to Emily Coleman, 9 February 1937.

51. DB to Ottoline Morrell, 24 November 1936 (Texas).

52. T. S. Eliot to DB, 28 January 1938.

53. DB to Emily Coleman, 1 November 1937.

54. Chitty, *Now to My Mother*, 335.

55. Emily Coleman to DB, 12 October 1936.

56. Emily Coleman to DB, 24 November 1936.

57. Emily Coleman to DB, 9 July 1938; Chitty, *Now to My Mother*, 105.

58. James B. Scott unpublished interview with Djuna Barnes, 2 April 1971. Barnes especially admired Joseph Frank's article "Spatial Form in Modern Literature, Miss Barnes' *Nightwood*."

59. Emily Coleman to DB, 12 August 1958.

60. Peter Hoare to DB, 12 February 1965.

61. Gene Montague makes the case that Dylan Thomas's poem "How Shall My Animal" (1938) derives from the imagery of Dr. O'Connor's monologues in *Nightwood*. See his "Dylan Thomas and *Nightwood*," *Sewanee Review* 76 (Summer 1968), 420–34.

62. On 23 July 1970, Caedmon Records wrote to Barnes wanting to issue a record of Dylan Thomas reading both from his own works and from the "Watchman, What of the Night?" chapter of *Nightwood*.

63. Gide declined in a letter to Barnes of 2 October 1937.

64. D. D. Paige, ed., *The Letters of Ezra Pound* (New York: Harcourt, Brace, 1950).

65. DB to Emily Coleman, 20 February 1937.

66. DB to Emily Coleman, ibid.

67. Chitty, *Now to My Mother*, 94.

68. DB to Emily Coleman, 30 November 1937.

69. DB to Emily Coleman, 21 May 1938.

70. Field, *Djuna*, 19.

71. At Glossop's request, Saxon Barnes destroyed all the letters from Glossop to Djuna Barnes that he could find after her death, but plenty of information remains.

72. Chitty, *Now to My Mother*, 93.

73. Chitty, *Antonia White: Diaries*, 85–86.

74. Lyndall Passerini Hopkinson, *Nothing to Forgive: A Daughter's Story of Antonia White* (London: Chatto & Windus, 1988), 61.

75. See DB to Emily Coleman, 4 February 1939.

76. DB to Emily Coleman, 10 September 1937.

77. DB to Emily Coleman, 20 March 1939.

78. DB to Emily Coleman, 19 August 1938.

79. DB to Emily Coleman, 4 February 1939.

80. Chitty, *Antonia White: Diaries*, 115.

81. Ibid., 152; 150.

82. DB to Emily Coleman, 30 October 1938.

83. Chitty, *Antonia White: Diaries*, 93–94.

84. DB to Antonia White, 24 June 1937.

85. DB to Emily Coleman, 21 May 1938.

86. The diaries of Marian Bouché, Archives of American Art, Reel 689, 174.

87. DB to Emily Coleman, 24 May 1938.

88. DB to Emily Coleman, 25 July 1938.

89. Ibid.

90. DB to Emily Coleman, 7 August 1938.

CHAPTER 12: STOP PRAYING FOR ME!

1. Djuna Barnes, "The Poisoned Tree."

2. DB to Emily Coleman, 11 May 1936.

3. DB to Emily Coleman, 4 October 1938.

4. DB to Emily Coleman, 3 August 1936.

5. DB to Emily Coleman, 30 October 1938.

6. Ibid.

7. Mellen, *Kay Boyle*, 200.

8. DB to Emily Coleman, 15 December 1938.

9. David Gascoyne to DB, 1951.

10. DB to Emily Coleman, 6 June 1941.

11. DB to Emily Coleman, 18 January 1939.

12. Ibid.

13. DB to Emily Coleman, 3 March 1939.

14. DB to Emily Coleman, 11 July 1939.

15. DB to Emily Coleman, 27 November 1939.

16. Peggy Guggenheim to Emily Coleman, 30 January 1940.

17. Peggy Guggenheim to Emily Coleman, 13 March 1940.

18. DB to Emily Coleman, 26 January 1940.

19. DB to Emily Coleman, 30 March 1940.

20. Elizabeth Barnes to Susanna Chappell, 17 June 1924.

21. DB to Emily Coleman, 13 August 1939.

22. DB to Robert McAlmon, undated (Yale).

23. Field, *Djuna*, 230.

24. Robert Giroux, " 'The Most Famous Unknown in the World'—Re-

membering Djuna Barnes," *New York Times Book Review*, 1 December 1985, 30–31.

25. Emily Coleman to DB, 8 January 1941.

26. T. S. Eliot to DB, 2 December 1940.

27. Laughlin wanted to provide Barnes with a small regular income whether or not royalties accrued, and then not publish a hardbound edition of *Nightwood* as long as the *Selected Works* was in print (Peter du Sautoy to DB, 2 January 1963).

28. One report was on Jean Toomer's *From Exile into Being*, one of three autobiographies Toomer wrote between 1928 and 1941. It tells of his career as a disciple of the mystic Georges I. Gurdjieff and as a spiritual reformer for idealist, spiritualist, transcendentalist consciousness.

29. DB to Emily Coleman, 24 September 1942.

30. DB to Emily Coleman, 3 February 1943.

31. DB to Emily Coleman, 28 October 1942.

32. DB to Barbara Rigney, 5 November 1973.

33. DB to T. S. Eliot, 12 November 1946.

34. A photo of this portrait appears in Broe, *Silence and Power*, photo no. 25.

35. Tate sent Barnes a copy of this letter, which is with her papers at the University of Maryland.

36. It appears that Cordelia Pearson was never given her portrait, for it went to the University of Maryland when Djuna Barnes sold her literary estate.

37. Cordelia Pearson to DB, 6 March 1950.

38. Cordelia Pearson to DB, 1 August 1963.

39. Interview with Irwin Cohen and Francesca Belanger, 8 April 1989.

CHAPTER 13: PRUSSIC ACID
IN DRAMATIC FORM:
THE ANTIPHON

1. The epigraph is from a Barnes letter to Emily Coleman, 28 October 1942: "I started out grimly sentimental—which is silly. How I would wish nothing better then to write logically & without emotion. Quite impossible for me of course. I even find in Shakespeare too great a sweetness. I know of no writer as mean as I would be! Proust, amid his icicles, drips sentimentality."

2. Richard Ellmann, *James Joyce* (New York: Oxford University Press, 1959), 215.

3. DB to Ellemira Zolla, 23 April 1968.

4. All references to Djuna Barnes's play *The Antiphon* are to *The Selected Works of Djuna Barnes* (New York: Farrar, Straus & Cudahy, 1962).

5. Barnes was proud of her English heritage. She told James B. Scott: "I'm English on my mother's side; my roots, my affinities are with England" (Scott's unpublished interview with Barnes, 2 April 1971).

6. In autobiographical terms, this abandonment has to do with Saxon's putting his mother in an apartment of her own, when she might have preferred to live with him and Eleanor. Djuna didn't really disapprove of this, knowing how difficult her mother was, but at the same time she thought it rather cruel, if practical.

7. A letter from Barnes to Natalie Barney of 1 May 1939 confirms that she has just seen Eliot's new play.

8. DB to Emily Coleman, 30 November 1937.

9. DB to Emily Coleman, 30 March 1940.

10. DB to Willa Muir, 23 July 1961.

11. On page of DB's notes (owned by Peter Barnes) beginning: "The Guise family persecuted the Huguenots." The "prince" was Lord Lonsdale (Hugh Cecil Lowther, of Penrich) as two pages of notes say.

12. One of Zadel Barnes's grandfathers was named Elisha.

13. Field, *Djuna*, 187.

14. DB to Karl Gierow, 5 October 1960.

15. Barnes's sexual violation will here be called "rape" regardless of any question of cooperation or volition. Legally it was a case of statutory rape, since Barnes was underage. Whether or not it was also incest is purely a speculative matter.

16. In the deleted pages from the "Go Down Matthew" chapter of *Nightwood*, Catherine (formerly Hess, who would become Nora) says: "And I was in bed that first night [with the Percy Faulkner figure], and he said, 'Christ! You don't bleed much.' And I said, 'It is all the blood it has.' And all before the door my mother had strewn flour—to give herself hope, hoping there would be no foot-mark in it going my way."

17. Emily Coleman to DB, 30 October 1937.

18. A letter of 15 June 1962 from Barnes to Wolfgang Hildesheimer says: "I am used to misunderstanding, and misjudging. One idiot says *Titus* rapes Miranda." To Christine Koschel, Barnes wrote: "But I am distressed to hear from you that you think *Titus raped his daughter!*" (29 December 1968). This was a frequent theme in her letters of the period.

19. DB to Karl Gierow, 5 October 1960.

20. Lynda Curry, " 'Tom, Take Mercy' ": Djuna Barnes' Drafts of *The Antiphon*," in Broe, *Silence and Power*, 290–91.

21. The published text has Miranda say: "Miranda damned, with instep up-side-down,/Dragging rape-blood behind her, like the snail—" (*SW* 185).

22. Valerie Eliot, review of "I Could Never Be Lonely."

23. On page of DB's notes on Eliot dated 1981, owned by Peter Barnes.

24. DB to Emily Coleman, 31 March 1949: "So I go on trying to write a play. What on earth I am doing in that medium I have not the slightest idea. Action, plot . . . exactly *not* what I am suited for. Well, Chaplin wanted to be Hamlet."

25. T. S. Eliot to DB, 19 December 1954.

26. Edwin Muir to T. S. Eliot, 13 January 1956. In P. H. Butter, ed. *Selected Letters of Edwin Muir* (London: Hogarth Press, 1974), 175–76.

27. Lynda Curry says: "during July and August 1956, Barnes rewrote and substantially shortened the first two-thirds of the second act of *The Antiphon*, leaving only the masked attack scene and the doll house scene uncut. Her severe editing in this fifth draft cost the play a great deal in character development, theme, and general information." (" 'Tom, Take Mercy,' " in *Silence and Power*, 295.)

28. DB to Solita Solano, 14 June 1956 (Library of Congress).

29. DB to Willa Muir, 20 August 1962.

30. T. S. Eliot to DB, 1 October 1956; 8 November 1956.

31. Page of DB's notes beginning: "the poor, who carry their house on a packing string," owned by Peter Barnes.

32. This appears on a sheet Barnes owned. At the top, she wrote: "Blurb by T.S. Eliot!" Below that is the play's title and author's name. Below Eliot's words are those of Muir's letter to him of 13 January 1956 praising the play as "one of the greatest things that have been written in our time, and it would be a disaster if it were never to be known."

33. This is precisely what Barnes's own blurb had done for Charles Henri Ford's *The Young and Evil*.

34. On page of DB's notes beginning: "Nuns & Priests attend Bull Fights," owned by Peter Barnes. Another note says: "Tom said he never knew what to think of a work until he had heard others' opinions."

35. Emily Coleman to DB, 26 May 1958.

36. Increasingly, with the impending publication of *The Antiphon*, Barnes began to leave notes for biographers and critics who would examine her work. She made notes on her copy of Muir's letter to Eliot of 13 January 1956 and on the ones Eliot sent her. At other times she would compile pages of notes cataloging various memories and remarks people had made about her work. These, taken together with her letters to Muir, Eliot, and Wolfgang Hildesheimer, give a clear idea of Barnes's stated intentions in the play and of the publishing history.

37. For instance, no publisher has done more to publicize Djuna Barnes than a Berlin firm called Wagenbach Verlag, which has published translations of works unavailable in English.

38. See Sherrill E. Grace, "About a Tragic Business: The Djuna Barnes–Dag Hammarskjöld Letters," *Development Dialogue* 2 (1987), 91–115.

39. Published in the Stockholm newspaper *Dagens Nyheter*, 24 May 1959, 29. Barnes wrote across the top: "Rather silly, & not much like me."

40. Barnes's first interview was conducted by Guido Bruno in December of 1919 (see *Interviews*); the second was done by her friend James Stern and published in *Time*, 18 January 1943; the last important one in English was by Henry Raymont, "From the Avant Garde of the Thirties," for the *New York Times*, published on 24 May 1971. The Raymont interview angered Barnes because he had said that she could approve his article before publication; if she had seen it, she would have deleted any reference to a recent autobiography of playwright Lillian Hellman, who was angered and hurt when she read of Barnes's disgust with Hellman's willingness to reveal all. Barnes was mortified and apologized.

41. Barnes told Hank O'Neal that she didn't much like Auden's poetry but felt "sorry for him because he became so ugly: 'a face like an elephant's ass' " (O'Neal 36).

42. Giroux, " 'The Most Famous Unknown in the World.' " The earliest letter from Hammarskjöld to Barnes seems to have been 7 June 1958.

43. It is interesting that Hammarskjöld did not send reviews from Sweden's two most prominent newspapers, *Svenska Dagbladet* and *Dagens Nyheter*, which could mean that he edited out the negative reviews. Since the premiere, there have been a few additional performances of *The Antiphon*—one in Paris directed by Daniel Mesguich (1990) and one in Frankfurt under the direction of Peter Eschberg. The premiere in English was done by the Noh Oratorio Society of San Francisco in February 1984 at the Studio Eremos, directed by Claude Duvall.

44. Emily Coleman to DB, 15 August 1940(?).

45. Thurn Budington to DB, 2 April 1958.

CHAPTER 14: OBSEQUIES AND MEETING THE NEW MRS. ELIOT

1. DB to Willa Muir, 20 August 1962.

2. DB to T. S. Eliot, 22 January 1949.

3. In Willa Muir, *Belonging* (London, 1968), and Peter Ackroyd, *T. S. Eliot, A Life* (New York: Simon & Schuster, 1984), 301.

4. Valerie Eliot to the author, 29 May 1990.

5. Frances McCullough, in Broe, *Silence in Power*, 367.

6. DB to Willa Muir, 20 August 1962.

7. On page of DB's notes beginning: "Nuns & Priests attend Bull Fights," owned by Peter Barnes, and also in DB to Natalie Barney, December 1964.

8. Ackroyd, *T. S. Eliot*, 298.

9. On page of DB's notes beginning: "her eyeball in the seam (gristle) of his wink," owned by Peter Barnes.

10. Valerie Eliot, review of "I Could Never Be Lonely."

11. DB to Valerie Eliot, 5 January 1965.

12. These two notes on page of DB's notes beginning: "Nuns & Priests attend Bull Fights."

13. On page of DB's notes headed "TREES," owned by Peter Barnes.

14. James Stern to DB, 24 February 1957.

15. On page of DB's notes headed "TREES."

16. Valerie Eliot in *The Mysterious Mr Eliot*, BBC program. In Ackroyd, *T. S. Eliot*, 320.

17. On page of DB's notes beginning: "her eyeball in the seam (gristle) of his wink," owned by Peter Barnes.

18. Ibid.

19. The German translators of *The Antiphon*, Inge von Weidenbaum and Christine Koschel, complained to Barnes that this misunderstanding occurred because Unseld wished to avoid paying fees to both Faber & Faber and Farrar, Straus & Cudahy (Christine Koschel and Inge von Weidenbaum to DB, 7 March 1977). In 1971, Unseld bought the German rights to *Nightwood* from Neske Verlag.

20. Hildesheimer gave 53 letters, postcards, telegrams, etc., to the archives of the Akademie der Künste, Berlin. A short critical biography of Barnes was published in German by Kyra Stromberg: *Djuna Barnes, Leben und Werk einer Extravaganten* (Berlin, 1989).

21. DB to Peter du Sautoy, 5 June 1971.

22. London *Times*, 5 January 1959.

23. Willa Muir to DB, 29 July 1962.

24. Interview with Irwin Cohen and Francesca Belanger, 8 April 1989.

25. Giroux, " 'The Most Famous Unknown in the World.' "

26. Ibid.

27. DB to Emily Coleman, 22 October 1961.

28. DB to Emily Coleman, undated.

29. Valerie Eliot, review of "I Could Never Be Lonely."

30. Valerie Eliot to DB, 14 October 1965.

31. Articles on Bouché appeared in *The Reviewer* (July 1922); *House Beautiful* (June 1928); *The New Yorker* (19 May 1930); *New York Times* (10 June 1937); *Life* (18 August 1941); and *Town & Country* (February 1947).

32. Peggy Guggenheim to DB, 25 October 1954.

33. Chitty, *Now to My Mother*, 181.

34. Peggy Guggenheim to DB, 26 April 1964.

35. DB to Peter Hoare, 27 May 1970. In Broe, *Silence and Power*, 338–39.

36. DB to Emily Coleman, 20–23 March 1936.

37. By his first wife he had a son, Andy, and by his second a daughter, Suzie.

38. On 12 December 1944, Zendon's photo appeared in the *New York Herald Tribune* as sales manager for the Mutual Broadcasting System.

39. For information on their father, I am grateful to Nicholas Barnes and Leigh Ponvert.

40. DB to Silas Glossop, 3 June 1967.

41. Thurn Budington to DB, 20 September 1952.

CHAPTER 15: MADAME VITRIOL

1. Djuna Barnes told James B. Scott and others that she was the "most famous unknown author in the world," in Broe, *Silence and Power*, 362. To Natalie Barney she wrote: "I am the most famous unknown of the century!" (10 September 1967). Chester Page recorded Louise Crane's epithet for Barnes, "Madame Vitriol" (C. Page 240).

2. These words are by Baroness Elsa von Freytag Loringhoven. Diaries of Emily Coleman, 5 July–1 September 1934, 30. I have learned of the late Barnes from several memoirs, especially Chester Page's unpublished "Memories of Djuna Barnes," the "Reminiscences" section of Broe's *Silence and Power*, 340–68, and Darryl Pinckney's *High Cotton* (New York: Farrar, Straus & Giroux, 1992), 194–203. The major published source of information on Djuna Barnes's daily life in the last few years of her life is Hank O'Neal's *"Life is painful, nasty and short . . . in my case it has only been painful and nasty"* (New York: Paragon House, 1990).

3. Valerie Eliot, review of "I Could Never Be Lonely."

4. DB to Natalie Barney, 31 May 1963.

5. Pinckney, *High Cotton*, 199. Frances McCullough's version is "All they want, Mrs. McCullough, is me upside down on 42nd Street, with my skirt over my head and my bum in the air" (in Broe, *Silence and Power*, 366). A similar version appears in a letter from DB to Phyllis Jones, 23 November 1977.

6. Louise Crane, the wealthy daughter of W. Murray Crane of the Crane Paper Company, was editor of the magazine *Iberica*.

7. DB to Natalie Barney, 2 October 1968.

8. DB to Susan Sontag, 24 February 1967.

9. Note by DB in the Marianne Moore file at the University of Maryland.

10. DB to Natalie Barney, 16 December 1965.

11. Interview with Irwin Cohen. At one point Beckett sent a book dealer a check for $3,375 with instructions that it be forwarded to Barnes.

12. O'Neal (140) says that Beckett's "letters were judged the most valuable when the second half of her papers were sold," presumably to the University of Maryland, but these letters have apparently disappeared.

13. Page of DB's notes beginning: "Shaks. Alls Well that . . .". On the next page the line appears again in the poem "An old man gives his terror, not his love."

14. Page of DB's notes beginning: "When Gheminda comes for damnation," owned by Peter Barnes.

15. DB to Natalie Barney, 8 April 1964.

16. DB to Phyllis Jones, 27 July 1975.

17. Pinckney made these observations over many months. See his novel *High Cotton*, 195–96.

18. In Broe, *Silence and Power*, 345.

19. Scott's short but lively memoir of Barnes appeared in Broe, *Silence and Power*, 341–45.

20. The American Academy and Institute of Arts and Letters sent her $500 in June of 1970 to help with medical expenses (she was elected a member in 1959), and in the years to follow there were more checks, the final one, for $3,500, being in May 1982. These loans were partially repaid. In 1959 and 1961, she received $2,500 from the Ingram Merrill Foundation to write a play (in 1962, it was $3,000). There were smaller grants as well. At one point she received $1,000 from the estate of Janet Flanner. In 1968, Barnes received $5,000 from the estate of the film producer Albert Lewin and $1,500 a year for life from the estate of Natalie Barney on her death. Barnes's monthly income during her final years included a social security check ($115) and $300 a month from Peggy Guggenheim, which the estate increased slightly. There was a monthly check for $25, first from Mary Reynolds (thanks to Marcel Duchamp), then from Reynolds's estate, and latterly $240 a month from Louise Crane. Most of these figures come from O'Neal's *Life is painful. . . .*

21. Barnes received another $2,000 for the papers of Countess Elsa von Freytag Loringhoven, which were in her possession. Robert L. Beare acted as Maryland's agent.

22. Yale, Harvard, Princeton, Syracuse, the University of Oregon, and the University of Texas all expressed interest in the Djuna Barnes papers. Bart Auerbach appraised the papers at $47,150 (Auerbach to Barnes, 26 February 1972). Syracuse University had at one time offered to purchase the papers but later found that they could not pay the price (letter to DB of 5 October 1963). A letter of 8 November 1972 from Ampersand Books says that the Beinecke Library at Yale, which had first refusal, had offered $30,000

and wanted three years to pay. The University of Maryland offered to pay the asking price. On 25 November 1972, Barnes accepted Maryland's offer for her papers, except for the ones she was currently using. Some five years later, the University of Maryland paid an additional $6,000 for those papers of Barnes that still remained in her possession.

23. Willa Muir commented on Barnes's critical eye: "Do you know (I suppose you do) that boots, well laced, obsess you a bit? and rumps—not only horse-rumps—and veils, of all things. What a noticing eye you have!" (Willa Muir to DB, 29 July 1962).

24. In addition, Barnes left money to Jussi Korzeniowski, Phyllis Jones, Chester Page, and Peter Heggie of the Authors Guild. To Saxon Barnes she left her household effects, books, and manuscripts.

25. DB to Emily Coleman, 10 January 1936.

26. Originally entitled "Transfiguration" and published in *London Bulletin* 3 (June 1936), 2, the poem was revised as "Fall-out Over Heaven." It appeared in Neville Braybrook, ed., *T.S. Eliot: A Symposium for His Seventieth Birthday* (New York: Farrar, Straus and Cudahy, 1958), 27.

27. DB to Willa Muir, 20 August 1962.

28. One journalistic piece on Paris, "Lament for the Left Bank" (1941); a short story called "The Perfect Murder" (1942); one play, *The Antiphon* (1958); a book review on Stein: "Matron's Primer" (1945); three poems: "Transfiguration" (1936), which she revised as "Fall-out Over Heaven" (1958), "Quarry" (1969), and "The Walking-mort" (1971); and the inconsequential *Creatures in an Alphabet* (1982).

29. O'Neal describes her health problems: 12, 37, 46, and passim.

30. DB to Mary Reynolds, 14 June 1949.

31. DB to Solita Solano, 24 May 1968.

32. DB to Phyllis Jones, 22 June 1974.

33. DB to Natalie Barney, 18 June 1968.

34. Scott's unpublished interview with DB, 2 April 1971.

35. Hank O'Neal to Fabienne Benedict, 15 February 1979.

36. Interview with Francesca Belanger, 8 April 1989.

37. DB to Natalie Barney, 23 May 1934.

Works by Djuna Barnes

∎ ∎ ∎

BOOKS

The Book of Repulsive Women. New York: Bruno's Chapbooks II, no. 6 (13 November 1915), 86–112; reprinted 1948. (Contains "From Fifth Avenue Up"; "In General"; "From Third Avenue On"; "Seen from the L"; "In Particular"; "Twilight of the Illicit"; "To a Cabaret Dancer"; "Suicide: Corpse A/Corpse B"; and five drawings.)

Vagaries Malicieux. *Double Dealer* III (May 1922), 249–60; New York: F. Hallman, 1974.

A Book. New York: Boni & Liveright, 1923.

Ladies Almanack. (Written by a lady of fashion). Dijon, France: Darantière (privately printed), 1928; New York: Harper & Row, 1972.

Ryder. New York: Boni & Liveright, 1928; St. Martin's Press, 1979; 1981; Elmwood Park, Ill.: Dalkey Archive, 1990.

A Night Among the Horses. New York: Boni & Liveright, 1929. (A new edition of *A Book*, with three stories added.)

Nightwood. London: Faber & Faber, 1936; 1950; New York: Harcourt, Brace, 1937; Cambridge, Mass.: Ryerson Press, 1936; New York: New Directions, 1946; New York: Farrar, Straus, 1962 (in *Selected Works*).

The Antiphon. London: Faber & Faber, 1958; New York: Farrar, Straus, 1958; 1962 (in *Selected Works*).

Spillway. London: Faber & Faber: 1962; New York: Farrar, Straus, 1962 (in *Selected Works*); New York: Harper & Row, 1972.

The Selected Works of Djuna Barnes (*Spillway, The Antiphon, Nightwood*). New York: Farrar, Straus & Cudahy, 1962.

Greenwich Village as It Is. Edited by Robert A. Wilson. New York: Phoenix Book Shop, 1978. (In *New York*.)

Creatures in an Alphabet. New York: Dial Press, 1982.

Smoke and Other Early Stories. Edited by Douglas Messerli. College Park, Md.: Sun & Moon Press, 1982; 2d ed., 1987.

Interviews. Edited by Alyce Barry. Washington, D.C.: Sun & Moon Press, 1985.

New York. Edited by Alyce Barry. Los Angeles: Sun & Moon Press, 1989.

STORIES

"The Terrible Peacock." *All-Story Cavalier Weekly* XXXVII (24 October 1914), 780–84. (In *Smoke.*)

"Paprika Johnson." *The Trend* VIII (January 1915), 417–22. (In *Smoke.*)

"What Do You See, Madam?" *All-Story Cavalier Weekly* XLIII (27 March 1915), 381–84. (In *Smoke.*)

"The Murder in the Palm Room; An Adventure in Silver and Black." *Vanity Fair* VII (December 1916), 47. (Attributed to Barnes by Messerli.)

"Who Is This Tom Scarlett?" *New York Morning Telegraph Sunday Magazine,* 11 March 1917, 5. (In *Smoke.*)

"The Jest of Jests." Ibid., 1 April 1917, 6. (In *Smoke.*)

"Prize Ticket 177: In the Lottery for the Sisterhood of the Single." Ibid., 8 April 1917, 5. (In *Smoke.*)

"A Sprinkle of Comedy." Ibid., 27 May 1917, 2. (In *Smoke.*)

"The Earth." Ibid., 10 June 1917, 4. (In *Smoke.*)

"The Head of Babylon." Ibid., 1 July 1917, 4. (In *Smoke.*)

"Fate—the Pacemaker." Ibid., 22 July 1917, 4.

"Smoke." Ibid., 19 August 1917, 2. (In *Smoke.*)

"The Coward." Ibid., 26 August 1917, 4. (In *Smoke.*)

"Monsieur Ampee." Ibid., 16 September 1917, 4. (In *Smoke.*)

"The Terrorists." Ibid., 30 September 1917, 4. (In *Smoke.*)

"The Rabbit." Ibid., 7 October 1917, 4. (In *Spillway.*)

"Indian Summer." Ibid., 14 October 1917, 6.

"A Night in the Woods." Ibid., 21 October 1917, 4. (In *Smoke.*)

"Finale." *Little Review* V (June 1918), 29–30.

"Renunciation." *Smart Set* LVI (October 1918), 65–69.

"A Night Among the Horses." *Little Review* V (December 1918), 3–10. (In *A Book*; *Spillway.*)

"The Valet." Ibid. VI (May 1919), 3–9. (In *A Book*; *Spillway.*)

"Beyond the End." Ibid. VI (December 1919), frontispiece and 7–14. (In *A Book.*)

"Oscar." Ibid. VI (April 1920), 7–23. (In *A Book.*)

"Mother." Ibid. VII (July–August 1920), 10–14.

"The Robin's House." Ibid. VII (September–December 1920), 31–38. (In *A Book*.)

"Katrina Silverstaff." Ibid. VII (January–March 1921), 27–33. (In *A Book*, as "The Two Doctors.")

(Lydia Steptoe) "The Diary of a Dangerous Child: Which Should Be of Interest to All Those Who Want to Know How Women Get the Way They Are." *Vanity Fair* XVIII (July 1922), 56; 94.

(Lydia Steptoe) "The Diary of a Small Boy." *Shadowland* IX (September 1923), 45; 72.

"Aller et Retour." *Transatlantic Review* I (April 1924), 159–67. In *Transatlantic Stories*, ed. Ford Madox Ford. London: Duckworth, 1926, 38–60. (In *Spillway*. A dramatic adaptation, called "A Mother Returns," was never published.)

"The Passion." *Transatlantic Review* II (November 1924), 490–501. In *Transatlantic Stories*, 38–60. (In *Spillway*.)

"Cassation." Formerly "A Little Girl Tells a Story to a Lady." In *Contact Collection of Contemporary Writers*. Paris: Three Mountains Press, 1925, 1–10. Also in *Americans Abroad: An Anthology*, ed. Peter Neagoe. The Hague: Servire Press, 1932, 1–19. (In *Spillway*.)

"The Little Girl Continues." *This Quarter* I (Fall 1925), 195–202; 346. In *Americans Abroad*, 20–26. (In *Spillway*, as "The Grande Malade.")

"Rape and Repining." *transition* IX (December 1927), 20–28. (Chapter 5 of *Ryder*.)

"A Duel Without Seconds; Wherein a Lady Discovers That an Ordinary Theft May Involve One's Honor in More Ways than One." *Vanity Fair* XXXIII (November 1929), 84; 116. In *Vanity Fair: Selections*, ed. Cleveland Amory and Frederic Bradlee. New York: Viking, 1960, 169–70.

"The Letter That Was Never Mailed; Wherein Friendship and Loyalty All but Droop Beneath the Hot Winds of Rivalry, but True Love, as Usual, Conquers All in the End." *Vanity Fair* XXXIII (December 1929), 68–69; 134.

"The First of April; Messages by Wire and a Rendez-vous in Rome Prove to Two Lovers That Love Is a Pleasant Habit." Ibid. XXXIV (March 1930), 69; 84.

"The Doctors." In *Spillway*.

"Spillway." In *Spillway*.

"Dusie." In *Americana Esoterica*. New York: Macy-Masius, 1927, 75–82.

"Run Girls, Run." *Caravel* II (March 1936), 1–7. (In *Vagaries Malicieux*.)

"The Perfect Murder." *Harvard Advocate* CXXVIII (April 1942), 6–9. In *Harvard Advocate Centennial Anthology*, ed. Jonathan D. Culler. Cambridge, Mass.: Schenkman, 1966, 249–55.

"Behind the Heart." Ed. Phillip Herring. *Library Chronicle*, Summer 1993, 3–17.

Saturnalia. Unpublished manuscript. University of Maryland.

Life Lasts Too Long. Unpublished story. Title deleted. Messerli.

"Tertium Organum," story with pictures, *McCall's*, 1923? Publication uncertain.

DRAMA

"The Death of Life: Death Is the Poor Man's Purse—Baudelaire." *New York Morning Telegraph Sunday Magazine*, 17 December 1916, 8.

"At the Roots of the Stars." Ibid., 11 February 1917, 8.

"Maggie of the Saints." Ibid., 28 October 1917, 4.

"A Passion Play." *Others* IV (February 1918), 5–17.

"Madame Collects Herself." *The Parisienne*, June 1918, 89–91.

"To Sublet for the Summer." *New York Morning Telegraph Sunday Magazine*, 21 July 1918, 6. (In *New York*.)

"Three from the Earth." *Little Review* VI (November 1919), 3–15. (In *A Book*.)

"Kurzy of the Sea." Unpublished manuscript. Library of Congress, 1920.

"An Irish Triangle." *Playboy* VII (May 1921), 3–5.

(Lydia Steptoe) "Little Drops of Rain: Wherein Is Discussed the Advantage of XIX Century Storm Over XXth Century Sunshine." *Vanity Fair* XIX (September 1922), 50; 94.

"Five Thousand Miles: A Moral Homily Inspired by All the Current Talk About the Wild Free Life in the South Seas." Ibid. XX (March 1923), 50.

"Ten Minute Plays II: Two Ladies Take Tea." *Shadowland* VIII (April 1923), 17; 70.

"Water-Ice: Wherein the Wintry Lady Fiora Silvertree Is Unexpectedly Thawed." *Vanity Fair* XX (July 1923), 59.

(Lydia Steptoe) "Ten Minute Plays VI: The Beauty." *Shadowland* IX (October 1923), 43; 74.

"She Tells Her Daughter." *Smart Set* LXXII (November 1923), 77–80.

"To the Dogs." *A Book*, 44–58.

"The Dove." *A Book*, 147–63. (Presented by Studio Theatre, New York, 6 May 1926.)

"The Biography of Julie von Bartmann." Full-length play, 1924. Unpublished manuscript. University of Maryland.

The Antiphon.

"Ann Portuguise." Unpublished manuscript.

POEMS

"The Dreamer." *Harper's Weekly* LV (24 June 1911), 9.

"Call of the Night." Ibid. LV (23 December 1911), 22.

"Serenade." *All-Story Cavalier Weekly* XXXII (16 May 1914), 228.

"Just Lately Drummer Boy." *The Trend* VIII (October 1914), 32.

"When Emperors Are Out of Men!" *All-Story Cavalier Weekly* XXXVIII (31 October 1914), 153.

" 'Six Carried Her Away.' " *The Trend* VIII (November 1914), 184.

"Solitude." *All-Story Cavalier Weekly* XXXIX (28 November 1914), 152.

"The Personal God." *The Trend* VIII (December 1914), 366.

"Jungle Jargon." In "Djuna Barnes Probes the Souls of the Jungle Fold." *New York Press*, 14 February 1915, 4:2.

"Who Shall Atone?" *New York Press Sunday Magazine*, 4 April 1915, 1.

"Vaudeville." *All-Story Cavalier Weekly* XLIV (24 April 1915), 375. In *Vanity Fair* XX (May 1923), 67.

"Harvest Time." *All-Story Weekly* XLV (22 May 1915), 369.

"The Master—Dead." Ibid. XLV (5 June 1915), 768.

"Tramp Summer." Ibid. XLVI (26 June 1915), 454.

"This Much and More." Ibid. XLIX (4 September 1915), 81.

The Book of Repulsive Women.

"Death." *All-Story Cavalier Weekly* LV (4 March 1916), 406.

"In Conclusion." Ibid. LVII (6 May 1916), 764.

"Dust." Ibid. LVIII (3 June 1916), 612.

"Birth." Ibid. LIX (24 June 1916), 442.

"The Yellow Jar." *Munsey's Magazine* LVIII (September 1916), 605.

"A Last Toast." *All-Story Cavalier Weekly* LXII (9 September 1916), 379.

"To an Idol." Ibid. LXII (16 September 1916), 480.

"Shadows." *Munsey's Magazine* LIX (November 1916), 272.

"Love-Song." *All-Story Cavalier Weekly* LXIX (18 November 1916), 744.

"Lines to a Lady." Ibid. LXXXIV (1 June 1918), 764.

"Antique." *Harper's Monthly Magazine* CXXXVII (August 1918), 330. (In *A Book*.)

"The Lament of Women" and "To ———." *Little Review* V (December 1918), 37–38.

"To the Hands of a Beloved." *All-Story Cavalier Weekly* XCVII (17 May 1919), 212.

"To One in Favour." *Smart Set* LIX (July 1919), 104.

"To a Bird." *All-Story Cavalier Weekly* CI (20 September 1919), 687.

"Two Poems" ("To the Dead Favourite of Liu Ch'e" and "Pastoral"). *The Dial* LXVIII (April 1920), 444–46. "Pastoral" reprinted in *Current Opinion* LXIX (August 1920), 268. (In *A Book*.)

"I'd Have You Think of Me." *Vanity Fair* XIX (October 1922), 67. (In *A Book*.)

"To One Feeling Differently." *Playboy* II (March 1923), 36.

"Two Lyrics" ("She Passed This Way" and "The Flowering Corpse"). *Vanity Fair* XX (March 1923), 14. ("The Flowering Corpse" in *A Book*.)

"Crystals." *New Republic* XXXV (20 June 1923), 101.

"The Child Would Be Older." *Shadowland* VIII (July 1923), 43.

"First Communion." *The Dial* (August 1923), 166. (In *A Book*.)

"Love Song in Autumn." *Vanity Fair* XXI (September 1923), 84. (In *A Book* as "Song in Autumn".)

"To One in Another Mood." Ibid. XXI (November 1923), 118.

"Hush Before Love." *A Book* 116.

"Paradise." *A Book* 131.

"Six Songs of Khalidine: To the Memory of Mary Pyne." *A Book* 145.

"Lullaby." *A Book* 179.

"Finis." *A Book* 220.

"Transfiguration." *London Bulletin* III (June 1936), 2. Revised as "Fall-out Over Heaven" in *T. S. Eliot: A Symposium for His Seventieth Birthday*, ed. Neville Braybrooke. New York: Farrar, Straus & Cudahy, 1958, 27.

"Galerie Religieux." In *The Wind and the Rain: An Easter Book*, ed. Neville Braybrooke. London: Secker & Warburg, 1962, 266.

"Quarry." *New Yorker* 45 (27 December 1969), 53. Reprinted in *A Festschrift for Djuna Barnes*, ed. Alex Gildzen. Kent, Ohio: Kent State University Libraries, 1972.

"The Walking-mort." *New Yorker* 47 (15 May 1971), 34.

"Rite of Spring." *Grand Street* (Spring 1982).

UNPUBLISHED POEMS

"Death and the Wood"; "Requiem"; "Archaic"; "Then Think of Her"; "Love and the Bird"; "Tally Ho"; "Exodus"; "Nightfall"; "Marine"; "Autumn"; "Death and the Boy"; "Love and the Beast"; "Death in the Wood"; "Canterbury Summer for Chaucer"; "Eve Before Eve"; "The Indexes"; "Portrait of a Lady Walking."

JOURNALISM AND INTERVIEWS

"You Can Tango—A Little—at Arcadia Dance Hall." *Brooklyn Daily Eagle*, 29 June 1913. (In *New York*.)

" 'Twingeless Twitchell' and His Tantalizing Tweezers: They Attract and Hold the Attention of Reginald Delancey and the Piquant Ikrima—A Midsummer Night's Entertainment on the Highways of the Great City, That, however, Has Elements of Tragedy—Digital Dexterity of the Dental Demonstrator Holds Audience in Awe." Ibid., 27 July 1913. (In *New York*.)

"Sad Scenes on Sentence Day in the Kings County Court." Ibid., 3 August 1913. (In *New York*.)

"The People and the Sea; How They Get Together." Ibid., 10 August 1913. (In *New York.*)

"Round Ben Franklin's Statue Forum Orators Fret and Fume." Ibid., 24 August 1913. (In *New York.*)

"Training Seals in Stage Stunts; Odd Antics Taught to Deep Sea Denizens in a Brooklyn Barn; Rewarded with Fish Treats; Trainer Demonstrates the Ease with Which His Pets May Be Instructed to Entertain." Ibid., 31 August 1913.

"No Turkey or Tango in Drag or Glide Dances." Ibid., 5 September 1913. (In *New York.*)

"Part Victory, Part Defeat at Suffrage Aviation Meet." Ibid., 7 September 1913. (In *New York.*)

"Our School's Open Again; We're Glad to Get Back." Ibid., 14 September 1913. (In *New York.*)

"Seventy Trained Suffragists Turned Loose on City." Ibid., 28 September 1913. (In *New York.*)

"Arbuckle 'Floating Hotel' to Be Closed." Ibid., 28 September 1913. (In *New York.*)

"The Home Club: For Servants Only." Ibid., 12 October 1913. (In *New York.*)

"Veterans in Harness." Ibid., 12 October–14 December 1913. (In *New York.*)

"Who's the Last Squatter?" Ibid., 2 November 1913. (In *New York.*)

"Mrs. Clinton Hoard Works for Uplift of Drama Here; Brooklyn Woman Outlines Plan for Carrying Propaganda of Stage Reform into Every Town on Long Island. Enlists Support of Women's Clubs." Ibid., 23 November 1913.

"Chinatown's Old Glories Crumbled to Dust." Ibid., 30 November 1913. (In *New York.*)

"Why Go Abroad?—See Europe in Brooklyn!" Ibid., 7 December 1913. (In *New York.*)

"Navy Yard Teems with Work Undone." Ibid., 21 December 1913. (In *New York.*)

"The Wild Aguglia and Her Monkeys Here." *New York Press*, 28 December 1913, 3: 2. (In *Interviews.*)

"Yes, the Vernon Castles Really Have a Home and They Occasionally Tango Past It; They Bought It to Keep Dogs In, and Sometimes, Small When They Haven't Anything Else to Do, They Sleep There from 2 a.m. till 11 a.m." Ibid., 18 January 1914, 5:3. (In *Interviews.*)

"Blanche Bates to Make Her Baby Violinist or Cubist; Husband Already Relying on Little Frances Virginia to Support Him." Ibid., 25 January 1914, 5:2; 5.

"Charles Maude Wears Clothes That Express Color of Soul." Ibid., 1 February 1914, 5:2.

"Charles Rann Kennedy Explains Meaning of Tangoism; 'It's a Mere Steaming

Up of Flaccid Souls and Represents Decadent America,' He Declares—
'Best of Us Can Go to a Cabaret for Awhile and Come Away Without Being
Crazed.' " Ibid., 29 March 1914, 5:3. (In *Interviews*.)
"Gaby's Reputation for Reckless Deviltry Is Shattered; Off the Stage Is Meek-
ness Personified and the World is 'Very Terrible and Very Sad and Hope-
less to Her'—She Doesn't Enjoy Any Part of Life, Because She Hasn't
Time." Ibid., 12 April 1914, 5:2. (In *Interviews*.)
"Surroundings Affect People More Than Anything Else, Declares Lillian Rus-
sell; 'I Could Never Be Lonely Without a Husband but It Would Almost
Be Abysmal Gloom to Have No Trinkets,' She Says." Ibid., 3 May 1914,
5:2. (In *Interviews*.)
"Diamond Jim Brady." 10 May 1914. (In *Interviews*.)
"Flo Ziegfeld Says He Selects His Chorus Girls by Looking at Their Feet and
Hands; Never Listens to Their Voices, Because Good Singers Seldom Have
Beautiful Faces; Billy Burke's Husband Used to Think Dark Hair Was
Pretty but He Has Changed His Mind—He's Tired of Buying Hosiery for
Entire Show—Says It Is Like Being Another Brigham Young; Declares
Wife Is Most Wonderful Woman in All the World." *New York Press*, 24
May 1914, 5:1. (In *Interviews*.)
"If Noise Were Forbidden at Coney Island, a Lot of People Would Lose Their
Jobs." Ibid., 7 June 1914, 5: 5. (In *New York*.)
"Come Into the Roof Garden, Maud." Ibid., 14 June 1914 6:1. (In *New York*.)
"Roshanara, a Wraithlike Reincarnation of the Ancient East." Ibid., 14 June
1914, 5:3.
"Plays That Rely on Upper Classes for Support Invariably Die a Quick and
Painful Death, Says Daniel Frohman; 'They Don't Support Anything, Not
Even the Pillars of Society,' He Says, and Adds That It's the Masses Which
Finally Determine the Success or Failure of a Play—Things Dramatic Are
Now Having Their Down Days, Declares New York Manager.' " Ibid., 28
June 1914, 5:1.
"Broadway Thinks It Is Only Street in Only City in the World, Says Atteridge;
Carroll His Co-Worker on 'The Passing Show,' Says It Never Thinks of
Yesterday or Tomorrow—But, After All It Is as Provincial as the Smallest
Town Found on Any Map in the Geography.' " Ibid., 5 July 1914, 5:2. (In
New York.)
"Desire to Live, Love and Achieve Elements of Successful Play, Paul Arm-
strong Says; Women Are Not the Vain Set—It's Men Who Think Every
Woman Who Looks at Them Loves Them; 'The More You Try to Say in a
Play, the Less You'll Be Noticed, so Be Wise Just at the End.' " Ibid., 12
July 1914, 5:2.
"Interviewing Arthur Voegtlin Is Something like Having a Nightmare, It Seems;
He Doesn't Care for the Stage—Wouldn't Let a Cat He Liked Chase a
Stage Rat—But He Longs to Produce 'Weird Plays with the Lure of a

Vampire-Woman's Eyes'—Friends Call Him 'Silver King.' " Ibid., 19 July 1914, 5:2. (In *Interviews*.)

"Mad, Bad, Glad, Raymond Hitchcock, with a Hundred Shattered Reputations, Is Beloved of His Wife's Kin; And That, After All, Is the Supreme Test of a Man's Humanity—Hitch Is So Happy This Summer He's Wasting Those Golden Baritone Notes Audiences Pay Money to Hear." Ibid., 26 July 1914, 5:1; 2. (In *Interviews*.)

"Great Success Made Joan Sawyer Timid." Ibid., 26 July 1914, 5:7.

" 'Tis the Season When a Chorus Girl Is Learning How a Manager Can Say 'No'; She Doesn't Much Care What Show She's in so Long as She Can Stay on Old Broadway; Lots of Them Go in Hopefully and Come out Heartbroken Because They Haven't Been Engaged." Ibid., 9 August 1914, 5:3.

"My Sisters and I at a New York Prizefight." *New York World Magazine*, 23 August 1914, 6. (In *New York*.)

"How It Feels to Be Forcibly Fed." Ibid., 6 September 1914, 5; 17. (In *New York*.)

"The Girl and the Gorilla." Ibid., 18 October 1914, 9. (In *New York*.)

"My Adventures Being Rescued." Ibid., 15 November 1914, 6. (In *New York*.)

"I'm Plain Mary Jones of the U.S.A." 7 February 1915. (In *Interviews*.)

"Djuna Barnes Probes the Souls of the Jungle Folk at the Hippodrome Circus; Broadway Mashers Wink Is Flung at Audience by Cynical Old Elephant—An Instance of Banter in the Balk; Camels Peer Out Through Invisible Lorgnettes, and Bears Lurch Along, Hands Raised as if They Were Praying." *New York Press*, 14 February 1915, 4:2.

"Billy Sunday Loves the Multitide, Not the Individual." 21 February 1915. (In *Interviews*.)

"Bunny Hopes to Outlive Booth; Not That He Deserves To, but Because There Is a Record of Him That Booth and Sir Henry Irving Did Not Leave—Has an Ambition to Improve the Scenario." *New York Press*, 14 March 1915, 4:2. (In *Interviews*.)

"Irvin Cobb Boasts He Is Still Just a Country Boy." 28 March 1915. (In *Interviews*.)

"A Visit to the Favored Haunt of the I.W.W.'s." *New York Press*, 11 April 1915.

"Jess Willard Says Girls Will Be Boxing for a Living Soon." 25 April 1915. (In *Interviews*.)

"Fashion Show Makes Girl Regret Life Isn't All Redfern and Skittles." *New York Press*, 25 April 1915, 4:4. (In *New York*.)

"Ruth Roye, Greatest 'Nut' in Vaudeville, Loves to Hear Man Out Front Laugh; No Girl's or Woman's Giggle Please Her Half as Much as the Hearty Guffaw of the Male Auditors." Ibid., 9 May 1915, 4:4. (In *Interviews*.)

"Lou-Tellegen on Morals and Things; Star of Much-Discussed 'Taking Chances'

Says as an Actor He May Be Vulgar or Inartistic, but Immoral, Never!" Ibid., 16 May 1915, 4:5. (In *Interviews*.)

"May Vokes in an Unguarded Hour; Tells Djuna Barnes Some of the Things Hidden Behind Her Funny Face; Yearns for a Shack; Scene from a Play That Took Place in a Dressing Room in the Longacre Theatre." Ibid., 23 May 1915, 19. (In *Interviews*.)

"A Philosopher Among Russian Dancers: An Interview with Adolph Bohm." *Bruno's Weekly* II (29 January 1916), 408–9. (In *Interviews*.)

"The Weavers, at the Garden Theatre." Ibid. II (5 February 1916), 433–34.

"Pet Superstitions of Sensible New Yorkers." *New York Tribune*, 20 February 1916. (In *New York*.)

"The Last Petit Souper—Greenwich Village in the Air—Ahem!" *Bruno's Weekly*, 29 April 1916 II: 665–70. (In *New York*.)

"Greenwich Village as It Is." *Pearson's Magazine*, October 1916. (In *New York*.)

"Becoming Intimate with the Bohemians." *New York Morning Telegraph Sunday Magazine*, 19 November 1916, 1, 4. (In *New York*.)

"How the Villagers Amuse Themselves." Ibid., 26 November 1916, 1. (In *New York*.)

"The Washington Square Players; What Is the Secret of the Organization That Started as a Whim in Boni's Bookshop and Now Threatens to Become Popular?" Ibid., 3 December 1916, 8.

"Wilson Mizner of Forty-Fourth Street; The Address Is Important for He Says He Has Not Been North, South, East or West of It in as Many Years." Ibid., 24 December 1916, 1. (In *Interviews*.)

"David Belasco Dreams; The Chronicles of One Who Wanders Among the Heavy Timbers of Antiquity." Ibid., 31 December 1916, 1. (In *Interviews*.)

"David Warfield—Optimist; Creator of the Music Master, Without His German Accent, Says He Is a Firm Believer in Happy Endings and Other Things." Ibid., 14 January 1917, 8.

"Found on the Bowery; The Italian Drama of Thundering Hate and Lightning Love." Ibid., 21 January 1917, 1. (In *New York*.)

"Frank Harris Finds Success More Easily Won Here in America Than in England." 4 February 1917. (In *Interviews*.)

"The Songs of Synge; The Man Who Shaped His Life as He Shaped His Plays." *New York Morning Telegraph Sunday Magazine*, 18 February 1917, 8.

"Giving Advice on Life and Pictures; One Must Bleed His Own Blood." (Alfred Stieglitz.) Ibid., 25 February 1917, 7. (In *Interviews*.)

"The Old Theatre in New Attire; As Pleasing To-days Are Painted for the World of Drama." Ibid., 18 March 1917, 8.

"Recruiting for Métachorie: Mme. Valentine de Saint-Point Talks of Her Church of Music." Ibid., 15 April 1917, 4. (In *Interviews*.)

"The Rider of Dreams Is Here: For This Is the Spirit of the Negro." Ibid., 22 April 1917, 1. (Interview in play form with Robert E. Jones. In *Interviews*.)

"Introducing Monsieur Copeau." Ibid., 3 June 1917, 4.

"The Artist's Place in War." Ibid., 17 June 1917, 2.

"Crumpets and Tea." Ibid., 24 June 1917, 5. (In *New York*.)

"When the Puppets Come to Town." Ibid., 8 July 1917, 4.

"Surcease in Hurry and Whirl—On the Restless Surf at Coney." Ibid., 15 July 1917, 2. (In *New York*.)

"The Hem of Manhattan." Ibid., 29 July 1917, 2. (In *New York*.)

"Three Days Out." Ibid., 12 August 1917, 4.

"On Going Fishing." Ibid., 2 September 1917, 2.

"Doing the Dunes." Ibid., 9 September 1917, 3.

"The Confessions of Helen Westley." Ibid., 23 September 1917, 5. (In *Interviews*.)

"Yvette Guilbert." Ibid., 18 November 1917, 2. (In *Interviews*.)

"Commissioner Enright and M. Voltaire." *New York Sun Magazine*, 17 March 1918. (In *New York*.)

"Woman Police Deputy Is Writer of Poetry." Ibid., 24 March 1918. (In *New York*.)

"Guardabassi, Soldier, Singer, and Artist." Ibid., 7 April 1918, 13–14. (In *Interviews*.)

"Soldier Thespians and 'You Know Me, Al'; New York's Own Division Raising Funds by Its Play to Provide Portable Theatre Over There and Relieve Trench Holders Mental Strain." Ibid., 21 April 1918, 15–16.

"City's War Camp Community Service Gives Our Boys Comforts." Ibid., 19 May 1918, 13–14. (In *New York*.)

"Seeing New York with the Soldiers." *New York Morning Telegraph Sunday Magazine*, 7 July 1918, 8. (In *New York*.)

"There's Something Besides the Cocktail in the Bronx." *New York Tribune*, 16 February 1919, III:6. (In *New York*.)

"Dempsey Welcomes Women Fans." 1921. (In *Interviews*.)

"James Joyce: A Portrait of the Man Who Is, at Present, One of the More Significant Figures in Literature." *Vanity Fair* XVIII (April 1922), 65; 104. (In *Interviews*.)

"Against Nature: In Which Everything That Is Young, Inadequate and Tiresome Is Included in the Term Natural." Ibid., XVIII (August 1922), 60; 88.

"Plays for Women." *New York Tribune*, 15 October 1922, 5:9.

"Floyd Dell as Playwright." Ibid., 12 November 1922, 5:10.

"Rudolph Schildkraut." *The Dial* LXXIV (April 1923), 420–21. (Pencil sketch.)

"What Is Good Form in Dying?: In Which a Dozen Dainty Deaths Are Suggested for Daring Damsels." *Vanity Fair* XX (June 1923), 73; 102.

(Lydia Steptoe) "Madame Grows Older," *Chicago Tribune*, Sunday Magazine, 9 March 1924 (C. Page).

"The Models Have Come to Town." November 1924. (In *Interviews*.)

"Do You Want to Be a Movie Actress?" February 1925. (In *Interviews*.)

(Lydia Steptoe) "A French Couturière to Youth" (Jeanne Lanvin). *Charm*, March 1925, 20–21; 71; 91?

(Lydia Steptoe) "The Romance of Beautiful Jewels." Ibid., May 1925, 44–47?

"How the Woman in Love Should Dress." October 1925. (In *Interviews*.)

(Lydia Steptoe) "Rome and the Little Theatre; Three Directors—Pirandello, Bragaglia and Ferrari—Have Created an Interest in This Art." *Charm*, August 1926, 15–17; 83.

"American Wives and Titled Husbands." June 1927. (In *Interviews*.)

"The Days of Jig Cook: Recollections of Ancient Theatre History but Ten Years Old." *Theatre Guild Magazine* VI (January 1929), 31–32.

"The Dear Dead Days: Love Is Done Differently on Our Current Stage." Ibid. VI (February 1929), 41–43.

"Portrait of a Crook: A Plea for Charm and Elegance in Stage Crime." Ibid. VI (April 1929), 35–37.

"Lady of Fourteenth Street." "Profiles," *New Yorker* V (6 April 1929), 29–32.

"Why Actors? Brother Sumac Searches for an Answer." *Theatre Guild Magazine* VII (December 1929), 42–43.

"When Stock Was Work: Sam Forrest Recalls What It Meant to Play Twelve a Week." Ibid. VII (February 1930), 33–34.

"Lord Alfred and Lady Lynn: An Interview to Prove That Marriage Is No Hindrance to Art." Ibid. VII (March 1930), 11–12. (In *Interviews*.)

"Just Getting the Breaks: Donald Ogden Stewart Confides the Secret of World Success." Ibid. VII (April 1930), 35–36; 57. (In *Interviews*.)

"The Green Pastures: Connelly's Biblical Play Discussed by Its Negro Actors." Ibid. VII (May 1930), 18–19. (In *Interviews*.)

"Alla Nazimova: One of the Greatest of Living Actresses Talks of Her Art." Ibid. VII (June 1930), 32–34; 61. (In *Interviews*.)

"Playgoer's Almanac." Ibid. VII–VIII (July 1930–March 1931).

(Lady Lydia Steptoe) "Hamlet's Custard Pie: Giles, the Butler, Learns What Is Wrong with the Drama." Ibid. VII (July 1930), 34–35; 48.

"Chester Erskin: A Young Stage Director with a Flair for the Theatrical Verities." Ibid. VII (August 1930), 32–33.

"The Stage Sets the Style: Margaret Pemberton, Who Costumes Many of Our Actresses, Talks of the Theatre's New Function." Ibid. VIII (October 1930), 38–39.

"Mordecai Gorelik: A Young Scene Designer Who Seeks, by Using 'Pretense' Rather Than 'Illusion,' to Parade on the Stage the Ceremonial Comedy of the Animal Called Man." Ibid. VIII (February 1931), 42–45.

"I've Always Suffered from Sirens: Raymond Sovey, However, Has Disciplined His Inspiration So Effectively That He Merges His Stage Settings Completely in the Author's Intention and the Play's Mood." Ibid. VIII (March 1931), 23–25. (In *Interviews*.)

"The Wanton Playgoer." Ibid. VIII (April–September 1931).

"The Tireless Rachel Crothers: That Vivacious Comedy *As Husbands Go* Is the Twenty-fourth Which She Has Written in Her Long and Methodical Career." Ibid. VIII (May 1931), 32–33. (In *Interviews.*)

"His World's a Stage: And so the Versatile Scene-Designs of Jo Mielziner Reflect with Artistic Fidelity the Moods and Manners of the World." Ibid. VIII (June 1931), 25–29.

"Nothing Amuses Coco Chanel After Midnight." September 1931. (In *Interviews.*)

"Lament for the Left Bank." In "Vantage Ground," *Town & Country* XCVI (December 1941), 92; 136–38; 148.

"Matron's Primer." (Review of Gertrude Stein's *Wars I Have Seen.*) *Contemporary Jewish Record*, June 1945, 342–43.

War in Paris. Unpublished typescript. University of Maryland.

INTERVIEWS WITH DJUNA BARNES

Åhman, Sven. "Omstritt geni i Greenwich Village: Exklusiv USA-forfattarinna i världspremiär på Dramaten." *Dagens Nyheter*, 24 May 1959, 29.

Bruno, Guido. "Fleurs du Mal à la Mode de New York—An Interview with Djuna Barnes." December 1919. (In *Interviews.*)

Raymont, Henry. "From the Avant Garde of the Thirties." *New York Times*, 24 May 1971, 24.

Stern, James. *Time*, 18 January 1943.

MISCELLANEOUS

"Foreword to the Selections from the Letters of Elsa Baroness von Freytag-Loringhoven." *transition* XI (February 1928), 19. (In Memoriam.)

"Response to Questionnaire." *Little Review*, May 1929, 12:2, 17.

Selected Bibliography*

■ ■ ■

Ackroyd, Peter. *T. S. Eliot: A Life*. New York: Simon & Schuster, 1984.

Anderson, Margaret. *My Thirty Years War*. New York: Horizon, 1970.

Barney, Natalie Clifford. *Adventures of the Mind*. New York: New York University Press, 1992.

Beach, Sylvia. *Shakespeare and Company*. New York: Harcourt, Brace, 1959.

Bercovici, Konrad. *It's the Gypsy in Me*. New York: Prentice-Hall, 1941.

Biddle, George. *An American Artist's Story*. Boston: Little, Brown, 1939.

Boyle, Kay. "Djuna Barnes: 1892–1982." *Proceedings of the American Academy and Institute of Arts and Letters*, 2d Series, no. 34, 79–82. New York, 1983.

Braude, Ann. *Radical Spirits: Spiritualism and Women's Rights in Nineteenth-Century America*. Boston: Beacon Press, 1989.

Broe, Mary Lynn, ed. *Silence and Power: A Reevaluation of Djuna Barnes*. Carbondale: Southern Illinois University Press, 1991.

———, and Angela Ingram, eds. *Women Writers in Exile*. Chapel Hill: University of North Carolina Press, 1989.

Budington, Henry Aaron. *The Leyden Branch of the Budington Family*. Springfield, Mass.: Privately printed, 1908.

Burke, Kenneth. "Version, Con-, Per-, and In- (Thoughts on Djuna Barnes' Novel *Nightwood*). *Southern Review* II (Spring 1966), 329–46. Also in his *Language as Symbolic Action* (Berkeley: University of California Press, 1968), 240–53.

Butter, P. H., ed., *Selected Letters of Edwin Muir*. London: Hogarth Press, 1974.

Callaghan, Morley. *That Summer in Paris: Memoirs of Tangled Friendships*. New York: Coward-McCann, 1963.

* These are works I actually quote from; excluded are works cited in passing.

Carrel, Alexis. *Man, the Unknown.* New York: Harper, 1935.

Charters, James. *This Must Be the Place.* London: Herbert Joseph, 1934.

Chitty, Susan. *Now to My Mother: A Very Personal Memoir of Antonia White.* London: Weidenfeld & Nicolson, 1985.

———, ed. *Antonia White: Diaries 1926–1957*, vol. I. New York: Viking, 1992.

Clark, Susan F. "Misalliance: Djuna Barnes and the American Theatre." Ph.D. diss., Tufts University, 1989.

Coleman, Emily Holmes. *Shutter of Snow.* London: Virago, 1981.

Commemorative Biographical Record of Middlesex County, Connecticut. Chicago: J. H. Beers, 1903.

Curry, Lynda. " 'Tom, Take Mercy': T. S. Eliot and *The Antiphon:* Djuna Barnes' Drafts of *The Antiphon.*" In Broe, ed., *Silence and Power*, 286–98.

Deutsch, Helen, and Stella Hanau. *The Provincetown: A Story of the Theatre.* New York: Farrar & Rinehart, 1931.

De Veer, Elizabeth, and Richard J. Boyle. *Sunlight and Shadow: The Life and Art of Willard L. Metcalf.* New York: Abbeville Press, 1987.

DeVore, Lynn. "The Backgrounds of *Nightwood*: Robin, Felix, and Nora." *Journal of Modern Literature* 10 (1983), 71–90.

Eckley, Grace. *Children's Lore in* Finnegans Wake. Syracuse, N.Y.: Syracuse University Press, 1985.

Eliot, Valerie. Review of Djuna Barnes, "I Could Never Be Lonely Without a Husband," *Financial Times*, 1 August 1987.

Ellmann, Richard. *James Joyce.* New York: Oxford University Press, 1959; 1982.

———. *Oscar Wilde.* New York: Alfred A. Knopf, 1988.

Ferguson, Suzanne C. "Djuna Barnes's Short Stories: An Estrangement of the Heart." *Southern Review* 5 (Winter 1969), 39.

Field, Andrew. *Djuna: The Life and Times of Djuna Barnes.* New York: G. P. Putnam, 1983. Rev. ed. (*Djuna: The Formidable Miss Barnes*) Austin: University of Texas Press, 1985.

Flanner, Janet. *Paris Was Yesterday.* New York: Viking, 1972.

Ford, Charles Henri. "I Will Be What I Am." Unpublished memoir in the Harry Ransom Humanities Research Center, University of Texas at Austin.

———, and Parker Tyler. *The Young and Evil.* Paris: Obelisk, 1933.

Friedman, Ellen G., and Miriam Fuchs, eds. *Breaking the Sequence.* Princeton: Princeton University Press, 1989.

Gildzen, Alex, ed. *A Festschrift for Djuna Barnes on her 80th Birthday.* Kent, Ohio: Kent State University Libraries, 1972.

Giroux, Robert. " 'The Most Famous Unknown in the World'—Remembering Djuna Barnes." *New York Times Book Review*, 1 December 1985, 30–31.

Glassco, John. *Memoirs of Montparnasse.* New York: Viking, 1973.

Grace, Sherrill E. "About a Tragic Business: The Djuna Barnes–Dag Hammarskjöld Letters." *Development Dialogue* (2) 1987, 91–115.

Greve, Felix Paul. *Fanny Essler: Ein Roman.* Stuttgart: Axel Juncker, 1905; English trans. Ottawa: Oberon, 1984.

———. *Maurermeister Ihles Haus: Roman.* Berlin: Karl Schnabel, 1906; English trans. Ottawa: Oberon, 1976.

Guggenheim, Peggy. *Out of This Century.* New York: Dial, 1946.

Hanfstaengl, Ernst. *Hitler Liederbuch 1924.* Munich: Hanfstaengl, 1924.

———. *Unheard Witness.* Philadelphia and New York: Lippincott, 1957.

———. *Zwischen Weisem und Braunem Haus.* Munich: Piper, 1970.

Hansen, Arlen J. *Expatriate Paris: A Cultural and Literary Guide to Paris of the 1920s.* New York: Arcade, 1990.

Harris, Frank. *England or Germany?* New York: Wilmarth Press, 1915.

Hartley, Marsden. *Adventures in the Arts.* New York: Boni & Liveright, 1921; reprint, 1972.

Herring, Phillip F. "Djuna Barnes and the Narrative of Violation." In Reingard Nischik and Barbara Korte, eds., *Modes of Narrative: Approaches to British, American, and Canadian Fiction,* 100–9. Würzburg: Königshausen & Neumann, 1990.

———. "Djuna Barnes Remembers James Joyce." *James Joyce Quarterly* 30 (Fall 1992), 113–17.

———. "Djuna Barnes and the Songs of Synge." *Éire-Ireland* 2:28 (Summer 1993), 157–62.

———. "Djuna Barnes and Thelma Wood: The Vengeance of *Nightwood.*" *Journal of Modern Literature,* 18:1 (Spring 1992) 6–18.

———. "Zadel Barnes, Journalist." *Review of Contemporary Fiction* (Djuna Barnes Centennial Issue, Fall 1993), 107–16.

Herzig, Carl. "Roots of Night: Emerging Style and Vision in the Early Journalism of Djuna Barnes." *Centennial Review* 31 (Summer 1987), 255–69.

Hjartarson, Paul, ed. *A Stranger to My Time: Essays by and About Frederick Philip Grove.* Edmonton (Canada): NeWest, 1986.

———, and Douglas O. Spettigue, eds. *Baroness Elsa.* Ottawa: Oberon, 1992.

Hodder, Edwin. *The Life of Samuel Morley.* New York: Randolph, 1888.

Hopkinson, Lyndall Passerini. *Nothing to Forgive: A Daughter's Story of Antonia White.* London: Chatto & Windus, 1988.

Howells, William Dean. *Literary Friends and Acquaintance.* New York: Harper, 1900.

James, Henry. *The Bostonians.* New York: New American Library, 1979.

Jay, Karla. *The Amazon and the Page: Natalie Clifford Barney and Renée Vivien.* Bloomington: Indiana University Press, 1988.

Joyce, James. *Ulysses* (The Corrected Text). New York: Vintage, 1986.

Kapp, Yvonne. *Eleanor Marx.* 2 vols. London: Lawrence & Wishart, 1972; 1976.

Kreymborg, Alfred. *Troubadour: An Autobiography*. New York: Boni & Liveright, 1925.

Lanser, Susan Sniader. "Speaking in Tongues: *Ladies Almanack* and the Discourse of Desire." In Broe, ed., *Silence and Power*, 156–69.

Larabee, Ann. "The Early Attic Stage of Djuna Barnes." In Broe, ed., *Silence and Power*, 37–44.

Le Goff, Denise-Claude. *Peter Neagoe: L'homme et l'oeuvre*. New York: Peter Lang, 1988.

Lemon, Courtenay. "The War and the Men of Thought." *Pearson's Magazine*, February 1917, 183–86.

Levine, Nancy J. " 'Bringing Milkshakes to Bulldogs': The Early Journalism of Djuna Barnes," in Broe, ed., *Silence and Power*, 27–34.

Lewis, Sinclair. *It Can't Happen Here*. New York: Doubleday, Doran, 1935.

Loeb, Harold. *The Way It Was*. New York: Criterion, 1959.

Loy, Mina. *The Last Lunar Baedeker*. Edited by Roger Conover. Highlands, N.C.: Jargon Society, 1982.

Ludington, Townsend. *Marsden Hartley: The Biography of an American Artist*. Boston: Little, Brown, 1992.

Mallalieu, H. L. *The Dictionary of British Watercolour Artists Up to 1920*. Woodbridge, Suffolk, England, 1976.

McAlmon, Robert. *Being Geniuses Together: 1920–1930*. Edited by Kay Boyle. New York: Doubleday, 1968.

———. *Distinguished Air*. N.p. 1925.

Macdougall, Allan Ross, ed. *The Letters of Edna St. Vincent Millay*. New York: Harper, 1952.

Mellen, Joan. *Kay Boyle: Author of Herself*. New York: Farrar, Straus & Giroux, 1994.

Metcalfe, Philip. *1933*. Sag Harbor, N.Y.: Permanent Press, 1988.

Montague, Gene. "Dylan Thomas and *Nightwood*." *Sewanee Review* 76 (Summer 1968), 420–34.

Muir, Willa. *Belonging*. London, 1968.

Nadel, Norman. *A Pictorial History of the Theatre Guild*. New York: Crown, 1969.

O'Neal, Hank. *Life is painful, nasty and short . . . in my case it has only been painful and nasty*. New York: Paragon House, 1990.

Page, Chester. "Memories of Djuna Barnes." Unpublished memoir.

Paige, D. D., ed. *The Letters of Ezra Pound*. New York: Harcourt, Brace, 1950.

Pinckney, Darryl. *High Cotton*. New York: Farrar, Straus & Giroux, 1992.

Plumb, Cheryl J. *Fancy's Craft: Art and Identity in the Early Works of Djuna Barnes*. Selingsgrove, Pa.: Susquehanna University Press, 1986.

Pullar, Philippa. *Frank Harris*. New York: Simon & Schuster, 1976.

Rascoe, Burton. *A Bookman's Daybook*. New York: Liveright, 1929.

———. *Before I Forget*. New York: Doubleday Doran, 1937.

———. *We Were Interrupted.* New York: Doubleday, 1947.

Roberts, Mary Fanlon. "Speaking of Art." *Arts & Decoration* 34 (January 1931), 70.

Roditi, Edouard. Interview by Daniel Halpern. *Antaeus* 2:99 (Spring 1971), 104–6.

Sarlós, Robert Károly. *Jig Cook and the Provincetown Players.* Amherst: University of Massachusetts Press, 1982.

Sawyer-Lauçanno, Christopher. *An Invisible Spectator: A Biography of Paul Bowles.* New York: Weidenfeld & Nicolson, 1989.

Scott, James B. *Djuna Barnes.* Boston: Twayne, 1976.

Sieveking, Lance. "Hugh Kingsmill and John Holms." *The Listener*, 31 January 1957.

Simon, Linda. *The Biography of Alice B. Toklas.* New York: Doubleday, 1977.

Singer, Alan. "The Horse Who Knew Too Much: Metaphor and the Narrative of Discontinuity in *Nightwood*." *Contemporary Literature* 25 (1984), 66–87.

Stanton, Elizabeth Cady. *Eighty Years and More.* New York: Schocken Books, 1971.

Stanton, Theodore, and Harriet Stanton Blatch, eds. *Elizabeth Cady Stanton as Revealed in Her Letters, Diary and Reminiscences.* New York: Harper, 1922.

Stearns, Harold E. *The Street I Know.* New York: Lee Furman, 1935.

Sterne, Maurice. *Shadow and Light.* New York: Harcourt, Brace & World, 1966.

Stromberg, Kyra. *Djuna Barnes, Leben und Werk einer Extravaganten.* Berlin: Wagenbach Verlag, 1989.

Thompson, Francis M. *History of Greenfield*, 2 vols. Greenfield, Mass., 1904.

Tobin, A. I., and Elmer Gertz. *Frank Harris: A Study in Black and White.* Chicago: Madelaine Mendelsohn, 1931.

Tyler, Parker. *The Divine Comedy of Pavel Tchelitchew.* New York: Fleet, 1967; London: Weidenfeld, 1969.

Vorse, Mary Heaton. *Time and the Town: A Provincetown Chronicle.* New York: Dial, 1942.

Watson, Steven. *Strange Bedfellows: The First American Avant-Garde.* New York: Abbeville Press, 1991.

Williams, William Carlos. *Autobiography.* New York: New Directions, 1967.

Wilson, Edmund. *The Twenties.* New York: Farrar, Straus & Giroux, 1975.

———. *The Fifties.* New York: Farrar, Straus & Giroux, 1986.

Wyndham, Horace. *Speranza: A Biography of Lady Wilde.* New York: Philosophical Library, 1951.

Index

...

Autobiographical sources of Barnes's works, 1. *See also* major works, by title

Aveling, Edward, 15

Les Aventures de l'Esprit, Barney, 148–149, 150

"The Bard of Abbotsford," Zadel Barnes, 2

Barker, George, 53, 225, 268; Coleman and, 228, 232–33

Barnes, Brian Eglinton, 25, 34. *See also* Barnes, Wald

Barnes, Buan, 32, 37, 42, 47–49, 321n51

Barnes, Culmer, 2

Barnes, Cynthia Sexton Turner, 1

Barnes, Djuna Chappell, xvi, xvii–xviii, xxiii, 32, 34–35, 59, 196–197, 254–55, 346n40; abortion, xxv, 151, 184, 197; alcoholism of, xx, xxv, 233, 237, 239, 241, 242, 244, 245, 248–51, 252, 258; appearance of, 68, 97, 131, 148–149, 295; Arizona trip, 250–51; and Barney, 148–52; in Berlin, 137–39; and Coleman, 189–91, 193–94, 197, 200, 254, 292; common-law marriage, xxiv, 59–63; death of, xx, xxvi, 311–12; divorce of parents, 40–41; dreams, 236; education of, 38–40; and Eliot, 233–34, 243, 273, 276–77, 282–86; family of, xviii–xix, xxiii–xxvi; and Fanny, 30–31, 44; finances of, xxvi, 65, 151, 202, 252–53, 303, 329n2, n5, 331n45, 340n31, 343n27, 349n11, n20, n21; genius of, 202, 203, 205; in Greenwich Village, xx, xxiv, xxv, 66, 103–4, 121, 128–29, 171–72, 218–20, 251–252, 295–310; Hammarskjöld and, 288–89; at Hayford Hall, 191–99, 204; as journalist, 68, 75–102; literary influences, 122–126, 134, 173; name of, 319n24; notes, 345n36; old age, 295–311;

in Paris, 131–37, 139–55, 217; pregnancy, 184; and publishers, 286; rape of, xvi, 53, 268–71, 344n15; revenge as motivation, 262–72; sale of papers, 303–4, 349–50n22; in sanatorium, 249–250; suicide attempts, 246, 295–296; and theater, 121–22, 126, 128, 179–80; wills of, 303, 305, 350n24; and World War II, 251; and WPA, 228–29; and Zadel, 1, 22

family relationships, xviii–xix, 33, 41, 42, 52–54, 66, 106, 220–21, 280–81; with mother, 49–50, 250; with Saxon, 241; with Zadel, 63

health of, xxvi, 233, 240, 244, 245–247, 274; appendectomy, xxv, 172; asthma attack, 191; in old age, 295, 301, 308–10

lovers, xxiv, xxv, 66, 106–7, 166, 221; Barney, 150; Ford, 71, 171–84; Glossop, 236–39, 245–246; Hanfstaengl, 66–73; Heap, 127; Lemon, 104, 110–12; Middleton, 220, 221; Neagoe, 166, 221–22; Oberlé, 184; Pyne, 73–74; Vail, 116–17; Wood, xvii, 135, 150, 156–62

Barnes, Duane (father of Zadel), 1, 314n5

Barnes, Duane (son of Fanny), 17, 22, 32, 35–38, 42, 49, 321n51; and spiritualism, 43–44, 47

Barnes, Eleanor, 241, 247

Barnes, Elisha, 1

Barnes, Elizabeth Chappell, xviii–xix, xxiii, 41–42, 49, 50–51, 64, 220–21, 241, 344n6; children of, 32–33; and Christian Science, 247–48; death of, xxv, 51; divorce of, xxiv, 40–41; and Djuna, 49–50, 66, 222, 250, 269; married life, 29, 34–35; and *Nightwood*, 203; portrayal in *The Antiphon*, 263, 265, 267, 280. *See also* Chappell, Elizabeth

Grateful acknowledgment is made for permission to use selections from the following copyrighted works:

Letters from Djuna Barnes to Robert McAlmon, June 14, 1928 and one undated. By permission of the Yale Collection of American Literature, Beinecke Rare Book and Manuscript Library, Yale University.

Other writings of Djuna Barnes. By permission of The Authors League Fund, as literary executor of the estate of Djuna Barnes; Papers of Djuna Barnes, Special Collections, University of Maryland at College Park Libraries; and Harry Ransom Humanities Research Center, The University of Texas at Austin.

Writings of Brian E. (Wald) Barnes, Duane Barnes, and Zadel Barnes Gustafson. By permission of Kerron Barnes.

Writings of Elizabeth C. Barnes. By permission of Peter Barnes.

Writings of Natalie Barney. By permission of the Literary Estate of Natalie Barney.

It's the Gypsy in Me by Konrad Bercovici, Simon & Schuster, 1941. By permission of the publisher.

Now to My Mother: A Very Personal Memoir of Antonia White by Susan Chitty. Copyright © Susan Chitty, 1985. Reprinted by permission of Weidenfeld and Nicolson and Curtis Brown, London, Ltd.

Letters and diaries of Emily Coleman. © Estate of Emily Holmes Coleman, 1995. By permission of the Estate of Emily Holmes Coleman and the University of Delaware Library, Newark, Delaware.

Letter from T. S. Eliot to Geoffrey Faber and editor's blurb by T. S. Eliot for *The Antiphon*. By permission of Mrs. T. S. Eliot and the Faber Archive.

Other letters of T. S. Eliot. By permission of Mrs. T. S. Eliot.

Review by Valerie Eliot of *I Could Never Be Lonely Without a Husband* appearing in *The Financial Times*, August 1, 1987. By permission of Mrs. T. S. Eliot.

"I Will Be What I Am" by Charles Henri Ford. By permission of the Yale Collection of American Literature, Beinecke Rare Book and Manuscript Library, Yale University.

Other writings of Charles Henri Ford. By permission of Charles Henri Ford.

Memoirs of Montparnasse by John Glassco. Copyright © Oxford University Press, Canada, 1970. Reprinted by permission of Oxford University Press, Canada.

Letters of Peggy Guggenheim. © Karole and Julia Vail, 1995. By permission of Karole Vail.

Life is Painful, Nasty and Short . . . In My Case It Has Only Been Painful and Nasty: Djuna Barnes, 1978–1981: An Informal Memoir by Hank O'Neal. By permission of Paragon House.

Writings of Chester Page. By permission of Chester Page.

Letters of James B. Scott and his interviews with Djuna Barnes. By permission of James B. Scott, Ph.D.